THE HEART

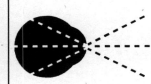

This Large Print Book carries the
Seal of Approval of N.A.V.H.

The Heart

Maylis de Kerangal

Translated from the French by Sam Taylor

THORNDIKE PRESS

A part of Gale, Cengage Learning

GALE
CENGAGE Learning·

Farmington Hills, Mich • San Francisco • New York • Waterville, Maine
Meriden, Conn • Mason, Ohio • Chicago

LIBRARY OF CONGRESS CATALOGING-IN-PUBLICATION DATA

Names: Kerangal, Maylis de, author. | Taylor, Sam, 1970– translator.
Title: The heart / by Maylis de Kerangal ; translated from the French by Sam
   Taylor.
Other titles: Râeparer les vivants. English
Description: Large print edition. | Waterville, Maine : Thorndike Press, 2016. |
   © 2016 | Series: Thorndike Press large print peer picks
Identifiers: LCCN 2016013366 | ISBN 9781410491282 (hardcover) | ISBN 1410491285
   (hardcover)
Subjects: LCSH: Heart—Transplantation—Patients—Fiction. | Organ
   donors—Fiction. | Large type books. | Psychological fiction.
Classification: LCC PQ2671.E64 R4713 2016b | DDC 843/.914—dc23
LC record available at http://lccn.loc.gov/2016013366

Published in 2016 by arrangement with Farrar, Straus and Giroux, LLC

Printed in Mexico
1 2 3 4 5 6 7 20 19 18 17 16

My heart is full.

— *The Effect of Gamma Rays on*
Man-in-the-Moon Marigolds
(dir. Paul Newman, 1972)

The thing about Simon Limbres's heart, this human heart, is that, since the moment of his birth, when its rhythm accelerated, as did the other hearts around it, in celebration of the event, the thing is, that this heart, which made him jump, vomit, grow, dance lightly like a feather or weigh heavy as a stone, which made him dizzy with exhilaration and made him melt with love, which filtered, recorded, archived — the black box of a twenty-year-old body — the thing is that nobody really knows it; only a moving image created by ultrasound could echo its sound and shape, could make visible the joy that dilates it and the sadness that tightens it; only the paper trace of an electrocardiogram, set in motion at the very beginning, could draw the shape, describe the exertion, the quickening emotion, the prodigious energy needed to contract almost a hundred thousand times a day, to pump nearly ten

pints of blood every minute, yes, only that graph could tell a story, by outlining the life of ebbs and flows, of gates and valves, a life of beats — for, while Simon Limbres's heart, this human heart, is too much even for the machines, no one could claim to really know it, and that night, that starless and bone-splittingly cold night on the estuary and in the Pays de Caux, as a lightless swell rolled all along the cliffs, as the continental shelf retreated, revealing its geological bands, there could be heard the regular rhythm of a resting organ, a muscle that was slowly recharging, a pulse of probably less than fifty beats per minute, and a cell-phone alarm went off at the foot of a narrow bed, the echo of a sonar signal translated into luminescent digits on the touchscreen — 05:50 — and suddenly everything raced out of control.

And so, that night, a van brakes in an empty parking lot, coming to a halt at a crooked angle, and as the front doors slam and a back door slides open, three figures emerge, three shadows outlined against the darkness and seized by the cold — icy February, runny noses, slept-in clothes — boys, it looks like, who zip their coats up to their chins, pull their hats down to their eyelashes, muffling the upper flesh of their ears with polar fleece, and — blowing into their cupped hands — turn toward the sea, which is at this hour nothing but noise and blackness.

Yes, they're boys, you can see that now. They are standing in a line behind the low wall that separates the parking lot from the beach, stamping their feet and breathing deeply, their nostrils sore from piping the iodine and the cold, and they survey that

dark expanse where the only rhythm is the roar of the crashing waves, that din made by the final collapse; they scan what is rumbling before them, that crazy clamor with nothing to see — nothing except perhaps the whitish, foamy edge, billions of atoms catapulted against each other in a phosphorescent halo — and, stunned by the winter cold outside the van, dazed by the marine night, the three boys now pull themselves together, see and hear clearly again, assess what awaits them — the swell — judging it by ear, estimating its breaker index, its depth coefficient, and remember that waves formed offshore always move more quickly than the fastest boats.

Looks good, one of the three boys muttered softly, should be a good one, and the two others smiled, then the three went back together, slowly, scraping the ground with their feet and pacing around like tigers. They lifted their eyes to penetrate the night beyond the town, the still-black night behind the cliffs, and the one who had spoken looked at his watch — another fifteen minutes, guys — and they climbed back into the van to wait for the nautical dawn.

Christophe Alba, Johan Rocher, and Simon

Limbres. The alarms went off and they pushed back their sheets and got out of bed for a session agreed upon only just before midnight with an exchange of texts, a mid-tide session, the kind you get only two or three times a year: heavy sea, regular swell, low wind, and not a soul around. In jeans and jackets, they crept outside without breakfast — not even a glass of milk or a bite of cereal, not even a slice of bread — and waited in front of their apartment building (Simon) or the gates of their house (Johan) for the van that was right on time (Chris), these boys who normally never emerge from their beds before noon, no matter how much their mothers nag them, these boys who usually don't have the energy to do more than crawl lethargically from the living room couch to their beds and back, here they are in the street at six in the morning, champing at the bit, laces undone, breath foul — beneath the street-lamp, Simon Limbres watched the cloud of air that rose from his mouth as it slowly expanded, dissolved, and vanished, remembering how as a child he had liked to pretend he was smoking, putting his index and middle finger to his lips, taking a breath so deep it hollowed his cheeks, and blowing out like a man — these boys, the *Three*

11

Caballeros, aka the *Big Wave Hunters,* aka Chris, John, and Sky, aliases that were less nicknames than pseudonyms, created as part of their reinvention from French high school kids to planetary surfers, so that calling them by their real names instantly brings them back to a hostile set of circumstances: the freezing drizzle, the gently lapping waves, the vertical cliffs, and the streets deserted as evening approaches, the parents' scolding, the demands of school, the complaints of the girlfriend left behind, abandoned once again in favor of the van and the waves, the girl who can never defeat the lure of the sea.

Inside the van: filth and damp, sand everywhere, harsh against the skin, brackish rubber, the stink of shellfish and kerosene, a pile of boards, a pile of wetsuits (different kinds for different seasons), gloves, socks, pots of wax, leashes. All three sat in front, shoulder to shoulder, rubbing their hands between their thighs while making monkey noises, shit man it's freezing, and then took a few bites of energy bars — taking care not to eat too much, because it's afterward that you wolf them down, afterward, when you've earned them — and passed around the bottle of Coke, the tube of Nestlé

condensed milk, the soft sweet cookies — Pépito and Chamonix — before one of them grabbed the latest issue of *Surf Session* from under the seat and they opened it out on the dashboard, their three heads close together above the pages that glowed in the dark, the glossy paper like skin slick with sunscreen and pleasure, pages thumbed a thousand times that they stare at once again, wide-eyed and dry-mouthed: a tsunami at Mavericks and point breaks in Lombok, rollers in Hawaii, tube waves in Vanuatu, all the greatest shores on the planet unfolding before them with the splendors of surfing. They point at the pictures with feverish fingers — there, yeah, and there, we'll get there one day, maybe even next summer, the three of them in the van setting off on a legendary surf trip, in search of the most beautiful wave in oceanic history, driving until they find that wild and secret place, which will belong to them the way America belonged to Christopher Columbus, and the three of them will be there, alone on the beach, when it finally appears on the horizon, the one they've been waiting for, the perfect wave, beauty incarnate, so huge and so fast that they will stand on their boards in an adrenaline rush, joy and terror electrifying every inch of their

13

bodies from the soles of their feet to the tips of their eyelashes, and they will ride it, rallying the world of surfers, that nomadic tribe with their sun-bleached, salt-washed hair, skin bronzed and eyes faded in the eternal summer of youth, boys and girls wearing only shorts printed with Tahitian flowers or hibiscus petals, turquoise or blood-orange T-shirts, shod only in flip-flops, a people aglow with sunlight and freedom, and they will surf that wave all the way to the shore.

As the sky outside lightens, the pages of the magazine are gradually illuminated, revealing their full spectrum of cobalt blues so pure they dazzle the eyes and greens so deep they look as if they have been painted in acrylics; here and there you can see the wake of a surfboard, a tiny white stripe traced across the vast wall of water, and the boys blink and mutter Jesus look at that, wow it's insane. Chris leans back to check his cell phone, and the screen light, shining from below, turns his face bluish, reveals the bone structure — the prominent arch of the eyebrows, lantern jaw, mauve lips — while he reads the news out loud: today in Les Petites Dalles, there's an ideal southwest/northeast swell, waves between

five and six feet, the best session of the year, each snippet of information punctuated with solemn cries of *yes,* man, we're gonna rule out there, we're gonna be kings! — their slangy French sprinkled with fragments of English, as if they're living inside a pop song or an American TV show, as if they were heroes, foreigners, the English words lightening deep, dark thoughts like *vie* and *amour* to the airy, meaningless "life" and "love," the English making them sound humbler — and John and Sky nodding in infinite agreement, *yeah,* man, *big wave riders,* we'll be *kings.*

It's time. The break of day, when the formless takes shape: the different elements coming into focus, sky separating from sea, the horizon growing visible. Methodically, the three boys get ready, following a precise order that is also a sort of ritual: they wax their boards, check the leashes are attached, put on their special polypropylene underwear before struggling into their wetsuits, their bodies contorted in the parking lot — the neoprene sticking to their skin, sometimes giving them friction burns — a choreography of rubberclad puppets asking each other for help, yanking and twisting. Rubber boots and hoods and gloves follow, then

they lock up the van and walk down to the sea, boards light under their arms, striding across the shingle where the pebbles collapse noisily underfoot. When they reach the shore, everything growing clearer in front of them — the chaos, the celebration — they attach the leashes to their ankles, reach back to zip their hoods so there's not an inch of bare skin on their necks — they have to make sure the suit is as watertight as possible to protect their young skin, often studded with acne on their shoulders and shoulder blades (where Simon Limbres has a Maori tattoo) — and then that movement of the arms, straight up in the air, meaning that the session is about to begin, *let's go!,* and now perhaps their hearts start to pump a little harder, shaking themselves slowly like waking animals inside their rib cages, now perhaps their mass and volume increase, their beating intensifies, two distinct sequences in every pulse. Two beats, always the same: terror and desire.

They enter the water. They do not scream as they throw their bodies into it, protected by that tight-fitting flexible membrane that conserves the warmth of their flesh, the explosiveness of their momentum. They don't loose a single cry, but pull faces as they cross the wall of rolling rocks, the

seabed steepening rapidly until, five or six yards from the shore, they can no longer touch it with their feet and they plunge forward, lying facedown on their boards, their arms cutting forcefully into the waves, driving through the backwash, heading out into the open sea.

Two hundred yards from the shore, the sea is just a wavelike tension, hollowing and bulging, billowing like a bedsheet. Simon Limbres becomes his movement, paddling toward the lineup, that zone in the sea where the surfer waits for a wave to rise. He checks that Chris and John are there, to his left, bobbing like little black corks, hardly visible as yet. The water is dark, marbled, veiny, the color of tin. There is still no sparkle or shimmer, only those white particles that powder the surface like sugar, and the water is icy, less than fifty degrees. Simon can never take more than three or four waves when it's like this, and he knows it: the cold wrings out the body. He has to choose carefully, seeking out the best-shaped wave, high-crested without being too sharp, with a curl that will open wide enough for him to take his place there, a wave that will last all the way to the shore, breaking and frothing only when it hits the shingle.

He turns back to the coast, as he always likes to before moving farther out: there is the land, stretched out like a black crust on the bluish glimmers where he floats, another world, a world to which he no longer belongs. The cliffs with their layers of different-colored rock mark the passing of time, but where he is, time no longer exists — there is no history here, only the randomness of the waves that buoy and whirl him. His gaze lingers on the vehicle made up to look like a California surfer van, parked on the lot by the beach — he recognizes the bodywork covered with stickers, all those names he knows by heart, Rip Curl, Oxbow, Quiksilver, O'Neill, Billabong, the psychedelic fresco mixing a hallucinatory vision of surf champions and rock stars, sprinkled with a nice heavy dose of siren-like, long-haired girls arching their backs in teenie-weenie bikinis, that van which they have created together, the antechamber to the wave — and then his gaze shifts to the taillights of a car climbing up to the plateau and disappearing inland, and he thinks of Juliette asleep, curled up in the fetal position beneath her kid's comforter. She looks so stubborn, even in sleep, and suddenly he turns the other way, leaving the continent behind, tears himself away from it with a

burst of energy, another sixty-five feet or so, and then he stops paddling.

Simon floats, arms resting but legs kicking, hands gripping the edge of the board, chest lifted slightly above the water, chin high. He waits. Everything around him is in flux: whole sections of sea and sky appear and disappear with each eddy of the slow, heavy, wood-like surface, like cool lava. The harsh dawn burns his face and his skin tightens, his eyelashes hardening into vinyl, the lenses behind his pupils icing over as if they'd been forgotten at the back of a freezer. His heart is beginning to slow down, in response to the cold, when suddenly he sees it, coming toward him, solid and homogenous, the wave, the promise, and instinctively he positions himself to find a way in, to slip inside like a thief entering a safe to steal its treasure — same balaclava, same precision of movement, down to the last millimeter — to slip in through the back, into that twist of matter where the inside turns out to be even huger and deeper than the outside. There it is, thirty yards away, coming toward him at a steady speed. Abruptly, concentrating his strength in his forearms, Simon sets off, paddling at full speed, and he is traveling quickly when he takes the wave, so he can be caught in its

slope, and now it's time for *takeoff,* that ultrafast phase when the whole world concentrates, speeds up, a temporal flash when you take a deep breath, hold it, and gather your body in a single action, giving it the vertical impetus to stand up straight on the board, feet nicely spread, the left in front, *settled,* knees bent and back flat, almost parallel to the board, arms open wide for balance. This is Simon's favorite second, the moment when he is able to seize the explosion of his existence, to win over the elements, to become part of the life around him, and, once he is standing on the board — guessing, in that moment, that the height of the wave from base to crest is about five feet — to stretch out the space, prolong the time, use up the energy of every atom of the sea until it breaks on the shore. To *become* the wave.

He lets out a yell as he takes this first ride, and for a moment of time he is in a state of grace — a horizontal vertigo: he is level with the world and feels as if he is coming out of it, part of its flux — the space closing in on him, crushing as it liberates, saturating his muscle fibers, his bronchial tubes, oxygenating his blood. The wave unfolds in a vague temporality — slow or fast, impossible to tell — suspending each second until the

surfer ends up pulverized, a senseless heap of flesh. And it's incredible but, no sooner has Simon Limbres crashed into bruising rocks in the gush of the climax than he is turning around and heading back out, without even a glance at the land or the fleeting figures glimpsed in the foam when the sea hits the earth, surface against surface; he paddles back out to the open sea, his arms windmilling fast, plowing a way to that threshold where it all begins, where it all gets going. He has rejoined his two friends, who will soon yell out just like he did as they descend the sequence of waves that march toward them from the horizon, exhausting their bodies, giving them no respite.

No other surfer came to that spot. No one else approached the parapet to watch them surf. No one saw them leave the water an hour later, worn out, spent shells, legs like jelly, staggering as they crossed the beach back to the parking lot, and back to the van. No one saw their hands and feet, blue with cold and purple with bruises, nor the dry patches that cut their faces, the cracks in the skin at the corners of their lips as their teeth chattered, their jaws trembling continually, like their bodies, all three of them

helpless to stop it. No one saw anything, and when they were dressed again — wool underwear beneath pants, layers of sweaters, leather gloves — no one saw them rubbing each other's backs, unable to say anything but oh God, shit man that was awesome, when they would so have liked to talk about it, describe the rides, immortalize the legend of the session. Shivering, they got in the van and closed the doors. The engine started, and they drove away.

Chris drives. He always drives: the van belongs to his father, and anyway, neither Johan nor Simon have their licenses yet. It takes about an hour and a half to reach Le Havre from Les Petites Dalles if you take the old road from Étretat, which passes through Octeville-sur-Mer, the valley of Ignauval, and Sainte-Adresse before depositing you at the estuary.

The boys have stopped shivering now. The van's heating is turned up as high as it will go; likewise the volume on the stereo. The heat pouring from the vents in the dashboard is, for them, probably another thermal shock. They are probably beginning to feel tired now too, mouths gaping in yawns, heads nodding gently, trying to find a comfortable position against the headrest of the seat, rocked by the vehicle's vibrations, noses swaddled in their scarves, and probably too they are starting to feel numb, their

eyelids closing intermittently. And so perhaps, after they had passed Étretat, Chris
accelerated without even realizing, shoulders slumping, hands heavy on the steering
wheel, the road straight. Yes, maybe he
thought, all right, we're on our way home
now, and the desire to get there quickly, to
knock back the aftereffects of the session,
its violence, weighed down upon the gas
pedal, and he let it happen, cutting through
the dark fields, the empty fields where nothing moved, and maybe the sight of the long,
straight highway — an arrow plunging
through the windshield as on the screen of
a video game — ended up hypnotizing him
like a mirage. Maybe he felt like he was
already home, practically there, and relaxed
his vigilance, though everyone remembers
that it had frozen the night before, winter
leaving its traces on the landscape, turning
it into wax paper. Everyone knows about
the patches of black ice on the asphalt, invisible under this dull-gray sky, blacking out
the edges of the road. Everyone can see the
compact patches of fog that hover above the
road at irregular intervals, the water evapo-
rating from the mud as the sun rises, dangerous pockets of mist that blind you as you
drive. Yes, everyone knows all that, but what
else might there be? An animal running

across the road? A lost cow? A dog that has scrambled under a wire fence? The sudden appearance of a fire-tailed fox or a ghostly human figure at the edge of the road that you must swerve to avoid at the very last moment? Or maybe a song? Yeah, maybe the girls in bikinis plastered across the van's bodywork suddenly came to life and climbed up the hood, lasciviously smearing the windshield with their bodies, their green hair falling over their shoulders, and their inhuman — or too human — voices filling the air, and maybe Chris lost his head, fell into their trap, hearing that song not of this world, the song of the sirens, the song that kills? Or maybe Chris just made one false move? Yes, that's it, a simple mistake, like a tennis player missing an easy shot, like a skier losing an edge, something dumb like that. Maybe he didn't turn his steering wheel when the road curved? Or maybe — because the possibility has to be raised — maybe Chris fell asleep at the wheel, left the drab countryside and entered the tube of a wave, entered the glorious and suddenly perceptible spiral that flashed past under his board, siphoning the world away with it, the world and the sky of the world.

The emergency services arrived at about

9:20 a.m. — ambulance, police — and signs were placed on the road in front and behind, directing traffic to smaller collateral roads. The main task consisted of removing the bodies of the three boys, imprisoned in their vehicle, mixed up with the bodies of the sirens who smiled on the hood or grimaced, deformed, crushed into each other, thighs, butts, and breasts all shredded and crumpled.

It was easily established that the little van was traveling too fast, at an estimated speed of 57 mph (12 mph above the speed limit for this section of the road), and it was also established that, for reasons unknown, it had swerved to the left and had been unable to straighten out again, that the driver had not braked — no tire marks on the asphalt — and that the van had smashed head on into this post. The absence of airbags was noted (this model van being too old), as was the fact that of the three passengers sitting in the front seat, only two were wearing seat belts — those sitting next to the doors, in the driver's seat and the passenger's window seat. It was established that the third person, sitting between the two others, had been propelled forward upon impact, his head colliding with the windshield. It had taken twenty minutes to

extricate him from the wreckage, and he had been unconscious, but his heart still beating, when the ambulance arrived. His student meal card having been found in his jacket pocket, it was lastly established that the third person's name was Simon Limbres.

Pierre Révol went on duty that morning at eight. As the night sky lightened to a pale dove gray above him, far from the grandiloquent choreographies of clouds that had made the estuary's picturesque reputation, he slid his magnetic card into the reader at the entrance of the parking lot and drove slowly across the hospital grounds, snaking between buildings that connected to each other according to a complex plan, and parked his car — a gunmetal-blue Laguna, quite old but still comfortable, leather interior and good sound system: the model preferred by taxi companies, he thinks, smiling — in his reserved spot, nose first. He entered the hospital, walking quickly across the vast glass-walled lobby toward the North Hall, where he reached the Intensive Care Unit.

He enters the department by pushing the door open with the flat of his hand, so hard

that it beats back and forth several times after he has gone. The men and women in white and green scrubs who are coming to the end of the night shift, exhausted and disheveled — tense faces, rictus grins, drum-tight skin, laughing too loud or coughing like smokers, voiceless — these people see him in the corridor and brush past him, or they see him from afar and glance at their watches, bite their lips, think, all right, only ten minutes to go and I'm out of here, and instantly their faces relax, change color, turn pale, the dark rings under their eyes suddenly deepening, eyelids blinking heavily.

Striding calmly, his pace unvarying, Révol reaches his office without deviating from his trajectory to respond to other people's greetings and remarks, to the papers that are already being handed to him, to the intern who is already dogging his footsteps, requesting his attention. Using his key, he enters through an unmarked door and prepares for the day's work: hangs his putty-colored trench coat on the hook stuck to the back of the door, puts on his white coat, switches on the coffee machine and the computer, drums his fingers on the paper-work that covers his desk, checks the cate-

gory of each pile, then sits down, connects to the Internet, scans the e-mails in his inbox, writes a couple replies — no hellos or best regards, no vowels or punctuation — then gets up and takes a deep breath. He is feeling good this morning.

He is a tall, skinny man, hollow-chested and round-bellied (solitude), long arms and legs, white lace-up Repetto shoes. There is something loose and vague about him, suggested perhaps by his youthful appearance and the way he leaves his coat open all the time, so that when he walks down a corridor it flaps to either side of him, like a pair of wings, revealing his jeans and the crumpled white shirt beneath it.

The little red light at the base of the coffee machine is illuminated and a bitter smell spreads through the room as the electric plate heats nothing: the glass pot sits on his desk, the last drops of coffee inside it turning lukewarm. However tiny — twenty square feet, tops — this private space is a privilege in the hospital, and it is surprising how impersonal, how messy, how frankly unclean it is: a swivel chair that is quite comfortable despite the high seat position; the desk where paper products of all kinds are piled up — loose sheets, notebooks,

Post-it notes — alongside plastic bags full of ballpoint pens bearing the acronyms of laboratories; a bottle of San Pellegrino, the water inside it flat; a framed photograph of Mont Aigoual. Punctuating the clutter, arranged in an isosceles triangle, a Venetian-glass paperweight, a stone tortoise, and a pencil holder bring perhaps the only hint of a personal touch. Along the back wall, a metal shelf supports archive boxes marked by year and various folders, a thick layer of dust, and some rare books whose titles you can read if you get close enough: the two volumes of *L'homme devant la mort* by Philippe Ariès; *La sculpture du vivant* by Jean Claude Ameisen; a book by Margaret Lock — *Twice Dead: Organ Transplants and the Reinvention of Death* — with a cover showing an illustration of a human brain in two colors; a back issue of the *Revue neurologique* from 1959; and a thriller by Mary Higgins Clark, *Moonlight Becomes You* — a book that Révol likes a lot, for reasons that will become clear. Apart from that, the room is windowless and fluorescent-lit, giving it the harsh luminosity of a kitchen at three in the morning.

The ICU is a place apart within the hospital, a place for tangential lives, deep comas,

terminal cases — for those bodies situated midway between life and death. A place of corridors and rooms, where all is in suspense. Révol works in this twilit territory — the underside of the diurnal world, where life is continuous and stable, where the days pass in light, rushing toward future plans — the way you might fiddle around in the dark pockets and hidden folds of a large, old overcoat. This is why he likes being on duty on Sundays, at night — has liked it since he was a young intern. You can imagine him then, a long-limbed student in love with the idea of duty itself, that feeling of being needed and yet independent, required to ensure the continuity of medical care for a given area, vigilant and responsible. He enjoys the intensity, the specific temporality, the fatigue that acts like a surreptitious stimulant, gradually rising through the body, accelerating and sharpening it, in a way that is almost erotic; he likes the vibratile silence, the half-lit atmosphere — machines with lights that blink in the darkness, bluish computer screens, desk lamps that glow like candles in a painting by La Tour (*The Newborn,* for example) — and the physical feeling of being on duty: the isolation, the sense of being cut off from the world, as if the department were a space-

ship entering a black hole, a submarine diving into the deepest abyss, into the Mariana Trench. But for a long time now, Révol has been drawing something else from it: the naked awareness of his existence. Not the feeling of power, a megalomaniac exaltation, but its very opposite: the influx of lucidity that regulates his actions and sifts his decisions. A fix of sangfroid.

Department meeting: the handover. The teams for both shifts are there, in a circle, some standing, some leaning against the walls, some holding mugs of coffee. The senior doctor who led the previous shift is a guy in his thirties, sturdily built, thick-haired, with muscular arms. Radiating exhaustion. He gives a brief rundown on the situation of each patient in the department — for example, the absence of any noteworthy change in that eighty-year-old man, still unconscious after sixty days of intensive care, whereas the neurological state of the young girl, admitted two months ago after an overdose, has deteriorated — before talking at greater length about the new arrivals: a homeless woman of fifty-seven with advanced cirrhosis, who was admitted after undergoing convulsions in the homeless shelter and whose hemody-

namic state remains unstable; a man in his forties, admitted in the evening after a massive coronary, who is presenting with a cerebral ischemia — he had been jogging on the seafront, toward the Cap de la Hève, wearing expensive running shoes, a fluorescent-orange bandana around his head, when he collapsed outside the Café de l'Estacade, and even though he was wrapped in a thermal blanket, his body had been blue by the time he reached the hospital, soaked with sweat, facial features sunken. What's happening with him? Révol asks questions in a neutral voice, leaning against the window. A nurse replies that the vital signs (pulse, blood pressure, body temperature, respiration) are normal, urine flow is weak, a peripheral venous catheter has been inserted. Révol doesn't know this girl. He inquires about the patient's blood tests and she responds that they are being carried out now. Révol checks his watch: all right, let's go. Everyone leaves the room.

Everyone except the nurse, who waits behind, intercepts Révol and puts out her hand: Cordélia Owl, I'm new, I was in the OR before. Révol nods: Okay, welcome to the team. If he took a closer look, he would see that she is rather strange-looking: not

drunk or hungover, but she has marks on her neck that look like hickeys, her lips are swollen and too red despite the absence of lipstick, her hair knotted, knees bruised; perhaps, if he looked closer, he would wonder at the source of that vague smile, that Mona Lisa smile which never leaves her face, even when she is leaning over her patients to examine their eyes and mouth, inserting breathing tubes, checking vital signs, administering drugs, and perhaps he would end up guessing that she had seen her lover again that night, that he had called her after weeks of silence, the bastard, and that she had gone to their date sober and ravishing, dressed to the nines, smoky-eyed, shiny-haired, hot-breasted, determined to maintain a friendly distance but not the greatest actress in the world, whispering Hi how are you? Nice to see you again, while her entire body radiated her arousal, incubated her excitement, an ember. They'd had a couple beers and made an attempt at conversation that never went anywhere, so she had gone outside for a smoke, telling herself I should go now, this is stupid, it's pointless, I should go, but he had joined her outside, I won't stay long, I want to get to bed early tonight, faking her out, and then he'd taken out his lighter and lit her ciga-

rette, she'd leaned her head down, sheltering the flame in her hands, and a few locks of hair had fallen over her face, flirting with the fire, and in an automatic gesture he'd brushed the hair back behind her ear, the flesh of his fingertips grazing her temple — all those well-worn seduction techniques — and, bang, she'd felt her legs go weak, as if someone shoved the backs of her knees forward. It was crazy: a second before there had been no spark between them, no chemistry, nothing, and then the next thing she knew they were staggering under a neighboring porch, sheltered by the darkness and the smell of cheap wine, knocking against trash cans, revealing the zones of white flesh, the tops of thighs appearing from under jeans or pantyhose, bare stomachs exposed by the lifting of shirts, buttocks by the unbuckling of belts, the two of them simultaneously freezing and boiling, desire crashing into desire . . . Yes, if Révol looked more closely, he would see a girl who was curiously alert and alive, despite her lack of sleep, a girl who was more ready for the day than he was, a girl he'd be able to count on.

We've got someone for you. A call at 10:12 a.m. Neutral, informative, staccato. A man, six feet, 150 pounds, about twenty years old, automobile accident, traumatic brain injury, in a coma — we know who this is, of course: his name is Simon Limbres. The call is barely over before the emergency medical team arrives at the ICU. The fire doors open and the stretcher is rolled through the department's main corridor, people moving out of its way. Révol appears. He has just examined the patient admitted in the night after convulsions and he is pessimistic: the woman was not given CPR in time; a scan revealed that liver cells died after the heart stopped beating, a sign that the brain cells were affected too. Now, after being alerted, he sees the gurney at the end of the corridor and thinks: This is going to be a long day.

The emergency team's doctor follows the

stretcher. Bald, in his mid-fifties, he has the physique of a mountain climber: zero body fat, hard as stone. He exposes pointed teeth when he shouts out: Glasgow 3! Then, to Révol: The neurological examination showed no spontaneous reaction to auditory, visual, or tactile stimulation; there is also ocular damage (asymmetrical eye movement) and respiratory autonomic dysfunction; we've intubated him. He closes his eyes and smooths his skull, from the forehead to the occiput: suspected cerebral hemorrhage after a TBI, nonreactive coma, Glasgow 3 — he uses this shared language, this language that banishes prolixity as time-wasting, forbids any notions of eloquence or seductiveness in articulation, abuses nouns, codes, and acronyms, this language where to talk is to describe or provide information about a body, to lay down the parameters of a situation in order that a diagnosis can be made, tests ordered, that the patient can be treated, saved: the power of concision. Révol absorbs each piece of information, then orders a body scan.

It's Cordélia Owl who takes charge of the young man, supervising the transfer to his room, to his bed. After that, the emergency team leaves the department, taking its

38

equipment — stretcher, mobile respirator, oxygen tank. Now she has to fit an arterial catheter, electrodes on the thorax, a urinary catheter, and to start up the monitor that displays Simon's vital signs — lines of various colors and shapes appear on the screen, superimposed, straight lines or broken lines, hatched derivations, rhythmic undulations: medical Morse. Cordélia works with Révol: her actions are assured, her movements fluid, relaxed, as if the viscous ennui that clogged her every gesture only yesterday has been purged from her body.

One hour later, death clears its throat, knocks politely on the door, a moving stain, irregularly shaped, opacifying a clearer, larger shape: yes, there it is, that's death. An abrupt vision, like a hard slap in the face, but Révol does not blink, concentrating on the body-scan pictures that appear on his computer screen: labyrinthine images, each with a key, like a map, that he has to rotate in every direction, zoom into, on which he must make reference points and measure distances, while close by on his desk lies a hospital-branded cardboard folder containing a paper printout of "relevant" images provided by the Radiology Department that scanned Simon Limbres's brain. To produce

these representations, the boy's head was scanned by X-rays, and then, using a tomographic analysis, the data was divided into "slices," each thinner than a sheet of paper, which could be analyzed in every spatial plane: coronal, axial, sagittal, and oblique. Révol can read these images, what they say about the patient's state and what they augur for his future; he recognizes those shapes, those marks and haloes, interprets those milky rings, deciphers those black spots, those legends and codes; he compares, checks, recommences, continues his investigation until the inevitable conclusion: Simon Limbres's brain is dying; it is drowning in blood.

Diffuse lesions, early cerebral swelling, and there is nothing they can do to control intracranial pressure, already way too high. Révol leans back in his chair. His gaze lingers on the disorder of his desk while he thumbs his jaw; he surveys the scrawled notes, the administrative newsletters, the photocopy of an article sent by the Ethics Unit of the Paris Hospital Administration on tests carried out in the moment of heart failure; his eyes glide over the various small objects that cover the desk, including that tortoise carved in jade, a gift from a young female patient who was suffering with severe

asthma, then suddenly halt at the streaming purplish slopes of Mont Aigoual. In all likelihood, Révol is remembering, in a flash, that September day when he first used peyote in his house in Valleraugue. Marcel and Sally had arrived in late afternoon in an emerald sedan, its wheel rims caked with dry mud. The vehicle had come to a juddering stop outside his house and Sally had waved through the open window Hello! Hey! It's us!, her snow-white hair flying, revealing her wooden earrings — a pair of lacquered scarlet cherries. Later, after they'd eaten, as night was falling over the limestone plateau, a rain of bright stars, they had gone out into the garden and Marcel had unwrapped a parcel containing a few little grayish-green cactuses, round and thornless, which the three friends rolled around in their palms before inhaling the bitter smell. These plants had come a long way: Sally and Marcel had gone to a mining desert in northern Mexico to find them, had smuggled them illegally out of the country, and had carefully brought them here, to the Cévennes. Now Pierre, who studied hallucinogenic plants, was impatient to try them: the combination of powerful alkaloids contained in peyote, a third of which were mescaline, provoked visions that seemed to

come from nowhere, unrelated to memories, visions that played a major role in the ritual use of this cactus, which the indigenous Americans most often consumed during shamanic ceremonies. But, even more than this, what interested Pierre was the synesthesia that manifested during these hallucinations: psychosensory vividness was supposed to increase in the first phase of ingestion, so he hoped to be able to see tastes, to see odors and sounds, tactile sensations, and he hoped that this translation of the other senses as images would help him to understand, even to solve, the mystery of pain. Révol thinks of that brilliant night, when the celestial vault had split open above the mountains, releasing unsuspected places they had tried to dive into, lying in the grass, faces to the sky, and suddenly the idea crosses his mind of a constantly expanding universe, a place where cellular death will be the operator of metamorphoses, where death will shape the living like silence shapes noise, or darkness light, or the static the mobile — a fleeting intuition that persists on his retina even as his eyes refocus on the computer screen, that sixteen-inch rectangle irradiated with black light where the cessation of all mental activity in Simon Limbres's brain is an-

nounced. Unable to connect the young man's face with death, he feels his throat tighten. And yet he's been working in this area for nearly thirty years. Thirty years.

Pierre Révol was born in 1959. The Cold War, the Cuban Revolution, Swiss women voting for the first time in the canton of Vaud, the shooting of Godard's *Breathless,* the publication of Burroughs's *Naked Lunch* and the release of Miles Davis's mythical opus *Kind of Blue* — just the greatest jazz album of all time, according to Révol, who likes to glorify his own vintage. Anything else? Oh yes — he puts on a casual air in order to increase the power of the revelation: you can imagine him looking away as he speaks to you, turning his attention to something else altogether, perhaps rummaging in his pocket or dialing a phone number or reading a text — yes, it's the year when death was redefined. And in that moment, he is not displeased by the mixture of stupor and dread that he sees on the faces of the people around him. Then, lifting his head and smiling vaguely, he adds: Which is not exactly insignificant when you happen to work in Intensive Care.

In fact, Révol often thinks that in 1959, rather than being a mere placid baby with

the triple chin of a provincial politician, bundled up in a onesie, rather than spending two-thirds of his life asleep in a pale-straw, gingham-lined Moses basket, he would have preferred to be in that room, at the Twenty-third International Congress of Neurology, on the day when Maurice Goulon and Pierre Mollaret took the podium to present their findings; what wouldn't he have given to see them speaking to the medical community — or, in other words, to the world itself — those two men, the neurologist and the specialist in infectious diseases, aged about forty and sixty, dark suits and polished black shoes, bow ties; he would have loved to have observed what he could of their relationship, the mutual respect that bridges the age gap, the silent hierarchy that always exists at meetings of scientists, my esteemed colleague, my esteemed colleague — but who speaks first? who has the privilege of concluding? Yes, the more Révol thinks about this, the more sure he feels that he would have liked to be there, that day, sitting among the pioneers of resuscitation — men, mostly, feverishly concentrated — would have liked to be one of them, in that place, the Hospital Claude-Bernard, a trailblazing hospital where Pierre Mollaret had created, in 1954, the first

modern Intensive Care Unit in the world. He had formed a team, renovated the Pasteur Building so it could hold nearly seventy beds, ordered the famous Engstrom 150 electric ventilators, developed to deal with the polio epidemic that was raging in the north of Europe, and that would replace the "iron lungs" that had been used since the thirties. And, the more Révol concentrates, the better he is able to visualize this scene — this seminal scene that he never experienced in reality — the more he can hear the two professors whispering to each other, arranging their papers on the lectern, clearing their throats behind the microphones, waiting impassively for the hubbub to die down and silence to descend so that they can finally begin speaking in that cold, clear tone unique to those who, aware of the fundamental importance of what they are saying, feel no need to add anything, content simply to describe, describe, describe, laying down their conclusions the way you lay down four aces in a poker hand. Even now, the enormity of their announcement stupefies him. Because what Goulon and Mollaret said that day could be summarized in a single phrase that was like a cluster bomb exploding in slow motion: the moment of death is no longer to be consid-

ered as the moment the heart stops, but as the moment when cerebral function ceases. In other words: *I no longer think, therefore I no longer am.* The heart is dead, long live the brain — a symbolic coup d'état, a Revolution.

So the two men stood on the podium, facing their peers, and described the outward signs of what they now call the *coma dépassé.* They detailed several case histories in which patients, placed on ventilators, maintained their cardiac and respiratory functions without showing any cerebral activity — patients who, without new machines and techniques enabling a blood supply to their brains, would have suffered cardiac arrest. From there, they established that the development of medical resuscitation had changed everything, that progress in their field had led them to formulate a new definition of death, and that they assumed this scientific breakthrough — with its startling philosophical repercussions — would also have the consequence of authorizing and enabling organ transplants.

Goulon and Mollaret's speech was followed by the publication of a crucial article in the *Revue neurologique* detailing twenty-three cases of *coma dépassé.* You undoubt-

edly remember the description of the books on Révol's metal shelf, mentioning a copy of an issue of that magazine from 1959, so you will have already guessed that the article appeared in that very issue. Révol bought the issue on eBay and picked it up from the seller at the Lozère-École Polytechnique station on the RER B train line. He spent a long time waiting in the cold for the seller to arrive — a little lady in a topaz turban who trotted along the platform until she reached him, pocketed his cash, then extracted the magazine from a tartan shopping bag and craftily attempted to swindle him.

Révol, eyes riveted once again to his computer screen, duly records the boy's death, closes his eyes, opens them, and suddenly sits up. It is 11:40 a.m. when he calls the department office. Cordélia Owl answers. Révol asks her if Simon Limbres's family has been informed and the young nurse says yes, the police called his mother. She's on her way now.

Marianne Limbres walks through the main entrance of the hospital and heads straight to the reception desk. There are two women there, sitting behind computer screens, two women wearing pale-green scrubs and speaking in low voices. One of them — the one with a thick black braid curled over her shoulder — looks up at Marianne: Hello! Marianne does not reply at first. She doesn't know which department she should go to — Emergency, Intensive Care, Trauma Surgery, Neurobiology — and, struggling to decipher the list of departments listed on a large sign fixed to the wall, as if the letters, words, lines are overlapping and she can't separate them, put them back in order, find any meaning in them, she ends up blurting out: Simon Limbres. Sorry? The woman frowns — her eyebrows thick and black too, meeting in a furry clump at the top of her nose — and Marianne tries again, manag-

48

ing two brief sentences this time: I'm looking for Simon Limbres. He's my son. Ah.
On the other side of the counter, the woman
leans over her computer and the tip of her
braid caresses the keyboard like a Chinese
paintbrush. What was the last name again?
Limbres — *l, i, m, b, r, e, s* — Marianne
spells out and then turns toward the vast
lobby, with its pillars, its cathedral-high ceiling and skating-rink floor: the acoustics, the
gleam. It is silent here, hardly anyone
around. A man in a bathrobe and flip-flops
walks with the aid of a crutch toward a
telephone on the wall; a woman in a wheel-
chair is pushed by a man wearing a felt hat
with an orange feather — a neurasthenic
Robin Hood — and, farther off, near the
cafeteria, in front of a row of doors barely
visible in the dimness, three women in white
have gathered, holding plastic cups. I don't
see him. When was he admitted? The woman
keeps her eyes on the screen, clicking her
mouse. This morning, Marianne sighs, and
the woman looks up again. Ah, so it's ER.
Lowering her eyelids, Marianne nods while
the woman sits up, flicks her braid back
behind her head, and points over to the
elevators at the back of the lobby, then
explains how to get to the Emergency
Department without having to go outside in

the cold and walk all around the buildings. Marianne thanks her and sets off again.

She had fallen back asleep when the telephone rang, buried in an interlacing of pale dreams that sifted the light of day and the shrill computerized voices coming from a Japanese cartoon on the television — later, she would unsuccessfully search the dream for signs: the harder she tried to gather her memories of it, the more it dissolved and she was left without anything tangible, nothing that could make any sense of the terrible shock occurring about twenty miles away, at that very moment, on a muddy road — and she wasn't the one who answered, but seven-year-old Lou, running into the bedroom because she didn't want to miss a second of what she was watching in the living room and simply dropping the phone on her mother's pillow before running back out again, so that the voice on the other end of the line seemed to weave itself into Marianne's dreams, speaking louder, insistent, and in the end it was only when she heard those words please, madame, answer me: Are you the mother of Simon Limbres? that Marianne sat up in her bed, her brain suddenly awakened by a rush of fear.

■ ■ ■ ■

She must have screamed quite loud. Loud enough, in any case, for her daughter to re-appear, slow-moving and serious-faced, eyes wide, standing in the doorway of the bed-room, her head leaning against the door frame, staring at her mother, who didn't see her but was panting like a dog, movements frenzied and face twisted, tapping franti-cally at her cell phone to call Sean, who wasn't answering — pick up, pick up for fuck's sake — her mother hurriedly dress-ing, in boots, winter coat, scarf, then diving into the bathroom to splash cold water on her face, not bothering with any moisturizer or makeup, and only then, lifting her face from the sink, did she see her reflection in the bathroom mirror — irises frozen under swollen eyelids, as if she had suddenly got bags under her eyes, Signoret eyes, Ram-pling eyes, the green flash at the level of her eyelashes — and feel a sudden dread at not recognizing herself, as if her disfigurement had begun, as if she was already another woman. Part of her life — a huge part, still warm, compact — was detaching itself from the present, toppling into the past, where it would fall away, disappear. She sees falling

rocks, a landslide, fault lines dividing the earth beneath her feet: something closes, something is now out of reach. Part of the cliff separates from the plateau and collapses into the sea; a peninsula slowly moves away from the continent and drifts toward the horizon, alone; the door to a cavern of wonders is suddenly obstructed by a rock; in the blink of an eye, the past has grown larger, an ogre gobbling up life, and the present is now a line so thin it is barely visible, beyond which lies the great unknown. The ringing of the telephone broke the continuity of time, and, standing in front of the mirror, where her reflection stares back at her, hands clinging to the edge of the sink, Marianne is petrified by the shock.

Picking up her bag, she turned around and fell over her daughter, who had not moved. Oh Lou. The child lets herself be hugged without understanding, but everything in her look, her attitude, is interrogating her mother, who evades the question — put on your socks, take a sweater, come along — and, as the door bangs shut at the top of the stairs, the thought suddenly enters Marianne's head — an icy slash — that the next time she unlocks this door she will know the truth about Simon. On the next floor down, Marianne rings the door-

bell of the apartment below hers, then rings it again — it's Sunday morning, everyone's sleeping — and a woman answers it. Marianne mutters the words hospital, accident, Simon, serious, and the woman, wide-eyed, nods her head and whispers gently I'll take care of Lou. In her pajamas, the little girl enters the apartment, waving to her mother through the half-open doorway, then suddenly changes her mind and rushes out to the staircase, calling: Mama! So Marianne runs back upstairs, kneels next to her daughter and hugs her tight, then, looking deep into her eyes, repeats the cold litany: Simon, surfing, accident, I'll be back, back soon. Unfazed, the child kisses her mother's forehead and returns to the neighbor's apartment.

After that, she had to fetch her car from the underground parking garage: panic-stricken, she'd had to make two attempts to extricate the vehicle from its narrow space, maneuvering it carefully, millimeters to spare on either side, until she reached the ramp that sloped up to the street. The garage door opened and, dazzled, she blinked several times. The daylight was white, the sky that milky color it has when it snows, though there was no snow — a dirty trick. Marshaling her forces, her

reason, she concentrated on where she had to go, driving east through the upper part of town, following the perfectly straight roads — Rue Félix-Faure then Rue du 329 then Rue Salvador-Allende — the way arrowing forward and only the names changing as she reached the suburbs of Le Havre. Opulent villas overlooking the garbage dump of the poor part of town, vast and perfectly apportioned gardens, private institutions, and somber-colored sedans, gradually changing to decrepit buildings and suburban houses with verandas and little gardens, small cement courtyards where mopeds and beer crates stood in puddles of brown rainwater, and now delivery vans were weaving slowly past sidewalks too narrow for two people to walk side by side; she drove past the Tourlaville Fort, the funeral parlors across from the cemetery, the marble headstones behind tall windows, spotted a bakery with lit windows in Graville, an open church — and crossed herself.

The city was sleeping, but to Marianne there was something menacing about it; she had the sailor's fear of a calm, flat sea. It even seemed to her that the space around her was bulging slightly, as if to contain the phenomenal energy lurking inside the matter, that internal power that might easily

turn to dazzling destructive power with the splitting of a few atoms; but the strangest thing — she came to this conclusion when she thought about it later — was that she saw no one else at all that morning, not a single other car, not a single human being, not a single animal — no dog, cat, rat, insect. The world was deserted, the city as empty as if its inhabitants had all taken refuge in their homes to protect themselves from a catastrophe, as if the war had been lost and they were all hiding behind their windows to watch the enemy troops file past, as if they were all quarantined out of fear of some contagious fate, as if they sensed her anguish and fled from it. Metal shutters were closed behind store windows, blinds lowered. The only things that greeted Marianne as she drove were the seagulls, breaking ranks above the estuary, circling above her car, which, seen from above, was the sole moving object in the entire landscape, a little rectangle that seemed to gather up what little life remained on earth, powered forward like a pinball — irreducible, solitary, shaken by spasms. The outside world slowly expanded, seemed to tremble palely, the way the air above a desert or a sun-baked road trembles palely. The landscape changed into something fleeting and

distant, turning white, almost vanishing completely, while Marianne drove with one hand on the steering wheel, the other hand wiping away the tears that ran down her face, eyes on the road, and her mind tried to ward off the intuition that had been solidifying inside her ever since the phone call, an intuition that shamed her, hurt her, and then the road dipped down toward Harfleur, the exit for Le Havre, the expressway interchanges where she carefully overtook the car in front of her, passed a forest, motionless and enclosed, and finally reached the hospital.

In the parking lot, she turned off the engine, then tried again to make a phone call. Sitting tense, she listened to the quick, regular ringing noises that the call produced and visualized its progress: the sound speeding away to the south of the city, carried on one of those radio waves that formed the invisible matter of the air, crossing from one relay mast to the next, riding an ever-changing frequency, entering the port area, then an industrial wasteland located near the oceanside dock, snaking past the construction sites of buildings under renovation until at last it connected to that freezing warehouse where Marianne had not been

for a long time; she tracked the call as it weaved between the pallets and the wooden beams, between chipboard planks and plywood sheets, merging with the sound of the wind as it was gobbled up there by the sound of splitting tiles, mixing with the whirlwinds of sawdust in the corners, with the smells of polyurethane glue, marine varnish and resin, piercing the fibers of the piled-up work T-shirts, the thick leather gloves, ricocheting between the tin cans used as paint-brush holders, ashtrays, kitchen drawers — a shooting gallery at the fair — the continual vibrations of the circular saw, against the vibrations of the song blasting from an old stereo — Rihanna's "Stay" — against everything that juddered, pulsated, whistled, including the man working there, Sean, who was at that moment leaning over a cradle with an aluminum rail and stops set at a certain distance for cutting slats of the same width. He was a supple, muscular man with tanned hands who moved slowly, leaving footprints on the powdered floor. Wearing a face mask and ear protectors, he was whistling, the way a decorator whistles as he stands at the top of a ladder, paintbrush in hand, the same shrill melody over and over again. The call reached the inside pocket of a parka hang-

ing close by and triggered a ringtone in the casing of a cell phone — the sound of rain landing on a lake or a sea — a ringtone he had downloaded the week before, and which he did not hear now.

The ringing ended, and the call went through to voicemail. Marianne closed her eyes, and saw the warehouse in her mind's eye. In particular, she saw Sean's treasured *taonga,* shining golden-brown on the metal hanging rails that ran along the wall: the clinker-built skiffs from the Seine Valley, the sealskin kayak made by the Yupik in northwest Alaska, and all the wooden canoes he had made there — the biggest of them had a finely sculpted stern like those you find on *waka,* those outrigger canoes used by the Maoris in their ritual ceremonies; the smallest was light and supple, the hull made of birch bark and the interior covered with strips of pale wood, Moses' basket when he was left on the Nile to save his life, a nest. It's Marianne — call me back as soon as you get this message.

Marianne crosses the lobby. It seems to take her forever, each footstep weighed down by urgency and fear. Finally she reaches the huge elevator, which takes her belowground, to a wide landing, the floor paved with large

white slabs. She sees no one, but hears women's voices. The corridor turns sharply, and then she sees a crowd of people, walking in different directions, sitting, standing, lying in mobile beds parked against the walls. Something happens and there are murmurs, complaints, the voice of a man losing his patience, I've been waiting here for an hour, the moaning of an old woman in a black veil, the weeping of a child in his mother's arms.

A door is opened. Inside she sees a glass desk. Behind it, another young woman, sitting in front of a computer screen: she looks up, her face round and very open. A student nurse, she cannot be more than twenty-five. Marianne says the words I am Simon Limbres's mother, and the young woman frowns, disconcerted, then swivels on her chair and addresses someone behind her: Simon Limbres, young man, admitted this morning, know anything about it? The man turns around, shakes his head and, seeing Marianne, says to the nurse: Call the ICU. The woman picks up the phone, has a brief conversation, hangs up, nods, while the man comes out from behind the desk in a movement that sets off a surge of adrenaline somewhere in Marianne's guts. Suddenly she feels hot. She loosens her scarf and

unbuttons her coat, wipes the sweat from her forehead, it's like a sauna in here. The man offers his hand. He is small and frail-looking, his neck thin and creased, like a small bird's, inside the overlarge collar of a pale-pink shirt. His white coat is clean and buttoned to the top, with his name tag in its correct place on his chest. Marianne shakes his hand but can't help wondering if this is how hospital staff greet all visitors or if this ordinary gesture somehow manifests an attitude on the man's part — solicitude or something else — motivated by Simon's condition. She doesn't want to know, doesn't want to hear anything, not yet, that belies in any way the unspoken statement "Your son is alive."

The doctor leads her through the corridor toward the elevator. Marianne chews her lip as she follows him: He's not here, he was admitted directly to Intensive Care. His voice is nasal-sounding, the tone neutral. Marianne stops, staring at him, her voice broken: He's in Intensive Care? Yes. The doctor moves soundlessly, his footsteps small in his rubber soles, his white coat seeming to hover above the ground, the waxy skin of his nose gleaming in the fluorescent light, and Marianne, who is a head taller than him, can see his scalp

through the thin covering of hair. He crosses his hands behind his back: I can't tell you anything, but come with me, they'll explain everything, I assume his condition required admission to that department. Marianne closes her eyes and grits her teeth. Suddenly her whole being draws back. If he says anything else she will scream, or cover his big mouth with her hand to shut him up, please stop, I'm begging you, and then, as if by magic, he leaves his sentence unfinished, dumbfounded, he stands in front of her, frozen to the spot, his head wobbling above the pink shirt collar, and, stiffly, as if made of cardboard, his hand rises, palm up, toward the ceiling, in a vague gesture that somehow expresses the contingency of this world, the fragility of human existence, before falling back down to his side: They're expecting you in ICU. As they arrive in front of the elevator doors, their conversation comes to an end; gesturing with his chin to the end of the corridor, the doctor concludes in a calm but firm voice, I have to go, it's Sunday, the ER is always crazy on Sundays, people don't know what to do with themselves. He presses the call button, the metal doors open slowly, and, suddenly, as they shake hands again, he smiles at Marianne, a bleak smile, goodbye, Madame,

be brave, and turns back toward the sound of shouting.

Be brave, he said. Marianne repeats this word to herself as the elevator takes her to the next floor up. How long it is taking her to get to Simon, the damn hospital is like a labyrinth. The walls of the elevator cabin are covered with medical advice and union announcements. Be brave, he said, be brave, her eyes are gluey, her hands damp, and the pores of her skin are dilating in the too-warm air, ruining her features. Screw bravery, screw this stupid heating system, she can hardly breathe in this place.

The Intensive Care Unit takes up the entire south wing of the ground floor. Access is strictly controlled — there are signs on all the doors forbidding entry to non-personnel — so Marianne waits in the hallway, eventually leaning against a wall and letting herself slide down until she is squatting, her head moving left and right, the back of her skull hard against the wall, lifting her gaze toward the fluorescent tubes on the ceiling. Closing her eyes, she listens: still those voices busily teasing or informing each other from one end of the corridor to the other, still those rubber-soled feet, ballet slippers or ordinary

sneakers, those metallic chimes, alarms going off, the wheels of carts rolling on the
floor, the continual hum and buzz of the
hospital. She checks her phone: Sean hasn't
called. She decides to move — she can't
just wait here — and, standing in front of
the double fire doors edged with black rubber, stands on tiptoes to look through the
window. All is calm. She pushes the door
open, and enters.

He knew instantly that it was her — the stunned look, the staring eyes, the way she chewed her cheeks — so he did not even ask if she was Simon Limbres's mother, simply offered her his hand with a nod: Pierre Révol, I'm the senior doctor here, I admitted your son this morning, please come with me. Instinctively she walks on the linoleum floor with her head lowered, not even glancing sideways in case she sees her child at the back of a dark room. They walk side by side for twenty yards in the lavender-blue corridor, and then there's an ordinary door with a label the size and shape of a business card stuck to it. She doesn't notice the name.

Today, Révol forsakes the Family Room, which he has never liked much, and receives Marianne in his office. She stands for a moment, then sits on the edge of the chair, while he walks around the desk and sits op-

posite her, in his swivel chair, chest thrust forward and elbows to the sides. The more Marianne looks at him, the more she forgets the people she has seen so far in her time at the hospital — the woman with the mono-brow at reception, the student nurse in the ER, the doctor in the pink shirt — as if they were merely links in a chain leading her to this face, their features superimposed one upon the other to form a single face — that of the man sitting in front of her now, about to speak.

Would you like a coffee? Surprised, Mari-anne nods. Révol stands up and, turning the other way, picks up the pot from the coffee machine, which she hadn't seen, and — silently, with broad, sweeping gestures — pours the coffee into two white plastic cups. Steam rises from them. He is playing for time, searching for the right words; she knows this but does not object, although she feels a paradoxical tension, because time is dripping away, like coffee into the pot, while she is fully aware of the urgency of the situation, its seriousness, its closeness. Now Marianne closes her eyes and drinks, concentrating on the burning liquid in her mouth, dreading the first word of the first sentence — the doctor's jaw tensing, his lips

opening, stretching, teeth appearing, the end of the tongue flickering into sight occasionally — that tragedy-soaked sentence that she knows is about to be spoken. Everything in her withdraws, stiffens, her spine pressing against the back of the (wobbly) chair, her head driven back: she would like to get out of here, run to the door and escape, or disappear through a trapdoor opening suddenly beneath her feet, so she can enter a black hole of forgetfulness, so no one in this building can find her, so she need never know anything other than the fact that Simon's heart is still beating; she would like to flee this cramped room, this sordid light, and run away from the news. Because no, she is not brave. She is slippery as a snake, would do anything to make him reassure her, say her fears are unfounded, tell her a story — a suspenseful story, sure — but a story with a happy ending. She's a disgusting coward, but she does not back down from her stance: each second that passes is a hard-won treasure; each second slows her approaching fate, and, observing her writhing hands, her legs knotted under the chair, those closed eyelids, swollen, darkened by the previous night's makeup — a streak of kohl that she applies with her fingertip, in a single movement — seeing

those murky-jade, watery irises, the trembling of those splayed lashes, Révol knows she has understood, that she knows, and so with infinite gentleness he allows the time before his first word to stretch out, picks up the Venetian paperweight and rolls it in the palm of his hand, the glass ball sparkling under the cold fluorescent light, flashing colors over the walls and the ceiling, lines of light like veins, moving across Marianne's face, teasing her eyes open. And this, for Révol, is the signal that he can begin speaking.

Your son is in critical condition.

Hearing those first words — limpid tone, calm tempo — Marianne's eyes, which are still dry, rest on Révol's, which hold her gaze, while he begins his next sentence and she composes herself. His words are crystal clear without being brutal — his semantics correct and precise, *largos* woven into the silences, pauses that closely fit the deployment of meaning — and spoken slowly enough that Marianne can repeat each syllable she hears internally, engrave them in her memory: Your son suffered a cranial trauma in the accident. The scanner shows a major injury in the frontal lobe — he touches his hand to his skull, to the side of

his forehead, to illustrate what he means —
and this violent shock provoked a cerebral
hemorrhage. Simon was in a coma when he
arrived at the hospital.

Révol takes a sip of his now-lukewarm coffee. Across from him, Marianne has turned
to stone. The telephone rings — one, two,
three times — but Révol does not pick it
up. Marianne stares into his face, absorbing
it whole: silky-white complexion, mauve
rings under transparent gray eye bags, heavy
lids wrinkled like walnut shells, a long and
mobile face — and the silence swells, until
Révol speaks again: I'm worried — the sudden, inexplicable loudness of his voice
surprises her, as if someone has nudged the
volume control — we are carrying out
examinations at the moment, and the first
results are not good. Even though his voice
makes an unknown sound in Marianne's
ears, and instantly accelerates her breathing, it is not enveloping, it does not sound
like those horrific voices that purport to
comfort while leading you to a mass grave;
on the contrary, his voice designates a place
for Marianne, a place and a line.

He is in a deep coma.

The seconds that follow open up a space
between them, a naked and silent space.

They wait on the edge of this space for what seems a long time. Marianne Limbres begins to turn the word "coma" slowly in her head while Révol once again approaches the darkest part of his profession. Still rolling the paperweight in the palm of his hand — a veiled and solitary sun — he thinks that there is nothing as violent, as complex as this: placing himself next to this woman so that they can, together, penetrate that fragile zone of language where death is declared, so that they can move forward, in synchrony. He says: Simon is not reacting to painful stimuli anymore. His eyes are nonreactive and he is in a vegetative state; with regard to his breathing, we are beginning to see fluid accumulating in his lungs, and the first scans are not good. He speaks slowly, his phrases punctuated by intakes of breath: a way of making his body, himself, present in his words, a way of adding empathy to this clinical sentence. He speaks as if carving the words into stone, and now the two of them are face-to-face, confronting the truth — this is it, the ultimate face-to-face — and it has been accomplished unswervingly, as if speaking and looking were two sides of the same coin, as if they had to face each other as much as they will have to face up to what awaits in one of the rooms of this hospital.

I want to see Simon — voice distraught, eyes and hands wandering. I want to see Simon — that is all she had said, when her cell phone rang for the umpteenth time from the depths of her coat pocket: the neighbor who's looking after Lou, Chris's parents, Johan's parents, but still no word from Sean. Where is he? She sends a text: Call me.

Révol looked up. Now? You want to see him now? He glances at his watch — 12:30 — and replies, calmly, I'm afraid it's impossible at the moment. You'll have to wait a while: he's in treatment right now, but as soon as we've finished, you will of course be able to see your son. And, placing a yellowish sheet of paper between them, he continues: If it's all right with you, we need to talk about Simon. Talk about Simon. Marianne tenses. What does he mean, "talk about Simon"? Are they going to fill out one of those forms like they often do in hospitals? List the operations he's had? — adenoids, appendix, nothing else — the bones he's broken? — a radius fractured in a bicycle accident the summer he turned ten, that's

all — any allergies? — no, none — diseases he's contracted in the past? — that staph infection the summer he turned five, which he told everyone about because that fabulous name (*Staphylococcus aureus*) made it seem so rare; the mononucleosis he suffered at sixteen, the kissing disease, the lovers' disease, and his lopsided smile when teased about it, the strange pajamas he wore then, like a pair of Hawaiian bermudas matched with a quilted sweatshirt. Are they going to list his childhood illnesses? Talk about Simon. The images speed through her mind and Marianne panics: a baby with roseola lying on a garter-stitch baby blanket; a three-year-old boy with measles, brown scabs on his scalp, behind his ears, and that fever that dehydrated him, turning the whites of his eyes yellow and his hair sticky for ten long days. Marianne speaks tersely while Révol takes notes — date and place of birth, weight, height — and seems in fact not really to care about those childhood illnesses once he has written on his form that Simon has no particular background of serious diseases, rare allergies, or malformations of which his mother is aware. At these words, Marianne becomes flustered, a memory flash, ten-year-old Simon on a school ski trip, afflicted with violent stomach

pains, and the doctor who examined him palpating his left side and, assuming it was appendicitis, diagnosing an "inverted anatomy," the heart on the right side, not the left, etc., a statement that no one questioned, and that fantastical anomaly had turned him into a special person for the rest of that ski trip.

Thank you, Mme Limbres. Then, after smoothing the sheet down with the flat of his hand, he returns it to Simon's dossier, a pale-green folder. He looks back up at Marianne: You can see your son as soon as we have completed the examinations. What examinations? Marianne's voice sounding suddenly alert in the office, and the vague idea that if they are conducting examinations, then all is not lost. The glimmer in her eyes warns Révol, who makes an effort to bring the situation under control, stemming the tide of hope: Simon's situation is developing, but not in the way we would want it to. Marianne's face registers the pain of this blow. Ah, she says, so how is Simon's condition developing exactly? In speaking like this, she knows she is leaving herself open to another blow, that she is taking a risk. Révol inhales deeply before replying.

Simon's injuries are irreversible.

■ ■ ■ ■

He has the unpleasant sensation of having
kicked this woman when she was down, of
having delivered a death blow. He stands
up. We'll call you as soon as we can. Then,
in a louder voice, Does Simon's father
know? Marianne stares at him and answers
he'll be here this afternoon — but Sean still
hasn't called or texted, and suddenly she is
seized with panic, begins wondering if
maybe he isn't in the warehouse today, or at
home, if maybe he's gone to Villequier or
Duclair or Caudebec-en-Caux to deliver a
skiff, or if he's at the rowing club on the
Seine, in fact maybe at this very moment
he's trying out the boat with the buyer, and
they're rowing, sitting on the sliding seat,
Sean watching and quietly making remarks,
impressing with his expert terminology, and
little by little Marianne sees the river narrowing between high, mossy rock walls
covered with plants growing out horizontally, giant ferns and fleshy vines, peat moss
and acid-green grass all tangled up along
the vertical cliffs or bowing toward the river
in leafy cascades, then the light dims, the
geography leaving only a narrow corridor of
milk-white sky above the boat, the water

becoming heavy, flat, slow, the surface aswarm with insects — iridescent-turquoise dragonflies, transparent mosquitoes — the river turning bronze, scattered with silver reflections, and suddenly, in horror, Marianne imagines that Sean has returned to New Zealand, that he is rowing up the Whanganui River, from the Cook Strait, leaving from another estuary and another city, and heading inland, alone in his canoe, fully at peace, the way she had known him, gazing straight ahead; he rowed steadily, passing Maori villages along the riverbank, climbing down the waterfalls, carrying the light boat on his back, advancing ever northward, toward the central plateau and the Tongariro volcano, where the sacred river drew its source, retracing the path of migration to the new lands. She can see Sean precisely, she can even hear his breath echoing in the canyon. Everything is calm there, suffocatingly calm. Révol watches her, concerned by the panic he can see in her eyes, but when he says I'll see you with him, then, when he arrives, Marianne nods, okay.

The scraping of chair legs on the floor, the creak of the door, now they are walking toward the other end of the corridor, and once they are on the landing, without adding a word to their meager dialogue, Mari-

anne turns on her heel and slowly walks away, with no idea where she is going. She passes the waiting room with its straight-backed chairs and its coffee table strewn with old magazines, where mature women with healthy teeth and shining hair and firm perinea smile at her, and soon she is back in the vast glass-and-concrete lobby, on the skating-rink floor. She walks past the cafeteria — multicolored packs of chips, candy, and chewing gum fill the display racks, brightly printed posters of burgers and pizzas are stuck to the wall, bottles of water and soda stand in glass-fronted refrigerators — then suddenly stops, staggering on her feet: Simon is lying helpless somewhere back there, how can she leave him behind like this? She wants to turn around, go back to him, but she continues on her way. She has to find Sean. She has to.

She heads to the main exit, the doors slowly opening in the distance, and four figures enter the building, move toward her. Soon the figures emerge from the blur of her myopia: it's the parents of the other two *caballeros,* Christophe and Johan, walking in a line, wearing the same winter coats that weigh heavy on their shoulders, the same scarfs wrapped around their necks like

braces to hold up their sagging heads, the same gloves. They recognize her, slow down, then one of the two men breaks step and comes toward Marianne, takes her in his arms. The other three wait in line to embrace her. How is he? Chris's father is speaking. All four of them are looking at her. She is paralyzed. Whispers: He's in a coma, no news yet. Shrugging, her mouth twisted: And you? How are the boys? Johan's mother speaks: Chris has fractures in his left hip and fibula; Johan, fractures of both wrists and his clavicle, his rib cage was crushed but no organs were punctured — she speaks plainly, with an outrageous lack of emotion designed to show Marianne that all four of them are aware how lucky they are, how monstrously lucky, because their children are only a little broken, their children were wearing seat belts, they were protected from the collision, and if this woman is downplaying her anxiety to this degree, abstaining from all commentary, it is also to let Marianne know that they know, about Simon, they know it's serious, very serious — a rumor that's spread from the ICU to the Department of Orthopedic and Trauma Surgery, where their sons are — and that she would never be so indecent as to rub it in. And then there is the awkward-

ness she feels, the guilt that holds her back, because it was fifty-fifty between their two sons as to who got the seat belt, with Chris having one automatically as the driver — Johan might well have sat in the middle of the bench, in which case she would be standing in Marianne's shoes at this very moment, in exactly the same situation, staring down into the same chasm of misery, her mouth twisted with the same pain, and at the mere thought of this she is suddenly dizzy, her legs weakening and her eyes rolling back in their sockets. Her husband, sensing that she is about to keel over, puts his arm under hers to steady her, and Marianne, seeing this woman on the verge of collapse, also becomes aware of the chasm between them, between the four of them and her, the abyss that separates them now, thank you, I have to go, let's talk later.

It hits her that she doesn't want to go home. She is not ready yet to see Lou again, to call her mother, to tell Simon's grandparents, her friends; she is not ready to hear them panic and suffer. Some of them will scream into the phone — no, my God, I can't believe it, no no no — some of them will sob inconsolably while others bombard her with questions, mentioning the names

of medical examinations that she knows nothing about, telling her about a case involving someone they know who came out of a coma after the doctors thought it was all over, talking about all the spectacular remissions they've heard about, questioning the hospital, the diagnosis, the treatment, even asking for the name of the doctor in charge of Simon, ah, really, no, I don't know him, oh but I'm sure he's very good, insisting that she writes down the number of this famous surgeon who has a two-year waiting list, suggesting that they could call him on her behalf, because they know him or have a friend who, and maybe she'll even get someone stupid enough, crazy enough to inform her that, hang on, it's possible, you know, to confuse a *coma dépassé* with other states that resemble it, an ethylic coma, for example, or an overdose of sedatives or hypoglycemia, even hypothermia, and then, remembering that Simon surfed in cold water that morning, she will feel like throwing up, then pull herself together to remind the person who's tormenting her that he was in a major road accident, and even if she resisted, repeating to everyone that Simon was in good hands and all they could do was wait, she knew they would want to show their love by covering her with words.

No, she is not ready for that yet. What she wants is somewhere to wait, somewhere to kill time, a shelter from the storm. She reaches the parking garage, sees her car, and abruptly breaks into a run, diving inside it, and then her fists are pounding the steering wheel and her hair is lashing against the dashboard, her hands shaking so much that she can hardly fit the key into the ignition, and when the engine does finally start, Marianne has trouble controlling her speed, her tires squealing as she pulls out of the parking garage. After that, she drives straight ahead, toward the west, where the sky is brighter, while in his office, Révol does not sit down but does what the law obligates him to do when declaring brain death in the ICU: he picks up the phone and calls the Coordinating Committee for Organ and Tissue Removal. Thomas Rémige is the one who answers.

And yet he almost misses the call, he almost doesn't hear it, and it is only as he gets his breath back after a long, turbulent phrase — a vocal polyphony, a flight of birds, Benjamin Britten, *A Ceremony of Carols,* opus 28 — that he hears the trill of his cell phone, distorting the brilliant, delicate song of a caged goldfinch.

This Sunday morning, in a first-floor efficiency apartment on Rue du Commandant-Charcot, Thomas Rémige is making the strips of his venetian blinds vibrate; alone, and naked, he is singing. He began by standing in the center of the room — always in the same spot — his weight evenly distributed on his two feet, back straight, shoulders slightly thrown back, rib cage open in order to clear his chest and neck. Once he felt balanced, he started making slow circular movements with his head

to relax his neck, repeating the same rotations with each shoulder, then focused on visualizing the column of air rising from the pit of his stomach to his throat, that internal ductwork propelling the breath and vibrating his vocal cords. He adjusts his posture and at last opens his mouth, an oven — a little odd in that moment, vaguely ludicrous — fills his lungs with air, contracts the muscles of his abdomen, then exhales like the opening of a passage, sustaining the action as long as possible, utilizing his diaphragm and his zygomatics — a deaf person could hear him simply by putting their hands on his body. Watching this scene, it would be possible to draw an analogy with the sun salutation or the morning chants of monks and nuns, the same lyricizing of the dawn. You might imagine such a ritual to be aimed at the maintenance and conservation of the body — like drinking a glass of cool water, brushing your teeth, unrolling a rubber mat in front of the television to do floor exercises — but for Thomas Rémige it is something else altogether: an exploration of self — the voice as a probe infiltrating his body and transmitting to the outside world echoes of everything that animates it. The voice as stethoscope.

■ ■ ■ ■

He was twenty years old when he left the prosperous family farm, which was taken over by his sister and her husband. He bid goodbye to the school bus and the muddy courtyard, the smell of wet hay, the lowing of a lone cow waiting to be milked and the hedge of poplars grown close together on a grassy bank; after that, he lived in a tiny efficiency in the center of Rouen rented to him by his parents, with an electric radiator and a sofa bed, and he rode a 1971 Honda 500. He started nursing college, loved girls, loved boys, couldn't decide, and one night — during a trip to Paris — entered a karaoke bar in Belleville: it was full of Chinese people, vinyl hair and waxy cheeks, regulars come to polish their performances, couples mostly, admiring and filming each other, reproducing the movements and postures they'd seen on television, and then, suddenly, yielding to the pressure of the people there with him, he had chosen a song — something short and simple, Bonnie Tyler's "It's a Heartache," I think — and, when it was his turn, had taken the stage and slowly metamorphosed: his sluggish body beginning to move, a voice coming

from his mouth, a voice that was his but which he didn't recognize, a voice with amazing timbre, texture, range, as if other versions of himself had been hiding there inside his body: a tiger, the sea crashing against a cliff face, a prostitute. Realizing that there was no mistake — it really was him singing — he seized upon his voice as his bodily signature, as the form of his singularity, and decided he wanted to get to know it. So he began to sing.

By discovering song, he discovered his body. Like a sports enthusiast the day after an intense run or bike ride or gym session, he felt tensions he had never felt before, knots and currents, points and zones, as if his body were revealing to him unexplored possibilities within himself. He undertook to identify everything of which he consisted, to map out a precise anatomy, the shapes of organs, the variety of muscles, their unsuspected powers; he explored his respiratory system, and how the action of singing gathers and controls it, constructing himself as a human body and, perhaps even more than that, as a singing body. It was a second birth.

The time and money that he devoted to singing grew through the years, and it ended up dominating a large part of his daily life, and of a salary swelled by extra shifts at the

hospital: he practiced his singing exercises every morning, studied every evening; twice a week he took lessons with a bulb-shaped opera singer (giraffe-necked, reed-armed, large-breasted, flat-bellied, wide-hipped, with wavy hair down to her knees, swaying around in her flannel skirts), and at night he would find recitals, operas, new recordings on the Internet, download them, pirate them, copy them, archive them; in the summer, he traveled all over France, attending opera festivals, sleeping in tents or sharing a bungalow with fellow buffs; one day he met Ousmane, a Gnawa musician and shimmering baritone, and that summer — last summer — he went to Algeria and bought a goldfinch in the Collo valley, spending all the money he inherited from his grandmother on it: three thousand euros in cash rolled up in a batiste handkerchief.

His early years working as a nurse in Intensive Care reinvigorated him: he entered an underworld, a parallel universe, a subterranean space on the edge of the ordinary world, stirred by continual overlappings at their border, this world suffused by a thousand sleeps where he himself never slept. To begin with, he roamed the department as if mapping it internally, aware that, here, he

inhabited the other half of time, the cerebral night, the core of it all. His voice became clearer, more nuanced. At that time, he was studying his first *lied,* a Brahms lullaby, a simple song that he sang for the first time at the bedside of an agitated patient, the melody working like an analgesic. Flexible hours, heavy workload, everything in short supply: the department was a world apart, obeying its own rules, and Thomas had the feeling that he was, little by little, cutting himself off from the outside world, living in a place where the separation between night and day no longer made any difference to him. Sometimes he felt that he was in too deep. To clear his head, he took more singing lessons, emerging from them exhausted but with an ever deeper insight and a richer voice, continuing to work with an energy which began to be noted at staff meetings, becoming expert at dealing with patients in every grade of coma and sedation, including awakening, carefully handling the machines that monitored patients and kept them alive, showing an interest in pain management. He worked like this for seven years before deciding he wanted to change jobs but remain in the same sector. He became one of the three hundred nurses who coordinate organ and tissue removal

for the entire country, based at the hospital in Le Havre. He is twenty-nine years old and he is at the peak of his powers. When people ask him about this new line of work, which naturally involved extra training, Thomas talks about relationships with loved ones, psychology, law, the collective aspect, all of which is central to his work as a nurse, of course, but there is something else, something more complex, and if he trusts the person he is talking to, if he decides to take the time, he will tell them about that singular uncertainty on the threshold of the living, about his questioning of the human body and its uses, about an approach to death and its representations — because that is what it's all about. He ignores those who tease him — what if the electroenceph-alogram messed up, what if it broke down, an electrical fault or whatever, and he wasn't really dead? Huh? It's not impos-sible, is it? Ooh, you've gone over to the dark side, Tom! — and just keeps smiling, coolly chewing another matchstick, until the night he receives his master's in philosophy from the Sorbonne and buys everyone a drink. Famous for swapping shifts with his coworkers, he would often manage to be replaced for the five half-day seminars at Rue Saint-Jacques, a street he liked to fol-

low down to the Seine, where he would listen to the hum of the city, and sometimes sing.

Impossible to plan anything today: Thomas Rémige is on call, so the ICU could summon him at any time during the next twenty-four hours. As always, he has to find a way to cope with this dead time, vacant without being free — this paradoxical time that is perhaps another name for boredom — by trying to organize it, an attempt that often ends up completely screwed, with Thomas incapable of either relaxing or doing something useful, suspended by the uncertainty, paralyzed by the procrastination. He gets ready to go out, then decides to stay home; begins baking a cake, watching a movie, archiving sound recordings (the song of the goldfinch), then gives up, leaving it until later . . . but there is no such thing as later: later is an abstract concept, thrown into flux by his random hours. So, seeing the hospital's number on the screen of his cell phone, Thomas feels a simultaneous twinge of disappointment and a pang of relief.

The organization he runs functions independently from the hospital even though it

is situated within its walls. But Révol and Rémige know each other, and the young man can guess exactly what Révol is about to tell him; he could even say it for him, this phrase that standardizes tragedy in the name of increased efficiency: One of the department's patients is in a state of brain death. An observation that sounds conclusive, terminal, but for Thomas it has a different meaning altogether, announcing the beginning of a movement, the first step in a process.

One of the department's patients is in a state of brain death.

Révol's voice recites precisely the wording that he expected. Rémige nods without a word, instantly going through the finely calibrated operation that he will soon set in motion within a legal framework that is both dense and strict, a high-precision movement that must be unfolded in accordance with a very specific time line, which is why he now looks at his watch — something he will do many times in the hours that follow, something they will all do, repeatedly, endlessly, until it is all over.

They begin a rapid dialogue, alternating questions and statements about Simon Limbres's body. Rémige sounds out Révol on

three main points: the context of the diagnosis of brain death (where are we with that?), the medical evaluation of the patient (cause of death, background check, feasibility of transplantation), and, lastly, the situation regarding next of kin: Has he been able to talk to the boy's family about the brutality of the event? Are his next of kin present? To this last question, Révol replies in the negative, then clarifies: I've just talked to the mother. Okay, I'll get ready now. Rémige shivers with cold. He is naked, remember.

A few moments later, wearing a helmet, gloves, and boots, his jacket zipped up to the collar and his indigo scarf wrapped around his neck, Thomas Rémige mounts his motorcycle and sets off in the direction of the hospital. Before putting on his helmet, he listened to the echo of his footsteps in the silent street, attentive to that sensation of being inside a canyon, a bottleneck of sound. A flick of the wrist and the engine roars; after that, he too heads east, following the straight road that splits the poor part of town — a road parallel to the one taken earlier by Marianne — swallowing up the miles on Rue René-Coty, Rue du Maréchal-Joffre, Rue Aristide-Briand — bearded names, mustachioed names, names with

paunches, names wearing pocket watches and fedoras — Rue de Verdun and so on, as far as the expressway interchanges, as far as the city limits. His full-face helmet makes it impossible for him to sing, and yet some days, overcome by some mixed emotion midway between fear and euphoria, he lifts his visor in these urban corridors and lets the space vibrate in his vocal cords.

Later, in the hospital. Thomas knows every inch of this vast, oceanic lobby, this void that he crosses diagonally from the end of the path to the stairs that lead up to his office, the Coordinating Committee for Organ and Tissue Removal, on the second floor. But this morning, he goes in as a stranger, as vigilant as if he did not belong to this organization; he goes there as he goes to other hospitals in the area — institutions unauthorized to remove organs. Speeding up as he passes the reception where two men wait, red-eyed and silent, wearing big black down jackets, he waves to the monobrow woman, who, seeing him hurtling into view when she knows he is on call, guesses that a patient in the ICU has just become a potential donor, and responds to his wave with just a look. The arrival in the hospital of the coordinating nurse is always a delicate

matter: the patient's next of kin, unaware of what is about to happen, might hear him talking to someone else about the reason for his presence and make the connection to the condition of their child, their brother, their lover, the news coming as a terrible shock — a situation that would not augur well for the interviews that follow.

In his lair, Révol, sitting behind his desk, hands Simon Limbres's medical file to Thomas. He raises his eyebrows as he does this — eyes widening, forehead wrinkling — and continues their earlier telephone conversation as if no time has passed: a nineteen-year-old boy, nonreactive to neurological testing, no reaction to pain, no cranial nerve reflexes, fixed pupils, hemodynamically stable, I've seen the mother, the father will be here in two hours. The nurse glances at his watch — two hours? The last of the coffee in the pot is poured into a plastic cup, which makes a little crumpling noise. Révol goes on: I've requested the first EEG, they're doing it now — words that are like the pistol shot at the start of a race, because, by ordering this exam, Révol has triggered the legal procedure for recording the death of this young man. There are two kinds of protocol for this: either a CT an-

giography (or, in the event of brain death, a scan confirming the absence of intracranial blood flow) or two thirty-minute EEGs, carried out at four-hour intervals, showing the flat line that signifies the disappearance of all cerebral activity. Thomas receives this signal and declares: We'll be able to carry out a complete evaluation of the organs. Révol nods: *I know.*

Out in the corridor, they go their separate ways. Révol goes up to the recovery room to check on the patients admitted that morning, while Rémige returns to his office, where he immediately opens the green folder. He immerses himself in it, reading each page attentively — the information provided by Marianne, the emergency team's report, today's scans and analyses — memorizing the figures and synthesizing the data. He gradually forms a precise idea of the condition of Simon's body. He is not without apprehension, though, for while he knows all the different stages, the signs that line the route he must take, he is also well aware that this is no well-oiled machine, no simple chain of events, no mere checklist of items to be crossed off one by one. This is terra incognita.

When he's gone through the dossier, he

clears his throat and calls the Biomedical
Agency in Saint-Denis.

The street is silent too, as silent and color-less as the rest of the world. The catastrophe has spread through everything — places, objects — like a plague, as if the world were adapting itself to what happened this morning, the brightly painted van crashing at full speed into the post, the young guy propelled headfirst through the windshield, as if the surrounding landscape had absorbed the impact of the accident, had swallowed the aftershock, muffled the last vibrations, as if the shock wave had grown smaller, spread itself thin, weakening until it was a flat line, a simple line rushing into space and merg-ing with all the other billions and billions of lines that formed the violence of the world, this pin cushion of sadness and ruin, and as far as the eye can see, nothing: no glimmer of light, no burst of bright color, no gold or crimson, no music drifting from an open window — no pounding rock tune, no

melody to which you might sing along, laughing, happy, and vaguely ashamed at knowing the lyrics to such a sentimental song — no smell of coffee or flowers or spice, nothing, not a red-cheeked child running after a ball or crouching, chin on knees, eyes magnetized by the progress of a marble rolling along the sidewalk, not a sound, not a single human voice calling out or whispering words of love, no newborn baby's cry, not a single living being caught in the continuity of time, occupied in some simple, insignificant act on a winter's morning. There is nothing to disturb Marianne's suffering as she moves forward like a robot, her movements mechanical, her expression vague. *On this fateful day.* She repeats these words to herself, under her breath, unsure where they came from, saying them as she stares down at her boots, as if the words were lyrics accompanying her muffled footsteps, a regular sound that spares her from thinking that, for the moment, there is only one thing to do: take one step and then another step and then another and then sit down, and drink. She heads slowly toward a café that she knows is open on Sundays, a shelter she reaches on the verge of collapse. On this fateful day, I pray to you, my Lord. She whispers the words over and over again,

enunciating their syllables like the beads of a rosary. How long is it since she said a prayer out loud? She wishes she could never stop walking.

She opens the door. It is dark inside, marked by the night's excesses, smelling of cold ash. A song by Alain Bashung. *"Voleur d'amphores au fond des criques."* She approaches the bar, leans over the counter. She's thirsty, she doesn't want to wait. Anyone there? A guy comes out of the kitchen: he is huge, wearing a skintight sweater and baggy jeans, just-got-out-of-bed hair, yes, yes, there's someone here, and now, standing in front of her, he asks her, formally: So, miss, what would you like to drink? A gin — Marianne's voice barely audible, not much more than a pant. The man smooths his hair back with his hands, the fingers heavy with rings, and then rinses a glass, all the while checking out this woman, whom he knows he has seen here before. How's it going, miss? Marianne looks away. I'm going to sit down. In the large mirror hung at the far end of the room, she sees a face she doesn't recognize, and looks away again.

Don't close your eyes. Listen to the music. Count the bottles above the bar. Observe

the shapes of the glasses. Read the posters on the wall. *"Où subsiste encore ton écho."* Send out decoys, divert the coming violence. She builds a dam against the flood of images of Simon that roll over her in waves, like a bombing raid, tries to push them back, to beat them back, even though she's already organizing them in her mind, nineteen years of memories, a vast mass. Keep all of that at arm's length. The memories that flashed through her while she was talking about Simon in Révol's cubbyhole of an office lodged in her chest with a pain she is powerless to control or reduce. For that, she would have to situate the memory in her brain and inject some numbing fluid into that precise spot, the needle of the syringe aimed by computer, but even then that would only paralyze the driving force — the capacity to remember — because the memory itself fills her entire body, though Marianne doesn't know this. *"J'ai fait la saison dans cette boîte crânienne."*

She has to think, to gather and order her thoughts, so she can say something clear to Sean when he arrives, relate the facts in an intelligible manner. First: Simon has had an accident. Second: He is in a coma — gulp of gin. *"Dresseur de loulous, dynamiteur*

97

d'aqueducs." Third: The situation is irreversible — she swallows as she thinks of this word she must pronounce, "irreversible," five syllables that freeze the state of affairs forever, a word she never utters, because she believes in the continual movement of life, the possibility of turning any situation around, nothing is irreversible, nothing, she proclaims at every opportunity — speaking the words in a lighthearted tone, gently shaking the words, the way she would the shoulders of someone who's feeling down, nothing is irreversible, apart from death, or disability, and maybe then she might spin around, begin dancing. But Simon . . . no. Simon is irreversible.

Sean's face — those catlike eyes — lights up the screen of her cell phone. Marianne, you called me? Instantly she bursts into tears — the chemistry of pain — incapable of uttering a word while he repeats: Marianne? Marianne? He probably imagines the echo of the sea in the harbor is interfering with the signal, probably hears her spit and snot and tears as so much static while she bites the back of her hand, rendered speechless by the horror she feels at hearing that voice she loves so much, that voice familiar to her as only a voice can be, but become

suddenly strange, abominably strange, because it comes from a space-time where Simon's accident never occurred, an intact world light-years away from this empty café; and now it was dissonant, this voice, it dis-orchestrated the world, tore apart her brain: it was the voice of life before. Marianne hears this man calling her and she weeps, filled by the emotion we sometimes feel when confronted by something that, in the past, survived unscathed, something that triggers the pain of impossible journeys back in time. One day, she must find out what direction time flows in — whether it's linear or the quick circle of a hula hoop, whether it curls and loops or is coiled like the spiral of a snail's shell, whether it can take the form of a tube wave, sucking up the sea, the entire universe, into its dark flip side. Yes, she needs to understand what it is that makes up the passing of time. Marianne grips her phone in her hand: fear of speak-ing, fear of destroying Sean's voice, fear that she will never again be able to hear it as it is now, that she will never again be able to experience that vanished time when Simon was not in an irreversible condition, al-though she knows that she has to put an end to the anachronism of this voice, to bring it up to date, reinstate it in the tragic

present, she knows she has to do it, and when she finally manages to speak, her words are not simple or precise, but incoherent, to the point where Sean loses his calm, he too is overcome by dread — something has happened, something serious — and he starts to question her, exasperated: Is it Simon? What about Simon? What about surfing? An accident? Where? In her mind, his face stands out from the sonic texture, as clearly as on the photograph on her cellphone screen. She imagines he might think that Simon has drowned and corrects him, her monosyllables lengthening into sentences that gradually become more organized and meaningful. Soon she is able to tell him everything she knows in the right order, closing her eyes and placing the phone flat against her sternum as Sean cries out. Then, recovering herself, she quickly explains that, yes, his condition is life-threatening, that he is in a coma but still alive, and Sean, his voice deformed as hers was earlier, says I'm on my way, I'll be there in two minutes, where are you? — and his voice has defected now, leaving the land of the innocent and joining Marianne, piercing the fragile membrane that separates the lucky and the damned — wait there for me.

Marianne found the strength to tell him the name of the café and its precise location. It was pouring rain the day she came here for the first time — four months ago, in October. She was working on an article, something she'd been commissioned to do by the local Heritage office; she had revisited the Saint-Joseph church, Oscar Niemeyer's Volcan, a sample apartment in a building designed by Perret — all these buildings whose architectural movement and radicalism she loved — but her notebook had begun to get soaked, and, sitting in the bar, dripping rainwater onto the floor, she had downed a whiskey, neat; Sean had started sleeping in the warehouse back then, having left the apartment without taking anything with him.

She sees her outline in the mirror at the back of the room, then her face, which he will soon see after all this time, after so much accumulated silence; she had long imagined this moment, promising herself she would be beautiful when it came, beautiful as she still could be, and that he would be dazzled, or at least moved, but the dried tears have tightened her skin, as if

covered with a clay mask, and he will hardly even be able to see her pale-green eyes, whose depths he loves to look into, because her eyelids are so puffy.

She downs the glass of gin and then he is there, standing in front of her, his face haggard, tiny particles of wood dusting his hair, encrusted in the folds of his clothes, in the stitching of his wool sweater. She stands up abruptly, and her chair tips over backward — landing with a clatter — but she doesn't turn around: she stands facing him, one hand lying flat on the table to support her unsteady legs, the other hanging down at her side. They look at each other for a fraction of a second, then one step forward and they embrace, hug each other so hard it's as if they're being crushed together, heads pressed firmly enough to crack their skulls, shoulders bruised, arms aching from gripping so tightly, their scarfs, jackets, and coats merging into one, the kind of embrace you share to protect yourself from a tornado or to prepare for a fall into an abyss, an end-of-the-world type thing, and yet, at the same time, at exactly the same time, it is a gesture that reconnects them — their lips touch — that emphasizes and abolishes the distance between them, and when they free them-

selves from the embrace, when they finally let go of each other, stunned and exhausted, they are like shipwreck survivors.

When they sit down, Sean sniffs Marianne's glass. Gin? Marianne's smile turns to a pained grimace and she hands him the menu. Then she starts to read out a list of everything he could order for lunch, for example croque-monsieur, croque-madame, salade périgourdine; haddock and potatoes, a plain omelet, tartine provençale, sausages and fries, crème caramel, crème vanille, apple tart . . . If she could, she would read out every item on the menu and then start over again at the beginning just in order to delay the moment when they would have to face up to the misery, to the darkness and tears. He lets her do it, watching her without a word. Then, suddenly losing his patience, he grabs her wrist, pressing down on the artery. Stop. Please. He orders a gin too.

So, Marianne arms herself with courage — armed, yes, that's exactly it: a sort of naked aggression has been growing since their embrace, and she covers herself in it, protects herself like someone brandishing a dagger — and, sitting up straight on the bench, she announces the three statements she has prepared, her eyes staring straight

ahead. When he hears the last one — "irreversible" — Sean shakes his head and his face crumples, convulses, no, no, no, then he stands up heavily, knocks the table — the gin jumping inside its glass — and walks toward the door, arms hanging by his sides and his fists balled as if he were carrying something heavy, with the tread of a man who has just beaten the shit out of someone, some guy who was asking for it. As soon as he's outside, on the doorstep, he abruptly turns around and goes back to the table they were sitting at, moving forward through the ray of sunlight painted on the floor, and his silhouette, backlit, is haloed with a grayish film — the sawdust that covers him sprayed up into the air each time his foot hits the ground. His body is smoking. He leans his torso forward, as if he's about to charge. When he gets to the table, he grabs the glass of gin and downs it, then barks at Marianne, who is already tying her scarf around her neck. Come on.

The room is bathed in half-light, the floor reflecting the frozen sky from between the slats of the blinds. He has to wait for his eyes to adjust before he can make out the machines, the furniture, and the body that inhabit this room. Simon Limbres is there, lying on his back in a bed, a white sheet pulled up to his chest. He is on a ventilator, and the sheet lifts slightly with each inhalation, a small but perceptible movement that makes it look as if he's asleep. The sounds of the hospital are muffled here, and the constant beeping and buzzing of the electrical equipment seems only to heighten the silence. It might easily be a normal patient's room, were it not for the subdued lighting, that impression of withdrawal, as if the room were situated outside the hospital, in a depressurized cell where nothing more was at stake.

■ ■ ■ ■

They didn't speak in the car — not a word.
There was nothing to say now. Sean left his
car parked outside the bar — located at the
end of the road where the skiffs he made
and the surfboards that Simon picked up or
borrowed, "shortboards" or "fishes," dug
into the water — and got into Marianne's
car, a first, and she drove, her forearms
straight and rigid as matchsticks, while Sean
kept his face turned to the glass, occasionally commenting on the traffic, which wasn't
too bad — a fact that helped them, carrying
them hurriedly to their son's bedside, but
which also delivered them inexorably into
blackness and sadness: there was nothing to
hinder their progress, delay their arrival. Of
course, they both think about a dramatic
turnaround, the miraculous idea of this all
being a mistake — the images in the scanner being accidentally inverted, an error of
interpretation, a computer bug, a simple
typo, these things happen, just like people
sometimes take home the wrong baby from
a maternity ward, or the wrong patient is
taken to the operating theater: hospitals are
not infallible, after all — but without really
being able to believe in the possibility, and

above all without being able to communicate their thoughts to each other. Soon the smooth, glass-covered buildings are growing bigger, filling the windshield of the car, and now they are fumbling through that semi-dark room.

Marianne approaches Simon. She is as close as possible to his body, which has never seemed so long to her before, and which she has not seen this closely in such a long time — Simon's embarrassment causing him to lock the bathroom door, demanding that people knock before entering his bedroom, walking through the apartment wrapped in towels like a young Buddhist monk. Marianne leans over her child's mouth to feel his breath, places her face sideways on his chest to hear his heart. He is breathing, she can feel it; his heart is beating, she can hear it. Does she think, then, of the first time she heard his heart beat, at the ultrasound center in Odéon one fall afternoon, the sound of a stampede in the speakers while the luminescent smears on the screen marked out his tiny body. She stands up. Simon's head is bandaged, but his face is intact. But is it still *his* face she sees? The question haunts her while she examines her son's forehead, his temples,

the shapes of his eyebrows, the bulge of his eyeballs beneath the lids — the smooth, little concave patch of skin at the inside corner of the eye — while she recognizes the strong nose, the fleshy, prominent lips, the hollowed cheeks, the lightly bearded chin, yes, all this is familiar, but Simon's face — everything in him that lives and thinks and moves — will she ever see that again? Her legs weakening, she staggers, grips the bed, which moves on its wheels, pulling the drip with it, and the space reels around her. Sean's figure loses its clarity, as if behind a rain-blurred window. He has walked to the other side of the bed, standing directly across from Marianne, and now he takes his son's hand while from the icy hollow of his guts to the edge of his barely open lips he struggles to sound his name: Simon. We're here, we're with you, you can hear me, Simon, my boy, we're here. He touches his forehead to his son's: his skin is still warm, and it smells of him, the smell of wool and cotton, the smell of the sea, and he probably begins to whisper words intended only for the two of them, words no one else can hear and that we will never know, the ancient babble of the Polynesian islands, or words of *mana* that have crossed unaltered through all the layers of language,

reddening rocks from a still-burning fire, that dense, slow, inexhaustible matter, that wisdom — he speaks for two or three minutes, then stands up straight and his eyes meet Marianne's and their fingers brush lightly above their child's chest, moving the edge of the sheet, which slides off the young man's chest, revealing the Maori tattoo that neither of them has ever touched, the drawing that comes from his shoulder, then spreads over the hollow of the clavicle and then the scapula. Simon got it done the summer he turned fifteen, at a surfing camp in the Basque Country. It was his way of saying this is my body and I do what I want with it. Sean, whose own back was completely covered with tattoos, had calmly asked him about the meaning, choice, and positioning of the image, seeking to find out if this was some expression of his mixed heritage; but Marianne had taken it badly: Simon was so young, she said anxiously, this tattoo of yours, you do realize it's for life? And the word comes back at her, like a boomerang: "irreversible."

Révol enters the room. Sean turns and calls out: I can hear his heart beating — the buzzing of the machines in the room seems to grow louder in that instant — then he

says it again, insistent: His heart is beating, isn't it? Yes, Révol says, his heart is beating, because of the machines. Later, as they're about to leave the room, Sean interrogates him again: Why didn't you operate on him when he first arrived? The doctor can sense the aggression, the tension, the despair that turns to anger, and he can also tell that the father has been drinking — he can detect the faint smell of alcohol on his breath — so he explains, carefully: It wasn't possible to operate on him, monsieur. The hemorrhage was too widespread, too advanced, you could see it on the scan we took as soon as Simon was admitted, it was too late. Is it this certainty shown in the face of disaster, this imperturbable calm that borders on arrogance, even while the tremors are intensifying, that causes Sean to raise his voice? In any case, he yells: You didn't even try to save him! Révol grimaces but does not blink. He wants to say something, but senses that all he can do is stay silent, and anyway there is a knock at the door. Without waiting for a response, Cordélia Owl enters the room.

Having splashed some water on her face and downed a cup of coffee, she is beautiful the way certain young women are after a night without sleep. She greets Marianne

and Sean with a brief smile, and then, concentrating fully, walks up to the bed. I'm going to take your temperature. She speaks to Simon. Révol freezes. Marianne and Sean stare at her in amazement. The young nurse turns her back to them, all right, that's good, then checks his blood pressure and says I'm going to look at your catheter now, to see if you've peed — she is so gentle, it is almost unbearable. Seeing the shocked expressions on Marianne and Sean Limbres's faces, Révol thinks about interrupting the nurse, ordering her to leave the room, but finally decides in favor of movement: We should go to my office to talk, come with me if you would. Marianne rears up, shakes her head, unwilling to leave the room, I'm staying with Simon — a few strands of hair hang over her face, swinging from side to side — and Sean stands stubbornly alongside her, but Révol insists: Come with me, the nurse needs to take care of your son now, you'll be able to see him again afterward.

Once again they are back in the maze, in the intersecting corridors, amid the figures of people at work, echoing voices, waiting patients, nurses checking drips, blood pressure, dealing with bedpans and bedsores,

airing rooms, changing sheets, washing floors, and once again Révol with his gangling stride, the sides of his white coat flapping at either side of him like wings, once again the tiny office and the icy chairs, the swivel chair behind the desk and the paperweight rolling in the palm of his hand when, at that very moment, Thomas Rémige knocks on the door, then opens and walks right in. He introduces himself to Simon Limbres's parents — I'm a nurse, I work in this department — then sits next to Révol, on a stool that he puts there. So, there are now four of them sitting in this cubbyhole, and Révol realizes he needs to speed things up because they are suffocating here. So, taking care to look them in the eyes again, individually — this man and this woman, Simon Limbres's parents, the look a way of giving his word — he tells them: Simon's brain no longer shows any activity. We've just carried out another thirty-minute EEG and it shows a flat line. Simon is now in a *coma dépassé.*

Pierre Révol has physically collected himself — back straightened, neck thrust tall — contracting his muscles as if moving up a gear and accelerating, as if saying to himself at that moment, okay, no more beating

112

around the bush, let's just get on with it, and it is probably this effort that enables him to pass beyond Marianne's involuntary shudder and Sean's exclamation, both of them realizing the significance of the term *"dépassé,"* understanding that the end of the story is close, and for them the imminence of this announcement is unbearable. Sean closes his eyes, bows his head, pinching the inside corners of his eyes with his thumb and index finger and murmurs I want to be sure that you've done everything you can, and Révol gently assures him: The violence of the accident was too great. Simon's condition was hopeless by the time he was admitted this morning. We sent the scan to several neurosurgeons, who unfortunately confirmed our view that a surgical intervention would accomplish nothing. I give you my word. The moment he said the word "hopeless," Simon's parents stared at the floor. Something inside them cracks and collapses. Then, suddenly, as if to delay the final sentence, Marianne says: Yes, but people sometimes wake up from comas, don't they, even if it's years later? There are lots of cases like that, aren't there? Her face is transformed by this idea, a burst of light, and her eyes grow wide. Yes, with comas, nothing is ever lost. She knows this: there

113

are so many stories on blogs, on forums, of people waking up after years of silence, these little miracles. Révol looks into her eyes and firmly replies: No — the fatal syllable. He continues: All the functions that comprise your son's consciousness, awareness, mobility have ceased, and the same is true for his vegetative functions: his breathing and heartbeat are entirely dependent on machines. Révol talks and talks, gathering evidence, enumerating facts, pausing after each piece of information, his intonation rising — a way of saying that the bad news is accumulating, piling up over Simon's body — until finally his sentence comes to an end, exhausted, suddenly indicating the void stretching out before it, like a dissolution of space.

Simon is in a state of brain death. His life is over. He is dead.

After delivering such a message, it is only natural to take a moment to get your breath back, stabilize the oscillations in your inner ear so you don't fall off your chair. Their gazes become unglued. Révol ignores the beep that his pager makes, opens his hand and examines the orange-ish paperweight that lies warm in his palm. He is worn out. He has announced the death of their son to

114

this man and this woman, without clearing his throat or lowering his voice; he has pronounced the words — the words "death" and "dead" — words that freeze the blood. But Simon's blood is not cold, that is the problem. The notion of his death is contradicted by the way he looks, because, when it comes down to it, his flesh is warm, it moves, instead of being cold, blue, and immobile.

Looking sideways, Révol watches Marianne and Sean: she is burning her retinas on the yellow fluorescent tube fixed to the ceiling, while he rests his forearms on his thighs and leans forward, staring at the floor, head withdrawn into his shoulders. What could they have seen in their son's room? What could they have gleaned with their ignorant eyes, incapable of understanding the relationship between Simon's destroyed insides and his peaceful exterior, between reality and appearance? There was nothing visible on their son's body, no physical sign that would enable a diagnosis to be made, as if reading the body — nothing like the brilliant Babinski reflex, which could be used to detect brain disease simply by stimulating the sole of the foot. No, for them, he lay there mute, indecipherable, as impenetrable as a safe. Rémige's cell phone

rings, excuse me, he jumps to his feet and instantly switches it off, then sits down again. Marianne shivers, but Sean does not even lift his head, sitting there motionless, his back wide, bulging, dark.

Révol keeps them in his field of vision, trying to understand them, his gaze like a lens that he runs over their presence. These two are a little younger than him, children of the late sixties, and they have spent their lives in a corner of the globe where life expectancy, already high, keeps growing, lengthening, where death is kept hidden in the shadows, where it is erased from the places of everyday life, evacuated to hospitals, where it is dealt with by professionals. Have they ever even seen a corpse before? Sat by a grandmother's deathbed, dragged a drowned man from the water, cared for a dying friend? Have they ever seen a dead person other than in American TV shows like *Body of Proof, CSI, Six Feet Under*? Révol likes to visit these televisual morgues occasionally, these worlds populated with emergency physicians, medical examiners, funeral directors, embalmers, and forensics experts, among them always a good number of sexy, eccentric, near-hysterical females, most often a gothic vamp with pierced lips or a classy but bipolar blonde, always

116

desperate for love; he likes listening to these people chatting around a stiff laid out on a mortuary slab, the camera lens covered with a blue filter, telling each other secrets, shamelessly flirting, even working sometimes, formulating hypotheses over a strand of hair trapped in a pair of tweezers, a button examined under a magnifying glass, a sample of mucous analyzed with the aid of a microscope, because the clock is always ticking, the night coming to an end, because there is always an urgent need to solve the mystery of the traces on the epidermis, to take a stab at deciphering the victim's corpse to find out if they had gone clubbing or eaten candy or too much red meat, if they had drunk whiskey, were afraid of the dark, combed their hair, handled chemicals, had promiscuous sex; yes, Révol enjoys watching these shows sometimes, although in his opinion such scenes say nothing about death. Even if the corpse is the camera's main focus, even if it fills the screen, even if it's examined, sliced up, turned over, it is all a charade, and the stories reflect this. So the dead body, a repository of unrevealed secrets, of narrative and dramatic possibilities, is ultimately used to keep death at a distance.

Sean and Marianne have still not moved.

Despondency? Courage? Dignity? Révol has no idea, and is half-expecting them to suddenly explode, leap over his desk, sending his papers flying, knocking over his stupid ornaments, maybe even hit him, insult him — you bastard, you piece of shit. God knows they have reason enough to go crazy, to bang their heads against the wall, to scream with rage. Instead of which, the two of them appear to be slowly dissociating themselves from the rest of humanity, migrating toward the edge of the earth, leaving this time, and this place, to drift among the stars.

How could they even think about the death of their child when what was a pure absolute — death, the purest absolute of all — had been reformulated, newly defined, in different bodily conditions? Because it was no longer that beating rhythm in the hollow of the chest that confirmed life (a soldier removing his helmet and leaning down to put an ear to the breast of his comrade lying in mud at the bottom of the trench), it was no longer breath exhaled by the mouth that signified life (a dripping lifeguard giving mouth-to-mouth to a young girl with a greenish complexion), but the electrified cerebrum, activated by brain waves, prefer-

ably beta waves. How could they even contemplate it, this death of their Simon, when his skin was still pink and soft, when, as Rimbaud wrote, the nape of his neck was bathed in cool-blue cresses and his feet were stretched out in the yellow flags? Révol gathers the representations of corpses that he knows about, and they are always images of Christ — pale-bodied crucified Christs, foreheads spiked by the crown of thorns, hands and feet nailed to the black, glistening wood, or Christs taken down from the cross, heads laid back and eyes half-closed, white-skinned and emaciated, hips covered by a thin shroud, in the style of Mantegna, or *The Body of the Dead Christ in the Tomb* by Holbein the Younger — a painting of such realism that Dostoyevsky warned believers if they look at it, they risk losing their faith — or they are kings, prelates, embalmed dictators, cinematic cowboys collapsed on the sand and shot in close-up, and he remembers that Christlike photograph of Che, his eyes open, exhibited in a morbid mise-en-scène by the Bolivian junta, but he can think of nothing analogous to Simon, this intact and calmly athletic body, free of blood or wounds, resembling a young god in repose, Simon who looks like he is sleeping, who looks alive.

How long do they stay seated like this after the announcement, slumped on the edges of their chairs, held captive in a mental experience of which their bodies had, until that moment, not the slightest inkling? How long does it take them before they accept death's new regime? For now, there is no possible translation for what they are feeling; it strikes them down in a language that precedes language, from before words, before grammar, an unshareable language that is perhaps another name for pain. Impossible to extricate themselves from it, impossible to substitute another description for it, impossible to reconstruct it in another image. They are, at once, cut off from themselves and from the world that surrounds them.

Thomas Rémige has remained silent, sitting on the metal stool next to Révol, legs crossed at the knees, and perhaps he is thinking about the same things as the doctor, forming the same mental visions. He has put his box of matches away and now waits, with them. Time passes. Their minds whirl and the room fills with their silent screams. Then Révol stands up, tall and pale, his long, sorrowful face indicating that he must leave them now, I have to be

somewhere, so Thomas Rémige remains alone with Simon's parents, who do not stand up but move closer to each other, shoulder to shoulder, and weep in silence. He waits for a moment, then asks them, in a kind voice, if they would like to go back to Simon's room. Without replying, they stand up and leave the room, the nurse following, but as soon as they are in the corridor, Sean shakes his head, no, I can't, not yet. He is breathing loudly, filling his lungs and swelling his chest, one hand covering his mouth, and Marianne slides under his shoulder — to support him, to protect him — and the three of them come to a halt. Thomas goes up to them and explains: I'm here to accompany you, to be with you; if you have any questions, please ask me. Sean sounds like he's suffocating, then — how does he find the strength to speak? — he demands: What's going to happen now? The nurse swallows while Sean continues, his voice ravaged by grief and disgust: Why are you keeping him alive if there's no hope? What are we waiting for? I don't understand. Marianne, staring vacantly through the lock of hair that has fallen over her face, seems not to hear any of this. Thomas is searching for a way out, a way to formulate his answer: Sean's question has severed the

121

usual chronology of the protocol, designed to protect the grieving from the sudden shock of the tragedy, the brutality of the announcement, by giving them time. But the question must be answered. He decides to speak to them now.

Cordélia Owl plumps Simon's pillow, smooths the sheet over his chest, draws the curtains, leaves the room, closes the door behind her, and walks toward the reception desk, tracing arabesques on the floor of the corridor — damn these tight, fitted scrubs: she would have liked more room right now, to be able to hear the rustling of the folds, feel the fabric rubbing against the bumps and indentations on her knees, which she knew to be supple and reliable. On the way, she puts her hand in her pocket and pulls out her phone: no messages. *Nyet. Nada de nada.* 2:40 p.m. He must be asleep. Yes, he's sleeping. Lying on his back somewhere, bare-chested, abandoned. She smiles. Don't call.

Underwear back in place, buttons rebuttoned, belt buckles adjusted, they stood facing each other on the sidewalk, well, I should go, wow it's late, um it's actually

pretty early isn't it?, yeah, okay bye, a kiss on the cheek, a kind smile, and then they separated, following the appropriate ballet steps — smooth *balancé, dégagé arrière, tour piqué* — and moved away from each other along the same line, before both melting into darkness. Cordélia had walked slowly to begin with, clacking her heels like a fifties starlet in a pencil skirt, one hand holding her coat collar tight to her throat. She didn't turn around — absolutely not — but once she had rounded the corner, she began to spin like a top, face to the sky, mouth open to the wind, arms held wide like a whirling dervish, then, once she was facing the right way, started to run, speeding between buildings, occasionally leaping a gutter as if it were a river she had to cross, her arms waving like ribbons, the cold night air lashing her face, blowing open her coat, which she hadn't buttoned up, and it was good, she felt beautiful, supple, felt like she'd grown at least seven inches taller since the two of them had gone clattering into garbage cans, since her panties had slid to the floor and he had put his hand under her mound, his palm hollowed so he could raise her up the wall, and she had lifted herself on the toes of one foot, wrapping the knee of her other leg behind his back and draw-

ing him toward her, his cock inside her, tongues clamoring in their mouths like fire in furnaces, teeth finally biting into flesh. She laughed as she walked, the hot-cold shivers of a girl who had overplayed her role as a solitary heroine, in the eyes of the world, now thawed, the amazon of the city assuming her desire and controlling her actions, she moved forward through the windy boulevards, the deserted five a.m. streets, broke into a run, indifferent to the car that slowed down next to her, to the windows that lowered, to the sexual insult that was bellowed from within, hey slut, you want some?, devouring the space in front of her, burning it up, so she almost crossed Rue d'Étretat just as Chris's van pulled out to her left on the Quatre-Chemins crossroads, stopping dead by the sidewalk, the fresco on the bodywork filling her vision — it seemed to her that the California surfer girls in triangular bikinis were winking and smiling at her as if she were a possible sister — and a few strides later, she was home, buried under the down comforter, eyes closed, although she couldn't sleep. She had not asked anything of that guy who had been tormenting her for so long, had not posed a single question — brave girl.

■ ■ ■ ■

She enters the glass-walled, aquarium-like room, grabs a chair and collapses, suddenly exhausted. Clown fish crisscross the computer screen. She checks her phone again. Zilch. Of course there's nothing. An unwritten rule that she wouldn't break, not for all the gold in the world. The idea that, however quickly and coolly she spoke it, the slightest word to come out of her mouth would inevitably be smarmy, fake, overbearing, that any sentence she might pronounce would reveal the anxious sentimental cretin that lurked inside her. Don't move a muscle. Swallow some coffee, a few nuts, a vial of royal jelly, don't do anything stupid. Switch off that damn phone. Fuck, I'm so tired.

Pierre Révol walks in as she is examining the purplish marks on her neck, twisting herself in front of the Photo Booth app on her computer. Seeing his face appear in the image, leaning over her shoulder like an indiscreet neighbor reading her newspaper on a metro ride, she cries out. So, you were saying you've just started in the department? Révol stands motionless behind her as she jumps up and turns around, her head swimming, a black veil obscuring her vi-

sion, I need to eat something. She pushes her hair behind her ears in an attempt to clear her messed-up face — yes, I started two days ago — and with a firm hand she adjusts her collar. I need to talk to you about something important, something you'll have to face here. Cordélia nods, okay. Now? It won't take long, it's about what just happened in the room back there, but at that very moment — *bzzz bzzz* — Cordélia's cell phone vibrates inside her pocket and she stiffens suddenly as if she's been electrocuted, oh God, no, I don't believe it, fuck! Révol sits on the edge of a table and begins to speak, looking down at the floor, arms crossed over his chest, legs crossed at the ankles: The boy you saw in a state of brain death — *bzzz bzzz* — Révol is articulating very clearly, but for Cordélia his words are like a phonetics exercise in a foreign language. No matter how hard she tries to focus all her attention on that face, to make her brain concentrate on what that voice is saying, it's as if she's swimming against the current, against that warm wave that swells against her hip at regular intervals — *bzzz bzzz* — that runs between her thighs, into the hollow of her anus. She fights against it, trying to return to that man who seems to be growing ever more distant

from her, as if she's caught in rapids, becoming ever more inaudible as he explains: So, that young man is dead; now, grasping the reality of that death is difficult for his parents, because the appearance of his body seems to contradict the facts, you understand? Cordélia makes an effort to listen, articulating a yes like she's bursting a bubble, I see, but in truth she doesn't see anything, the scatterbrain, in fact there's a stampede inside her head now — *bzzz bzzz* — the tiny vibrations of the phone provoking a flood of sexual images, frames from the movie of the night before — that oh-so-soft mouth open on the nape of her neck, the breath warm, and now her forehead, her cheek, her stomach, and her breasts are being scraped against the wall, skin reddened by the contact with the grainy mortar, the jutting bricks, while he moves behind her, and her hands grab his butt to pull him even closer, even deeper, harder — *bzzz* — the final palpitation, that's it, she doesn't blink, swallows before replying, tight-voiced, yes, I understand exactly what you mean. Révol glances at her a little suspiciously before concluding: So, when you're looking after a patient here, please don't talk to them the way you did to Simon Limbres: his parents were in the room, and for them it was a

contradictory signal in an extreme situation; such words, spoken in the context of treatment, blur the message we are trying to communicate to them, when the situation is already upsetting enough, okay? Yes — Cordélia's voice, agonized. She is waiting for only one thing now, for Révol to leave the room, go on, get the hell out of here, I get it, just go, and then suddenly, without warning, she balks, lifts her head: You didn't involve me in the patient's care; you saw the parents on your own; we're not going to work like that anymore. Révol looks at her, amazed: Oh? So how are we going to work? Cordélia takes a step forward and replies: We're going to work as a team. The silence lengthens. They look at each other, then the doctor jumps back to his feet: You look a little peaked, do you know where the kitchen is? They have cookies there. You need to be careful, young lady; twelve hours in the ICU is a marathon, not a sprint, you need to stay the distance. Yeah, yeah, okay. Finally, Révol leaves the room and Cordélia shoves her hand into her pocket. She closes her eyes, thinks about her grandmother in Bristol, whom she talks to every Sunday evening — it can't be her, she tells herself, it's too early. She would willingly undergo a superstitious test (he loves me he loves me not) before

opening her eyes and reading the numbers on the touchscreen. She would willingly put all her money, as on a roulette board, on a single number, a room number, would throw a ball of paper into a wastepaper basket or simply call heads or tails on a coin toss. Oh, don't be an idiot — what's the matter with you?

Cordélia Owl stands in the center of the room, head high and shoulders back, and slowly lifts up her fingers, one by one, to reveal the number of the person who called her. Unknown. She smiles with relief. In fact, she is no longer so certain she wants him to contact her, no longer so eager to hear his voice again. Suddenly she feels cruel; thinking of him, she is lucid and cheerful. She is twenty-five years old. With a feeling of disgust, she anticipates the gradual loss of romantic tension, this mountain of fatigue — exaltation, anxiety, craziness, squalid impulsiveness — and wonders again why this intensity remains for her the most desirable part of her life, then suddenly spins around and turns her back on this question, the way you might remove your foot from the muddy pond where you've just put it, felt it being sucked down. Unable to rest, what she must do is prolong

the previous night, let it infuse her, celebrate it. Maintain her girlish grace and irony. When she reaches the little kitchen, she takes a packet of raspberry wafers from a cupboard, tears open the paper, which rustles like silk under her voracious fingers, and slowly devours every single one.

Révol moves through the corridor, ignoring the people who call out to him, try to hand him papers as they jog alongside him: Three minutes, just give me three minutes for Christ's sake, he mutters, holding up three fingers while emphasizing the word "three" in an authoritative voice. His colleagues know that gesture; they know that once he's in his office the doctor will gravitate to that rolling, swaying chair of his, check his watch, start a countdown — three minutes, the time it takes to boil an egg: the perfect measurement — and, profiting from this moment of solitude, will rest his cheek against his elbow, flattened and bent on the desktop, just like a kid in kindergarten taking a nap in the classroom after lunch, and will sink into this brief crevice of sleep to shed the trauma of what has just occurred. Exhausted, he leans his head on his crossed arms and falls asleep. He makes the very

most of those three minutes: after so many years — twenty-seven — spent putting other people to sleep, it's not surprising that he has developed a highly efficient technique for taking a micro-siesta, even if it lasts only a fraction of the time usually recommended for recharging a human body. Everyone knows that Révol long ago lost that other sleep: nocturnal, horizontal, deep. In the apartment where he lives, on Rue de Paris, there is no bedroom anymore, in the strict sense of the word, only one large room in which the double bed is used as a coffee table, a place to store his collection of vinyl records — everything by Bob Dylan and Neil Young — and his paperwork, and long trays containing his botanical experiments with psychotropic plants. It's for professional usage, he tells those — rare — visitors who are amazed to see cannabis plants being openly cultivated, along with poppies, lavender, and *Salvia divinorum,* known as "diviner's sage," a hallucinogenic herb whose curative virtues he has described in articles published in pharmacological magazines.

The night before, alone in his apartment on Rue de Paris, he watched the Paul Newman movie *The Effect of Gamma Rays on Man-in-the-Moon Marigolds* for the first

time. The title had suggested some kind of botanical fantasy, but the film itself was something else altogether, a powerful combination of hallucination and science, which Révol loved. Moved and captivated, he formed the idea — why not? — of reproducing the experiment conducted by Matilda, the movie's young heroine, in his living room. She had given varying doses of radium to marigold seeds in order to observe their growth, the way their shapes changed through time under the influence of the gamma rays, some becoming huge, others puny and crumpled, and still others simply beautiful. Little by little, this solitary kid began to understand the infinite variety of life, at the same time learning to take her place in the world, declaring onstage at her school's science fair that it was possible, one day, that a wonderful mutation would transform and improve the human species. After that, he dreamily fried eggs, their yolks as dazzlingly yellow as the centers of the marigolds in the movie, grabbed a bottle of blond beer from the refrigerator door, uncapped and slowly drank it, then rolled up inside a goose-down quilt, his eyes wide open.

Révol sleeps. There is a notebook close by on the desk so that he can, upon waking,

write down the images he's glimpsed, the sequences of actions and faces, and perhaps Simon's will be among them — his black hair rigid with dried blood, his olive skin tumid, the pale domes of his eyelids, forehead and right temple covered by a beet-red halo, the stain of death — or perhaps he'll see Joanne Woodward, alias Beatrice Hunsdorfer, Matilda's borderline insane mother, rushing into the auditorium after the science fair is over, emerging from the shadows in a formal evening dress, sequins and black feathers, staggering drunk, glassy-eyed, and declaring in a slurry voice, one hand planted on her chest: *My heart is full, my heart is full.*

They held hands as they followed Thomas Rémige, and, deep down, the reason they accompanied him, walking once again through this maze of corridors and sterile zones, waiting patiently as they entered each new level, holding doors open with their shoulders, in spite of the black meteor that had just crashed into their lives, in spite of their obvious exhaustion, the reason they did all this was because of the look in Thomas Rémige's eyes — that look which kept them in the land of the living, that look which already seemed priceless. And so, as they walked, the two of them moved closer, interlacing their fingers, touching together the fleshy pads of their fingertips and their bitten nails edged with dead skin, brushing their dry palms, the rings on their fingers, and they did it without thinking.

Yet another part of the hospital: a place

styled after the living room of a sample apartment, light and airy, with elegant if unexceptional furniture — an apple-green couch in a synthetic fabric that feels like velvet, and two stuffed vermilion chairs — the walls bare apart from a color poster for a Kandinsky exhibition — Beaubourg, 1985 — and, sitting on the coffee table, a green plant with long, thin leaves, four clean glasses, a bottle of mineral water, and a small potpourri dish that smells of orange and cinnamon. The curtains stir gently in the breeze that comes through the cracked-open window, and the few cars that come and go in the hospital parking lot below are clearly audible, as is the screech, like sonic scratches over all of this, of seagulls. It's cold.

Sean and Marianne are sitting next to each other on the couch, awkwardly, intrigued in spite of being so shaken, while Thomas Rémige sits on one of the vermilion chairs, holding Simon Limbres's medical file. Even though they are sharing the same space, however, inhabiting the same time, at that precise moment, nothing in this world could be more distanced than those two beings, in their pain, and this young man who has placed himself before them with the aim — yes, with the aim — of gaining their

consent for the removal of their child's organs. Here are a man and a woman caught in a shockwave, at once thrown into the air and smashed down into a broken temporality — a continuity brutally severed by Simon's death but which, like a headless duck running around the courtyard, keeps going senselessly — a temporality woven from pain, a man and a woman in whose heads are concentrated the whole tragedy of the world. And here is this young man in a white coat, cautious but committed, determined not to jump the gun, but highly aware of the silent countdown in a corner of his mind, knowing all too well that a body in a state of brain death quickly deteriorates, that time is of the essence — and torn between these two imperatives.

Thomas pours water into three glasses, stands up, and crosses the room to close the window. As he moves, he observes the couple carefully, never takes his eyes from them — this man and this woman, Simon Limbres's parents — and in this moment he is undoubtedly preparing himself mentally, conscious of the fact that he is about to mistreat them, to carve into their pain with questions they know nothing about right now, asking them to think and to

formulate responses when they are zombies, stunned by pain, hurtling through black space. In all probability, he prepares to speak the same way he prepares to sing, relaxing his muscles, regulating his breathing, aware that punctuation is the anatomy of language, the structure of its meaning, visualizing his opening phrase as a sound line, weighing the first syllable he will pronounce, the one that will break the silence, slicing instead of cracking the eggshell, quick and precise as a blade stroke rather than a fissure that meanders slowly up the wall when the earth trembles. He begins slowly, reminding them methodically of the context of the situation: I think you understand now that Simon's brain is being destroyed; nevertheless, his organs continue to function; this is an unusual situation. Sean and Marianne blink in acknowledgment. Encouraged, Thomas goes on: I'm aware of how painful this is for you, but I have to broach a delicate subject — his face is haloed by transparent light and his voice becomes imperceptibly louder. It sounds absolutely clear when he declares:

We are in a context where it would be possible to consider the donation of Simon's organs.

■ ■ ■ ■

Wham. In that instant, Thomas's voice hits the right frequency and the room seems to resonate like a gigantic amplifier. It is a high-precision delivery, as perfect in its timing as the wheels of a jet landing on the flight deck of an aircraft carrier, the paintbrush of a Japanese calligraphist, a tennis player's drop shot. Sean lifts his head, and Marianne jumps, their eyes capsizing in Thomas's calm gaze — they are beginning to comprehend, with terror, what they are doing here, sitting in front of this handsome young man with his classical features, this handsome young man who continues speaking in a composed voice: I would like to ask you if your son ever talked to you about this, if he ever expressed his views on the subject.

The walls dance, the floor rolls. Marianne and Sean are in shock, their mouths agape, eyes staring emptily at the coffee table, hands writhing, and the silence that fills the room is thick, black, vertiginous, a mix of panic and confusion. A chasm has opened up, here, in front of them, a chasm that they can only imagine as "something," because "nothing" is unthinkable. They struggle with this, facing that black hole, together, even if

they are not feeling the same emotions or posing the same questions — Sean has become solitary and silent over the years, combining clear-headed unbelief with a sort of lyrical spirituality, based in the myths of Oceania, while Marianne had her first communion in a flowered dress and tennis socks, wearing a crown of fresh flowers on her head, the host stuck to the roof of her mouth, she prayed for a long time each evening in the bunk bed she shared with her sister, kneeling on the upper bunk, saying the words out loud in those pajamas that made her itch, and even now when she enters a church, she explores the silence as if it's the texture of a mystery, seeks out the little red light shining behind the altar, inhales the heavy odor of wax and incense, observes the daylight filtering through the rose window in colored rays, the wooden statues with painted eyes, but remembers the intense sensation that ran through her in that moment when she removed the halter of faith from her neck. The two of them conjure visions of death, images of beyond, postmortem spaces deep in eternity: it's a gulf hidden in a fold of the cosmos, a black and rippling lake, it's the kingdom of the believers, a garden where beings move, their flesh resuscitated by the

hand of God, it's a lost valley in the jungle where forsaken souls flutter aimlessly, it's a desert of ashes, a sleep, a diversion, a Dantean hole at the bottom of the sea, and it's also a hazy shore reached in a delicately worked wooden canoe. They are leaning forward, arms crossed over their stomachs, nursing the shock, and their thoughts converge in a funnel of questions that they do not know how to ask.

Thomas starts again, trying a different tack: Was your son on the national organ donation refusal registry? Or do you know if he's ever expressed his opposition to the idea, if he's against it? A complicated question; their frowns deepen. Marianne shakes her head, I don't know, I don't think so, she stammers, while Sean suddenly moves, his dark squarish head turning slowly toward Thomas, and says, his voice muffled: Nineteen years old — he inclines forward and gathers together these poorly articulated words, spoken without really opening his mouth — are there any nineteen-year-olds who make the necessary arrangements regarding, for that sort of, does that even exist? "Necessary arrangements" — his voice is menacing, contained, the S's sinisterly snakelike. It can happen, Thomas replies softly, sometimes. Sean swallows a

mouthful of water, bangs the glass back on the table: Maybe, but not Simon. And so, stealing in through what he identifies as a breach in the dialogue, Thomas asks, in a slightly louder voice, why "not Simon"? Sean chews silently: Because he loves life so much. Thomas nods, I understand, but does not give up: Loving life doesn't mean he never thought about death; he might have talked about it to his friends or family. Filaments of silence are spliced together, and then Marianne reacts, foggily, the words tumbling fast: Friends, family, yeah, I don't know, actually yes, his sister, yes he really loves his little sister, Lou, she's seven, they're like day and night but they're really close, and his friends, well, there's his surf buddies, Johan, Christophe, and his high school friends, but, I don't know, we don't see them very often, but friends and family, yeah, I don't know, well there's his grandmother, his cousin who lives in the United States, and there's Juliette too, his first love, and there's us.

They are talking about their son in the present tense; not a good sign. Thomas continues: I'm asking you these questions because if the deceased — in this case, your son, Simon — has not made known his refusal,

if he has not expressed his opposition, we need to think about what he would have wanted: Would he have consented? "The deceased — in this case, your son, Simon." Thomas had raised his voice and distinctly pronounced each word of this phrase, hammering in the final nails. Consented to what? It's Marianne who asks the question, lifting her head, but in truth she already knows the answer; she wants to hear those final nails go in. Thomas replies: Consented to the removal of his organs, for transplant operations. He has to use these brutal phrases, unfolded like slogans on banners; he has to utilize their heavy impact, their blunt power; Thomas knows all too well how much suffering can be caused by ambiguity, misplaced subtlety, in these kinds of interviews.

The tension has very quickly risen at this point on the earth's surface. The plant's leaves seem to tremble, the water in the glasses to ripple; the light in the room seems to grow suddenly brighter, making them blink, and the air to vibrate as if the motor of a centrifuge was slowly turning above their heads. Thomas is the only one to remain completely immobile, to show no emotion. Keeping his gaze steady on their

pain-creased faces, ignoring the tremors of their jaws, the shaking of their shoulders, he goes on unflinchingly: The purpose of this interview is to discover and formulate the expression of the dead person's wishes — Simon's wishes; we are not here to consider what you yourself would do in this situation, but to think about what your son would have wanted. Thomas holds his breath, assessing the stealthy violence of these words, words that force a radical distinction between their bodies and the body of their child, words that create a distance, but which also, at the same time, allow them to think clearly. In a weak drawl, Marianne asks: How can we know?

She is asking for a method. Sean watches her, and Thomas reacts unhesitatingly. In that moment he wonders if Marianne might be, in the words of an expression he learned at a seminar, the "resource person"; in other words, the person who might create a wake effect. We are here to think about Simon, he says, about the person he was; the removal process is always connected to a unique individual, to our reading of his existence; we have to think about this together; for example, we can ask whether Simon was religious, whether he was generous. Generous? Marianne repeats, stunned. Yes, gener-

ous, Thomas confirms, how he was in his relationships with other people, whether he was curious, whether he liked traveling; these are the kinds of questions we need to ask.

Marianne glances over at Sean; his face is haggard, muddy skin and black lips, his eyes focused slantingly on the green plant. She can't see the link between the nurse's questions and organ donation. Finally, she whispers: Sean, was Simon generous? They look away, unsure how to respond, the two of them breathing heavily. She puts an arm around the neck of this man with thick, black hair like her son's, pulls him toward her, their heads touch, and he lowers his while a yes slides from his dry throat — a "yes" that, in all honesty, has little to do with their son's generosity, because, when it came down to it, Simon was not especially generous: he was more catlike, lighthearted and selfish, grumbling with his head inside the fridge Jesus don't you have any Coke in this house? rather than a young man of lavish gestures and kind thoughts. This "yes" is more a description of Simon as a whole, lifting him up to let him shine, a modest, direct boy who devoured the intensity of his youth.

Suddenly Marianne's voice breaks through

in a rush of breath, the words coming out in jolts: There is something — we're Catholics — Simon was baptized. She stops dead. Thomas waits for her to continue, but the silence lengthens, so he asks her — a life buoy thrown in the sea — Was he a believer? Did he believe in the resurrection of the body? Marianne looks at Sean, though all she can see of him is his profile, leaning forward, then bites her lips, I don't know, we don't go to church very often. Thomas is tense — last year, a dead girl's parents refused the removal of any organs from their daughter's body on the basis that they believed in the resurrection of the flesh and considered this a mutilation that rendered any other form of existence impossible, and when Thomas gave them the Church's official position — in favor of donation — they replied: No, we don't want her to die a second time. Marianne rests her head on Sean's shoulder, then starts to speak again: Last summer he read this book on a Polynesian shaman, the coral man or something, he was planning to go there to meet him, you remember? It was a book about reincarnation. Sean nods, eyes closed, and adds in a barely audible murmur: Simon had so much energy, he liked to exert himself, he was a physical being, that's it,

that's how he was, living in his body, that's how I see him, natural, living in nature, he wasn't afraid. Marianne waits a few seconds and then asks, uncertain: Is that what it is, being generous? I don't know, maybe. And now she is crying.

They are speaking in the past tense now, the father and the mother. They have begun the story. For Thomas, this is a tangible step forward, the signal that the idea of the death of their child is slowly crystallizing. He places the case file on the table, rests his hands flat on his thighs, and opens his mouth to continue speaking. But then, without warning, everything is up in the air again: Sean leaps to his feet and begins pacing around the room, agitated, abruptly declaring this is bullshit, all this crap about generosity, I don't see why Simon being generous or liking to travel should give you the right to think he'd want to donate his organs, that's too easy, and anyway, what if I said he was selfish, would that be the end of it? He stops pacing around, approaches Thomas, and whispers in his ear: Just tell us if we can say no, go on. Marianne, shocked, turns to him and cries out Sean! But he doesn't hear her, he is striding around the room again, his pace increasing.

Finally he leans against the window, his back to the glass, his silhouette black and huge against the daylight: Go ahead, just tell us the truth, are we allowed to refuse or not? He is snorting like a bull. Thomas doesn't blink; his spine stays straight, his clammy hands remain glued to his jeans. Marianne stands up and walks toward Sean. She holds out her arms but he turns away, walks three paces along the wall, spins on his heels, and punches the wall with all his might: the window shudders above the Kandinsky poster, then he groans: Fucking hell, I don't believe this! and, devastated, turns to face Thomas, who is now standing up, white as a sheet, frozen, immobile, and announces in a decisive tone: Simon's body is not just a box of organs that you can help yourself to.

The process is suspended if the attempt to discover the deceased's wishes, carried out in tandem with his loved ones, ends in refusal.

At last, Marianne grasps Sean's hand. Fantastic, she whispers, stroking it, that's just what we need, then leads him over to the couch, where the two of them sit down, take deep breaths. There's a lull. Marianne and Sean each drink a glass of water; neither

is particularly thirsty, but they need to buy time, to keep moving, rediscover the right frequency so they can speak again.

At this point, Thomas thinks the whole thing is screwed. Too tough. Too complex, too emotional. The mother maybe, but the father . . . there's no way back, it's all going too fast. They'd barely had time to realize their tragedy before they had to decide about organ removal. He sits down too. Picks up the file from the coffee table. Does not insist, or seek to influence them, manipulate them, use his authority. Does not act as the agent for a silent but oppressive game of emotional blackmail, a pressure that is all the more powerful on Simon's parents because young, healthy donors are so rare. He does not, for example, tell them in no uncertain terms that French law prescribes the principle of presumed consent in the absence of membership in the national organ donation refusal registry. Spares them the tortured question of how presumed consent can be the rule when the donor was dead and could no longer speak, could no longer consent to anything. Spares them the legal fact that, by never having said anything on the subject to his family, Simon has effectively said yes, another rephrasing of the dubious dictum *silence implies consent.* Yes,

in the end, he keeps quiet about those texts that would so easily have undercut the meaning of this dialogue, making it a mere formality, a hypocritical convention, when the law as a whole suggested something more complex, based on reciprocity and exchange: as each person is considered a potential organ recipient, is it not logical that each person should also be considered a potential organ donor after his or her death? Once the conversation takes this turn, he will only mention the legal context to people who are neutral on the question of donation, or in order to comfort families after they have already agreed, using the law like a handrail to support them as they move forward.

He closes Simon's file and rests it on his knees again, signaling to Sean and Marianne Limbres that they may quit this dialogue if they desire and leave the room. They've refused — it happens. There has to be a place for such a decision: the possibility of refusal is also the condition for donation. He should shake hands and say goodbye now. The interview has failed, and he has to accept that fact. Thomas's principle is absolute respect for the wishes of loved ones, and he also understands the indisput-able nature of that which makes the body of

the deceased sacred for those who loved him. It's his way of preventing an approach that risks becoming — supported legally and ethically by the letter of the law and the shortage of transplant organs — a steam-roller. His gaze sweeps the walls of the room: from behind the window, a bird is watching them. A passerine. Seeing it, Thomas immediately wonders if Ousmane will drop by his apartment to feed Mazhar, the goldfinch, fill its trays with clean water and organic grains, those multicolored grains grown on a balcony in Bab El Oued. He closes his eyes.

Okay, what would you remove? Sean asks this, head down, eyes to the ground, and Thomas, surprised by this change of course, frowns and then instantly adjusts to this new tempo: The heart, the kidneys, the lungs, and the liver; if you agree to this, you will be kept fully informed and your son's body will be restored. He lists the organs unwaveringly, a symptom of the urge he always feels to favor dry precision over evasive vagueness.

The heart? Marianne asks. Yes, the heart, Thomas repeats. Simon's heart. Marianne is dazed. Simon's heart — clusters of blood cells merge in a little sac to form the first

vascular network on the seventeenth day; pumping begins on the twenty-first day (very weak contractions, but audible on highly sensitive equipment designed expressly for heart embryology); the blood flows through the growing vessels, nerves form in tissue, veins, tubes, and arteries, the four chambers develop, and by the fiftieth day everything is in place, if unfinished. Simon's heart — a round belly rising gently at the bottom of a portable crib; the bird of night terrors flapping distraught inside a child's chest; the staccato drumbeat syncopated with Anakin Skywalker's destiny; the riff under the skin when the first wave rises — feel my pecs, he said to her one evening, muscles tensed, monkey face, he was fourteen years old and in his eyes she could see the new glow of a boy taking possession of his body, feel my pecs, Mom — the diastolic melt when he saw Juliette at the bus shelter on Boulevard Maritime, stripy T-shirt dress, red Doc Martens, art portfolio tucked under her arm; held breath on Christmas Eve, the surfboard unwrapped in the middle of the freezing warehouse, opened with that mixture of meticulousness and passion, the way you slice open an envelope containing a love letter. The heart.

But not his eyes — you don't take his eyes,

do you? Her scream stifled with a palm held to her own mouth. Sean shudders, instantly shouts no, never, not his eyes. His groan dies to silence and Thomas looks at the ground, I understand.

This is another area of turbulence, and he shivers, swims through it, knowing that the symbolic significance differs from organ to organ — Marianne reacted only to the idea of removing her son's heart, as if removing his kidneys, liver, or lungs was more conceivable, and she refused the removal of the corneas, which, like the muscle tissue and the skin, are rarely the subject of the family's consent — and understands that he must compromise, make an exception to the rule, accept their restrictions, respect this family. It's empathy. Because Simon's eyes were not only his nervous retinas, his taffeta irises, his pure black pupils in front of the natural lens; his eyes were his gaze, the way he looked at you. His skin was not only the mesh of his epidermis, his pores, it was his light and his touch, the living sensors of his body.

Your son's body will be restored.

It is a promise and it is perhaps also the death knell for this dialogue — who knows? Restored. Thomas looks at his watch, makes

a quick calculation — the second thirty-minute EEG will take place in two hours — would you like some time alone? Marianne and Sean share a glance, both nod. Thomas stands up and adds: If your son is a donor, it will enable other people to live, other people who are waiting for an organ. The parents pick up their coats and bags, their movements slow even though they are in a rush to leave this place now. So he wouldn't have died for nothing, right? Sean lifts the collar of his parka and looks Thomas in the eye: We know, we know all that, transplants save lives, the death of one person can give life to another, but Simon is our son, don't you understand? I understand. As she walks through the doorway, Marianne turns and she too looks Thomas in the eye: We're going to get some fresh air, we'll be back.

Left alone in the room, Thomas collapses into a chair. He rests his head in his hands, runs his fingertips through his hair, massaging his skull, and exhales a long breath. No doubt he is thinking how tough his job is; maybe he too would like to talk, to punch walls, throw things at wastepaper baskets, break glasses. Maybe it will be a yes, more likely a no. It happens — a third of interviews end with a refusal — but for Thomas

Rémige, a clear-headed refusal is better than an agreement torn from confusion, extracted with forceps, and regretted two weeks later by people ravaged with remorse, people suffering with insomnia, drowning in grief. You have to think about the living, he often says, chewing the end of a matchstick, you have to think about those who are left — in his office, on the back of his door, he has stuck a photocopy of a page from *Platonov,* a play he has never seen, never read, but this fragment of dialogue between Serguey Voinitzev and Nicolas Triletzki, seen by chance in a magazine he'd found at the local Laundromat, had thrilled him the way a kid is thrilled when he discovers some glorious treasure: a Charizard in a packet of Pokémon cards, a golden ticket in a chocolate-bar wrapper. What shall we do, Nicolas? Bury the dead and mend the living.

Juliette is in her room. From the window, if she angles herself slightly sideways and stands on tiptoes, she can see the roof of Simon's building. The first time Simon came here, into her girlish lair, he stared out the window and then suddenly turned back to face her: We can see each other, you know, and he had spent a long time guiding her until she spotted it, among the marquetry of gray surfaces that stretched out below, a zinc-colored patch scattered with chimneys where some seagulls were perched: Down there . . . Her gaze rests there softly.

They argued last night. They lay there on their sides, face-to-face, naked, holding each other tight under the warm comforter. They had just made love, and they continued tenderly caressing each other, and talking in the dark — strangely voluble, their words always more limpid in moments like that —

then the sound of a text arriving had pierced the calm, and the echo of the sonar didn't make her laugh that time; she saw it as a hostile intrusion — the surf session agreed, 6 am outside your place. She hadn't needed to wait for him to read the message to know what it was about, and to understand that he had been waiting for this signal since the beginning of the evening. Something snapped inside her then: she jumped out of bed and got dressed, tight-lipped, panties, T-shirt, what's the matter? he asked, sitting up and leaning on an elbow, frowning — but he knew what the matter was. Don't pretend you don't know, she should have said, instead of just muttering nothing, nothing, nothing's the matter, her face concealing the bitterness she felt. Then he'd gotten dressed too and followed her to the kitchen, where it all degenerated.

Today, in the silence of the empty apartment, leaning over the three-dimensional labyrinth she has just begun making in a Plexiglas case, she thinks about it again, about what made her take on that pathetic role — of the woman who stays home while the man goes out to enjoy the world; this conjugal pose, this adult thing, this thing that old people do, when she is just eighteen

— and about what made her lose control to the point where she was insisting, by turns loving and violent, stay, stay with me, speaking in a way that was foreign to her, like an actress playing a fragile, passionate character, a cliché, reminding him that she would be alone this weekend, her parents weren't coming back till Sunday night so they could be together all that time, but Simon had dug his heels in: That's surfing, that's just how it is, it's always a last-minute thing, he was also playing a role, playing the man, and they had festered, barefoot on the tiles, hard-eyed and mottle-skinned; he had tried to hug her, an urge, his hands touching her slender waist under the tank top, touching her slightly jutting hip bones, but she had pushed him away, roughly, don't bother, go ahead, I won't make you stay, and he had left, okay, I'll go, had even slammed the door after telling her, on his way out, I'll call you tomorrow, after blowing her a kiss from the doorway.

She has been steadily building her labyrinth since returning to school after the Christmas break. Students in the Art Section have to present a personal project at the end of the year. She had begun by building the Plexiglas cube — three feet by three feet by three

feet, with two of the faces not being enclosed until the end — after spending a long time studying different material samples, and now she is building the interior. Diagrams in different scales are pinned to the wall above her desk; she looks at them, moving closer to the wall, then she places a sheet of white foam board on the worktable and prepares the pencils, two metal rulers, the clean erasers, a pencil sharpener and a hot glue gun. She goes to the bathroom to wash her hands before putting on transparent plastic gloves, given to her by the local hairdresser — they had been on the colorist's cart, under the trays of dye, between the hair curlers, the multicolored clips, and the little sponges.

She begins, making a notch in the white board and cutting it with a utility knife with different-shaped blades that she notes down afterward, following the template she traced with exacting precision, and which is supposed, when the model is finished, to show this rhizomic star-shaped branching, this complex interlacing where each path will cross another, where there will be no entrance or exit or center, just an infinity of routes, connections, junctions, vanishing points, and perspectives. She is so absorbed in her work that she ends up perceiving a

faint buzz, as if the silence were vibrating, saturated, and forming a protective bubble around her, situated now at the center of the world. She likes drawing, folding, cutting, gluing, sewing, designing, has always liked it; her mother and father often remember the little building projects she used to do, even before she could read, the bits of paper she used to tear up and assemble all day long, those mosaics stitched together with thick wool threads, those puzzles, those increasingly sophisticated mobiles she would balance with modeling clay. What a creative child she was, always so passionate and painstaking, an extraordinary little girl.

The first time she showed the transparent case to Simon, explaining her project to him, he had looked baffled and asked: Is it a map of the brain? She had looked at him in surprise, then, speaking quickly, self-assured, had replied: In a way, yeah, that's what it is, it's full of memories, coincidences, questions, it's a random space where things come together. She didn't know how to explain what the experience meant to her, how each time she worked on it she would feel herself coming unstuck and carried far, far away, far at least from her hands which kept moving under her eyes, her thoughts escaping ever further as

the strips of board piled up on the table, then took their place inside the case, glued to the structure with a repetitive gesture — the pressure of her index finger on the glue-gun trigger applying exactly the right quantity of that hot, white substance with its smell that got her slightly high — drifting slowly toward the entrance of the labyrinth, in a mental haze where extremely precise memories mixed with spirals of desire and daydreaming, coming back always to Simon at the end of the trajectory, tracing the lines of his tattoo, the points and subtle curls in green ink, inevitably bringing his image back to her mind, because she was in love.

The hours pass in Juliette's room and, little by little, the white labyrinth opens up a passage to that day in September, that first day, the material of the air gradually structuring itself so that, at last, they are walking together, side by side, as if invisible particles were joining together around them under the influence of a sudden acceleration, their bodies having signaled to each other as soon as she walked through the open school gates in that ancient, voiceless language of desire. And so, letting her friends go on ahead of her, she had slowed down until she was alone on the sidewalk with Simon, who had

sensed her in the rearview mirror of his mind, standing on his bicycle, right foot on the left pedal, then sliding to the ground so he could escort her, pushing his bike with one hand on the handlebars — all this to talk to her, all this so they can talk to each other. Do you live far? I live up there, what about you? Really close, just around that corner. The light is insanely clear after the storm and the sidewalk is scattered with yellow leaves, torn from the trees by the rain. Simon risks a sideways glance: Juliette's skin is very close, finely grained beneath the blush she wears, her skin is alive, her hair is alive, her mouth is alive and so is her earlobe, pierced with cheap earrings; she has drawn a line in eyeliner level with her lashes, a fawn. Do you know François Villon, the *Ballade des pendus*? He shakes his head, I don't think so, she is wearing raspberry lip gloss, "Brothers and men that shall after us be, / Let not your hearts be hard to us," you see what I mean or not? Yeah, I see, but he doesn't see anything, he is blinded, thousands of mirrors have formed in the quivering drops of water, they lean their foreheads toward the ground and slalom between the puddles, the bike jingling in unison with the rest, each word and each gesture weighted with boldness and

reserve, like two sides of the same event. They are blooming, held in a hothouse light. They walk up the avenue like princes, nervily excited but moving as slowly as possible, *pianissimo, pianissimo, pianissimo, allargando,* engulfed in the astonishment of what they are for each other. Their sensitivity is amazing, almost molecular, and whatever circulates between them pulses and swirls, leaving them breathless at the foot of the funicular railway, blood beating in the veins of their temples and their palms clammy, because everything is on the verge of disintegration now, and at the moment when the alarm rings, signaling the train's departure, she kisses him on the mouth — the briefest of kisses, over in the blink of an eye — and then she is on the train, where she turns to face him, leaning against the window, forehead suckered to the dirty glass. He sees her smile and then kiss the window, pressing her lips against it, eyes closed, hands flattened against the glass, he can see the purplish lines that code her palms, then she turns around and he is left paralyzed, his heart incredibly dilated — what happened? — and the funicular moves off, up the slope, sluggish but unrelenting, and Simon decides to do exactly the same thing, only better, so he gets on his bike

and begins riding up the hill. A wide bend in the road takes him away from her, but he pedals hard, crouched forward like a Tour de France rider, his schoolbag making him look like a hunchback, then the sky grows darker, the shadows on the ground vanish, and it rains again — a heavy, coastal rain — and in a few minutes the asphalt is streaming, slippery, so Simon changes gear and stands on his pedals, blinded by the drops of liquid hanging from the arch of his eyebrows, but so happy that he could, in that moment, lift his face to the sky, open his mouth, and drink everything that is pouring from above. The muscles of his thighs and calves are tensed with the effort, his forearms ache, he spits and gasps, but finds within himself the necessary momentum to follow the right line through the final curve, angled so exactly that he is able to speed up and he is freewheeling when he reaches the plateau at the top, and he charges into the funicular station just as the train brakes with a loud screech, skidding in front of the doors, soaked to the bone, jumps off his bike, and his legs buckle. Hands on his knees, head facing the ground, his lips foamed with spit, hair stuck to the edges of his face like a young marshal of the Empire, he parks his bike next to a bench

and gets his breath back, opening his jacket and the top buttons of his shirt, his heart rate gradually slowing beneath the exposed tattoo — it is the heart of a swimmer in the high seas, an athlete's heart with a resting pulse of less than forty beats per minute, a superhuman bradycardia, but barely has Juliette gone through the turnstile at the exit than it accelerates again — a wave, a surge — and he walks toward her, hands in his pockets, head withdrawn into his shoulders. She smiles, and lifts her oilskin as high into the air as she can: it's an awning, an umbrella, a canopy over a bed, a solar panel capable of harnessing all the colors of the rainbow, and once he is standing next to her, she stands on tiptoes to cover him with it — and herself too, the two of them contained inside the sweetish odor of the plastic, their faces reddened by the waxed fabric, their lashes dark blue, their lips purple, their mouths deep, and their tongues infinitely curious. They stand under the tarpaulin as in an echoing tent, the rattling rain above them forming the soundscape against which can be heard the breaths and hissings of saliva; they stand under the tarpaulin as if under the surface of the earth, submerged in a damp, humid space where toads croak, where snails crawl,

where magnolias, brown leaves, linden blossoms, and pine needles rot into humus, where old bits of chewing gum and rain-soaked cigarette butts slowly molder, they are there as under a stained-glass window that recreates an earthly day, and the kiss doesn't end.

Juliette looks up, breathless. The light has dimmed; she switches on the lamp, and shivers. Before her eyes, the labyrinth has grown. She glances at her watch — nearly five p.m. Simon should be calling soon.

When they step outside, they are dazzled by the defiantly pale, gray-milk sky, and look down at their shoes, walking side by side to the car, hands in their pockets, noses, mouths, and chins covered by scarfs, collars turned up. The car is freezing. Sean is in the driver's seat and they slowly exit the parking lot — how many times will they have to go past this stupid barrier today? They take minor roads, not wanting to go far from the hospital, just remove themselves from the world for a while, sink below the waterline of this unimaginable day, disappear into an undefined, fibrous space, into a translucent infrageography that matches their despair.

The city stretches out, becomes looser, the last suburbs fraying its edges, the sidewalks emptying; there are no more picket fences, only high chain-links, a few warehouses and

the remains of old, blackened urban settlements under the freeway exchanges. After that, it is the contours of the land that steer their trajectory, guiding their drifting progress like lines of force; they drive on the road under towering cliffs, along the hillside covered with caves where isolated hobos and gangs of teenagers hang out — smoking grass, spraying graffiti — they pass houses at the foot of the hill, the Gonfreville-l'Orcher refinery, then finally turn off toward the river, as if snatched up by the sudden opening of space, and now they reach the estuary.

They drive for another mile or two. The asphalt ends, so they cut the engine: emptiness all around them, disused space, a no-man's-land between the industrial zone and the pasture fields, and it is difficult to understand why they stop here, under a sky furrowed with dense smoke clouds that twirl fast from the refinery chimneys, then spread into dreary smears, secreting carbon monoxide dust — an apocalyptic sky. Within seconds of parking the car by the side of the road, Sean takes out his pack of Marlboros and starts to smoke without even opening the window. I thought you'd stopped, Marianne says, gently removing his cigarette from his fingers to take a drag herself —

169

she smokes in a peculiar way, palm over her mouth, fingers tightened, the cigarette held between two metacarpal joints — exhales the smoke without swallowing, then puts it back between Sean's fingers as he mutters no, didn't feel like it. She shifts in her seat: Are you still the only guy in the world to brush his teeth while smoking? — summer 1992, camping in the desert near Santa Fe, a tie-dyed dawn, coral-red and monkey-palm pink, coffee in tin cans, the fear of scorpions crouching in the cold shadows of rocks, the song from *Rio Bravo* — "My Rifle, My Pony, and Me" — sung together, and Sean with the toothpaste-stained handle of a toothbrush sticking out from one corner of his mouth while at the other side of his smile he was smoking his first Marlboro of the day — he nods: yes — the ridge tent streaming with dew, Marianne naked under her fringed poncho, hair down to her butt, and reading in an exaggerated declamatory tone a collection of poems by Richard Brautigan they'd found at the back of the Greyhound bus that had dropped them in Taos.

I should never have made him that surfboard. Sean takes the time to stub out his cigarette in the ashtray, then abruptly leans

over the steering wheel and bangs his head against it, thud, his forehead rebounding violently from the hard rubber. Sean! Marianne squeals in surprise, but he does it again and again, faster and faster, repeatedly banging the same part of his forehead against the wheel, thud, thud, thud, stop it, stop that now. Marianne grabs his shoulder to hold him back, but he elbows her away, knocking her into the passenger-side door, and while she is recovering from this, he grips the steering wheel with his teeth, biting into the rubber, and emits a deafening roar, a wild, dark roar, something unbearable, a noise she doesn't want to hear, anything but that, she wants him to shut up so she grabs him by the neck, sinks her fingers into his hair, into his scalp, and shouts through gritted teeth: Stop it now!, pulling him backward until his jaw unclenches from the steering wheel, until his back is touching the seat, until his head bangs into and then stabilizes against the headrest — his eyes closed, his forehead burned red between his eyes by the collisions — until the roar becomes a wail. After that, she lets go, trembling, and whispers you mustn't do that, you mustn't hurt yourself, look at your hand — his fingers are clamped onto his knees like pliers —

Sean, I don't want us to go crazy. In that precise moment, it is possible she is talking to herself, measuring the madness that is rising inside her, inside them both, this shared madness the only form of thought possible, as if it were the only rational way out of this unimaginably vast nightmare.

They slump into each other, curling up together inside the car. But this apparent return to calm is merely an illusion, because Sean's lamentation is worming its way into Marianne's mind, and now she begins to think what might have been, this Sunday, without the accident, without the driver's exhaustion, without the lure of surfing, without her son's obsession with those god-damn waves, and at the end of this thread of dark thoughts, which she follows wearily through the labyrinth of her mind, there is Sean. Yes, Sean, that's it, it was him, it was Sean who had encouraged that inclination in Simon, who had sparked and nurtured it, all of it, canoes and Maoris, tattoos and surfboards, the ocean, the migration to new lands, the osmosis of nature, that whole jumble of myths that so fascinated her little boy, that whole widescreen fantasy in which he grew up. She grits her teeth, fighting the impulse to hit the man next to her, this man who is groaning and whining. Yes, thinking

back, it was those trips they took together to deliver skiffs, leaving behind her and Lou, "the girls"; it was their shared addiction to riding waves that led Simon, later, to take risks on his own, going out more and more often in conditions that were too cold, too stormy, and his father never saying a word about it, because he was a laidback, solitary father, an enigmatic father who had isolated himself from them to the point where, one evening, she told him go, I don't want to live with you anymore, not like this, a man she loved but . . . fuck it. Yes, it was surfing that was to blame — that dangerous folly — but how had she, Marianne, how had she allowed that addiction to adrenaline to grow to such dimensions inside her own home? How had she allowed her son to fall into that vertiginous spiral, into that endless tube wave, that insanity? Yes, she was to blame too, for not doing anything, not saying anything, when her son started living his life at the whim of weather systems, dropping everything when a swell was forecast, his homework, everything, sometimes getting up at five in the morning to drive fifty miles in search of a wave; she had done nothing, because she was in love with Sean, and probably fascinated, herself, with that whole stupid fantasy — the man who

built boats and fires under snow, who knew the name of each star and each constellation in the sky, who whistled complex melodies, enthralled that her son could also live his life so intensely, proud that he was so different from the others . . . so, yes, they were both to blame, because they had done nothing to stop this, they had failed to protect their child.

The mist that has formed on the windows is starting to trickle in drips when Marianne says, surfing was the best thing you ever gave him. He says, oh I don't know, and they both fall silent. The best thing had been the process of making things, what it moved inside him, the use of foam and resin instead of supple wood to build canoes. In early December, he had gone to the Landes to pick up polystyrene boards from a "shaper" on the coast — a wiry-bodied man in his fifties with a red Apache scarf tied around his head, gray-bearded and pony-tailed, wearing Tahitian bermudas, a specialist fleece, and fluorescent flip-flops: an old hippie, basically, who barely said a word and never made eye contact, who surfed whenever he could, the luminescent screen of a portable weather station constantly relaying wind and swell forecasts; Simon had spent

a long time thinking about those materials, which were new to him, studying their density, their resistance, before opting for the extruded polystyrene boardstock foam rather than polyurethane, before choosing epoxy resin rather than the cheaper polyester resin; he had spent a long time watching the shaper as he planed and sanded, and had then loaded everything in his station wagon, driving through the night, thinking about making his board, mentally tracing its shape, obsessing about its solidity, and all this in secret.

They get out of the car to go for a walk — let's go outside, Marianne said, opening the door. They leave the car behind on the path, parked against a thicket of brambles, and cut across a field, taking turns to clamber through the barbed-wire fence — first her, then him, one foot, then the other, back held flat, each holding the wires above the other's head, below the other's stomach, watch out for your hair, your nose, your eyes, don't get your jacket caught.

Winter woods and fields. The ground is a cold soup that slops and sucks at their shoes, the grass crunches, and the cow pies, hardened by frost, are like scattered slabs of black rock. The branches of the poplar trees

175

scratch the sky like talons, and the copses are full of crows as big as chickens. This is all a bit much, Marianne thinks, we're going to freeze to death out here.

Finally, they reach a place where they can see the river, the vastness of the sky coming as a shock. They are out of breath, their feet soaked, but they move toward the riverbank, drawn close to the water as if magnetized, stopping only when the field begins to slide slowly into the water, which is black here, tangled with wet branches and decomposing stumps, with the corpses of insects that winter has killed and rotted, a brackish mire, completely still, a fairy-tale pond beyond which the estuary is slow, dull-colored, pale like sage, the fold of a shroud. Crossing it seems possible but dangerous: there are no wooden pontoons here, no boats moored nearby, no kids with pocketfuls of flat rocks come to skim them on the water's surface, tracing a trajectory of low, graceful bounces, making the aquatic spirits dance in their wake; they are trapped here by these hostile waters, hands sunk deep in their pockets and feet sunk deep in mud, facing the river, chins buried in their collars. What are we doing here? Marianne thinks, wanting to scream, but her mouth,

wide open, makes no sound at all, like in a nightmare. But then, far off to their left, they spy a dark ship, the sole means of embarkation visible in either direction, a solitary craft that, by its presence, points out the absence of all the others.

I don't want them to cut him open, I don't want them to skin and gut his body. The chromatic purity of Sean's voice, toneless, sharpened by cold like a blade in ashes. Marianne slips her left hand into the right pocket of Sean's parka, her index and middle fingers burrowing into the black hollow of his fist, opening it up, carving out enough space for her other two fingers to join them in there — all this without Sean turning his head. To their left, the rumble of the freighter grows closer, and the color of its hull comes into focus: an oily red, the exact color of dried blood. A bulk carrier with a cargo of grain, it goes down the river toward the sea, holding to its channel while here everything widens — a confluence of rivers and consciences — toward the formless and the infinite, toward disappearance. And suddenly it looms huge, so close that they imagine they could reach out a finger and touch its hull; it passes, casting a cold shadow over them, the water frothing, fold-

ing, turning turbid in its wake, and Marianne and Sean watch its long body — 260 feet, at least three thousand tons — as it files past, a red curtain sliding gradually over reality, and I don't know what they are thinking about at that second: probably about Simon — where he was before he was born, where he is now — or maybe they're not thinking about anything, their minds entirely captured by this vision of the world slowly vanishing and then reappearing, tangible, utterly mysterious, and the ship's prow cleaving through the water affirms the searing pain of the present moment.

The wake bubbles and then grows calm, smooth. The freighter moves away, taking its noise and its movement with it, and the river regains its original texture, the estuary setting everything ablaze, a radiance. Marianne and Sean turn toward each other, holding hands, their arms stretched out to the sides, and caress each other with their faces — what could be more tender than this gentle brushing of skin on skin, the edges of cheekbones sliding beneath flesh? — and end up leaning into each other, forehead to forehead, and Marianne's words imprint the static air.

They won't hurt him. They won't hurt him

at all. Marianne's voice is muffled, and Sean lets go of her hands and takes her in his arms, his sobs melt into the breathing of nature, and he nods, okay, we should go back there now.

He's a donor.

Sean is the one who makes this declaration, and Thomas Rémige jumps up from his chair, shaky and red-faced, his chest expanding with an influx of heat, as if his blood had sped up. He moves toward them, suddenly stops. Thank you. Marianne and Sean look down, the two of them rooted to the spot in the doorway of the office, speechless, their shoes soiling the floor with mud and black grass, barely able to comprehend what they have just done, just said — their son is a donor, they are giving him away, abandoning him, the thoughts and words echoing inside their eardrums. The telephone rings — it's Révol. Thomas quickly tells him that it's okay, three quickly spoken words in an encrypted language that Sean and Marianne do not understand, the acronyms and hurried speech intended to scramble meaning, and soon they leave

180

Rémige's office and are taken back to the interview room. Révol is there waiting for them. There are four of them in the room now, and the dialogue begins again immediately, with Marianne asking: What happens now?

It is 5:30 p.m. The window is open, as if the room had needed airing, a cool blankness replacing the stale, ruined dialogue that had filled the space before — the exhaled breaths, the spilled tears, the odor of sweat. Outside, a strip of lawn running perpendicular to the wall, an asphalt driveway, and, between the two, a hedge the height of a man. Thomas Rémige and Pierre Révol sit on the vermilion chairs while Marianne and Sean return to the apple-green couch, their anguish palpable — still their eyes are so wide open that their brows are creased, the area of white around the pupil enlarged, still their mouths are half open, ready to scream, their bodies tense with waiting, with fear. They are not cold, though, not yet.

We will make a comprehensive evaluation of the organs and we will transmit that evaluation to the doctor from the Biomedical Agency. Based on that information, he will be able to suggest one or several removals, after which we will organize the opera-

tion itself. Your son's body will be returned to you tomorrow morning. As Révol speaks, he accompanies each phrase with a hand gesture, tracing in the air the steps of the next sequence. His words contain a great deal of information, even if they also suggest ellipses, things left unsaid, an opaque area that catalyzes their fear: the operation itself.

Suddenly Sean breaks his silence: What will be done to him exactly? He asks his question clearly, not in a strangled stammer, showing the courage of a soldier going over the top, exposing himself to machine-gun fire, while Marianne bites her coat sleeve. What will happen that night in the operating theater, the image they have of it — this carving up of Simon's body, its dispersal — all of this horrifies them, but they want to know. Rémige takes a deep breath before answering: Incisions will be made in the body, the organs will be removed, the body will be closed up again. Simple verbs, atonal information, intended to counteract the emotional drama linked to the sacredness of the body, to the transgression suggested by its opening.

Are you going to perform the operation? Sean lifts his forehead — still the impression that he might charge from below, like a

boxer. Simultaneously Révol and Rémige discern in this interrogation the visible tip of an iceberg of ancient terror: being declared dead, by doctors, when you are still alive. Let us not forget that Révol has a copy of Mary Higgins Clark's thriller *Moonlight Becomes You* in his office, a book that involves a funerary practice once common in England: a ring is placed on the finger of the person to be buried, a ring attached to a cord that will ring a bell on the surface if the dead person wakes up underground. The definitions of the various criteria for death, developed in order to allow organ removals, contribute to this age-old fear. The nurse turns to Sean and, with his thumb and index finger, draws a solemn sign in the air: The doctors who declare a patient's death never take part in the process of organ removal — never. In addition — his voice deepens, his tone grows firmer — there is always a dual procedure: two doctors observe the same protocol and two distinct signatures are required for the official report of the patient's death. This demolishes the scenario of the criminal doctor who knowingly decrees his patient's death in order to dispossess him afterward, destroys the rumors linking the medical mafia to international organ trafficking,

183

invisible dispensaries located in the chaotic suburbs of Pristina, Dhaka, or Mumbai, and discreet clinics protected by security cameras, shaded by palm trees, installed in the upper-class areas of western cities. Gently, Rémige concludes: The surgeons who remove the organs will come from the hospitals where there are patients waiting for transplants.

A drift of silence, and then Marianne's voice again, muffled as if she were speaking through a caul: But who will be with Simon then? — that "who" emphasized, naked. Me, Thomas replies, I will be there. I will be there for the entire operation. Marianne slowly moves her gaze toward his — the transparency of crushed glass — so you will tell them about the eyes, that we don't want them to, you'll tell them. Thomas nods, I'll tell them, yes. He stands up, but Sean and Marianne continue to sit still, some force weighing down on their shoulders and holding them to the ground. This lasts for a while, and then Marianne says: So we don't know who will get Simon's heart, is that it? I mean, it's anonymous, we'll never know, right? Thomas goes along with these questioning declarations, these declaratory questions, but clarifies: You will be able to find

out the sex and age of the people who will receive the organs, but you will never learn their identity; if you wish, however, you can be given news about the transplant. He goes on: The heart, if it is transplanted, will be given to a patient according to established medical criteria — and gender is irrelevant to compatibility. Bearing in mind Simon's age, however, his organs should be offered first to children. Sean and Marianne listen, then confer in low voices. It is Sean who next speaks to the doctor: We would like to be with Simon again now.

Révol is needed elsewhere, so he leaves them while Thomas accompanies Marianne and Sean to the door of the room. They walk in silence, and then: I'm going to leave you with Simon now, I'll be back later.

The room has darkened as evening falls, and the silence seems to have thickened. They approach the bed with its motionless folds. They probably imagined the announcement of Simon's death would be followed by an alteration in his appearance, or at least that some aspect of the way he looks would have changed since the last time they saw him — skin color, texture, glow, temperature. But no, nothing has changed at all. Simon lies there, and the infinitesimal

movements of his body still make the sheets rise and fall weakly; what they have been through finds no correspondence here, no echo or reflection, and this is a blow so violent that their thoughts are unhinged, they fidget and stutter, talk to Simon as if he could hear them, talk about him as if he couldn't hear them, seem to struggle to remain within the realms of language while their phrases become dislocated, their words bang together, fragment, and short-circuit, while their caresses become collisions and then breaths, sounds and signs soon tapering off into a continual buzz inside their chests, an imperceptible vibration, as if they had now been expelled from all language and their acts now had no time or place in which to occur, and so, lost in the cracks in reality, they themselves cracked and broken and fragmented, Sean and Marianne find the strength to lift themselves onto the bed so that they can be as close as possible to their child's body. Marianne ends up lying on the edge of the bed, her hair falling over the side, while Sean half-sits on the mattress, resting his head on Simon's torso, his mouth at the exact location of the tattoo, and the parents close their eyes together and are silent, as if they too were sleeping.

Night has fallen now, and they are in darkness.

Two floors above, Thomas Rémige is glad to be alone so he can concentrate, take stock, and call the Biomedical Agency: the next step is an in-depth evaluation of the organs. The woman who answers the phone is one of the founders of the organization; Thomas recognizes her deep, husky voice, visualizes her at the center of a classroom, the tables arranged in a U, the large plastic amber-colored chain attached to her glasses, which hide her face. Then, sitting at his computer, following a complex process that involves entering a series of identification numbers and encrypted passwords, he opens a software application in the database and creates a new document into which he carefully copies all the information regarding Simon Limbres's body: this is the Cristal file, an archive and dialogue tool that is now connected with the Biomedical Agency, guaranteeing the traceability of the organ and the anonymity of the donor. He looks up: a bird is hopping about on the window ledge — the same bird as before, with a round, staring eye.

The day Thomas acquired the goldfinch, Algiers was sweltering under a cloud of vapor. Inside his indigo-shuttered apartment, Hocine lay on the couch, legs bare beneath a striped djellaba, fanning himself.

The stairwell was painted blue; it smelled of cardamom and cement. Ousmane and Thomas climbed three flights in the dimness: a yellow, trembling light filtered through the panes of frosted glass in the roof, barely penetrating down to the first floor. Thomas sits quietly while the cousins greet each other, embracing warmly, then a rapid conversation in Arabic that sounds like pistachio shells being bitten apart. He doesn't recognize Ousmane's face when he speaks his native language; it takes on new shapes — his jaw retracting, gums exposed, eyes rolling and sounds emerging from the back of his throat, from a complicated area far behind the tonsils, new vowels held then

clicked under the palate — so that he almost looks like someone else, like a stranger, and Thomas feels flustered. The tone of the exchange alters when Ousmane announces in French the reason for their visit: my friend would like to hear the goldfinches. Ah, Hocine turns toward Thomas, and maybe adopt one? he asks craftily, with a wink. Maybe. Thomas smiles.

Arriving the day before, after crossing the Mediterranean for the first time, the young man was bewitched by the perfectly curved bay of Algiers and by the city ranged beyond it, the blues and the whites, the crowds of young people, the smell of the water-sprayed sidewalks, the dragon trees in the Jardin d'Essai, their interlacing branches creating a sort of fantastical vault. A beauty that was not voluptuous but stripped bare. He felt intoxicated. New sensations called to him and turned his world upside down in a mixture of sensory excitement and a super-charged awareness of what surrounded him: life was unfiltered here, and so was he. He tapped euphorically at the bulge in his pocket formed by the cash rolled up inside a little handkerchief.

Hocine walks to his balcony, pushes open the shutters, and leans out into the street, clapping his hands, shouting orders. Ous-

mane shouts back at him in Arabic, apparently begging, please, no, don't go to any trouble, but here they are, being brought up to the room, soups and skewered meats, bowls of cereal as light as foam, orange salads with mint leaves, and honey cakes. After the meal, Hocine places the cages on the ceramic tiles that cover the floor, using the patterns on the cages to align them properly. The birds are tiny — four or five inches high — with disproportionately large throats and abdomens. Their plumage is unspectacular, their claws matchstick-thin, their eyes staring. They stand on gently swinging little wooden trapezes. Thomas and Ousmane crouch a few feet away from the cages while Hocine collapses onto a pouffe at the back of the room. He makes a sound a little like a yodel and the recital begins: the birds sing, each in turn and then all together — a canon. The two young men dare not look at each other or touch each other.

And yet, everyone said that the goldfinch was vanishing from the face of the earth. The goldfinches from Bainem Forest, from Kaddous, from Dely Brahim, from Souk Ahras — all gone. Those populations, once so dense, were now threatened with extinc-

tion by intensive hunting. The cages hung by the doors of houses in the Casbah squeaked as they moved in the wind, all empty, while the merchants' cages were now filled with canaries and parakeets; the only goldfinches to be found were kept in dark back rooms, guarded like treasure, the birds' value swelling with their rarity — simple capitalist logic. You could maybe buy some on Friday evenings in El Harrach, in the east of the city, but everyone knew that the specimens exhibited there, just like those at the Bab El Oued market, had never fluttered over Algerian hills, nested in the branches of the pines and cork oaks that grew there, had not been captured in the traditional manner, with birdlime, the non-singing females immediately released in order to ensure reproduction; those birds did not sing. They came from the Moroccan border, from the Maghnia region, where they were hunted in their thousands, caught in nets that made no distinction between males and females, then brought to the capital through shady channels where opportunist guys under twenty maneuvered and manipulated, young unemployed men who had given up their dead-end jobs and fought like demons to gain a foothold in this business, drawn by the juicy rewards on

offer, guys who knew nothing about birds — and, anyway, most of the specimens, tangled in the nets, died of stress during transportation.

Hocine kept his expensive birds behind the Place des Trois-Horloges — real Algerian goldfinches. He always kept at least ten of them and had never had any other profession, being recognized as an expert throughout Bab El Oued and beyond. He knew every species, its characteristics and metabolism, could tell from the way it sang the provenance of each bird, even the name of the forest where it was born; people came from afar to solicit his services, authenticating, assessing, spotting fakes — Morocccan specimens sold as Algerian ones, which were often ten times more expensive; females sold as males. Hocine did not work with the networks, but did the hunting himself, alone, with birdlime, going off for several days to "his places" in the Béjaïa and Collo valleys, and when he got home he would spend most of his time treasuring his captures. As goldfinches were judged by the beauty of their songs, he worked hard to teach them melodies — the birds from Souk Ahras had a reputation for being able to memorize the highest number of songs — using an old tape player that played the

music in a loop as soon as the sun rose (he did not subscribe to the methods of the younger breeders: covering the cage with a blanket, making two slits in it, and running MP3 earbuds through the holes so the birds would hear the song all night). But the appeal of the goldfinch went beyond the musicality of its song and was linked, above all, to geography: its song was the manifestation of a territory. Valley, city, mountain, forest, hill, stream. It brought a landscape to life, evoked a topography, gave the feeling of a soil and a climate. A piece of the planetary puzzle took form in its beak, and just as the witch in the fairy tale would spit out toads and diamonds, just as the crow in the fable released the morsel of cheese from its beak, so the goldfinch expectorated something solid, scented, tactile, and colored. So it was that Hocine's eleven birds sang the cartography of a vast territory.

His customers — businessmen in ties, wearing beige or pale-gray suits and round, gold-colored metal-framed sunglasses — would turn up at his house in the middle of the afternoon like junkies in need of a fix. The birds sang, and the buyers remembered walking in sandals over pine needles, bunches of cyclamens and pink milk-cap mushrooms; they loosened their ties, drank

lemonade, and — with the bird's song determining its value — prices were discussed. Hocine made a good living. One day, the young heir to an oil company swapped his car, a Peugeot 205, for the last Bainem goldfinch Hocine ever possessed, a deal that gave rise to the legend of this otherwise stoic breeder: the bird was easily worth that, more fabulous than the genie of the magic lamp, it was not only a bird, but a whole threatened forest, and the sea that bordered it, and everything that lived inside it, the part for the whole, it was Creation itself, it was childhood.

When the concert ended, the debate began. Which one do you like? Hocine asked, speaking with his mouth close to Thomas's face. Ousmane watched his friend with amusement, enjoying the situation. Which one do you like? Tell him! Don't be afraid! I like them all! Thomas pointed to a cage — inside it, the bird ceased swinging on its perch. Hocine glanced at Ousmane and nodded. They exchanged a few words in Arabic. Ousmane started to laugh. Thinking he was being taken for a ride, Thomas took a step back, behind the cages. Silence spread through the room. Thomas's hand slipped inside his pocket and his fingers fiddled with the handkerchief. He stamped

his feet pointedly, not daring to say let's go. Hocine announced the price of the bird he had chosen. In a soft voice, Ousmane explained: It's a bird from Collo, ash, elm, eucalyptus, it's young, you'll be able to raise it yourself, teach it, this bird is from my village. Thomas, suddenly filled with wonder, stroked the bird's back through the bars of the cage; he thought for a long time, and then unfolded the roll of bills. I hope you took your commission, he told Ousmane as they walked downstairs.

Sean and Marianne leave the room. Thomas is waiting for them in the doorway. They open their mouths but remain silent, it looks as if they have something to say — something they've agreed — so Thomas tells them: You can ask me anything, that's why I'm here. Sean, articulating with difficulty, makes their request: Simon's heart, at the moment it, tell Simon, when you stop his heart, I, you, I want you to say to him, we're there, with him, that we're thinking of him, our love, and Marianne interjects: And Lou, and Juliette too, and Grandma. Then Sean takes over again: The sound of the sea, so you can let him hear it, and he hands Thomas an iPod with earphones, it's track 7, just press play, we want him to be able to hear the sea — strange loops in their brains — and Thomas agrees to carry out these rites, in their name, it will be done.

They start to walk away, but Marianne

turns one last time toward the bed and what paralyzes her in that moment is the solitude that emanates from Simon, now as alone as an object, as if he had jettisoned his human essence, as if he were no longer linked to a community, connected to a network of intentions and emotions, but was wandering, lost, metamorphosed into an absolute thing. Simon is dead — she pronounces these words for the first time, suddenly horrified — then looks for Sean, doesn't see him, rushes into the corridor and finds him crouching motionless against the wall, irradiated, just like her, by Simon's solitude, crushed just like her by the certainty of his death. She squats next to him, cups his jaw and tries to lift his head, come on, let's go, let's get away from this place, when what she would like to tell him is: Come on, it's over, Simon no longer exists.

His cell phone rings: Thomas unlocks the screen and hurries toward his office, suddenly wanting to plow ahead without delay, and Sean and Marianne, who are walking beside him, sense this acceleration, understanding instinctively that they must yield to it, and suddenly they feel cold: these same overheated corridors that dried their skin and their mouths before have become

icy hallways where they button up their coats, lift their collars. Simon's body is going to be spirited away; it will disappear to a secret place with limited access — the operating room — where it will be opened, stripped of its organs, sewed back together, and for a period of time — one night — the course of events will be out of their hands completely.

Suddenly the situation tilts toward a different sense of urgency; the pressure in their movements and gestures falls, it ceases throbbing in their consciences and flees elsewhere — to Thomas Rémige's office, where he is already talking to the doctor from the Biomedical Agency; to the movements of the attendants who are transferring their son's body; to the eyes that analyze the images appearing on screens; and also far off, to other hospitals and other departments, to other white-sheeted beds in other understaffed buildings — and now they no longer know what to do, they feel lost. Of course, they could stay in the department, sit next to a table covered with old newspapers and dog-eared magazines, wait until 6:05 p.m., when the second EEG will be completed, marking the legal time of Simon's death, or they could go downstairs to get a coffee from the vending machine,

they are free to do what they want, but they should keep in mind that a multiple-organ removal takes several hours, they must understand that it's a long and complex operation, so they might well be advised to go home, perhaps you should get some rest, you'll need all your strength, we'll take care of him — and when they pass through the automatic doors at the hospital's main entrance, they are alone in the world, and exhaustion breaks over them like a tidal wave.

She left the RER suburban train station La Plaine-Stade de France at dawn and walked in the opposite direction from that now being taken by the mass of people surging in a continuous flow, increasingly compact as kickoff time approaches, joined in a collective fever — pregame excitement and speculation, rehearsals of songs and insults, Delphic oracles. She turned away from the enormous, naked stadium, indifferent to its massive bulk, as absurd and indisputable as a flying saucer that had landed in the night, and sped up as she walked through the short tunnel beneath the tracks. Coming outside again, she walked up Avenue du Stade-de-France for two hundred yards, passing the headquarters of banks, insurance companies, and other organizations, passing their smooth walls — white or metallic or transparent — and arrived at number 1. There, she rummaged inside her

purse for a while, then removed her gloves so she could search more easily, and finally knelt down on the freezing sidewalk and emptied the purse's contents, watched expressionlessly by the guy on the other side of the door who was very carefully peeling back the cover from a bottle of yogurt drink, terrified that a drop might spurt onto his beautiful navy-blue suit. And then, as if by a miracle, she felt the outline of her magnetic card at the bottom of a pocket, took it out, gathered her belongings, and entered the lobby. I'm on duty, I'm a doctor at the Biomedical Agency, she told him haughtily, without looking at him, and was crossing the lobby when she noticed the pack of Marlboro Lights lying next to the digital tablet that he must have used to watch TV all night — probably soccer games or trashy movies, she thought, annoyed — and, having reached the second floor, she walked about fifty feet, then turned to her right and pushed open the door of the National Center for the Allocation of Transplants.

Marthe Carrare is a small woman in her early sixties, olive-skinned and round-faced, with auburn hair, large breasts, and a spare tire contained inside a skin-tight beige-pink cardigan, a spherical butt bulging in brown

wool pants, fairly slim legs, and tiny rounded feet in flats; she feeds on cheeseburgers and nicotine chewing gum, and at this moment her right ear is red and swollen from having various telephone receivers pressed against it all day long — work cell, private cell, landline — and, if you know what's good for you, you won't disturb her for anything, you will make yourself invisible and silent while she asks Thomas about the situation: So, what's happening? Thomas replies: It's okay. She is calm: All right, send me the report of his death so I can check the file, and Thomas says I just faxed it to you, and I also filled out the donor's Cristal file.

Marthe hangs up and walks over to the fax machine, frown lines arrowing down toward the top of her nose, thick-framed glasses attached to a chain, lipstick leaking into the little wrinkles around her mouth, a heady perfume and cold tobacco fumes trapped beneath her collar: yes, the sheet is there — the official report of Simon Limbres's death, filed at 6:36 p.m. Now she enters the adjoining office, which contains the national organ donation refusal registry, a file so high-security that only about ten people in the country are authorized to consult it, and only then after the legally attested death of the person in question.

■ ■ ■ ■

Back in her office, Marthe Carrare tells Thomas it's fine, then stares at her computer screen, opens the Cristal file, clicks on the various documents that comprise it — general information sheet, a medical evaluation of each organ, scans, ultrasounds, other analyses — and examines it all, immediately noting Simon Limbres's relatively rare blood group (B negative). The file is complete. Marthe approves it and assigns it an identification number, a code that will guarantee the donor's anonymity: from this point on, Simon Limbres's name will not be mentioned in any future discussions between the agency and the various hospitals with which it is in contact. Thus begins the protocol for the allocation of transplant organs. Namely, one liver, two lungs, two kidneys. And one heart.

Night falls. At the end of the avenue, the stadium is illuminated, and its outline — like an oblong ring, like a bean — traces a grayish halo in the sky through which the Sunday-evening airplanes leave their vapor trails. It is time, now, to turn our attention to those who are waiting, scattered through-

out the country and sometimes even beyond its borders, people whose names are on lists, classified by organ, to be transplanted, and who, every morning, ask if their position has changed, if they have moved up the ladder, people with no conception of the future, whose lives are restricted, suspended by the condition of one particular organ in their body. People living their lives with the sword of Damocles hanging above their heads. Imagine that.

Their medical files are centralized in the computer that Marthe Carrare is consulting at this moment, while sucking a nicotine lozenge. She checks her watch and thinks that she has forgotten to cancel her dinner date, two hours from now, at her daughter and son-in-law's apartment. She doesn't like going there — the phrase pops into her head that very second: I don't like going there, it's cold in that place — but can't be sure if it's the apartment's walls, plastered with an expensive white milk paint, that make her shiver, or if it's the absence of ashtrays, of a balcony, of meat, disorder, tension, or if it's the Malian stools and the designer fainting couch, the vegetarian soups served in Moorish bowls, the scented candles — "cut hay," "wood fire," "wild mint" — the domesticated satisfaction of

people who go to bed early under Indian velvet bedspreads, the tender lifelessness that stretches throughout their kingdom. Or maybe it's the couple that appalls her — the couple that, in the space of less than two years has swallowed up her only daughter, dissolving her in a safe, soothing conjugality, a balm after years of nomadic solitude: her hot-headed, polyglot daughter now grown unrecognizable.

In a specially programmed software, Marthe Carrare enters all the medical data concerning the heart, the lungs, the liver, and the kidneys of Simon Limbres, then searches her databases to find patients able to receive them — the list of matches being shorter when it comes to the liver and the kidneys. The short list of compatible recipients is then combined with the realities of geography, the location of the organs and the locations of possible recipients producing an operational cartography involving distances to be covered within a limited time frame, relating to the the viability of the organs. This leads to a logical evaluation of miles and journey times, the pinpointing of airports and highways, stations, pilots and planes, specialized vehicles and experienced drivers, so that the territorial aspect of the

enterprise adds a new parameter, narrowing the list of possible patients even further.

The first compatibility issue between donor and recipient involves blood — ABO compatibility. Cardiac transplants require strict Rh compatability, and with Simon Limbres being B negative, an initial cut is made, considerably reducing the list of nearly three hundred patients waiting for a transplant. Marthe Carrare's fingers tap more furiously at the keyboard, and her face shows the urgency of finding a recipient, perhaps some slight intoxication, the forgetting of everything else. Next, she uses the HLA system to examine tissue, which is equally essential. The human leukocyte antigen code is the patient's biological identity card and relates to the immune system. While it is practically impossible to find a donor with an identical HLA to that of the recipient, their codes must be as close as possible in order for the organ transplant to take place under the best conditions and with the lowest risk of rejection.

Marthe Carrare entered Simon Limbres's age into the software, so the list of pediatric recipients was searched first. Next she checks if there is a compatible patient in a

state of HU (high urgency) — in other words, a patient whose life is in danger, who might die at any moment. She also carefully applies a sophisticated protocol in which each stage is connected to the previous one and is used to determine the next one. For the heart, in addition to blood and immune-system compatibility, factors such as the organ's physical conformation, its shape, size, and weight come into play — the heart of a big, strong adult cannot be transplanted into the body of a child, for example, and vice versa — while the geography of the transplant is circumscribed by one unalterable limitation: there must be a maximum of four hours between the moment when the heart is stopped inside the donor's body and the moment when it is restarted in the recipient's body.

The search progresses and Marthe moves her face closer to the screen, her eyes enormous and distorted behind the lenses of her glasses. Abruptly, her yellowed fingertips immobilize the mouse: a high-urgency case has been identified for the heart — a woman, 51 years old, blood group B, 5' 8", 143 lbs., in the hospital at Pitié-Salpêtrière, in Professor Harfang's department. She carefully reads and rereads the information,

knowing that the call she is about to make will provoke a general acceleration at all levels on the other end of the line, an influx of electricity into people's brains, an injection of energy into their bodies — otherwise known as hope.

Hello, this is the Biomedical Agency — an increase in diligence and attention at the department's reception — the call is transferred several times until it reaches the surgical unit, then a formal voice says Harfang, and Marthe Carrare begins, quickly, directly, Doctor Carrare, Biomedical Agency, I have a heart — yes, that really is how she phrases it: her vocal cords, coated with forty years of cigarette smoke and nicotine gum, vibrating in her palate with every movement of her tongue — I have a heart for a patient in your department on the transplant waiting list, a compatible heart. Instant reaction — not even the briefest silence: Okay, send me the file. Already done, Carrare replies. You have twenty minutes.

After that, Marthe Carrare moves down one line on the list of recipients on her screen and calls the teaching hospital in Nantes, another cardiac surgery unit where the same dialogue is exchanged, this time regarding a seven-year-old child who has

been waiting for a heart for nearly forty days. Marthe Carrare specifies: We are waiting for a response from Pitié, then, once again: You have twenty minutes. Then a third department is called at the Timone hospital in Marseille.

The waiting begins, punctuated by telephone calls between the doctor in Saint-Denis and the coordinator in Le Havre, intended to synchronize the planning of the operation, to organize the surgical unit in advance, and to provide updates on the donor's hemodynamic status — nice and stable, for now. Marthe Carrare knows Thomas Rémige: she's met him on several occasions during training courses organized by the agency and at seminars where she has spoken, both as an anesthesiologist and as one of the agency's founding members, and she is glad that she will be dealing with him today. She trusts him: he is a safe pair of hands, professional and sensitive, the kind of guy you can rely on, and she is probably even more glad that his emotions are well contained by his unwavering concentration, his intensity always carefully channeled, never giving way to hysteria in spite of the human tragedy that acts as the fuse to every transplant operation. It's a stroke of luck for everyone, having a guy

like that around.

The responses about the liver, the kidneys, and the lungs quickly follow after a round of the same procedures — Strasbourg takes the liver (a six-year-old girl), Lyon the lungs (a seventeen-year-old girl), Rouen the kidneys (a nine-year-old boy), while down the road, in the stands of the soccer stadium, spectators are unzipping their jackets — leather biker jackets, khaki bomber jackets with orange linings — and covering their faces with scarfs like highwaymen about to attack a stagecoach, or like student protesters protecting themselves from teargas, and hundreds of hands are taking out smoke bombs that were hidden under sweaters or tucked in the back of their jeans — but how did those objects get through security? Pins are pulled from the first grenades as the players' buses are announced at Porte de la Chapelle — red smoke, green smoke, white smoke — and the clamor intensifies in the bleachers when a huge banner is unfurled: "Directors, players, coaches, everyone out!" The section where the hard-core *ultras* gather is impressive: all of them crammed into the small space, a unified block of aggression, a hostile mass, and the spectators coming into

the stadium walk faster, enthralled, while the suited security guards frown and start to run, jackets unbuttoned and ties flapping against their bellies, mouths pressed to walkie-talkies, the North End's getting messy, don't let too many in. Chanted insults burst into the air as the buses, with their tinted windows, comfortable seating and remarkably silent engines, leave the main road and enter the VIP area that surrounds the arena, coming to a halt by the players' entrance. Marthe stands up and opens the window: figures rush past the agency building and up the avenue, toward the stadium, local youths who know the area, and she sends a brief text to her daughter — emrgncy at BMA, call u tmrw, mom — then taps the chewing-gum box against the balcony railing and holds her hand under the opening, but the box is empty. She bites her lip: she knows she has cigarettes hidden in various places all over her office, the precise locations forgotten, but for the moment she decides to keep chewing.

She imagines thousands of people gathered around the field over there, with its grass so brilliantly green it looks like it's been varnished, each blade illuminated with a mixture of resin and turpentine or laven-

der oil, which, after the solvent has evaporated, forms a solid, transparent film like a silverish reflection, like a preparation on a new cotton ball, a layer of wax polish, and she thinks that in the same moments when Simon Limbres's living organs are being matched, in the moment when they are shared out among different sick bodies, thousands of lungs will swell as one across the way, thousands of livers will be soaked with beer, thousands of kidneys will, simultaneously, filter bodily substances, and thousands of hearts will pump blood, and suddenly she is struck by the fragmentation of the world, by the absolute discontinuity of reality in this small area, by the thought of humanity being sprayed in an infinite divergence of trajectories — an anguished feeling she has already experienced, that day in March 1984, when she was sitting in a number 69 bus, on her way to a clinic in the 19th arrondissement to have an abortion, less than six months after the birth of her daughter, whom she was bringing up on her own, rain streaming over the windows, and she looked at the faces of the passengers who surrounded her, one by one, those faces that you see in Paris buses in mid-morning, eyes gazing into the distance or staring at the safety pictograms on the walls

or riveted on the call button, or straying into the auricle of a human ear, eyes that avoided each other, old ladies with shopping bags, young mothers with babies held in slings, retired people traveling to the municipal library to read their usual magazines, unemployed men in dubious suits, noses deep in their newspapers but unable to read a word, unable to make the slightest sense of any of those headlines, but hanging on to the paper as if it were their only connection to a world where there was no longer a place for them, where soon they would no longer have enough to live on, these people sometimes sitting only six inches away from her, none of whom had any idea what she was about to do, the decision she had made and which, in two hours, would be irreversible, these people who were living their lives and with whom she shared nothing, nothing at all except this bus, caught in a sudden downpour, these worn seats and these sticky plastic grip straps that hung from the ceiling like nooses, nothing at all, each keeping to themselves, isolated and alone, and she had felt her eyes welling up with tears, had gripped the metal pole tightly so she wouldn't fall, and in that instant she had experienced solitude.

The first police sirens are heard around seven-thirty. She closes the window — it's cold outside — still an hour to go before kickoff and apparently it's proving difficult to contain the supporters' excitement: all these hearts together, it's too much. She wonders who's playing tonight. Time passes. Marthe Carrare examines the first file again, strangely satisfied by its concordance with the donor's file. It could hardly be any more perfect — what the hell are they doing at the Pitié? Just then, the telephone rings. It's Harfang: We'll take it.

Marthe Carrare hangs up and immediately calls Le Havre, warning Thomas that a team from Pitié-Salpêtrière will be contacting him to organize its arrival. The recipient is a patient in Harfang's department — do you know him? By name. She smiles. Says: They've got a good team there, they know what they're doing. Thomas checks his watch and replies: Okay, we'll get ready for the removal, we should be going into the OR about three hours from now, I'll call you back. They hang up. Harfang. Marthe says the name out loud. Harfang. She too

knows him. Knew of him before she knew him — that beautiful name, that strange name doing the rounds of hospital corridors for more than a century, so that people said simply he's a Harfang as a way of summarizing a discussion about a practitioner's excellence, or they talked about the "Harfang dynasty" as a way of describing the family that had provided the faculty with dozens of professors and practitioners, men named Charles-Henri and men named Louis, men named Jules, Robert, Bernard, and now men named Mathieu, Gilles, and Vincent, all doctors who had worked, were working in public hospitals — we're servants of the state, they liked to think as they ran the New York Marathon, went skiing in Courchevel, or sailed in the Gulf of Morbihan on carbon monohulls, distinguishing themselves in this way from the grasping medical masses, many of whom, including the youngest, opened private practices in calm, leafy quarters as soon as they had completed their training, sometimes going into partnership with Harfangs in order to cover the whole spectrum of pathologies affecting the human body, and offering quick checkups to overweight businessmen, guys who worked crazy hours and worried about cholesterol levels, hardened arteries, pros-

tate troubles, and declining libidos — among them five generations of pulmonologists following a patrilineal filiation that prioritized male primogeniture when handing out chairs and department directorships; among them one girl, Brigitte, ranked first in the internship entrance examination in Paris, in 1952, but who abandoned her studies two years later, persuaded that she was in love with a protégé of her father's when the truth was she was yielding to surreptitious pressure ordering her to make way, to leave more room for the young males of the clan; including this one, Emmanuel Harfang, the surgeon.

She remembers that during her internship, she had hung around for a while with a gang led by two Harfang cousins. One was in pediatric cardiology, the other in gynecology. They both had the famous "Harfang cowlick," a shock of white hair growing over their forehead which they slicked back over the dark hair that covered the rest of their head, a distinguishing feature of the clan, a legendary family seal, rally around my white plume and all the ad hoc swagger intended to loosen the panties of the girls they met; they wore 501 jeans and oxford shirts, tartan-lined beige raincoats with the collars turned up; they never went out in sneakers,

always Church's shoes, though they absolutely scorned tassel loafers; they were of medium height, wirily built, pale-skinned and golden-eyed, thin-lipped, with prominent Adam's apples that would make Marthe involuntarily swallow whenever she saw them sliding up and down under the skin of their throats; they looked like each other, and they also resembled this Emmanuel Harfang, ten years their junior, who repairs and transplants hearts at Pitié-Salpêtrière.

Emmanuel Harfang would descend the steps of the auditorium perfectly on time for his symposiums, staring straight ahead and jumping the final steps so that his momentum would carry him up to the lectern with an athletic bound, holding a sheet of paper that he wouldn't read, beginning his speech without even greeting his audience, favoring direct openings and abrupt attacks, getting straight to the point without bothering with the usual civilities, without bothering to state his name, as if everyone in the room was supposed to know who he was — a Harfang, son of a Harfang, grandson of a Harfang — a tactic that was also designed, in all probability, to wake up an audience who had a tendency to nod off early in the afternoon, pleasantly drowsy after eating those famous meals in the

nearby restaurants reserved for the occasion, where the carafes of red wine would be lined up on paper napkins, always that modest Corbières wine that went well with red meat, because as soon as Harfang pronounced his first words, the auditorium would snap out of its digestive torpor, every person in the audience remembering, when they looked at this slender, athletic man, that he was the pillar of a first-class cycling squad, part of a team that represented the hospital in various criteriums, filled with guys capable of riding 120 miles on Sunday morning, regardless of how difficult it was to combine such endeavors with their professional lives, guys ready to get up early to race, no matter how desperately they yearned for more sleep, for the chance to caress their wives, make love, play with their children, or simply just lie around listening to the radio, the light in the bathroom always brighter, the smell of toast always more desirable on mornings like that; guys who hoped to join this elite club and who would give anything, would elbow others out of the way, to be chosen by Harfang — "singled out" was the term they used, as Harfang, suddenly noticing their presence, would point at them with his index finger and, leaning his head to one side to assess

their physical condition, checking out a possible rival, would ask them, a strange smile twisting across his face: You like cycling?

Pedaling alongside Harfang, riding on his wheel for a few hours, was worth all the fury it provoked in their wives at being left alone with the kids on a Sunday until the middle of the afternoon, it was worth all the sarcastic comments — don't worry, darling, I know you're sacrificing yourself for the family — worth their more direct reproaches — you only ever think about yourself — worth the cutting remarks as they scornfully watched their husbands sucking in their paunches — careful you don't have a heart attack! — worth coming home crimson-faced, exhausted, legs barely holding up their body and their backsides so sore that they dreamed of taking a sitz bath but collapsed onto the first couch they spotted, or onto their bed for a well-earned siesta — and, of course, this quickly grabbed nap would trigger their spouses' ire once again, would fuel endless diatribes about men's selfishness, their idiotic ambitions, their submissiveness, their fear of aging, would make the wives lift up their arms and yell loudly or put their hands on their hips, elbows out, stomach thrust forward, teasing them theatrically — and, once they had

recovered from their efforts, it was worth wasting away the afternoon on their computers, buying a chamois on a specialized site, a matching bib, and all the other appropriate gear, finally screaming shut up! at the wife nagging from the other end of the apartment, making her cry, because — curiously — not a single wife ever supported this masculine obsession, not one, out of careerism or simple docility, ever encouraged her husband to straddle a bike and follow Harfang on the roads of the Chevreuse valley, to show off his speed, lightness, endurance, no, not one woman was ever fooled by this nonsense, and when they talked among themselves, the wives, deploring the insidious dragooning of their husbands, they would sometimes cite *Lysistrata,* plan a mass sex strike to make the men give up their extravagant toadying, or they would fall about laughing as they took turns describing how haggard their husbands looked after finishing a race, and in the end it was just funny, so let them go if they really wanted to, let them go and exhaust themselves, allies and adversaries, favorites and competitors, because soon not one woman would wake up at six in the morning to make coffee and hand the cup lovingly to her husband: instead, they would

stay in bed, curled up under the comforter, hair tangled, skin warm, purring with pleasure.

The last time Marthe Carrare heard Harfang speak, he had delivered a sparkling lecture about the uses of cyclosporin in antirejection treatments that had revolutionized transplant operations in the early 1980s, setting out in just twelve minutes the history of this immunosuppressant — a product that weakened the immune system of the recipient's body, thereby reducing the risk of the transplanted organ being rejected — after which he ran a hand through his hair, sweeping that famous white cowlick off his forehead, that distinctive shock of hair which allowed him to dispense with introductions, and barked out *questions?,* counted one, two, three in his head, and concluded his speech by foreshadowing the end of cardiac transplants, suggesting they would soon become obsolete because the time had come to consider the virtues of artificial hearts, technological wonders invented and developed in a French laboratory, with initial tests having already been authorized in Poland, Slovenia, Saudi Arabia, and Belgium. The nine-hundred-gram bioprosthesis, developed over twenty years

by an internationally renowned French surgeon, will be implanted into patients with serious heart failure whose lives are considered to be in danger. A murmur ran through the auditorium, waking up the drowsier students. Harfang's audience was disconcerted by this conclusion, by the idea that a prosthetic heart could rob the organ of its symbolic power, and while most of the heads obediently bowed down toward the spiral notebooks held below them, concentrating as the hands took notes of Harfang's words, a few shook from side to side, signaling sadness, or even vague dissent, while some slid hands inside jackets, behind ties, under shirts, touching bare skin so they could feel their hearts beating.

The game has kicked off and the rumble rising from the stadium has become a ceaseless roar, growing even louder at certain moments — a shot on target, a suddenly threatening counterattack, a piece of sublime skill, a violent clash, a goal. Marthe Carrare leans back in her chair: the donor's organs have been allocated, the trajectories calculated, the teams organized. Everything is on track. And Rémige is in control. As long as there are no unexpected problems during the removal operation, she thinks, as

long as the physiognomy of the organs does not reveal something not spotted or even suspected by the scans and the ultrasounds and the analyses, it should all be fine, and she will smoke a cigarette, drink a beer, eat a cheeseburger with barbecue sauce. She chews a little harder in order to squeeze out the last atom of nicotine from the gum, even if it's just the faintest memory of a taste, a smell, and she thinks about the security guard who by now must be bent over his tablet, following the soccer game, his pack of Marlboro Lights within reach.

Cordélia Owl is shaking a pack of cigarettes at Révol as the elevator doors close — I'm going downstairs for a break, five minutes — she gestures to him through the rapidly narrowing gap, and then her own face appears in front of her, a blur. The metal surface does not offer a clear reflection, only a vague mask, erasing her supple skin and shining eyes, the banding effect of her sleepless night, that still excited beauty: her face has turned like milk turns, features subsiding, complexion muddied, the rings under her eyes an olive gray verging on khaki, the marks on her neck almost black. Once she is alone in the elevator, she shoves the pack of cigarettes back in one pocket, takes her cell phone from the other, glances at it — still nothing — checks the bars at the top of the screen, squints, ah, no service, not even the hint of a signal. Immediately she feels hopeful again — he might have tried to call,

without success — and when the elevator arrives at the first floor, she runs to a side exit reserved for hospital staff, pushes the panic bar on the door, and she's outside. There are three or four of them there, smoking while they stamp their feet in the whitish zone that the luminous sign traces in the cold — nurse's aids and a nurse she doesn't know — and the air is so icy that it's impossible to tell the cigarette smoke apart from the carbon dioxide they are exhaling at the same time. She switches off her cell phone, then switches it on again, just to make sure. Her bare arms are turning visibly bluish, and soon her whole body is shivering. Do any of you have a signal? She turns toward the group, their voices responding, merging into one another, yeah, it's fine, I've got service, me too, and when her phone is on again, she checks it for messages. She does all this without hope, certain now that there is nothing on her voicemail, certain that she must stop thinking about it before anything can happen.

Strong signal, no messages. She lights a cigarette. One of the guys in the group says you're in the ICU, aren't you? He's a tall redheaded guy with a crew cut, an earring in his left lobe, and long hands with bright-

red fingers and neatly trimmed fingernails. Yeah, Cordélia replies, her little chin trembling. She feels weak, numb, goose bumps on her arms, stomach muscles aching from shivering under her thin blouse; she clings to her cigarette, sucks hard at the filter, and suddenly her eyes are burning, tears forming. The guy looks at her, smiling, hey, are you okay? what's up? Nothing, she replies, nothing, I'm just cold, but the guy has moved closer to her: The ICU's tough, isn't it? Some of the things you see . . . Cordélia sniffs and takes another drag: No, it's not that, I'm okay, just the cold, and tiredness. The tears roll down her cheeks, slowly, mascara-dyed, the eyes of a kid who's sobering up.

All the vivacity and passion that crackled inside her, that high-speed lightheartedness, playful and ferocious, that queenly gait she'd still had this afternoon in the corridors of the ICU: all of this suddenly becomes waterlogged, dangling sodden and heavy in her brain. No sooner was she twenty-three years old than she was twenty-eight; no sooner twenty-eight than thirty-one: time is speeding past her while she examines her existence with a cold, deadly gaze that takes aim at the different areas of her life, one by one — the damp studio

crawling with roaches, mold growing in the grout between tiles; the bank loan swallowing all her spare cash; close, intense friendships marginalized by newborn babies, polarized by screaming sweetness that leaves her cold; stress-soaked days and canceled girls' nights out, but, legs perfectly waxed, ending up jabbering in dreary wine bars with a bevy of available women, shrieking with forced laughter, and always joining in, out of cowardice, opportunism; occasional sexual adventures on crappy mattresses, or against greasy, sooty garage doors, with guys who are clumsy, rushed, stingy, unloving; an excess of alcohol to make all this shine; and the only encounter that makes her heart beat faster is with a guy who pushes back a strand of her hair to light her cigarette, his fingers brushing her temple and the lobe of her ear, who has mastered the art of the sudden appearance, whenever, wherever, his movements impossible to predict, as if he spent his life hiding behind a post, coming out to surprise her in the golden light of a late afternoon, calling her at night in a nearby café, walking toward her one morning from a street corner, and always stealing away just as suddenly when it's over, like a magician, before returning . . . That deadly gaze strips away everything, even her face,

even her body, no matter how well she takes care of it — fitness magazines, tubes of slimming cream, and one hour of floor barre in a freezing hall in Docks Vauban. She is alone and disappointed, in a state of disgrace, stamping her feet as her teeth chatter and disillusionment invades her territories and her hinterland, darkening faces, ruining gestures, diverting intentions; it swells, this disillusionment, it multiplies, polluting the rivers and forests inside her, contaminating the deserts, infecting the groundwater, tearing the petals from flowers and dulling the luster in animals' fur; it stains the ice floe beyond the polar circle and soils the Greek dawn, it smears the most beautiful poems with mournful misfortune, it destroys the planet and all its inhabitants from the Big Bang to the rockets of the future, and fucks up the whole world — this hollow, disenchanted world.

I'm gonna go. She tosses her cigarette to the ground, crushes it with the toe of her canvas ballet pump. The tall ginger guy watches her: You feeling better? She nods, I'm fine, see you later, turns on her heels and rushes inside. The walk back to the department is an interlude, which she uses to pull herself together before being en-

gulfed once again in work. Everything becomes more intense at this time of day: the evening edginess, restless patients, the final treatments before bedtime — changing the drip bags, distributing pills — and the organ removal that will take place in a few hours: Révol had come to see her, to ask if she could sub in at the last minute, stay beyond her shift to help out in the OR, an unusual request, which she agreed to.

She stops by the cafeteria to grab a cup of hot tomato soup from the vending machine — she looks so tiny, walking through the vast, icy lobby, her jaw tensed, then shoving her fist into the machine in an effort to make the drink come out more quickly. The soup is disgusting, so hot that the plastic cup half-melts in her hand, but she drinks it down quickly, and is just feeling warm again when she sees them walk past her — the mother and the father: the parents of the patient in room 7, the young man she fitted a catheter to that afternoon, the one who's dead and whose organs will be removed tonight, yes, those are his parents — following them with her eyes as they move slowly toward the tall glass doors. She leans against a pillar to get a better view of them: the glass is a mirror at this time of night, and the parents are reflected in it like ghosts

glimpsed in the surfaces of lakes on winter nights. If you wanted to describe them, you would say that they are shadows of themselves, the banality of the expression not so much revealing their internal disintegration as emphasizing what they were just this morning — a man and a woman standing tall in the world — and seeing them walk side by side across the floor tiles lacquered by cold light, it is easy to guess that, from now on, the two of them are pursuing a new trajectory begun only a few hours before, that they are no longer living in the same world as Cordélia and the planet's other inhabitants but are moving away from it, absenting themselves, drifting toward another domain, the place where, perhaps, for a time, all those people would survive, together and inconsolable, all those people who had lost a child.

Cordélia watches the figures grow smaller as they enter the parking lot, then vanish into the night. With a cry, she tears herself from the pillar, shakes herself like a foal, and picks up her cell phone. Her face regains its usual features and colors, and — with a mighty swing of the pendulum inside her — she makes an about-face that sets her on the right path again, quickly typing the number of that man who disappeared at

five in the morning. Surprised by her own action, she nimbly manipulates the keys on her phone, as if wanting simultaneously to get this thing out of the way and defy the submissiveness that is holding her sadness hostage, as if she wants to fight back against the morbidity assailing her and to remember the possibility of love. One, two, three rings, and then the guy's voice suggests in three different languages that she should leave a message. I love you, she says, and hangs up, oddly reinvigorated, divested of a weight. Suddenly, she sees life stretching out before her again, thinks that she always cries when she's tired, and that she should take a magnesium supplement.

Lou. They haven't called Lou. They haven't tried to speak to her, have not thought about her at all, except to ask that her name be spoken into her brother's ear at the moment when his heart is stopped. But they haven't thought about Lou herself, that little seven-year-old girl, her distress at watching her mother leave suddenly for the hospital, her long wait, her solitude, all of that, and even though they have been caught in death's oppressive whirlwind, dragged into tragedy, they can find no excuses and are thrown into a panic when they see the neighbors' number on Marianne's cellphone screen, along with a notification for a voicemail message that they do not have the strength to listen to, and now Marianne steps on the accelerator, whispering into the windshield, we're coming, we'll be home soon.

■ ■ ■ ■

The bells of the Saint-Vincent church are ringing and the sky has a creased appearance, like a melting altar candle. It is 6:20 p.m. when they climb the curving road that leads up the hill to Ingouville and drive into the building's underground parking garage. We're home, let's stay together tonight, Marianne said as she switched off the ignition — but would they even have had the strength to go their separate ways tonight, Marianne staying here with Lou, Sean returning to that one-bedroom apartment in Dollemard, rented in haste last November? Marianne struggles to fit the key into the lock, can't turn it — the metallic grating noise repeating inside the hole as Sean stamps his feet close behind her — and when she does finally get the door open, the two of them, off balance, fall forward into the room. They don't switch on a light, just collapse onto the couch — that couch they found by the side of a country road one rainy day, wrapped up like a giant piece of candy in a transparent tarp — and around them the walls turn to blotting paper, absorbing the colors of coffee and scrap-metal that signal the dying of the day: on

the few pictures that line the walls, other figures appear, other forms, while the chairs and tables swell, the patterns in the carpet fade; the room is like a sheet of photographic paper forgotten in a tray of developer, and this metamorphosis — this gradual darkening of the atmosphere in the room — sends them into a trance that deepens as the world around them slips away. The physical suffering they feel is not enough to keep them moored to reality: this is a nightmare, we'll wake up from it, is what Marianne thinks as she stares at the ceiling. And if Simon did come home, then, at that very moment — if his key made the same metallic grating noise in the lock as hers had made and then the door opened and he entered the apartment, slamming it behind him, the way he always did, invariably making his mother yell, Simon stop banging the damn door! — if he turned up right now, his surfboard under his arm, squeaking in its slip cover, his hair damp, hands and face still blue from the cold, exhausted by the sea, Marianne would be the first to believe it: she would stand up, move toward him, and offer him scrambled eggs with paprika, or pasta, something hot and energizing, yes, what she saw would not be a ghost but her child, home at last.

■ ■ ■ ■

Marianne's hand creeps across to touch Sean's hand, or his arm, or his thigh, any part of his body she can reach, but that hand creeps into emptiness because Sean has stood up and is taking off his parka. I'm going down to see Lou. He walks toward the door, but before he reaches it the doorbell rings. He opens it and Marianne cries out — it's her little girl.

Excited, Lou runs into the apartment dressed in a long colorful T-shirt worn over her clothes, with a scarf tied in her hair and iridescent tulle butterfly wings stuck to her back with the aid of Velcro ribbons — Lou too has straight black hair, olive skin, and mixed-race, delicately slanting eyes — and suddenly comes to a halt in front of her father, amazed to see him wearing a sweater inside the apartment. Are you back? Behind her, the neighbor remains on the threshold but pokes her head inside, like a giraffe, her face a question: Sean, have you come home? We just got here, he says brusquely: does not feel like talking. In front of him, Lou hops about while rummaging in her bag, then hands him a sheet of white paper: I did a drawing for Simon. She walks farther

235

into the living room and, seeing her mother sprawled on the couch, asks: Where is Simon? Is he still in the hospital? Without waiting for a reply, she turns around and rushes into the hallway, wings flapping and feet hammering. They hear a door being opened, Lou calling out her brother's name, then other doors banging, and his name called again. At last, the child reappears in the living room, where her two parents stand waiting, distraught, unable to speak, unable to say anything but — in a soft voice — Lou, while the neighbor, white-faced, steps back into the stairwell, indicating with a movement of her hand that she understands, won't disturb them, and closes the door.

The child stands facing her parents while the day dies in the west, little by little plunging the city into darkness, and now they are visible only as silhouettes. Marianne and Sean walk toward her: unblinking, she remains silent as her eyes devour the darkness — the whites of her eyes like china clay — and Sean lifts her up and Marianne hugs them both, their three bodies joined together, eyes closed, like those monuments in memory of the drowned that you find in ports in southern Ireland. They stagger back to the couch and lie diagonally across it

without letting go of each other, a Roman triad protecting itself from the outside world; they curl up inside their own breathing and the odors of their skin — the little girl smells of brioche and gummy bears — and this is the first time they have got their breath back since the announcement of the disaster, the first little nest they have been able to create in a quiet hollow of their devastation. And if you could only approach them, gently and silently, you would hear their hearts pumping, together, the life that remains, and hammering tumultuously, as if high-tech sensors had been placed on the valves and they were emitting infrasonic waves, those waves that run through space, plow through matter, sure and precise, zeroing in on Japan, the Seto Inland Sea, an island, a wild beach, and that wooden cabin where human heartbeats are archived, those cardiac fingerprints gathered from all over the world, deposited there by people who have made the long journey, and while Marianne and Sean's beat in time, Lou's is drumming fast, until she suddenly stands up, forehead damp with sweat: Why are we sitting in the dark? Catlike, she slips away from her parents' embrace and moves around the room, switching on all the lamps, one by one, then turns to her parents

and declares: I'm hungry.

Their phones beep more and more often now, alerting them to new voicemail messages. The time has come when they must think about talking, informing people — another ordeal looming into view. Marianne goes out onto the balcony, still wearing her coat, and lights a cigarette, readying herself to hear the news about Chris and Johan, then sees that she has a message from Juliette. She is paralyzed: fear of speaking, fear of hearing, fear that the words will get stuck in her throat, because Juliette was special. Simon had grudgingly introduced her one Wednesday in December when Marianne arrived home earlier than usual and found them in the kitchen. He hadn't said "my mother," but simply "Juliette, Marianne," immediately muttering let's go, we have stuff to do, as Marianne was engaging the girl in conversation: So you're in the same school as Simon? She had been stunned to discover what she looked like, this girl who had a place in her son's heart, this girl who looked like no one else, least of all a beach groupie, with her waiflike, flat-chested body and her strange, sweet little face — eyes so large they seemed to eat up her face, ears pierced with multiple holes, a gap-toothed smile and pale blond

hair cut like Jean Seberg's in *Breathless;* that day, she was wearing slim-fit, pale-pink corduroy jeans, bright-green high-top sneakers, and a twinset Fair Isle sweater under a red oilskin. Simon had waited impatiently while she replied to Marianne, then led her by the elbow to the door; later on, he had started dropping her name here and there, scattering Juliettes through the few conversations he agreed to participate in, until in the end she was mentioned almost as often as his friends and the names of beaches in the Pacific; he's changing, Marianne had thought, as Simon gave up McDonald's for an Irish pub that smelled of wet dog, began reading Japanese novels, gathering driftwood from the beach, and sometimes doing his homework with her — chemistry, physics, biology: subjects he was good at and she wasn't — and then one evening Marianne heard him telling her how a wave was formed: look (he must have been drawing a diagram), the swell moves toward the shore, it contracts as the water becomes more shallow, this is called the levee zone, that's where the waves arch their backs, sometimes it's quite violent, then the swell reaches the breaking zone, which can cover about a hundred yards if the sea floor is rocky, those are called point breaks, after that the waves

break in the surf zone but continue to mutate toward the shore, you see? (she must have nodded), and at the end, if you're really lucky, there's a girl there, on the beach, a pretty girl in a red oilskin. They used to stay up late, talking into the night while the house was asleep, and maybe they would even whisper I love you, not really knowing what it was they were saying, only that they were saying it to each other, that was what mattered, because Juliette — Juliette was Simon's heart.

Marianne stands on the balcony, the cold sealing her fingers to the metal guardrail. From here, she can see the city, the estuary, the sea. The main roads, the port, and the coastline are illuminated by the orange glow of streetlamps, cold flames creating powdery Payne's gray haloes in the sky, the lights signaling the entrance of the port at the end of the main pier, while beyond the waterfront it is black tonight — not a single boat left stranded, not a single flashing light, only a slowly pulsing mass, only darkness. What will become of Juliette's love when Simon's heart starts to beat inside a stranger's body? What will become of everything that filled that heart, its emotions slowly deposited in strata since the first day, inoculated here

and there in a rush of enthusiasm or a fit of rage, its friendships and enmities, its grudges, its vehemence, its serious and tender inclinations? What will become of the bursts of electricity that rushed through his heart when a wave approached? What will become of this full, this too-full, this overflowing heart? Marianne looks out at the courtyard: the pines still, the copses retracted, the cars parked under streetlights, the windows of the apartments opposite spilling warm light into the darkness, the reddish glows of living rooms and the yellows of kitchens — topaz, saffron, mimosa, and that even brighter Naples yellow behind the misted windows — and the neon-green rectangle of a sports field. It's almost time for Sunday supper — that reduced meal, that TV dinner of self-service snacks, leftovers, pancakes, boiled eggs, a ritual that meant: this evening, she didn't have to cook anything, and they would all sprawl in front of the TV to watch a soccer game or a movie, and Simon's outline appears clearly in the lamp. She turns around: Sean is there, looking at her, forehead pressed to the window, while behind him, on the couch, Lou has fallen asleep.

Another call. Another telephone trembling on a table and another hand picking it up — this one has a large, dark gold ring on one of its fingers, ribbed with spirals. Another voice succeeding the electronic growl — this one sounds nervous, and we understand why when we see the name on the cell phone's screen: "Harfang surg." Hello? And then another announcement — we can read the contents of this one on the face of the woman who is listening to it, emotion rushing beneath her skin, and then her features contracting again in furls.

"We have a heart. A compatible heart. A team is on its way to remove it. Come now — we'll do the transplant tonight. You'll go into the OR around midnight."

She hangs up, breathing heavily. Turns toward the room's only window and gets up to open it, both hands leaning on the desk

as she struggles to her feet, walking the three steps with difficulty, and then grunting as she forces the latch. Behind the window, winter is massing: a hardened landscape, glacial and translucent. The cold turns the sounds of the street to glass, each one isolated like the murmur of evening in a provincial town; it neutralizes the screech of the elevated railroad car as it comes to a halt at the Chevaleret station; it muzzles the air's odors and presses an icy film over her face. Shivering, she looks slowly over toward the other side of Boulevard Vincent-Auriol, to the windows of the building, directly across from where she stands, that hosts the Cardiology Department of the Pitié-Salpêtrière hospital. She had been there, three days earlier, for exams that showed her heart to be in a state of severe deterioration, enabling the cardiologist to request she be put on the priority list of recipients at the Biomedical Agency. She thinks about what she is living through, now, at this second. I'm saved, she thinks: I'm going to live. Someone, somewhere, has died suddenly, she thinks. Now, this evening, she thinks. She experiences the full force of the announcement, thinking that she doesn't ever want the spark of this present moment to fade into the past, into the realm of

memory: she wants it to endure, sharp and new. I am mortal, she thinks.

She takes a deep breath of winter, eyes closed: the bluish planet is drifting through a fold in the cosmos, suspended in silence amid gaseous matter; the forest is starred with straight-lined gaps; red ants are writhing under trees in a sticky frost; the garden expands: mold and stones, grass after rain, heavy branches, palm tree claws; the lidded city incubates the masses; children in bunk beds open their eyes in total darkness; she imagines her heart — a chunk of dark-red flesh, oozing and fibrous, pipes running in all directions — this organ riddled with necrosis, this organ that is failing. She closes the window. She has to get ready.

It is nearly a year since Claire Méjan rented this one-bedroom apartment without having even seen it — the mentions in the ad of the Pitié-Salpêtrière and its second-floor location being enough to make her sign a check, then and there, for the exorbitant sum demanded by the guy at the real estate agency. It's a small, dirty, dark place, the balcony on the third floor obscuring the view from her window like a helmet visor. But she has no choice. This is what it means to be sick, she thinks — not having a choice.

Her heart has left her no choice.

It's myocarditis. She found out about it three years ago, during a cardiology consultation at Pitié-Salpêtrière. Eight days before that, she'd stayed at home with flu, poking the crackling fire in the hearth, a blanket over her shoulders, while outside in the garden, snapdragons and foxgloves cowered in the wind. She had gone to see a doctor in Fontainebleau and told him about the fever, the aches, and the tiredness, but she had neglected to mention the short-lived palpitations, the pain in her chest, and the breathlessness she experienced during exercise, ascribing these symptoms to weariness, winter, the lack of light, a sort of general exhaustion. She left the doctor's office with a prescription for flu medicine, and decided to stay home and work from bed. A few days later, dragging herself through the streets of Paris to see her mother, she collapsed in shock: her blood flow decreased dramatically, her skin became pale, cold and clammy. She was taken to the ER in an ambulance, sirens screaming — like she'd found herself in an American soap opera — and they resuscitated her, then began the first tests. Blood analysis confirmed the existence of an inflammation, so they examined her heart. After that, she underwent a series

of exams: the electrocardiogram detected an electrical anomaly; the X-ray showed her heart to be slightly enlarged; then, finally, the ultrasound established heart failure. Claire stayed in the hospital. She was transferred to the coronary care unit, where more specific exams took place. The coronary catheterization was normal, reducing the likelihood of it being cardiac arrest, so they decided to carry out a heart biopsy: Claire received an injection in the cardiac muscle via the jugular. A few hours later, the results concluded with a hostile-sounding nine-syllable diagnosis: myocardial inflammation.

The treatment was two-pronged: the first dealt with the heart failure (the organ no longer pumping efficiently), and the second the rhythm disorder. Claire was ordered to rest — no physical strain whatsoever — and to take antiarrhythmic drugs and beta-blockers, while she was implanted with a defibrillator in order to prevent sudden death. At the same time, the viral infection was treated with powerful immunosuppressants and anti-inflammatories. But the disease persisted in its severest form: it spread into the muscle tissue, the heart grew even more distended, and every second the risk of death hung over her. The organ's

destruction was now considered irreversible: she needed a transplant. A new heart. The heart of another human implanted in the place of her own — the doctor's gestures seemed to mime the surgical act. In the long term, this was, for her, the only solution.

She goes home that evening. Her youngest son came to fetch her from the hospital; he will be the one who drives her back there. You're going to agree, aren't you? he asks quietly. She nods mechanically — she feels overwhelmed. Arriving at her house on the forest's edge — this fairy-tale house where she now lives alone, her children having all grown up — she goes straight to bed: lying on her back, staring at the ceiling, fear pins her in place, infects all her future days with no possible escape. Fear of death and fear of pain, fear of the operation, fear of the postoperative treatments, fear that the organ will be rejected and she will have to start over again, fear of a foreign body intruding in hers, fear of becoming a chimera, of no longer being herself.

She has to move. She's taking a risk, living in that village fifty miles from Paris, a long way from any main road.

Claire feels an immediate loathing for her

new apartment. Too warm, in both winter and summer; the need for lights even in the middle of the day; the noise from the street. A final airlock before the operating theater, she envisages it instead as an antechamber of death, thinking she will die here because — even though she isn't bedridden — she feels trapped in this place: she can't leave it without what seems a superhuman effort, climbing the stairs gives her pain, each movement making her feel as if her heart is separating from the rest of her body, slipping from its perch inside the thoracic cage and falling to pieces. This feeling turns her into a shaky, limping creature, on the verge of a breakdown. Day after day, the space seems to close in around her, limiting and reducing her gestures, restricting her movements, narrowing her entire world, as if she has a stocking or a plastic bag over her head — something fibrous that stifles her breathing — as if her feet are caught in quicksand. She grows somber. To her youngest son, who comes to see her one evening, she admits that it disturbs her, the thought of waiting for someone to die so she can have their heart: It's a strange situation, you know, and it wears me out.

To begin with, she is reluctant to really

move in. What's the point? Live or die, she won't be staying here long — it is temporary, no matter what. But she doesn't let her fears show — she acts tough. Her first weeks in this apartment alter her relationship with time. It's not that it changes speed — slowed down by paralysis, by the dread of her suspended sentence, by her debilitating circumstances — nor that it stagnates, like the blood in Claire's lungs stagnates; no, time seems rather to disintegrate in a bleak continuity. Partly due to the unending darkness of the place, the alternation of day and night soon loses its distinction: all she does is sleep, with the excuse that she is channeling the shock of this forced move. Her two eldest children gradually come to regard Sundays as her visiting day, a fact that makes her sad without her really knowing why. Sometimes they reproach her for her lack of enthusiasm: across the road from the hospital, it could hardly be better, they say to her straight-faced. The youngest, on the other hand, turns up at any time and gives her long hugs. He is a head taller than her.

Sinister winter, cruel spring (she cannot see the greenness returning to the forest, the pure colors bursting forth again, and she

misses the undergrowth: the golden stumps and the ferns, the light probing in vertical rays, the multitude of noises, the foxglove scattered in semishade behind flower beds, on secret paths), hopeless summer. She is withering away (you need some sort of structure, meals at fixed times, a daily routine, repeats everyone who comes to see her, finding her depressed, distracted, vague, even a little creepy, her blond-haired black-eyed beauty altered, corroded by anxiety and the lack of fresh air), her hair is dull, eyes glassy, breath sour, and clothes shapeless. Her two eldest children try to find someone who can look after her — a home helper who can take care of the housework, the shopping, monitor her intake of medicine. When she learns about this plan, anger brings her back to life — are they trying to hack away at the little freedom that remains to her? White-faced and bitter, she rants about being under house arrest, no longer able to bear healthy people's opinions about sickness.

The first call comes on the night of August 15. The window is open: it's 8:00 p.m. and the room is suffocatingly hot. This is the Pitié, we have a heart for you, tonight, now — always the same phrasing. She's not

prepared. Putting her fork back on her untouched plate, she looks at her family, gathered around her, reunited for her birthday — you have to celebrate your fiftieth — they all stand with their arms dangling at their sides like birds' wings: her mother, her three boys, the young woman who lives with her eldest and their little boy, all frozen except for the child with his garnet-colored eyes, all listening: I'm going, I have to go, chairs shoved backward, champagne flutes trembling, spurting, spilling, a bag packed with toothpaste and eau de toilette, the stairs descended with that rushed slowness that makes people trip and yell at each other — we forgot the sorbets in the kitchen, forgot the medical card, forgot the cell phone — then the sticky asphalt, the smoky sky, people leaning through open windows, a shirtless guy walking his dog, the little boy running on the sidewalk, grabbed by his mother, the tourists checking their maps as they emerge from the metro, and at last the hospital, ringed with little lamps, the admissions process, the newly scoured room where she waits again, sitting on the edge of the bed that she will never open because, finally, there is movement in the corridor, the sound of heavy footsteps, and Harfang appears. He stands before her, thin and

pale, bags under his eyes: In the end, we decided to refuse the organ.

She listens as he explains his decision, her face blank: The heart wasn't good, too small and poorly vascularized, there's no point taking a risk like that, we'll just have to keep waiting. Harfang imagines she must be in shock from the disappointment, her hopes dashed, but in fact she is stunned, stupefied, and soon she has only one thought in mind: to get away from here. Her feet hang in the void, her backside slips insensibly off the edge of the bed, and she lands softly on the floor, then stands up — I'm going home. Outside, her sons kick bushes that instantly give up clouds of burning dust, her mother bursts into tears, comforted by her youngest son, the eldest son's girlfriend keeps running after the little boy, who refuses to go back to the house, and everything falls apart. The group crosses the road in the opposite direction, no longer feeling hungry: it seems impossible to start eating the meal where they had left it. But they can still drink — a pink champagne served in bubble-glass flutes — and Claire ends up lifting her full glass above the table, arm outstretched and smiling, looking beautiful now: Come on, put your heart into it! You're not funny, you know, her

youngest son mutters.

After that, the nature of time changes — it regains its shape. Or, rather, it takes the shape of waiting: hollow and stretched out. From that point on, the only purpose of hours is to be available during them, knowing that the transplant operation could suddenly become reality, a heart might appear at any moment: I must stay alive, I must be ready. Minutes become supple, seconds ductile, and finally fall arrives, and Claire resolves to bring her books and lamps to this tiny apartment. Her youngest son installs Wi-Fi for her, and she buys an office chair, a wooden table, gathers together a few objects: she wants to start translating again.

Her editor is delighted by this news, and sends her Charlotte Brontë's first publication, a collection of poems published under her and her sisters' masculine pseudonyms: Currer, Ellis, and Acton Bell. She spends the fall in an icy cottage, battered by the wind, where three sisters and a brother write and read together by candlelight, communing with each other through books: feverish, exalted, tortured geniuses, inventing worlds, walking the moors, drinking quarts of tea, and smoking opium. Their intensity wins

Claire over, and she gradually perks up. Each day spent working yields a slender batch of pages, and as the weeks pass she finds her rhythm, as if it's a question of synchronizing the waiting — which becomes sharper and clearer as the state of her heart declines — with another kind of time: that of translating poems. Sometimes she feels she is replacing the painful contractions of her sick organ with a fluid back-and-forth, between her native French and the English she has learned, and that this reciprocal movement is digging a cradle-shaped crevice inside her, a new cavity. She'd had to learn a new language in order to understand her own, so she wondered if this new heart would allow her to better understand herself: I'm clearing a space for you, my heart, I'm making you a home.

On Christmas Eve, a man resurfaces, placing a bouquet of purple foxgloves on her bed. She has known him since childhood: they grew up together — lovers, friends, brother and sister, partners in crime. They are, for each other, almost everything a man and a woman can be.

Claire smiles and taps her chest: it's not a good idea to surprise me, you know. In fact, she has to sit down and recover while he

takes off his coat. The flowers are from her garden, she can tell from their scent. You know they're poisonous? she says, pointing at them. One of those flowers that children are forbidden to touch, breathe, gather, taste — she remembers staring, fascinated, at her fingers, coated with fuchsia powder, alone in the street, and the word "poison" appearing in a thought bubble above her head while she lifted her hand to her mouth. The man slowly pulls off a petal and places it in the palm of her hand: Look at that. The petal is so brightly colored that it looks artificial, made of plastic. Trembling in her palm, it is covered with microscopic wrinkles. Actually, he tells her, the digitalin contained in the flowers makes the heartbeat stronger, slower, steadier. It's good for you.

She sleeps with the flowers that night. The man carefully undresses her, removing the petals one by one, then placing them on her naked skin like the scales of a fish, a sort of organic jigsaw puzzle that he painstakingly perfects into a ceremonial gown, whispering don't move from time to time, even though she has long been asleep, in a luxuriant catalepsy, nursed and ornamented like a queen. It was still night when she awoke, but the children in the apartment above hers were already running around excitedly,

shouting, their footsteps hammering the floorboards, rushing into the living room to tear the wrapping paper from the presents that had appeared during the night around the ectoplasmic Christmas tree. Her friend had gone. She shook the petals from her body and made them into a salad that she seasoned with truffle oil and balsamic vinegar.

A T-shirt, a few pairs of underwear, two nightgowns, a pair of slippers, beauty products, laptop, cell phone, chargers. Her medical file — administrative printouts, latest exams, and those large, rigid envelopes containing scans, X-rays, and MRIs. She is glad she's alone to pack her bag, to walk cautiously downstairs, to take her time outside. She crosses the road diagonally, trying to catch the eyes of drivers who slow down when they see her, listening to the hot rail tracks vibrating over her head; she would like to see an animal — a tiger, ideally, or a barn owl with a heart-shaped face, but a stray dog would be fine, and bees would be wonderful. She is more terrified than she has ever been; she is anesthetized by terror. But she should call to let people know, she thinks, as she enters the hospital grounds. She looks up her sons' numbers

and sends them a text — it's now, tonight — then calls her mother, who must already be asleep, and lastly her foxglove friend on the other side of the world: signals sent in this very instant that stretch out a long way through time. She turns back one more time, looks at the window of her apartment, and suddenly all the hours that she has spent behind that pane of glass, waiting, are condensed into a single shard of time, converging at the base of her skull at the precise moment when she walks through the hospital gates, a lightning-quick finger snap that launches her into the enclosure, onto the asphalt ribbon that runs beside the buildings. Then, as the path bends to the left, she enters the Cardiology Institute: a lobby, two elevators — she forces herself not to think about choosing the one that will bring her good luck — up to the fourth floor and that corridor illuminated like a space station, the glass-walled workstation, and Harfang standing there, in a clean and neatly ironed shirt, white cowlick combed back off his forehead: I've been expecting you.

The Margherita splats against the apartment wall, landing on the carpet and leaving a Neapolitan sunset above the television set. Having cast a satisfied glance at the effect she has produced, the young woman turns toward the pile of white boxes on the breakfast bar of the American kitchen, patiently opens a second perfectly square, flat box, slides the burning disc of Americana onto her palm, then stands facing the wall, elbow bent, hand flat, and — with a rapid extension of her arm — throws the pizza with all her strength between the room's two windows, creating another action painting, slices of pepperoni scattered in a curious constellation across the wall. As she is preparing to open the third box, a blistered four-cheese, thinking that the yellowish sludge of melted mozzarella, parmesan, gorgonzola, and ricotta might well act as a sort of adhesive paste, a man comes

out of the bathroom, face aglow, stops dead in the doorway, sensing a threat, and — seeing the young woman getting ready to send a third hot circle flying straight at him — instinctively falls to the ground. Lying prone, he soon rolls over onto his back so he can watch her from below: she smiles, turns away from him, her eyes surveying the room, and — taking care to target a new area — throws the pizza against the front door. After that, she steps over the shocked young man and goes to wash her hands behind the breakfast bar. The man gets up, checks that there are no stains on his clothes, then takes note of the damage, turning in a circle until he is once again facing the woman as she stands at the sink.

She drinks a glass of water. Her pearl-white shoulders emerge from a soccer shirt in the colors of the Squadra Azzurra with a scoop neck that gives a glimpse of the tops of her small breasts; her immensely long legs emerge in the other direction from a pair of baggy, satiny blue shorts; a delicate film of perspiration pearls above her mouth: she's so beautiful when she's angry, the skin below her jaw pulsing. She doesn't even look at him as she crosses and uncrosses her long arms — things of classical beauty — lifting them as she does so, in order to

remove the now pointless soccer shirt, revealing a glorious torso that is a sum of various circles (breasts, areolae, nipples, stomach, belly button, the twin bait of her buttocks), of various triangles pointing toward the ground (the isosceles of the sternum, the convex of the pubis, the concave of the hips), and of various lines (the dorsal midline that divides the body in two identical halves, and the furrow, in a woman, that is reminiscent of a leaf's vein or a butterfly's symmetry axis), the whole punctuated by a little diamond shape in the area of the sternal crest — the dark keel — a collection of perfect forms whose balance of proportions and ideal arrangement he admired with a professional eye, prizing the anatomical exploration of the human body above all, and of this particular human body in particular, savoring its examination, searching passionately for the slightest disharmony in its construction, the tiniest defect, the faintest discrepancy: a curve of scoliosis above the lumbar vertebrae, that sporulating beauty spot, there, under the armpit, those calluses between the toes where her feet are compressed into the sharp points of her high-heeled shoes, and the slight strabismus that made her squint when she was short of sleep, the source of

that dissipated air, that look of a feral girl, which he loved so much.

She slips on a turtleneck sweater, removes her shorts and climbs into a pair of skintight jeans. The show is over. Then, having put on a pair of high-heeled boots, she heads toward the front door, where grease trickles down the wooden surface, opens it, and slams it behind her without a backward glance at the young man standing in the center of the messed-up apartment, who sighs with relief as he watches her go.

You're going to the hospital in Le Havre for an organ removal — a heart, now. When he heard these words in Harfang's mouth, enunciated just the way he had imagined during the past few months — brief and emotionless — Virgilio Breva almost choked on the bitter ball of happiness and disappointment that formed in his throat. Because, although of course he was on call, and although he was excited by his mission, the truth was that this announcement could hardly have come at a worse time — the rare conjunction of two unmissable events: a France versus Italy game + a horny Rose at home. All the same, he wondered for a long time afterward why Harfang had bothered to call him in person, detecting in that

fact a perverse desire to humiliate him on a historic evening, knowing perfectly well that the Italian was obsessed by soccer, his Sunday-morning training sessions having given him a legitimate excuse not to join the cycling squad: torture, Virgilio had once muttered, bemused, watching the throng of tadpoles in pointy helmets and multicolored cycling shorts set off down the road, with Harfang the queen bee at their center.

Sitting in the backseat of the taxi as it heads toward Pitié-Salpêtrière, Virgilio folds his fur-lined hood back over his shoulders and gets his breath back. The tensions of the last hour have left him in a state of disturbance, when he needs to be at the top of his game, more than ever before. Because tonight will be his night; tonight will be a big night. The quality of the transplant depends entirely on the quality of the removal — it's the fundamental law of his profession — and tonight, he is in the front line.

It's time to get a grip, he thinks, interlacing his leather-gloved fingers, it's time to dump that girl, that crazy bitch, time for his survival instinct to assert itself, even if that means being deprived of her hyperactive body and the glory of her presence. He

relives the alarms of the previous hour: Rose surprising him at home when he had planned to go to the soccer game with some friends, then demanding — adorable yet vaguely threatening — that the two of them stay at home to watch it and order pizza, arguing her case silently with the Italian soccer outfit she wore, the erotic tension gradually insinuating itself into the belligerent, upper-case tension of the France–Italy game, this embrace of opposites exuding a possible — and incredibly intriguing — happiness, to which Harfang's call, on the stroke of eight, had added an excess of feverish agitation, emotions shooting through the roof. Immediately, he had jumped to his feet and replied I'm here, I'm ready, I'm on my way, avoiding Rose's eyes but putting on an exaggeratedly tragic face — eyebrows like circumflex accents, lower lip rolled up over upper lip, the oval of the chin lengthened sadly — an expression that signified disaster, rotten luck, and was intended for Rose, grimacing for her at that moment, fanning the air with his hand like a clown, a thrift-store tragedian, while his eyes lit up with joy — a heart! She wasn't fooled. He backed out of the room to take a shower and dress in clean, warm clothes, and when he came out of the bathroom, the

situation had spiraled out of control. It had been a wonderful and overwhelming spectacle, but mentally replaying it now in slow-motion, perceiving its logical majesty, only seemed to accentuate Rose's supremacy, her incomparable beauty, and her fiery temperament, her ability to channel her rage into a regal body language, maintaining a royal silence where so many others would merely whine. Splat! Splat! Splat! The more he thinks about it, the more impossible it seems to break up with that highly flammable and utterly unique creature. No, he will never give her up, no matter what other people say, all those who think she's insane, or "borderline," as they put it, with a knowing look, when they would give anything to touch that trapezoid of warm skin in the hollow at the back of her knee.

She had first made her appearance at the start of the university year, during one of the classes taken by medical interns at the Pitié. The instruction given during the day-school years took the form of tutorial classes of one particular type: the study of clinical cases. The students attended long sessions, where real situations experienced by the departments or scenarios invented on the basis of particular questions that required study were "replayed," so that they could

learn to listen to the patient, become acquainted with the methods of auscultation, practice diagnoses, identify a pathology, and decide on a treatment protocol. This practical work, developed around the patient/doctor duo, took place in public and sometimes required the setting up of bigger groups, in order to encourage an aptitude for working together, for dialogues between the different disciplines. It was intended to resist the compartmentalization of medical specialties, which divided the human body into a collection of rules and practices, with no flow of knowledge between them, making it impossible to see the patient as a whole person. Because it was based on simulation, however, this new teaching method provoked a degree of mistrust: the use of fiction in the process of acquiring scientific knowledge, the very idea of "play-acting" a situation — you be the doctor and you be the patient — was enough to make the faculty skeptical. They did agree to it, though, acknowledging that this teaching technique brought together some very interesting material, including subjectivity and emotion, and emphasizing the importance, in the patient/doctor dialogue, of understanding and deciphering that fragile, often distorted communication. In this role-

playing game, it was decided that the students, carrying out their future function, would take on the part of the doctor, which meant that the hospital had to hire actors to play the patients.

They turned up to the audition after a small ad appeared in a weekly paper for performing-arts professionals. Most of them were theater actors, highly promising newcomers or eternal bit-part players from television shows, commercial veterans, understudies, walk-ons, extras, doing the rounds of casting sessions in order to pick up hours, to earn enough money to pay their rent — generally a shared apartment in an arrondissement in the northeast of Paris or a nearby suburb — or reinventing themselves as coaches for training days on sales techniques (at home or elsewhere), and perhaps ending up as human guinea pigs, tasting new yogurts, testing moisturizers or lice-repellent shampoos, experimenting with diuretic pills.

There were too many, so there was a selection process. The jury was made up of medical professors and practitioners, some of them theater aficionados. When Rose entered the audition room and walked past the workbenches, wearing platform sneak-

ers, burgundy Adidas sweatpants, and a sunshine-colored Lurex top, the men in the room were stirred into murmurs, their interest sparked by her face and her body. She was given a list of actions and words to help her improvise the part of a patient rushed to the gynecology department after the discovery of a suspicious lump in her left breast, and, during the fifteen minutes that followed, her commitment to the role elicited widespread admiration: she lay on her back, topless on the cold tile floor, and guided the student's hand — here, here, that's where it is, yes, there — and then, as the scene dragged on, a disturbance arose: the student, it was true, palpated her chest rather longer than was strictly necessary, moving from one breast to the other and then starting over, ignoring the dialogue guidelines, not listening to the essential information that she provided him with — including the intense pain she felt at the end of her menstrual cycle — so that she finally stood up, purple-faced, and slapped him. Bravo, mademoiselle! She was congratulated, and hired on the spot.

From the very beginning, Rose secretly disregarded the terms of the contract, believing that this job as a "patient," which she had landed for the entire academic year,

would be a learning opportunity for her, the chance to increase her range, the power of her art. Foolishly, she scorned ordinary pathologies — or what she considered ordinary pathologies — preferring to monopolize madness, hysteria, and melancholy, a register in which she excelled — romantic and mysterious heroines — sometimes allowing herself diversions not mentioned in the prescribed scenario (an effrontery that shocked the psychiatrists and neurologists who were running the classes and created confusion among the students, forcing them to ask her to take it down a notch or two); she played drowned women, attempted suicides, bulimics, erotomaniacs, diabetics, taking particular pleasure in mimicking people with limps, people in pain (a case of coxalgia in Brittany providing the opportunity for a very nice dialogue about inbreeding in Finistère Nord), people with hunchbacks (she succeeded in imitating the rotation of the vertebrae in the thoracic cage), and anything that required her to twist or unhinge her body; she liked interpreting a pregnant woman with premature contractions, but was less convincing in her incarnation of a young mother describing the symptoms of a three-month-old baby, which brought the pediatric intern out in a

cold sweat; superstitious, she refused to play cancer patients.

However, she was never better than on that December day when she had to simulate angina. The renowned cardiologist who was leading the course had described the pain to her in these terms: A bear is sitting on your chest. Rose's almond-shaped eyes had widened in awe: A bear? She had to gather her childhood memories — the vast, foul-smelling cage with its crudely modeled, cream-colored plastic rocks, and the huge animal, half a ton, with its triangular muzzle and its close-set eyes that gave a false impression of nearsightedness, the rust-brown fur dusted with sand, and the yells of the children when it stood up on its hind legs, six and a half feet tall; she recalled the scenes of Ceauşescu hunting in the Carpathian Mountains — the bears subdued by peasants and lured with buckets of food, emerging from the back of the clearing close to a log cabin mounted on pilings, moving forward until it was perfectly framed by the open window where a Securitate agent prepared a rifle before handing it to the dictator as soon as the bear was close enough that he couldn't miss; lastly, she remembered a scene from *Grizzly Man*. Rose began at the back of the room, walked

toward the student who was going to partner her in the scene, and then stood still. Could she make out the beast at the edge of the undergrowth, its head poking between bamboo shoots, or nonchalantly swaying its rump on four feet, cashew-colored fur, lazily scratching a stump with its non-retractable claws, before turning toward her and standing up like a man? Did she see the monster emerging from its cave after months of hibernation, stretching its muscles, reheating the stalled fluids in its body, reactivating the taste for blood in its heart? Could she discern it at dusk, rummaging through supermarket trash cans, growling happily under a huge moon? Or was she thinking about a different weight altogether — a man's? She fell back onto the floor — the noise her body made when it hit the floor provoked a murmur in the room — and, stiffening convulsively, let out a cry of pain, soon muffled into a silent groan, and afterward stopped breathing, completely immobile. Her thoracic cage seemed to flatten and hollow out in a basin while her face swelled up, slowly reddening, her lips, held tight, soon turning colorless, eyes rolling back in her head, and her limbs began to fibrillate, as if electrocuted; such realism was not expected of these actors, and some

of the students in the room stood up to get a better view, alarmed by her crimson face and concave abdomen, and a figure hurtled down the steps of the amphitheater and knelt next to Rose — knocking over the student who had begun imperturbably to read through the first lines of his questionnaire in a droning voice — and leaned over her to resuscitate her while the eminent cardiologist also rushed over, shining a penlight at her irises. Rose frowned with one eyebrow, opened one eye, then the other, sat up with a jolt, looked questioningly at the crowd gathered around her, and, for the first time in her life, felt the pleasure of being applauded. She lay flat on her back in front of the students as they stood and clapped in the bleachers.

The young man who'd rushed over to her, furious at having been fooled, reproached her for overacting: angina is not cardiac arrest, you know, the two things are not the same at all, it should have been more subtle and complex, you messed up the exercise. In order to make her understand, he listed the symptoms of angina one by one — constrictive thoracic pain, the feeling of being crushed all across your chest, of being squeezed in a vise, and sometimes other pains, typically in the lower jaw, one of the

two forearms, or, more rarely, in the back, the throat, but anyway, you don't collapse. Then he detailed the symptoms of cardiac arrest: massively accelerated pulse rate, sometimes to more than three hundred beats per minute, a ventricular fibrillation leading to respiratory arrest, which in turn causes the patient to faint, all this in less than a minute. He now began detailing the treatments, listing the medicines, the anti-platelet drugs that facilitate blood circulation and the nitroglycerin that relieves the pain by dilating the coronary arteries, he was captivated, no longer had any idea what he was saying but was unable to stop talking, throwing out sentences like lassos in order to catch her and keep her close to him. Soon his heart rate was racing, abnormally fast, a tachycardia close to two hundred beats per minute; he risked suffering the ventricular fibrillation he had just described to her, risked fainting, risked almost anything, frankly; Rose turned slowly toward him with starlike disdain, looked him up and down, and smilingly explained to him that a bear had just sat on her chest, didn't he know? She then told him, slyly, that she was ready to go through it again, if he would agree to play the bear — he had the physique and the finesse, she would bet

her life on it.

Virgilio Breva was indeed rather bearlike in his supple slowness, his explosiveness. He was a swarthy blond with a stubbly beard, his soft hair swept back, piling up in curls on the back of his neck. His nose was straight, and he had the fine features of a Friulian. He had the light-footed gait of a sardana dancer despite the fact that he was close to two hundred pounds, with the corpulence of a former fat kid, toned to the point where he was thick-chested, full-bodied, without any visible excrescences — no flab or lumps, in other words — a body that was just a little fleshy, enveloped in a layer of fat of equal compactness, thinning toward the extremities of his limbs, toward his very beautiful hands. Although transformed into this seductive and charismatic colossus — with a stature that matched the eloquence of his warm voice, his enthusiastic if occasionally excessive moods, his bulimic appetite for knowledge, his extraordinary capacity for hard work — his body was prey to painful fluctuations, an elasticity that haunted him with feelings of shame and fear (the trauma of having been mocked as pudgy, chubby, plump, or simply fat; the anger at having been looked down on for

that, for the sexual difficulties it caused him; all kinds of apprehensions), his self-loathing gathered into a ball inside his stomach, like a torture device. This body was the great torment of Virgilio's life — constantly monitored, examined for hours if he got a speck of dust in his eye, taken to the ER if he got a sunburn, questioned intensely over a sore throat, a stiff neck, a tired feeling — it was his obsession, but it was also his triumph, because women liked it now, that was indisputable: all you had to do was see Rose's eyes as they wandered over it. Some spiteful people, jealous of his success, even said, with a snigger, that he had only become a doctor so he could learn to control that great body of his, balance his moods, tame his metabolism.

The best in his year at the internship entrance exam in Paris, he raced through his years of study, cramming everything — including spells as chief resident and surgical assistant — into twelve years, when most students in a similar situation would stretch it out to fifteen (but I also can't afford it, he liked to tell people, with a charming smile, I'm not part of the establishment, and this outraged the wop inside him, the immigrant son, the industrious scholarship student, the boy who did not belong: he always blew

things out of proportion). Creative on the theoretical side and prodigiously gifted on the practical side, flamboyant and proud, driven by vaulting ambition and inexhaustible energy, he often lost his temper, it's true, and remained widely misunderstood: his mother, panicked by his success, connecting intellectual hierarchies to social hierarchies, ended up regarding him suspiciously, wondering how he had done it, what stuff he was made of, who he thought he was, this kid who went into a rage watching her wring her hands then wipe them on her apron, or hearing her moan, the day he defended his thesis, that her presence was completely pointless, that she wouldn't understand anything, that it wasn't her place, that she would rather stay home and cook a feast just for him, the pasta and the cakes that he loved.

So, he chose the heart, and then cardiac surgery. People were surprised, thinking that he could have made a fortune examining suspicious moles, injecting hyaluronic acid into frown lines and Botox into cheeks, remodeling the floppy, stretch-marked stomachs of multiparous women, X-raying bodies, developing vaccines in Swiss laboratories, giving speeches in Israel and the United States on iatrogenic diseases, becom-

ing a high-flying nutritionist. Or he could have covered himself in glory by opting for neurosurgery, or even hepatic surgery — specialties that dazzle with their complexity, their use of cutting-edge technology — instead of which he chose the heart. The good old heart. The human engine. A creaking pump that gets clogged up, goes on the blink. I'm basically a plumber, he liked to tell people: I tap on the surface, listen to the echo, identify what's gone wrong, replace the faulty piece, repair the machine, it's perfect for me — hamming it up as he says this, hopping from one foot to the other, minimizing the prestige of the discipline when the truth was that all of this flattered his megalomania.

In fact, Virgilio chose the heart so he could exist at the highest level, reckoning on the idea that the organ's kingly aura would reflect on him, just as it reflected on the cardiac surgeons rushing through the corridors of the hospital, plumbers and demigods. Because the heart is more than the heart, as he knew perfectly well. Even deposed from its former throne — the muscle continuing to pump no longer being enough to separate the living from the dead — it was, for him, the central organ of the body, the place where the most crucial

operations, those most essential for life, took place, and to Virgilio its symbolic stratification was unaltered. More than that, as both a cutting-edge mechanism and the operator of mankind's supercharged imagination, Virgilio envisaged it as the keystone to representations ordering man's relationship with his body, with other humans, with Creation, with gods, and the young surgeon was awestruck by the idea that he would be a part of this, a recurrent presence at this magical point in language, permanently situated at the exact intersection of the literal and the figurative, of muscle and emotion; he was thrilled by the metaphors and figures of speech that made it appear as the very analogy of life and never tired of repeating the fact that, having been the first to appear, the heart would also be the last to disappear. One night at the Pitié, sitting at a table with some others in the duty room, in front of the huge mural painted by the interns — a spectacular tangle of sexual scenes and surgical operations, a sort of gory orgy, jokey and morbid, where a few representations of hospital bigwigs appeared between all the asses, breasts, and enormous erections, among them a Harfang or two, generally portrayed on the job, in obscene postures, doggy-style or missionary, scalpel

in hand — he told the story of the death of
Joan of Arc, his delivery theatrical, eyes
sparkling like obsidian balls, slowly recount-
ing how the captive was taken by cart from
her prison to the Vieux-Marché, where a
crowd had gathered to watch, describing
the slim figure in the tunic that had been
treated with sulfur so she would burn more
quickly, the pyre built too high, Thérage the
executioner climbing up to tie her to the
stake — Virgilio, encouraged by his listen-
ers' captivated faces, mimed the scene, tying solid knots in the invisible ropes —
before setting fire to the bundles of sticks
with an experienced hand, lowering the
torch to the coals and the oil-soaked wood,
the smoke rising, the screams, Joan's last
words before she suffocated, then the scaf-
fold blazing like a flare, and the heart that
they discovered intact after the body had
been consumed, red and whole in the ashes,
so they were forced to rekindle the fire to
be rid of it.

An exceptional student, an extraordinary
intern, Virgilio intrigued the hospital's
management but struggled to find a niche
for himself among groups of fellow
surgeons-to-be, professing with equal vehemence an orthodox anarchism and a hatred

of "families," those incestuous casts, those biological connivances — when, in truth, like so many others, he was fascinated by all the Harfangs in white coats, attracted by the heirs, mesmerized by their reign, their health, the power of their numbers, curious about their properties, their tastes, and their idioms, their sense of humor, their clay tennis courts, so much so that he became obsessed by the idea of being invited to their homes, sharing their culture, drinking their wine, complimenting their mother, sleeping with their sisters — a raw devouring — and he intrigued like crazy to make it happen, as concentrated as a snake-charmer, then hated himself when he woke up between their sheets, suddenly rude, unpleasantly insulting, a grumpy old bear kicking the bottle of Chivas under the bed, wrecking the Limoges porcelain and the chintz curtains, and he would always end up running away, a lost soul.

His acceptance into the cardiac surgery department of Pitié-Salpêtrière sent his emotions up a notch: aware of his value, he immediately despised the petty rivalries of the medical courtiers, ignored the docile heirs and heiresses apparent, and set to work on getting close to Harfang, getting so close to him that he could hear him think,

doubt, tremble, so that he could sense his decision in the very instant it was made and see it in the movement of his gesture. From now on, he knows, he is going to learn with this man what he could never learn anywhere else.

Virgilio checks the Italian team's roster on his cell phone — makes sure that Balotelli is playing, Motta too, yes, that's good, and Pirlo, and we've got Buffon in goal — then exchanges predictions and insults with two other chief residents who will be eating dinner in front of a giant plasma screen tonight and drinking his good health, both of them French guys who hate the defensive Italian style and support a team that is physically underprepared. The taxi glides in parallel with the Seine, as flat and smooth as a runway, and as he approaches the entrance to the hospital opposite the Chevaleret metro station, he tries to calm himself down. Soon he is not responding to his colleagues' messages, only smiling, dropping out of their gamblers' stake-raising frenzy. Rose's face reappears in his mind, and he is about to write her a gallant text — something along the lines of: the curve of your eyes encircles my heart — then changes his mind: that girl is a nutcase, a dangerous

nutcase, and tonight, nothing must disturb his concentration, his control, nothing must deflect the success of his work.

The organ-removal teams begin arriving at 10:00 p.m. The Rouen team turns up in a car, only one hour on the roads separating them from the hospital in Le Havre, whereas the teams from Lyon, Strasbourg, and Paris are all arriving by airplane.

The teams have organized their transportation, calling an airline company that will accept this Sunday mission, and have verified the nocturnal opening of the little airport at Octeville-sur-Mer, formalizing all the logistical details. At the Pitié, Virgilio paced impatiently around the duty nurse who was frantically calling everyone, and did not even look at the young woman in a white overcoat who was also standing there, in silence, and who, when their eyes did finally meet, moved away from the wall and advanced toward him, hello, Alice Harfang, I'm the new intern in the department, I'll

be doing the removal with you. Virgilio eyeballed her: she didn't have the giveaway white cowlick, but he could tell she was one of them — ugly, indeterminate age, yellow eyes and eagle-beak nose. He could almost see the strings that were pulled to get her here. His face darkened. He particularly disliked the beautiful white coat with the fur collar. Not exactly an appropriate outfit for traipsing around hospitals. She's the kind of chick who just comes along for the ride and thinks money grows on trees, he thought irritably. Okay, I assume you're not scared of flying, right? he questioned her curtly then turned away while she replied no, not at all. The duty nurse handed him a road map, hot off the printer: go ahead, the plane's on the runway, you'll be departing in forty minutes. Virgilio picked up his bag and headed toward the exit without even glancing at Alice, who was following him, then took the elevator, the taxi, the main roads to Bourget airport, where they passed jet-lagged businessmen in long cashmere overcoats, holding luxury briefcases, and soon the two of them were climbing into a Beechcraft 200 and fastening their seat belts, without having exchanged a single word.

The weather forecast is favorable: no snow

yet, and not much wind. The pilot, a man in his late thirties with perfectly straight teeth, announces good flying conditions and an estimated journey time of forty-five minutes, then disappears into the cockpit. As soon as he's sitting down, Virgilio has his nose in a financial magazine that someone had left on his seat, while Alice turns toward the window and watches Paris transformed into a sparkling tapestry as the little plane gains altitude — the almond shape, the river and its islands, the squares and the main roads, the bright zones full of exclusive stores, the dark zones full of tower blocks and forests, all of it shading into obscurity if you let your eyes move from the heart of the capital to its edges, beyond the luminous ring of the beltway; she follows the lines traced by those tiny red and yellow dots that run along invisible roads, the silent activity of the earth's surface. After that, the Beechcraft climbs through the clouds and into the celestial night. And so, probably because they are disconnected from the ground in this way, propelled far beyond all social markers, Virgilio thinks differently about his companion — maybe he is beginning to find her less repugnant — asking her, is this your first removal? Surprised, the woman turns her face from the window

and looks at him: Yes, first removal, and first transplant. Closing his magazine, Virgilio warns her: The first part of the night might be a little upsetting, it's a multiorgan removal, the kid's only nineteen, we're probably going to take everything — organs, blood vessels, tissue — we're just going to scrape everything out. His fist opens and closes very fast. Alice looks at him — her expression, enigmatic, might just as easily mean "I'm scared" as "So? I'm a Harfang, remember?" — then she sits up and re-attaches her seat belt, while Virgilio, suddenly destabilized, does the same: they are making their descent toward Octeville.

The little airport has been opened specially for them: the runway is lined with lights, the top of the tower illuminated. The aircraft touches down, shaken by spasms. The door slides open and the gangway unfolds. Alice and Virgilio walk down to the runway, and from that moment on they are propelled in a single movement, as if they are standing on a moving walkway, a magically fluid and unbroken trajectory, crossing through a deserted exterior (that asphalt perimeter where they can hear the sea), a mobile, cozy interior (the taxi), a freezing cold exterior (the hospital parking lot), and an interior whose codes they recognize

instantly (the surgery unit).

Thomas Rémige is waiting for them, like the master of the house. Handshakes, espressos, introductions made, connections created, and, as always, the Harfang name radiates its aura. He makes a head count: each team consists of two people, a senior surgeon and an intern, to which his own hospital has added the anesthesiologist and the nurse anesthetist, the OR nurse, the nurse's aid, and himself — thirteen altogether. It will seem like a crowd in the operating theater, the impregnable citadel, the secret zone accessible only to holders of multiple entry codes. Christ, it's going to be standing room only in there, Thomas thinks.

The theater is ready. The surgical lamp projects a white light, vertical and shadowless, over the operating table, the beams from its circle of spots converging on Simon Limbres's body, which has just been brought here and which still shows the same level of animation. It is still troubling, still moving to see him this way. He is placed in the center of the room — he is the heart of the world. A first circle around him delimits a sterile zone that cannot be crossed by anyone not involved in the operation: noth-

ing must be touched, soiled, infected; the organs that are about to be harvested here are sacred objects.

In a corner of the room, Cordélia Owl takes it all in. She has changed into scrubs and left her cell phone in a changing-room locker. Being separated from it — no longer feeling that hard rectangular shape vibrating against her hip, insidious as a parasite — has sent her into another reality: yes, it's here that it's happening, she thinks, eyes riveted on the body stretched out before her, this is where I am. Having gone through her training in the OR, the place itself is not alien to her, but she has only ever seen intense mobilizations aimed at saving patients, at keeping them alive, and she is struggling to comprehend the coming operation, because the young man is already dead, isn't he, and the objective of the surgery is to save other lives. She has prepared the equipment, arranged the tools, and now she is quietly repeating to herself the order in which the organs will be removed, lips barely moving behind her mask: (1) the kidneys; (2) the liver; (3) the lungs; (4) the heart. Then she starts over in reverse, reciting the order of the organs based on the duration of ischemia the organ will tolerate — in other words, how much time

it will survive once vascularization has been stopped — (1) the heart; (2) the lungs; (3) the liver; (4) the kidneys.

The body is lying flat, naked, arms extended to the sides, leaving clear the thoracic cage and the abdomen. It has been prepared, shaved, painted, then covered in a fenestrated drape that marks out a window of skin on the body, a cutaneous perimeter covering the thorax and the abdomen.

All right, here we go. Let's get started. The first team appears in the operating theater. The urologists will get the ball rolling — they will be the ones to open the body and they will close it again at the end. Two men get to work, a Laurel and Hardy–like odd couple, the tall, thin one being the surgeon, and the small, round one the intern. The tall, thin one bends over the body and makes an incision in the abdomen — a bilateral laparotomy below the ribs, tracing a sort of cross on the abdomen. In this way, the body is split in two distinct zones at the level of the diaphragm: the abdominal zone, where the liver and the kidneys are located, and the thoracic zone, home to the lungs and the heart. The men use self-retaining retractors on the incision, turning them by hand to widen the opening

— this action requires physical force, allied to meticulous technique, and suddenly the manual dimension of the operation shows through the massed technology, the physical confrontation with reality that is necessary in this place. The body's interior — the murky, oozing insides — glows red under the lamps.

The practitioners will prepare their organs in turn. Quick, meticulous blades move around the organs, freeing them from their attachments, their ligaments, their respective envelopes, but for the moment nothing is severed. The urologists, standing on either side of the table, talk to each other as this happens, the surgeon taking the opportunity to educate the intern: he leans over the kidneys, breaking down the movements he makes, describing the techniques he uses, while his pupil nods and sometimes asks questions.

One hour later, the Alsace team enters the room, both women, both the same height and build; the surgeon, a rising star in the relatively select world of hepatic surgery, does not utter a word, her gaze impassive behind her small, round, metal glasses, working at the liver with the determination of someone in a fight, fully committed to an

action that seems to find fulfillment in its own execution. Her colleague stares unblinkingly at the surgeon's unbelievably skillful hands.

Another thirty-five minutes pass and the thoracic team enters the theater. It's Virgilio's turn now; time for him to shine. He informs the Alsatians that he is ready to make the first incision, then immediately afterward makes the longitudinal section of the sternum. Unlike the others, he does not bend over the body, but remains upright, neck angled and arms held forward — a way of maintaining his distance from the body. The thorax is open and Virgilio can now see the heart — his heart — he can consider its volume, scrutinize the ventricles and auricles, observe its solid contractions. Alice sees the satisfaction in his face: it's a magnificent heart.

He proceeds with stunning speed — the arm of a quarterback and the fingers of a lacemaker — first dissecting the aorta, then, one by one, the venae cavae: untangling the muscle. Alice, standing directly across from him on the other side of the operating table, is gripped by what is unfolding: by the parade around this body, by the sum of actions of which it is the object; she watches Virgilio's face, wonders what it means to

him to operate on a dead person, what he's feeling, what he's thinking, and the space around her seems to reel, as if the separation between the living and the dead no longer exists here.

Once the dissection is completed, it is time for cannulation. The blood vessels are pierced with a needle and little catheters inserted into them, through which will pass the liquid that cools the organs. The anesthesiologist surveys the donor's hemodynamic status on the screens — perfectly stable — while Cordélia supplies the surgeons with implements as required, taking care to repeat the name of the compress, the number of the pliers or blade as she places them in the palm of the plastic-gloved hand held open in front of her, and the more she does this, the firmer her voice sounds, the more confident she feels of her place in this operation. It's ready now: cannulation is completed, and we can clamp the aorta — and every practitioner in the room checks the anatomical map they have just been given, identifying the part intended for them.

Can we clamp? Virgilio's voice, loud in the theater even though muffled by the mask,

startles Thomas. No, wait! He shouted, and everyone turns to look at him now, hands immobilized over the open body, elbows frozen at right angles: the operation is suspended while the coordinator weaves between them to reach the table, moving his mouth close to Simon Limbres's ear. What he whispers then, in his most humane voice, even though he knows that his words are falling into a deathly void, is the promised litany of names, the names of those who are escorting him; he whispers that Sean and Marianne are with him, and Lou, and Grandma, he whispers that Juliette is there by his side — Juliette who knows about Simon now: she got a call from Sean around 10:00 p.m. after leaving a succession of increasingly distraught messages on Marianne's cell phone, though what Simon's father said to her was incomprehensible, as his words seemed to wander beyond language; he seemed unable to formulate a sentence, only gasps, cracked syllables, stammered phonemes, sobs, till Juliette finally understood that there was nothing else to hear, that there were no words, that this was what she had to hear, and she replied I'm coming, in a breath, then rushed out into the night, running to join the Limbres family in their apartment, hurtling

down the steep hill, not wearing a coat or even a scarf, an elf in sneakers, keys in one hand and cell phone in the other, and soon the glass-sharp cold started to burn, she was consumed on the slope, a figurine broken into pieces, almost falling several times as she struggled to coordinate her strides, breathing badly — not at all the way Simon had taught her to breathe, with no regularity, forgetting to exhale — her tibias aching and heels burning, ears popping like they did in a landing plane, and a stitch stabbing at her side; bent double, she continued to run on the too-narrow sidewalk, grazing her elbow against the high stone wall that bordered the curve, rushing down this slope that he had climbed for her on his bike five months earlier — the same bend but in the opposite direction, that day of the *Ballade des pendus* and the red plastic lovers' shelter that they had raised together, that day, that first day — she was running so hard she couldn't breathe now, and the cars were driving past her, up the hill, catching her in the white glare of their headlights, slowing down, the startled drivers continuing to watch her in their rearview mirrors for a long time afterward — a kid in a T-shirt, out in the street, at this hour, in this cold, and the look of panic on her face! —

then she came into view of the unlit bay window of the living room and accelerated again, entering the grounds, crossing a clear space of flower beds and hedges that seemed to her like a hostile jungle, then sprinting up the steps, where she took a tumble, the carpet of leaves coagulated by the cold forming a layer of ice, and scraped her face, splashing mud on her temple and her chin, and then she was up again and climbing the stairs, three floors, and when she arrived on the landing, her face deformed like the others, unrecognizable, Sean opened the door to her before she even rang the bell and took her in his arms, holding her tight, while behind him, in the dark, Marianne was smoking a cigarette, wearing a coat, standing next to the sleeping Lou: Oh Juliette, and the tears began — then Thomas takes the earbuds from his pocket, the earbuds that he has sterilized, and inserts them into Simon's ears, switches on the iPod, track 7, and the last wave forms on the horizon, in front of the cliffs, it rises and rises until it fills the whole sky, forming and unforming, deploying the chaos of the matter and the perfection of the spiral in its metamorphosis, scraping the seafloor, stirring up the layers of sediment and shaking the alluvium, uncovering fossils and overturning treasure

chests, revealing those invertebrates sunk deep in the vastness of time, 150-million-year-old ammonites and bottles of beer, airplane wreckage and handguns, bleached bones like tree bark, the sea-bed as fascinating as a gigantic garbage dump and an ultrasensitive membrane, a pure biology, and the wave lifts up the earth's skin, digging into memory and turning it over, regenerating the soil where Simon Limbres lived — the soft dune in whose hollow he shared a packet of french fries and mustard with Juliette, the pine forest where they sheltered during the squall, the 150-foot bamboo stalks just behind them, swaying like they do in Asia, and the warm raindrops hitting the gray sand that day, the odors mingling, bitter and salty, Juliette's lips the color of grapefruit — and then finally it explodes and scatters, in an almighty splash, a conflagration and a shimmer, while around the operating table the silence thickens, they wait, eyes meeting over the body, toes twitching, fingers suspended, but they all accept that it is right to pause for a moment as they stop Simon Limbres's heart. Once the rite has been performed, Thomas removes the earbuds and returns to his place. Again: Can we clamp?

Clamp!

■ ■ ■ ■

The heart stops beating. The body is slowly purged of its blood, which is replaced by a refrigerated liquid that, injected in a fast flow, will rinse the internal organs, while in that instant ice packs are placed around them — and it is probably at this point that Virgilio will glance at Alice Harfang to make sure she's not about to faint, because the blood that flows from the body is pouring into a plastic tray that amplifies the sounds like an echo chamber, and it is this noise, more than the sight of the open body, that tends to upset people. But no, the young woman is still standing, perfectly stoical, even if her forehead looks rather pale and beaded with sweat, and he goes back to work as the countdown begins.

And so the thorax becomes, once again, a ritual battleground where cardiac surgeons and thoracic surgeons fight over who will get what length of that stump of vein, where they scrap over a few extra millimeters of pulmonary arteries. Virgilio is a good and generous colleague, but he's tense, and he ends up snapping at the man opposite him: Leave me something, will you? I don't think a centimeter or two is too much to ask!

■ ■ ■ ■

Thomas Rémige has slipped out of the operating theater to phone the several hospital departments where the transplants will take place: he has to inform them of the time when the aorta was clamped — 11:50 p.m. — a figure that instantly sharpens the timeline for the coming operation: prepping the recipient, transporting the organ, transplanting the organ. On his return, the first organ is being removed, in absolute silence. Virgilio now begins the ablation of the heart: the two venae cavae, the four pulmonary veins, the aorta, and the pulmonary artery are severed — perfect caesurae. The heart is explanted from Simon Limbres's body. It's crazy, you can see it — there, in the air — for a brief moment you can apprehend its mass and its volume, attempt to grasp its symmetrical form, its dual bulge, its beautiful color (crimson or vermilion), seek to match it to the universal pictogram of love, the playing-card emblem, the T-shirt logo — I ♡ NY — the bas-relief carved on tombs and royal reliquaries, the symbol of Eros the charlatan, the figurative representation of the sacred heart of Jesus in pious imagery —

the organ held in the hand and exhibited to the world, streaming with tears of blood but haloed with radiant light — or any text icon indicating the infinite variety of sentimental emotions. Virgilio picks it up and immediately plunges it in a jar filled with clear liquid, a cardioplegic solution that guarantees a temperature of 39 degrees — the organ has to be cooled down very quickly in order to conserve it — after which the whole thing is protected inside a sterile safety bag and then in another bag, which is buried in crushed ice within an isothermic box.

When the box has been sealed, Virgilio waves goodbye to everyone, but none of the people surrounding Simon Limbres's body looks up, no one reacts at all apart from the thoracic surgeon angled over the lungs, who barks out you didn't leave me much to work with, you bastard, with a jerky laugh, while the surgeon from Strasbourg prepares to cut out the liver, such a fragile organ, by concentrating like a gymnast about to leap onto the beam — for a second, you half-expect her to thrust her hands into a bowl of chalk and rub her palms — while the urologists wait patiently to appropriate the kidneys.

Alice hangs back. She is focused on the

scene in front of her, staring at the people, one after another, gathered around the table and the inanimate body that is its dazzling center — Rembrandt's *Anatomy Lesson* flashes through her mind and she remembers how her father, an oncologist with long, twisted fingernails, like claws, hung a reproduction of the painting in the entrance hall of the family apartment and would often exclaim, tapping it with an index finger: That is a man, that's what we are! But, being a daydreamer as a child, she preferred to see in it a council of wizards rather than the doctors who made up her kin. She would stand for long moments in front of those strange figures, admirably arranged around the cadaver, dressed in deep-black tunics, their wise heads posed on immaculate ruffs, the abundance of folds as delicate as wafer-paper origami, the lace trimmings and precise beards, and in the middle of all this, that pale body, that mysterious mask, and the slit in the arm through which could be seen the bones and the ligaments, the blade held by the man in the black hat plunged into the flesh. More than admiring it, however, she listened to the canvas, fascinated by the discussion represented there, and ended up learning that piercing the peritoneal wall was for a

long time considered an affront to the sacredness of the body of man, that divinely created being, and she understood that all forms of knowledge contain an element of transgression. So it was that she decided to "do medicine," supposing that she actually had a choice in the matter, because she was, after all, the eldest of four daughters, the one her father took to the hospital on Wednesdays, the one he gave a professional stethoscope to on her thirteenth birthday, whispering into her ear: Harfangs are jerks, little Harfang girl, and you're going to crush them all.

Alice withdraws gradually, and everything in her field of view becomes still and il-luminated, like a diorama. Suddenly, what she sees in place of the stretched-out body is simply matter, a substance to be used and shared; no longer a stopped mechanism peeled open to have its best parts removed, but a material of infinite potential: a human body, its power and its end, its human end — and it is the emotion she feels at this, rather than any fountain of blood splashing into a plastic bucket, that might make her pass out. Virgilio's voice, already far off, behind her back: Are you coming? What the hell are you doing? Get your ass in gear! She turns around and runs the length of

the corridor to catch up.

A specialized medical transport takes them
back to the airport. The vehicle speeds
through darkness while they watch the
movement of figures on the dashboard
clock, following the dance of the luminescent hands that point down and then up
again, while they are mesmerized by the
digital numbers on their cell-phone screens.
And then Virgilio's phone lights up. It's
Harfang. How is it?
Perfect.

They bypass the city by the north and take
the Fontaine-la-Mallet road, passing the
compact, indeterminate shapes of suburban
buildings, tower blocks planted in fields
behind the city, swarms of apartment towers around an asphalt loop; they drive
through a forest, still not a star in the sky,
no flashing airplane lights or flying saucers,
nothing at all. The driver speeds along this
secondary road, well above the limit; he's
an experienced driver, accustomed to this
type of mission; he stares straight ahead,
forearms rigid and immobile, muttering into
a tiny microphone attached to a high-tech
earpiece, I'm on my way, don't fall asleep,
I'll be there soon. The box is wedged in the

compartment behind them, and Alice visualizes the several hermetic walls surrounding the heart, those membranes that protect it; she imagines that it is a rocket engine propelling them through space. Turning around and lifting herself up on one side, she is able to see past the headrest; squinting through the dimness, she deciphers the words on the label affixed to the side of the box and notices, among the information necessary for the traceability of the organ, a strange phrase: "element or product of human body for therapeutic use." And, just below this, the donor's Cristal number.

Virgilio leans back in his seat and breathes out. His eyes linger on Alice's profile, a shadow puppet against the window, and, suddenly stirred by her presence, asks in a soft voice: Are you okay? The question is unexpected — this guy has been so unpleasant up to now — and Macy Gray's voice on the radio sings *shake your booty, boys and girls, there is beauty in the world,* and out of nowhere Alice feels like crying — an emotion that grabs her from within and lifts her up, quivering — but she holds back her tears, grits her teeth as she turns her face away: Yup, I'm fine. So he takes his cell phone out of his pocket for the thousandth time, but instead of checking the time he

taps at it, gradually becoming annoyed: It's not loading, he hisses, fuck it, fuck it. Feeling bolder, Alice asks, something wrong? Virgilio answers her without looking up, it's the game, I wanted to see the result of the game, and without turning around the driver announces coldly that Italy won, 1–0. Virgilio lets out a yell, raises a fist, then demands: Who scored? The driver signals and brakes: the whitish space of an illuminated intersection looms ahead. It was Pirlo. Alice, stupefied, watches as Virgilio rapidly types a couple of victory texts, muttering to himself yes, yes, yes, then he looks over at her, one eyebrow raised: Pirlo, eh? What a player! His smile overwhelms his face, and then they are at the airport, hearing the roar of the sea close by, at the foot of the cliffs, and rolling the box across the runway and up the gangway, hauling it into the plane, this Russian doll of a box which contains the transparent plastic safety bag which contains the receptacle which contains the special jar which contains Simon Limbres's heart, which contains nothing less than life itself, the possibility of life, and which five minutes later is airborne.

As you can imagine, Marianne cannot sleep. Torn up with pain, she has not taken sleeping pills or any other drug, but has sunk into a kind of trance; her way of coping. At 11:50 p.m., she jumps up suddenly from the couch. Is it possible she has sensed the moment when the blood ceased flowing in the aorta? Is it possible she had an intuition of that moment? In spite of all the miles stretching out across the estuary, between her apartment and the hospital, an impalpable closeness gives the night a fantastical mental depth, vaguely frightening, as if magnetic lines were hardening in a space-time fault line, and connecting her to that forbidden place where her child lay, allowing her to watch over him.

A polar night: the opaque sky seems to dissolve, the fleecy layer of cloud being torn away to reveal Ursa Major. Simon's heart is

migrating now, traveling on rails, on roads, inside that box with slightly bumpy plastic walls that glow in the beams of electric light, conveyed with incredible care, like the heart of a prince in times past, like his entrails and his skeleton, the body divided for distribution, interred in a basilica, a cathedral, an abbey, in order to guarantee rights to his lineage, prayers for his salvation, a future for his memory — the sound of hooves heard on sunken paths, on the dirt roads of villages and the cobblestone streets of cities, their rhythm slow and majestic, then the flames of torches were seen, making liquid shadows in the branches of trees, on the façades of houses, on the wild-eyed faces; people massed on doorsteps, towels around their necks, seeing each other and signaling silently to watch this extraordinary cortege move past, the black carriage drawn by six horses in full mourning attire, caparisoned in sheets and precious surplices, the escort of twelve knights bearing torches, long black coats and crepe hangings, and sometimes even pages and valets on foot, holding white wax altar candles, sometimes companies of guards too, and the knight in tears at the head of the procession, accompanying the heart in its tomb, advancing toward the back of the crypt, toward the

chapel of a chosen monastery or the castle of his birth, toward a niche carved out in black marble and decorated with twisted columns, a shrine surmounted with a radiant crown, ornamented with escutcheons and coats of arms, Latin mottos carved into stone banners, and often people tried to look through a gap in the curtains to the inside of the carriage, where the officer of the transaction sat — the man who would hand-deliver the heart to those who would, from now on, take care of it, and who would pray for the deceased; most often this man is a confessor, a friend, a brother, but it was always too dark to see this man, or the reliquary placed on a black taffeta cushion, and certainly not the heart inside it, the *membrum principalissimum,* the king of the body, placed at the center of the chest like the sovereign in his kingdom, like the sun in its cosmos, this heart nested in gold-stitched gauze, this heart for which everyone wept.

Simon's heart was migrating to one part of the country, his kidneys, liver, and lungs entering other regions, rushing toward other bodies. What would remain, in this fragmentation, of the unity of her son? How could she attach her singular memory to that diffracted body? What will become of his pres-

ence, of his reflection on earth, of his ghost?
These questions circle her like fiery hoops,
and then Simon's face forms before her
eyes, intact and unique. He is irreducible;
he is Simon. She feels a deep sense of calm.
Outside, the night burns like a gypsum desert.

At the Pitié, Claire finds herself surrounded. She is led into a room in the Cardiac Surgery Department where every inch has been scrubbed and disinfected: a transparent glaze covers every surface, and the air is thick with detergent fumes. A too-high mobile bed, a blue leatherette armchair, an empty table, and, standing ajar in a corner of the room, the door of a bathroom. She puts her bag on the floor and sits on the bed. She is dressed completely in black — an old sweater with sleeves slit to the shoulder — and she stands out perfectly in this pale room, like a shadow. Texts begin appearing on her phone — her sons, her mother, a female friend, they are all on their way, fast as they can — but no message from the foxglove man, who is squatting on his heels next to a bamboo hedge, amid stray dogs and wild pigs, in a village in the Gulf of Siam.

■ ■ ■ ■

The nurse who enters plants her fists on her hips and declares in a cheery voice: So, tonight's the big night! She has a helmet of salt-and-pepper hair, and wears square-framed glasses; her cheeks are colored by a slight rosacea. Claire shrugs her shoulders, her palms raised to the sky, and smiles: Yep, tonight everything is possible. The nurse hands her several flat transparent packets that shimmer under the ceiling light like sheets of gelatin, then leans over her and a pendant swings forward from her skin, a brief sparkle in the void — it's a little silver heart engraved with a pledge, *Today more than yesterday but tomorrow even more,* the kind of jewelry you can buy in mail-order catalogs; Claire, mesmerized, watches it swing in irregular circles — and then the nurse stands up again, points to the packets: These are your clothes for the OR, you'll have to put them on before you go in. Claire looks at them with a mixture of impatience and reticence — the same feeling that has gripped her for the past year; another name for waiting. Feigning composure, she replies: We are going to wait for the heart to get here, though, aren't we? The woman shakes

309

her head; with a glance at her watch, she says no, you'll leave for the OR in two hours, as soon as we've received your results; the organ will arrive around twelve-thirty, and you have to be ready then, the transplant will take place immediately afterward. And she leaves.

Claire unpacks her things, puts her toiletries in the bathroom, plugs in her phone charger, and puts her phone on the bed; she makes herself at home. She calls her sons — they are running down a long corridor of the metro: she hears the echoes of their footsteps, we're here, we're coming, panting with anxiety. They want to reassure her, support her. They don't understand: she's not afraid of the operation. That's not it. What torments her is the idea of this new heart, and that someone has died today so all this can happen; the idea that it will invade and transform her, convert her — she thinks of grafts, cuttings, fauna and flora.

She paces the room. If this is a donation, it's a pretty unusual one, she thinks. There is no donor in this operation — no one intended to make a donation — and likewise there is no donee, because she is not in a position to refuse the organ: she has to accept it if she wants to survive. So what is it

310

exactly? The recycling of an organ that can still be used, can still fulfill its function as a pump? She begins to undress, sitting on the bed: she removes her boots, her socks. The meaning of this transfer, for which she was selected by an incredible alignment of co-incidences — the almost perfect compatibility of her blood and her genetic code with those of someone who died today — all of this becomes hazy. She does not like this feeling of unearned privilege; this lottery, it's like winning a little stuffed animal snagged by the metal claw from a jumble of toys piled behind glass in one of those arcade games. Worst of all is that she will never be able to say thank you; that is the crux of the matter. It's simply impossible. Thank you — that radiant phrase — will fall into the void. She will never be able to express any kind of gratitude to the donor or the donor's family, never mind offer a gift in return in order to free herself from this infinite debt, and the idea that she will be permanently trapped crosses her mind. The floor is ice-cold under her feet. She is afraid. Her whole being flinches.

She walks over to the window. Figures hurry down paths in the hospital grounds; cars move slowly between the buildings that, in the night, redraw the anatomical map of

the human body, organ by organ, pathology by pathology, separate children from adults, bring together mothers, the aged, the dying. She hopes that she will be able to kiss her sons before she puts on this tissue-paper gown that flutters without covering her up, making her feel as if she is naked in a breeze. Her eyes remain dry, but she is struggling to get her head around the enormity of what she is about to go through. Placing her hand there, between her breasts, she feels her pulse, still slightly too fast in spite of the medication, still somewhat unpredictable too, and says its name out loud: heart.

All those hours being interviewed by doctors who were making a psychological assessment of her when she was first proposed as a transplant candidate — a summary of her emotional relationships, an evaluation of her social integration, an appraisal of her behavior when faced with fatigue and anxiety, of her likely willingness to deal with a postoperative treatment that would be long and tough — from none of that did she learn what will happen to her heart, afterward. Maybe there is a scrapyard for organs somewhere, she thinks, removing her jewelry and her watch, some sort of garbage heap

where hers will be dumped along with others, evacuated from the hospital through a back door in large trash bags; she imagines a container for organic matter where it will be recycled, transformed into paste, a flesh compost served by unimaginably cruel heirs of Atreus to their rivals, who enter the palace dining room with hearty appetites — served as pancakes or steak tartare, or slop fed to dogs in huge dishes, or bait for bears and dolphins — and maybe those dolphins will be transformed, after eating the substance, their rubbery skin covered with blond hair like hers, maybe they will grow long velvety eyelashes.

A knock at the door and Emmanuel Harfang enters without waiting for a response. He stands in front of her, tells her the heart will be removed around eleven, that the organ is in excellent health, and then he stops talking, observes her: You wanted to speak to me. She sits on the bed, shoulders hunched, hands pressed flat to the mattress, ankles crossed — her feet are beautiful, the toenails painted bright red, sparkling in the chlorotic room like foxglove petals — yes, I have questions, about the donor. Harfang shakes his head, as if he thinks she is being silly, that she knows the answer already. We've already talked about this. But Claire

does not give up. Her blond hair brushes her cheeks. I would like to be able to think about it. For example, she adds persuasively, where is this heart coming from? It's not from Paris. Harfang stares at her, frowning; how does she know that? Then yields: Seine-Maritime. Claire closes her eyes, accelerates: Male or female? Harfang, instantly: Male. He reaches the door, open onto the corridor, she hears him leave and opens her eyes: Wait, tell me his age, please. But Harfang has gone.

Her three sons arrive just after this, looking unhappy. The eldest is terribly anxious and won't let go of her hand, the middle son paces the room, repeating everything is going to be fine, while the youngest has brought her a packet of heart-shaped candy. Harfang's a brilliant man, the best in his field, seventy heart transplants a year, and the best team too, you're in good hands, he says in a small, trembling voice. She nods mechanically, watching his face without really listening to him: I know, don't worry. It's more difficult with her mother, who keeps sniveling that life is unfair, that she wants to take her place under the knife, implying that it would be more natural, more conceivable for her to die first, or at

least risk her life first. Claire loses her patience: But I'm not going to die, I have no intention whatsoever of dying. The boys, incensed, abuse their grandmother: For God's sake, just shut up, you're not helping! Returning to the room, the nurse taps her watch face and curtails the discussion: All right, it's time for you to get ready. Claire hugs her sons, stroking their cheeks, whispering to each one, see you tomorrow, my love.

Later, naked, she went into the shower cubicle and washed herself with Betadine for a long time, spraying the yellow liquid all over her body and vigorously rubbing it into her skin. When she was dry, she put on the sterile paper gown, then began to wait.

Around 10:00 p.m., the anesthesiologist comes into the room: Everything okay? She is a tall woman, narrow-shouldered and narrow-hipped, with a swan neck and pale smile and long-fingered cold hands that brush hers when handing her a first pill — to relax you. Claire lies back on the bed, suddenly exhausted, even though she is more excited than ever before. One hour later, the department orderlies enter the room, grab the handles of her bed — the operation will be performed on a table, but

315

you'll be returned to your bed afterward — then they transfer her without another word. She is wheeled through corridors, not knowing where to look, sees endless dull ceilings rush past, and coils of electric wire like water snakes. Her heartbeat accelerates as they draw closer to the surgical theater, going through doors requiring electronic pass codes that lead to sterile zones. The space divides again, and then she is taken to a small room where they make her wait. We'll come and get you. Time is diluted: soon it is midnight.

Behind the door of the operating room, the anesthesiologist checks the placement of the equipment that will monitor the patient's condition: electrodes to monitor the heart, catheters to provide a continual blood pressure reading, and that device that pinches the patient's fingertip and tracks oxygen levels in the blood. She sets up the drip, suspending the bag of clear liquid, checking the flow speed — simple gestures, perfectly executed, as you would expect after thirty years of experience — all right, we can get going, is everyone here? But no one is completely ready yet: the team is in the changing rooms, putting on their sky-blue scrubs, short-sleeved shirts, and long-sleeved jackets; everyone wears at least two

surgical caps to ensure their entire scalp is covered, and two masks over their mouth. Disposable slippers and overshoes, and multiple pairs of sterile gloves, changed on a regular basis. They wash thoroughly, lathering their hands and forearms up to their elbows with disinfectant soap, cleaning and recleaning their fingernails. Indistinct bodies move into place, check the equipment, but their faces have vanished, leaving only a general notion of appearance, height, shape, gait, mannerisms, and the expressiveness of eyes, which in this room forms the basis of another language. There is a perfusionist, the OR intern, two dressings nurses, and two anesthesiologists: Harfang has worked with these two women — old friends now — for thirty years; he performed his first transplant with them.

And so it begins, like the start of a race. He is wearing a sort of apron gown that covers almost his entire body; it goes on front first and knots in the back; one sleeve is tied to his thumb; with its mid-calf length, it is reminiscent of those straight, narrow aprons that butchers wear. He approaches Claire for one last word: The heart will be here in thirty minutes; it's a wonderful heart, perfect for you, the two of you will get along splendidly. Claire smiles: But you will wait

until it's in the operating room before you take mine out, won't you? Harfang stares at her, amazed — are you serious?

Claire is anesthetized. Soon, images appear under her eyelids, a gush of vague shapes and warm tones, an infinite metamorphosis of surfaces, a kaleidoscope of cells and fibers, while the nurses make her head and most of her body disappear under large yellow plastic sheets, which are in turn covered with surgical drapes: only a small area of skin remains visible, lit clearly by the lamps overhead; it is a moving sight, this zone where they will dig. Harfang begins; with a sterile pencil, he traces the lines of the incisions to come, marking out the precise spots where he will make small openings — they slide pipes into these holes, through which they will send a system of tiny cameras. Then the anesthesiologist, ear to the OR phone, announces: Okay, they're here.

Another surgical theater, in a nocturnal estuary, but this one is almost empty now, the teams having left in reverse order to that of organ preparation; the last ones there with Simon Limbres are the urologists, who have removed the kidneys and are now in charge of making the body appear externally whole.

Thomas Rémige is there too, his face gaunt and shining with fatigue, and even though the hour is late, time slowing and slackening as they near the end of the operation, the surgery becoming less urgent, his presence is now accentuated. Every move he makes, even the most imperceptible, expresses the idea that no, they are not finished yet. He exasperates the others, of course, leaning over their shoulders, pre-empting everything the surgeons and nurses do. It would be so easy now to relax, to cut corners, to rush through the final details

and get the thing done — what difference does it make, really? But Thomas silently resists this general exhaustion, maintaining the urgency, refusing to let up: this part of the operation — restoring the donor's body — cannot be trivialized; it is an act of repair; they must repair the damage they have caused. Put things back the way they were. Without that, it's barbarism. Around him, they roll their eyes and sigh — stop worrying, what do you take us for, we're not going to botch the job, everything will be done properly.

Simon Limbres's body is hollow; in places, his skin looks as if it's been sucked inside. And as this atrophied, mutilated appearance does not match the way he looked when he entered the theater, it breaks the promise that was made to his parents. The void must be filled. Quickly, the practitioners create a sort of lining, using fabrics and compresses, a crude stuffing that must be modeled as best it can to resemble the shape, volume, and position of the harvested organs. Their hands move rapidly in what is an act of restoration: Simon Limbres is being given back his original appearance, so that it is him — that image of him — that will be remembered by his family when they

see him tomorrow in the mortuary, so they can recognize him as the boy he was.

Now the body is being closed up — on its emptiness, its silence. The oversewing — with a single thread, knotted at either end — will be delicate, painstaking, the surgeon's needle, thin and precise, tracing a straight perforated line; but what is most striking is that stitching — that ancient craft slowly deposited in human memory since the Paleolithic age — can provide the conclusion to such a high-tech operation. The surgeon works on a wholly intuitive level, absolutely unaware of his own movements, his hand making regular loops above the wound, each loop small and identical, lacing up and closing the skin. Across from him, the young intern continues to watch and learn: for him too, this is the first time he has taken part in a multiorgan removal, and he would probably have liked to perform the suturing himself, to have placed his hand on the donor's body as part of this collective gesture, but his perceptions have been overwhelmed by the intensity of the operation, and — whether from fatigue or nerves — his vision is clouded by black fluttering butterflies. Tensing up, he tells himself that he didn't buckle when the blood poured into the bucket, that he's gotten through

the hardest part, and that what matters now is staying on his feet until the end.

At 1:30 a.m., the urologists put down their instruments, lift their heads, breathe out, lower their masks, and leave the theater, taking the kidneys with them. Thomas Rémige and Cordélia Owl remain, the latter apparently kept going by a residual tension; she has not slept in almost forty hours, and she has the feeling that if she slows down, she will collapse, fall flat on her face. She begins the night's final tasks — making an inventory of instruments, filling out labels, noting down figures on printed forms, recording the hours — and these administrative formalities, carried out with robotic rigor, leave her mind free to wander, memories flashing into her brain of body parts, fragments of speech, different places — a hospital corridor opens onto a vaulted passage of exquisitely vile smells, a shock of hair trembles over the flame of the lighter, orange streetlamps undulate vertically in her lover's eyes, green-haired sirens writhe on the side of a van, her cell phone finally vibrates in the night — a porous continuum superimposed by the face of Simon Limbres, whom she treated this afternoon, whom she examined and caressed, and this

young woman with her hicky-flecked leopard-print body, thinks suddenly of how long it will take her to decant these hours, to filter the violence, to make sense of the meaning — what have I just lived through? Her vision blurs as she checks her watch, lowers her mask: I have to go back to the department for a while, the intern's alone in there, I'll be back soon. Thomas nods without looking: That's okay, take your time, I can finish up. He hears the woman's footsteps fade and the theater door close. Now he is alone. He looks slowly around him, and what he sees makes him quail: the room is in chaos, a tangle of equipment and electric wires, screens facing the wrong way, used instruments, soiled cloths piled up on bench tops, the operating table dirty, and the floor splattered with blood. Anyone who looked in would blink in the cold light and then see what looked like a battlefield, an image of war and violence. Thomas shivers, then gets to work.

Simon Limbres's body is now a corpse. What life leaves behind it when it goes, what death leaves on the battlefield. It has been violated. Skeleton, tissue, skin. Simon's skin is slowly turning the color of ivory, seeming to harden, haloed in the raw gleam that pours from the surgical lamps, becoming a

dry shell, a suit of armor, with the scars on the chest and abdomen like those of a mortal wound — the spear point in Christ's side, the warrior's sword thrust, the knight's blade. And so, whether it is this stitching that has renewed the song of the *aoidos,* the rhapsodist of ancient Greece, or whether it is Simon's face, his youthful beauty fresh from the waves of the sea, his hair still sticky with salt and curly like those companions of yearning Ulysses, or whether it is this cross-shaped scar, Thomas begins to sing. A restrained song, that would barely have been audible to anyone else in the room with him, but a song that is synchronized to this posthumous cleaning, a song that accompanies and describes it, a song that testifies.

Arrayed on a cart is the equipment necessary for the cleaning of the body before it is taken to the mortuary. Thomas is wearing a disposable apron over his shirt, he has disposable gloves on his hands, and he has gathered a pile of towels — also disposable, to be used once only, for Simon Limbres — and soft cellulose compresses, a yellow trash bag. He begins by closing the boy's eyes, using a dry eye pad. To close his mouth, he rolls up two pieces of tissue, placing one beneath the back of his head to flex his cervical muscles, while the other lifts his

chin up from his thorax. Next, he removes everything that has been inserted into the body — those wires and tubes, those perfusions and the urinary catheter — getting rid of everything that is wrapped around his body, everything that obstructs his vision of Simon Limbres. When it is all gone, the body appears suddenly more naked than ever: a human body catapulted far from humanity, disturbing matter drifting through the magmatic night, through the formless space of non-meaning, an entity to which Thomas's song confers a presence, a new inscription. Because this body, fragmented and divided by life, becomes whole again under the hand that washes it, in the breath of the voice that sings; this body that has suffered something extraordinary is now united with the company of men, with common mortality. It is praised in song, made beautiful.

Thomas washes the body, his movements calm and loose, and his singing voice takes support from the cadaver so as not to waver, just as it grows stronger by dissociating itself from language, frees itself from terrestrial syntax so as to find the exact place in the cosmos where life and death meet: it inhales and exhales, inhales and exhales, inhales and exhales; it escorts the hand as it revisits

the body's contours one last time, recognizing each hill and valley of skin, including that tattoo on the shoulder, that emerald black arabesque that Simon had inscribed into his pores the summer he realized that his body was his, that it expressed something about him. Now Thomas presses down on the puncture points in the epidermis left by the catheters, he dresses the boy in a diaper, and even arranges his hair in a way that sets off his face. The song grows louder in the operating room as Thomas envelops the corpse in an immaculate white sheet — the sheet that will then be knotted at his head and feet — and, watching him work, it is impossible not to think of the funerary rituals that conserved the beauty of the Greek heroes who deliberately died on the field of battle; that particular treatment designed to restore their image, so that they are guaranteed a place in the memory of men. To do this, the families and the poets will sing the hero's name, commemorate his life. It is a good death, the song of a good death: not an elevation, a sacrificial offering, not an exaltation of the deceased's soul that will rise in circular clouds toward heaven, but an edification, reconstructing the uniqueness of Simon Limbres. It brings back the young man on the dune, surfboard under

326

his arm; it makes him run toward the shore with his friends; it makes him fight someone over an insult, his fists bouncing in front of his face, protecting it; it makes him leap into the mosh pit at a gig, pogoing like crazy and sleeping facedown in his childhood bed; it makes him spin Lou round in a circle, her little calves flying above the floorboards; it makes him sit down in the kitchen at midnight, across from his smoking mother, to talk about his father; it makes him undress Juliette, or give her his hand so that she can jump without fear from the beachside cliff; it propels him into a postmortem space where death can no longer touch him — the place of immortal glory, of mythography, the place of song and writing.

Cordélia reappears one hour later. She's done the rounds of the department, pushed open doors, walked around the recovery room, checking vital signs, the flow of electric syringe pumps and diuresis; she leaned over the sleeping patients, looking at their faces, which sometimes grimaced with pain, observing their posture, listening to them breathe; and then she went back downstairs to see Thomas. She catches him singing, hears him before she sees him in fact, because his voice is loud now. Moved,

she stands immobile, her back to the theater door, hands hanging by her sides, head tilted back, and listens.

Later, Thomas looks up: You're just in time. Cordélia moves toward the table. The white sheet covers Simon's body up to his sternum, chiseling the features of his face, the grain of his skin, the transparent cartilages, the flesh of his lips. How does he look? Thomas asks; perfect, she replies. They share an intense look, and together they lift up the body, inside the shroud, still heavy in spite of the night's events, each taking one end, and slide it onto a stretcher, before calling the funeral parlor. Tomorrow morning, Simon Limbres will be returned to his family, to Sean and Marianne, to Juliette and Lou, to his loved ones, and he will be returned to them *ad integrum.*

The plane lands at Bourget at 12:50 a.m. Time is becoming dictatorial. With perfect logistical coordination, a car is waiting for them: not a taxi, but a thermally regulated vehicle designed specifically for this type of mission. A sign on the doors reads: Priority Vehicle — Organ Donation. Inside the car, all is calm: while the tension is palpable, there is no trace here of the kind of urgency shown in televised reports on the glory of transplant surgeons, on human-chain heroics, no hysterical pantomime, no bright-red countdown in the corner of the screen, no flashing lights or sirens, no squad of motorcyclists in white helmets and black boots opening the road in a blaze of tensed thumbs and impassive faces, jaws contracted. The process is under way, it is under control, and, for the moment, traffic is flowing freely on the highway, the rush of people going home after a weekend away already

diluted: before them, Paris rises up under a dome of corpuscular light. The OR calls while they are passing Garonor: The patient is here, we're prepping her now, where are you? Ten minutes from La Chapelle. We're on time, Virgilio mutters, and looks over at Alice, her owl-like profile — concave forehead, beak-shaped nose, silky skin — leaning into the fur collar of her white coat. She certainly looks like a Harfang, he thinks.

Close to the stadium, they hit a traffic jam. Shit. Virgilio sits up, instantly tense. What the fuck are they doing? The driver is unfazed. It's the game — they don't want to go home. Many of the cars they can see have their windows open, and delirious young men swagger about, waving Italian flags on poles; there are buses chartered by supporters' groups, and long-distance refrigerated trucks caught up in the euphoric bottleneck. They hear the news: there's a pile-up on the road ahead. Alice cries out, Virgilio freezes. Inch by inch, the driver manages to widen the gap between the neighboring vehicles, passing through them until he reaches the emergency lane. He drives at a reduced speed for about a mile, passing the accident site, and after that the road is clear, the spaced-out spotlights on

the safety barrier now forming one long line of brightness through the dark night. Another slowdown at La Chapelle: Let's take the beltway. The city exits are strung out to the east, from Aubervilliers to Bercy, in a long bend, after which the car turns right again, entering the city, and now they can see the banks of the Seine, the towers of the National Library, then a curve to the left and they drive up Boulevard Vincent-Auriol, braking at Chevaleret and entering the hospital grounds, here we are. The vehicle stops in front of the building — thirty-two minutes, not bad. Virgilio smiles.

Inside the operating room, the team barely looks up when they arrive together, carrying the treasure to the foot of the table like an offering left at the feet of a master. Their arrival does not disturb the practitioners' focus on the operation, which has already begun. Virgilio and Alice are barely welcomed when they enter, already dressed in sterile scrubs, arms washed, hands disinfected, and now Virgilio can see nothing of Alice but her strange eyes, slow and dense-looking, flecked with yellow, chartreuse, and honey, smoky topaz. Harfang, though, does finally ask them: So, everything go okay with the heart? And Virgilio, in the same casual

tone, replies: Yeah, just some traffic on the way back.

The heart is placed in a cup, close to the bed. Alice climbs onto a small platform at the end of the table, so she can watch the transplant, her legs weakening as she hoists herself up the step. Meanwhile, Virgilio moves forward to take the place of the department's intern: it's all he can do not to start picking up tools, and everything in his body language and facial expression communicates his desire to be there, under the triple surgical lamps, above the thorax, across from Harfang. Now, they will work together.

Suddenly, uncovering Claire's heart, Harfang whistles and says Christ, it's really not in great shape, she'll be glad to get rid of it, and there is a hum of quiet, surprised laughter around him: Harfang has a reputation for the terrifying pressure he puts on all members of his team, seemingly aware of everything, eyes in the back of his head, so this levity is unexpected. But the surgical theater is the only place in the world where he feels truly alive, where he is able to express who he is, his atavistic passion for his work, his fanatical rigor, his faith in humanity, his megalomania, his love of power; it is here that he summons his

332

lineage and recalls, one by one, the men who created the science behind organ transplantation, the progenitors, the pioneers — Christiaan Barnard in Cape Town in 1967, Norman Shumway at Stanford in 1968, and Christian Cabrol, here, at the Pitié — the men who invented transplantation, who first conceived it, who mentally built it up and broke it down hundreds of times before performing it, those men from the 1960s, workaholics, charismatic stars, media rivals who were quick to argue and stole from each other without a qualm, Casanovas at multiple weddings, surrounded by girls in riding boots and Mary Quant miniskirts, made-up like Twiggy, insanely bold autocrats who were covered in honors but never lost their rage.

First they have to deal with the veins and arteries that carry blood into and out of the organ. One by one, the veins are severed and clamped — Harfang and Virgilio move quickly, but it's as if this rapidity drives their action, as if by slowing down they would risk trembling — and then, this is impressive, the heart is extracted from the body and an extracorporeal circulation takes over: for two hours, a machine replaces Claire's heart, a machine that will reproduce the

blood flow in her body. At that moment, Harfang asks for silence. He chimes a blade against a metal tube, then through his mask pronounces the phrase that is ritual at this stage of the operation: *Exercitatio Anatomica de Motu Cordis et Sanguinis in Animalibus* — an homage to William Harvey, who in 1628 became the first doctor to describe the entire blood circulation system of the human body, with the heart named as a sort of hydraulic pump, a muscle that — through its movements and beats — ensured the continuity of blood flow. In the theater, without stopping what they are doing, everyone replies: Amen!

The perfusionist is disconcerted by this strange ritual. He does not understand Latin and wonders what the hell is going on. He is a young nurse, twenty-five, twenty-six, with curled-up eyelashes, the only person in the room who has never worked with Harfang before. He is sitting on a high stool positioned in front of his machine, like a DJ with his turntables, and no one here would be more at home than him in the tangle of wires coming out of the large black boxes. Filtered and oxygenated, the blood runs through a jumble of thin transparent pipes, color-coded stickers specifying their direction. On the screen, the electrocardio-

gram is flat and the body temperature is 90 degrees, but Claire is perfectly alive. The anesthesiologists take turns checking her vital signs, to confirm she is receiving the necessary substances. They can continue.

So Virgilio leans down and picks up the cup containing the heart. The ties of the various bags that protect the organ are sprayed with disinfectant, then undone; after that, he extracts the heart from the jar, holding it in both hands, and places it at the edge of the thoracic cage. Alice, still perched on the metal step, now stands on tiptoes, staring, fascinated, and almost loses her balance when she moves her chin forward to get a better view of what's happening, there, inside the body. She is not the only one to crane her neck in this way: the department intern, who is standing next to Harfang, also moves forward, his face so covered in sweat that his glasses slide down his nose and he nearly loses them, drawing back at the last minute to push them up, knocking a drip with his elbow. Please be careful, the anesthesiologist says coldly, before handing him a compress.

Now the surgeons begin the long process of sewing: they labor to connect the new heart, going from bottom to top so that it is

anchored at four points — the recipient's left auricle is stitched to the complementary part of the left auricle of the donor's heart, same thing for the right auricle, then the recipient's pulmonary artery is attached to the end of the donor's right ventricle, and the aorta to the end of the left ventricle. At regular intervals, Virgilio massages the heart, using two hands to press down hard, so his wrists disappear inside Claire's body.

An almost routine atmosphere descends now, and there are snatches of conversation, sometimes a hubbub of voices, department in-jokes. Harfang asks Virgilio about the game, with that mixture of condescension and fake complicity that annoys the Italian: So what do you think of the Italians' tactics, Virgilio? Do you think it makes for an entertaining game? And the young man replies, tersely, that Pirlo is a truly great player. The body is kept in a state of hypothermia, but the air in the room is hot now, and the practitioners' foreheads, temples, and upper lips are regularly sponged, they are helped to change their clothes and their gloves — the nurse opens the bags then holds up the protective outfits horizontally and inside out. The human energy being spent here, the physical tension and the meaning of each action — nothing less than

a transfer of life — seems bound to produce this humidity, which starts to grow, to hover like a cloud in the room.

The suture is completed at last. The transplant organ is purged, the air evacuated so that no bubbles rise into Claire's brain: now the heart is ready to receive blood.

The tension around the table skyrockets. Harfang announces: Okay, we can fill it up now. This filling is measured to the nearest milliliter, requiring a carefully calibrated flow: if they go too fast, the organ might be permanently deformed. The nurses hold their breath, the anesthesiologists watch vigilantly, the perfusionist sweats — while Alice remains composed. Nobody in the theater moves a muscle; a dense silence covers the surgical bed while the heart is slowly irrigated. And now, at last, we reach the electric moment. Virgilio grabs the paddles and hands them to Harfang; the devices remain suspended in the air for a moment; their eyes meet, then Harfang motions with his chin to Virgilio, go ahead, you do it — and in that moment, maybe Virgilio gathers every prayer and superstition he knows, maybe he begs God, or maybe, on the contrary, he thinks back through everything they have achieved up to now, the sum of

their actions and the sum of their words, the sum of spaces and feelings — and he carefully places the electric paddles on either side of the heart, glancing at the screen of the electrocardiogram. Ready? Clear! The heart receives the electric shock, and the world stands still above what is now Claire's heart. The organ stirs weakly: two, three little jolts, and then it stops. Virgilio swallows, Harfang rests his hands on the edge of the bed, and Alice is so pale that the anesthesiologist, afraid she might collapse, takes her arm and helps her off the step. Second time. Ready?

Clear!

The heart contracts — a shudder — and then there are tremors, so tiny they are barely perceptible, but you can see them if you look closely, those feeble beats, and slowly the organ begins to pump blood into the body, as it used to. The beats, strangely fast but regular, soon form a rhythm, like an embryo's pulse, that jerky percussion heard during the first ultrasound, and what we are hearing is indeed embryonic — the first heartbeat, a new dawn.

Did Claire hear Thomas Rémige's voice during her anesthetic dreams, as he sang his

song of a good death? Did she hear him at four in the morning as she received Simon Limbres's heart? She is placed under extra-corporeal assistance for another thirty minutes, and then, like Simon, she is sewn up, the retractors releasing the tissue for a delicate ladylike suture. She remains in the theater under surveillance, surrounded by black screens that trace the luminous waves of her heart, while her body recuperates, while the bedlam of the room is tidied, while the implements and compresses are tallied, while the blood is wiped away, while the team breaks up, while everyone discards their surgical scrubs and dresses in their own clothes, while they splash water on their faces and wash their hands, then leave the hospital to catch the first metro, while Alice recovers and risks a smile as Harfang whispers into her ear, so, little Harfang girl, what did you think of all that?, while Virgilio takes off his surgical cap and lowers his mask and decides to ask her to join him for a beer somewhere in Montparnasse, for a plate of fries and a bloody steak, to prolong the atmosphere of this night, while she puts on her white overcoat and he strokes the fur collar, while the first rays of daylight touch the undergrowth and the moss turns bluish, while the goldfinch sings and the big surf

comes to an end in the digital night: it is 5:49 a.m.

PERMISSIONS ACKNOWLEDGMENTS

Grateful acknowledgment is made for permission to reprint lyrics from "La Nuit Je Mens": words and music by Alain Bashung, Jean-Louis Pierot, Edith Fambuena, and Jean Marie Fauque. Copyright © 1998 Universal Music Publishing SAS and Chaterton Prod. All rights for Universal Music Publishing SAS in the U.S. and Canada controlled and administered by Universal Musica, Inc. All rights reserved. Used by permission. Reprinted by permission of Hal Leonard Corporation.

Grateful acknowledgment is made to Dr. Wendy McLaughlin and Dr. Michael Metz for their advice on the medical terminology used in the book.

A NOTE ABOUT THE TRANSLATOR

Sam Taylor is an author and translator. He is the author of the novels *The Republic of Trees, The Amnesiac,* and *The Island at the End of the World,* and has translated several books from the French, including Laurent Binet's *HHhH,* Hubert Mingarelli's *A Meal in Winter,* and Joel Dicker's *The Truth About the Harry Quebert Affair.*

ABOUT THE AUTHOR

Maylis de Kerangal is the author of several novels in French: *Je marche sous un ciel de traîne* (2000), *La vie voyageuse* (2003), *Corniche Kennedy* (2008), and *Naissance d'un pont* (published in English as *Birth of a Bridge,* winner of the Prix Franz Hessel and Prix Médicis in 2010). She has also published a collection of short stories, *Ni fleurs ni couronnes* (2006), and a novella, *Tangente vers l'est* (winner of the 2012 Prix Landerneau). In addition, she has published a fiction tribute to Kate Bush and Blondie titled *Dans les rapides* (2007). In 2014, her fifth novel, *Réparer les vivants* (published in the United States as *The Heart*), was published to wide acclaim, winning the Grand Prix RTL-Lire and the Student Choice Novel of the Year from France Culture and Télérama. She lives in Paris, France.

The employees of Thorndike Press hope you have enjoyed this Large Print book. All our Thorndike, Wheeler, and Kennebec Large Print titles are designed for easy reading, and all our books are made to last. Other Thorndike Press Large Print books are available at your library, through selected bookstores, or directly from us.

For information about titles, please call:
  (800) 223-1244

or visit our Web site at:
  http://gale.cengage.com/thorndike

To share your comments, please write:
  Publisher
  Thorndike Press
  10 Water St., Suite 310
  Waterville, ME 04901

eBay®

Top 100
2nd Edition

Simplified®

TIPS & TRICKS

by Julia Wilkinson

Visual

WILEY

eBay®: Top 100 Simplified® Tips & Tricks, 2nd Edition

Published by

Wiley Publishing, Inc.

111 River Street

Hoboken, NJ 07030-5774

Published simultaneously in Canada

Copyright © 2005 by Wiley Publishing, Inc., Indianapolis, Indiana

Library of Congress Control Number: 2005921460

ISBN: 0-7645-9727-2

Manufactured in the United States of America

10 9 8 7 6 5 4 3 2 1

2K/RX/QT/QV/IN

Trademark Acknowledgments

Contact Us

For general information on our other products and services contact our Customer Care Department within the U.S. at 800-762-2974, outside the U.S. at 317-572-3993 or fax 317-572-4002.

For technical support please visit www.wiley.com/techsupport.

Permissions

Wiley Publishing, Inc.

U.S. Sales

Contact Wiley at (800) 762-2974 or fax (317) 572-4002.

Praise for Visual Books

"I have to praise you and your company on the fine products you turn out. I have twelve Visual books in my house. They were instrumental in helping me pass a difficult computer course. Thank you for creating books that are easy to follow. Keep turning out those quality books."
Gordon Justin (Brielle, NJ)

"What fantastic teaching books you have produced! Congratulations to you and your staff. You deserve the Nobel prize in Education. Thanks for helping me understand computers."
Bruno Tonon (Melbourne, Australia)

"A Picture Is Worth A Thousand Words! If your learning method is by observing or hands-on training, this is the book for you!"
Lorri Pegan-Durastante (Wickliffe, OH)

"Over time, I have bought a number of your 'Read Less - Learn More' books. For me, they are THE way to learn anything easily. I learn easiest using your method of teaching."
José A. Mazón (Cuba, NY)

"You've got a fan for life!! Thanks so much!!"
Kevin P. Quinn (Oakland, CA)

"I have several books from the Visual series and have always found them to be valuable resources."
Stephen P. Miller (Ballston Spa, NY)

"I have several of your Visual books and they are the best I have ever used."
Stanley Clark (Crawfordville, FL)

"Like a lot of other people, I understand things best when I see them visually. Your books really make learning easy and life more fun."
John T. Frey (Cadillac, MI)

"I have quite a few of your Visual books and have been very pleased with all of them. I love the way the lessons are presented!"
Mary Jane Newman (Yorba Linda, CA)

"Thank you, thank you, thank you...for making it so easy for me to break into this high-tech world."
Gay O'Donnell (Calgary, Alberta, Canada)

"I write to extend my thanks and appreciation for your books. They are clear, easy to follow, and straight to the point. Keep up the good work! I bought several of your books and they are just right! No regrets! I will always buy your books because they are the best."
Seward Kollie (Dakar, Senegal)

"I would like to take this time to thank you and your company for producing great and easy-to-learn products. I bought two of your books from a local bookstore, and it was the best investment I've ever made! Thank you for thinking of us ordinary people."
Jeff Eastman (West Des Moines, IA)

"Compliments to the chef!! Your books are extraordinary! Or, simply put, extra-ordinary, meaning way above the rest! THANKYOU THANKYOU THANKYOU! I buy them for friends, family, and colleagues."
Christine J. Manfrin (Castle Rock, CO)

Credits

Project Editor
Maureen Spears

Acquisitions Editor
Jody Lefevere

Product Development Manager
Lindsay Sandman

Copy Editor
Marylouise Wiack

Technical Editor
Ina Steiner

Editorial Manager
Robyn Siesky

Permissions Editor
Carmen Krikorian

Editorial Assistant
Adrienne Porter

Manufacturing
Allan Conley
Linda Cook
Paul Gilchrist
Jennifer Guynn

Special Help
Sherry Kinkoph
Nancee Reeves

Cover Design
Anthony Bunyan

Book Design
Kathie S. Rickard

Production Coordinator
Maridee Ennis

Layout
Amanda Spagnuolo

Screen Artist
Elizabeth Cardenas-Nelson
Jill Proll

Illustrator
Ronda David-Burroughs

Proofreader
Melissa D. Buddendeck

Quality Control
Susan Moritz
Robert Springer
Brian H. Walls

Indexer
Sherry Massey

Vice President and Executive Group Publisher
Richard Swadley

Vice President and Publisher
Barry Pruett

Composition Director
Debbie Stailey

Author's Acknowledgments

Thanks to my husband, Nick Gallagher, for his support during this book; and to my kids, Lindsay and Kyle, for understanding why I didn't cook as much. I'd also like to thank the folks at Wiley: to Project Editor Maureen Spears, for all her help and expertise; to Acquisitions Editor, Jody Lefevere, for her faith in me; and to Copy Editor Marylouise Wiack for her thoroughness. A big thanks to Ina Steiner, for her Technical Editing and great suggestions, and to David Steiner for his industry knowledge. Final, thanks to the gang on the eBay Clothing, Shoes, and Accessories board for their cheerful helpfulness.

How To Use This Book

eBay®: Top 100 Simplified® Tips & Tricks, 2nd Edition includes 100 tasks that reveal cool secrets, teach timesaving tricks, and explain great tips guaranteed to make you more productive with eBay. The easy-to-use layout lets you work through all the tasks from beginning to end or jump in at random.

Who is this book for?

You already know eBay basics. Now you would like to go beyond, with shortcuts, tricks and tips that let you work smarter and faster. And because you learn more easily when someone *shows* you how, this is the book for you.

Conventions Used In This Book

❶ Steps

This book uses step-by-step instructions to guide you easily through each task. Numbered callouts on every screen shot show you exactly how to perform each task, step by step.

❷ Tips

Practical tips provide insights to save you time and trouble, caution you about hazards to avoid, and reveal how to do things in eBay that you never thought possible!

❸ Task Numbers

Task numbers from 1 to 100 indicate which lesson you are working on.

❹ Difficulty Levels

For quick reference, the symbols below mark the difficulty level of each task.

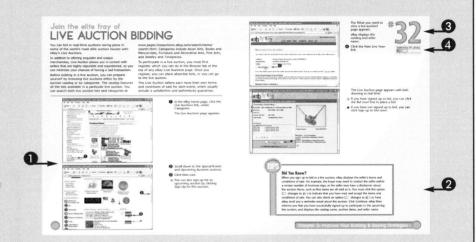

DIFFICULTY LEVEL	Demonstrates a new spin on a common task
DIFFICULTY LEVEL	Introduces a new skill or a new task
DIFFICULTY LEVEL	Combines multiple skills requiring in-depth knowledge
DIFFICULTY LEVEL	Requires extensive skill and may involve other technologies

Table of Contents

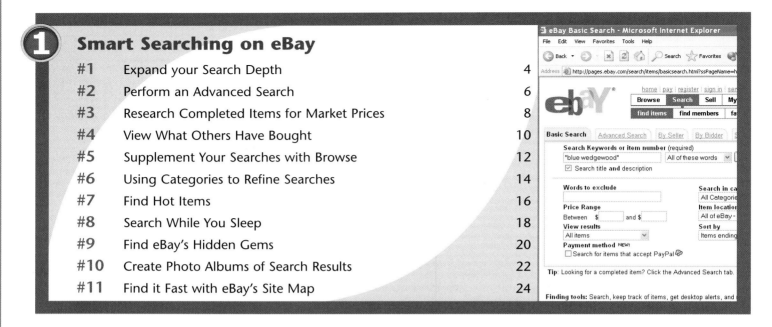

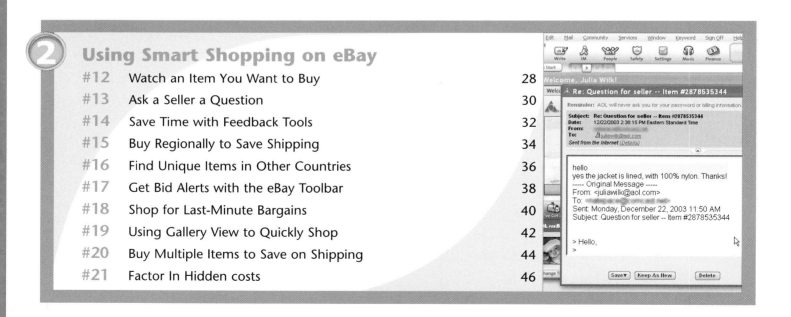

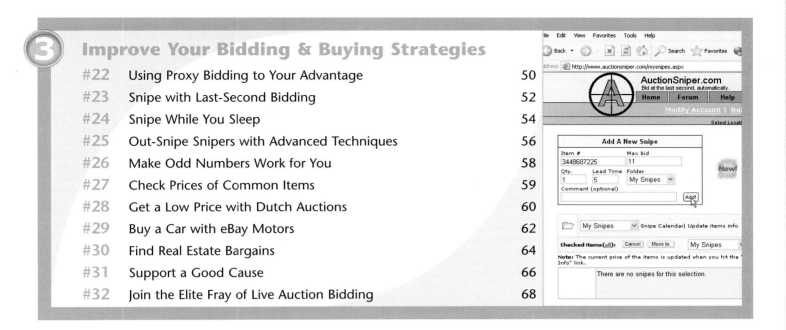
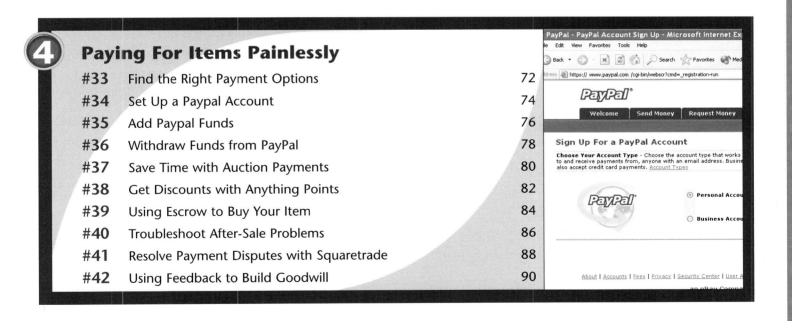

Table of Contents

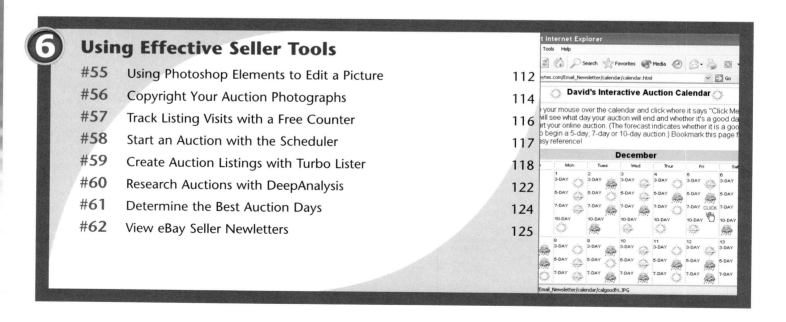

7 Boost Your Sales with Advanced Selling Techniques

8 Maximize Your Item's Exposure

Table of Contents

Smart Searching on eBay

With millions of items for sale on eBay, and more every day, finding what you want can be very time-consuming. Good search skills can help you find bargains and save time.

Although you can sort through listings using the eBay Browse feature, the huge number of items in many categories can make browsing overwhelming. Because of this, many people prefer to use searches rather than to browse on eBay.

However, you can use tips and tricks to make your searches more effective. The eBay search pages feature different parameters that narrow down your hunt for a specific type of item. You can even combine browsing and searching as a search strategy.

In addition to eBay's search features, you can use third-party tools such as timeBLASTER, to save time and more easily narrow down the items you seek from the millions of listings on eBay.

You can benefit from eBay's search features as both a buyer and a seller. As a buyer, you can use search tricks, such as searching for listings with typos and transpositions, to find items that other buyers may overlook. As a seller, you can use parameters, such as Completed Items only, to research items that are similar to those you sell. Because eBay shoppers expect good deals, it is critical for you to have a good idea of what kind of sales price you can expect for your items. That way, you know what you can afford to spend on inventory and still make a reasonable profit.

Top 100

Expand your
SEARCH DEPTH

You can increase the number of hits you receive on a search by searching items by both title and description. The Search title and description option on the eBay Basic Search tab allows you to retrieve items that contain keywords in both the item description and the item title.

If you search using titles only, you may miss a large percentage of the available items. For example, if you search for blue Wedgewood — a popular type of collectible china — with the title and description option activated, you may receive 50 items. A similar search without this option activated may result in 19 items, which would result in your missing more than half of the items you seek.

You may miss items when you use the titles-only search because sellers do not always include the keywords you expect in their titles. This occurs when sellers do not have enough space to fully describe their item in the title, do not choose the most appropriate words, or have several ways to describe the item.

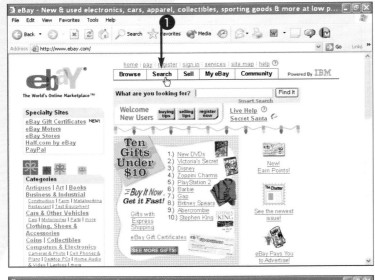

❶ In the main eBay home page, click Search.

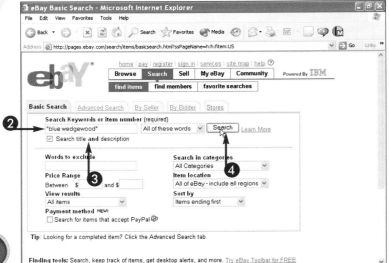

The Search tabs appear.

❷ Type the keywords that describe the item you want, leaving spaces between each keyword, and placing quotation marks around all the words.

❸ Click the Search title and description option.

❹ Click Search.

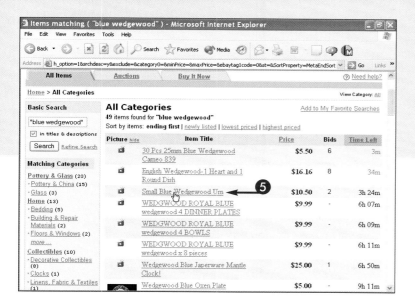

eBay retrieves and displays all item titles and item descriptions that contain your keywords.

5 Click a listing.

The details page appears for the listing.

● The page contains information including the item's current bid, the time left in the auction, how many bids the item has received, and the identity of the current high bidder.

 TIPS

Buyer Beware!

Carefully read the descriptions of items on which you intend to bid. Although your keywords may appear in an item description, you may not want the item. For example, if you type **"blue Wedgewood"** to look for that type of china, a search may yield an item with blue Wedgewood in its description, but the description may refer to an ottoman of blue Wedgewood color.

Did You Know?

You can also access the Basic Search tab by clicking the Smart Search link on the eBay home page, below and to the left of the Find It button. Or, you can simply type your search words into the text box located just to the right of the What are you looking for? prompt.

Perform an
ADVANCED SEARCH

You can perform a more powerful search on eBay by using the Advanced Search tab instead of the Basic Search tab. The Advanced Search tab contains all the features of eBay's basic search, as well as additional parameters that can narrow down your search.

Although using all of these options together may severely limit your search, you may want to combine some of them to optimize your search. For this reason, it is important to understand how each option can benefit you.

The Words to exclude option allows you to eliminate certain keywords from the search. For example, if

you know you want metal and not wooden toy trains, you can enter **wooden** in this option box.

The Buy It Now Items only option displays items for immediate purchase, and is especially useful if you see a bargain. For more on this feature, see Tasks #9 and #46.

The Gift Items only option yields listings that the sellers designate as gifts. In some cases, the seller may even offer gift wrapping, and shipping to the gift recipient.

The Advanced Search feature also facilitates international searching. For more information on international searching, see Task #16.

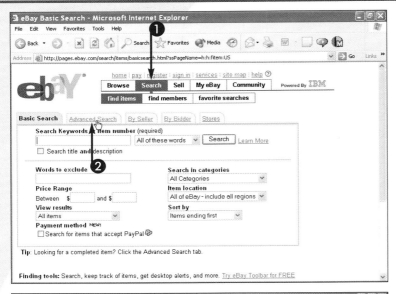

❶ In the eBay home page, click Search.

The Search tabs appear.

❷ Click the Advanced Search tab.

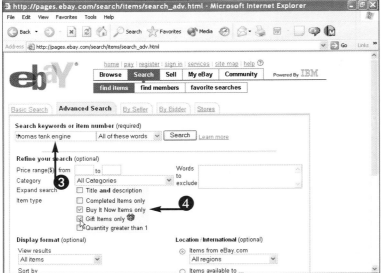

❸ Type the word or phrase for the item you want to find.

❹ Click the desired Expand search Item type options.

You can click the Buy It Now Items only option to show items for immediate purchase.

You can click the Gift Items only option to see items that make good gifts.

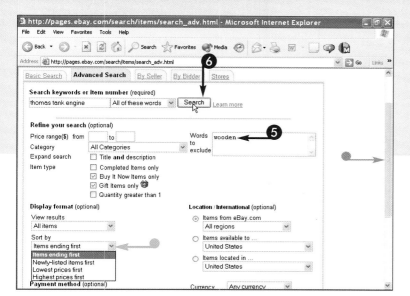

⑤ Type the words you want to exclude.

● You may need to scroll your screen.

● You can click here and select how to sort your list.

⑥ Click Search.

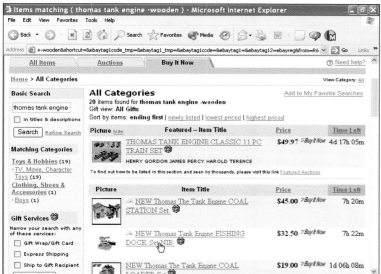

The search results appear.

This example lists all Buy It Now, non-wooden Thomas Tank engine gift items, with auctions that end first at the top of the list.

TIPS

More Options!

When you click the Completed Items only option, you receive hits for auctions that have ended. This is useful when you want to research how past items have sold. For more information on this option, see Task #3.

More Options!

In the Sort by list, on both the Basic and Advanced Search tabs, you can select different sort options. The Items ending first option lists auctions about to end first. The Newly-listed items first option displays auctions that have just gone live first, followed by those about to end. The Lowest prices first option shows items from the cheapest to the most expensive. The Highest prices first option shows items from the most expensive to the cheapest.

Research Completed Items for
MARKET PRICES

You can use the Completed Items only option in the Advanced Search tab to research the final selling prices for different types of items for the last two weeks. As a buyer, this information gives you an idea of what to expect as a final bid. As a seller, this information allows you to estimate what market prices you can expect for your own, similar items. Knowing an item's recent market price helps you avoid buying inventory at a price that is too high to yield a profit.

To see what has sold for the most and least money, you can use the Sort by menu to select either the Highest prices first or Lowest prices first option. Viewing the highest prices shows you the items that can make you the most money; viewing the lowest prices shows you what items to avoid selling.

Please note that items that do not meet their reserve, or asking prices, are not good reflections of a particular item's market value, nor should you use them for research purposes.

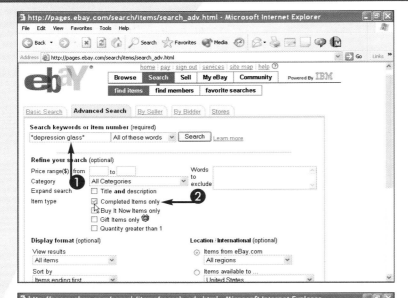

① In the Advanced Search tab, type a keyword or phrase.

Note: See Task #2 for more information on accessing the Advanced Search tab.

② Click the Completed Items only option.

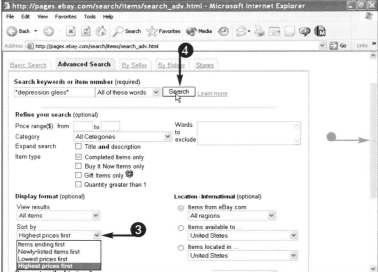

③ Click here and then click Highest prices first.

● You may have to scroll to see this option

④ Click Search.

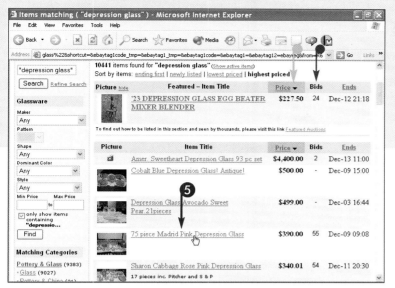

The search results appear.

● You can scan the price column to see which items resulted in the highest prices.

● You can scan the bid column for the highest number of bids, which indicates a popular item.

5 Click a listing.

● The details page appears for the item and contains a photo and a detailed description.

You should review the listing carefully to learn why the item sold for such a high price or had the highest number of bids.

● This example shows an item that sold — that is, met its *reserve* price.

Note: *Items that do not meet the reserve price are not accurate reflections of a market price.*

TIPS

Savvy eBaying!
For a thorough search, try different word combinations for items. For example, consider using the words antique glass as well as Depression glass, as different sellers may select different names or descriptions for their items.

Buyer Beware!
Various factors can influence the final sales price of an item, including condition, age, color, and season.

Buyer Beware!
Look at a variety of hits in the search returns, because the highest and lowest prices may not reflect the average sales price of a certain type of item. The Bids column on the results page shows the number of bids the item received and indicates the level of interest in it. Lower numbers in this column usually indicate lower interest.

View what
OTHERS HAVE BOUGHT

You can use the By Bidder tab in the eBay search page to view what other users bid on and buy. The By Bidder feature allows you to benefit from other people's shopping skills, because they may find a great item you would otherwise miss. If you often bid against certain users in key categories, take note of their user IDs and use them in a By Bidder search.

On the By Bidder tab, you can type the bidder's eBay ID, and a list of the items that person is bidding on appears, with information about those auctions, including an item number, a start and end date and time, price, title, current high bidder, and seller.

You can choose not to include completed items if you only want to see the items on which a user is currently bidding. You can also select the No, only if high bidder option to eliminate auctions the user lost. Finally, you can select how many results you want per page: 5, 10, 25, 50, 75, 100, 200, or All items on one page.

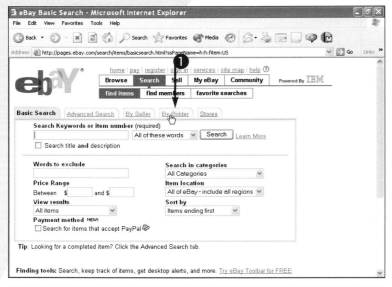

① In the search page, click the By Bidder tab.

The By Bidder tab appears.

② Type the bidder's user ID.

③ Click whether you want to include or exclude completed items.

● You can click here and select the number of results you want to see on a page.

④ Click Search.

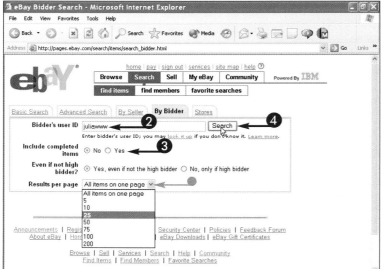

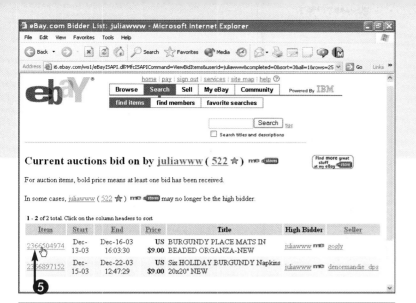

The titles appear for auctions bid on by the user.

5 If eBay lists any item on which you want to bid, click an item number.

● You can view an item on which the bidder is bidding.

● You can click Place Bid to begin bidding.

TIPS

Savvy Selling!

The By Bidder tab is a good tool to learn what your customers want. For example, if you sell bubble wrap, and you see your repeat customers bidding on tape and envelopes, consider adding those items to your inventory.

Did You Know?

Have you received e-mails from an eBay member who does not specify his or her user ID? If you have completed previous transactions with this member, you can look up the corresponding user ID. In the By Bidder tab, click the **look it up** link, then type the e-mail address in the Request user ID option box. eBay prompts you through a security screen, at which point you can click Search to retrieve the user's ID.

Supplement your searches with
BROWSE

You can increase your chances of finding items if you supplement your searches by browsing in the appropriate eBay category. This is because some sellers use titles or descriptions that you may not find when you perform a search for them.

Some eBay treasure-hunters actively use this search method to find listings where a seller has an item whose true value they do not realize. For example, one eBay browser bought an old manuscript written by a famous author; the seller did not know that the writer of the manuscript was famous. The buyer found this manuscript by looking for clues to its origin from the seller's description.

Because eBay offers a steadily growing number of category choices, you must check similar categories to obtain a thorough search. For example, under the Jewelry and Watches category, some items make sense in both the subcategories of Loose Beads and Loose Gemstones. Although some sellers list items in a second category, not all sellers do. Sellers sometimes have items that can belong in more than two categories.

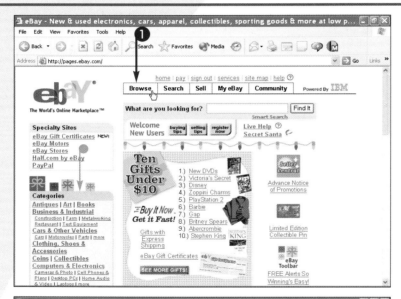

① In the eBay home page, click Browse.

● Another way to begin browsing for an item is to click a main category in the list under the Categories heading.

The list of categories appears.

② Click a category or subcategory.

● Because eBay can have long category lists, you may need to scroll down through the page.

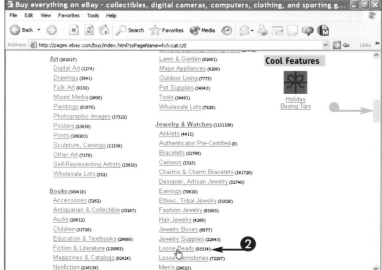

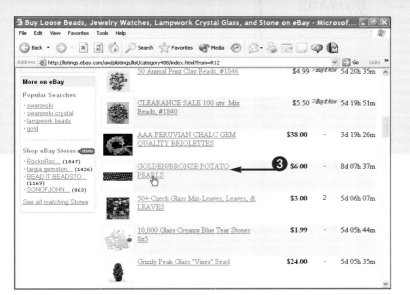

The results list appears, displaying all the items in the category you selected.

Review the different types of auctions that are available.

③ Click a listing.

The details page appears for the listing.

You may find an unusual item that you may otherwise not find when you do a search.

● In this example, the listing does not contain the word bead, but is for potato pearls.

More Options!

To get a quick overview of eBay's categories, click the see all eBay categories link, located beneath the Everything Else link on the eBay home page. The see all eBay categories link allows you to see all the first-and second-level eBay categories on one page, which can quickly help familiarize you with the various category options as they currently stand.

Using categories to
REFINE SEARCHES

You can combine browsing and searching to narrow down your search. This technique allows you to take advantage of eBay's large category hierarchy by moving through the many category layers — sometimes referred to as *drilling down* — to access the items you want. Because eBay's categories can consist of many layers, you may need to drill down into several subcategories before you find the item you want.

Combining the Search and Browse features is especially useful when you want to browse for a specific item, but do not know in which category

that item belongs. You may also find this technique useful if the item can potentially fall into several different categories. For more information on browsing, see Task #5.

You can combine the Browse and Search features by using the Matching Categories list, which appears on the left side of the page after you do a search. eBay often lists more than one category here, and presents you with a list of matching categories.

When you perform a search and then enter a matching category, eBay's search continues to filter out items according to your search words.

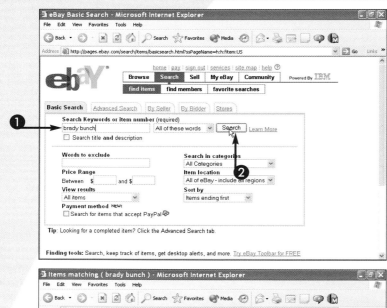

① In the Basic Search tab, type a search word or phrase.

② Click Search.

The search results appear.

● Matching Categories appears on the left side of the page.

These categories vary, depending on what search words you type.

③ Click the category you want.

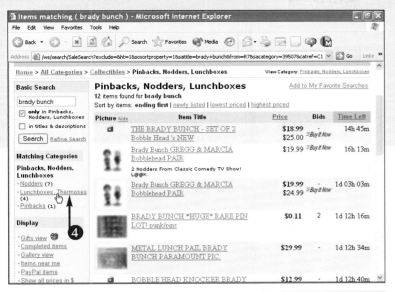

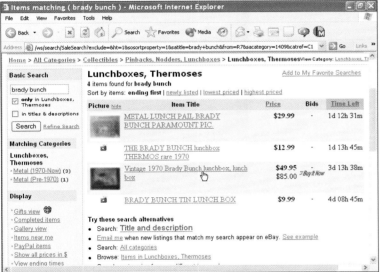

The search results appear.

eBay narrows down the Matching Categories to smaller categories.

4 Click another category under Matching Categories.

eBay displays the search results, further narrowing down the items.

TIPS

More Options!

You can also perform a search within any given category. In the eBay home page, click Browse. Once you drill down into a category with actual auction listings on the right, you can type search words into the Basic Search box on the upper left, and then click the Only in this category option (□ changes to ☑) directly beneath it.

Did You Know?

You can find search results grouped by category for eBay's top keyword searches at keyword. ebay.com. From there, you can browse a list of keywords that eBay buyers and sellers use most often. If you click a keyword, you receive a list of categories containing the keyword along with a Gallery containing photos of items related to that keyword.

Find
HOT ITEMS

You can read the Hot Items by Category document, located in Seller Central, to determine which items sold well recently. eBay staff creates a list of items they deem hot sellers in each category. eBay defines *hot items* as recent items whose bidding growth significantly outpaces new listings growth, or where the bid-to-item ratios are higher than other products in the same parent category.

As a seller, you can read the Hot Items by Category list to get ideas for things you can sell that can make you the most money. You can put the hot items

information to work and experiment with new types of products, and see what sells.

Because the hot items list changes regularly, it is a good idea to check it frequently to get the best idea of what sells well in a particular category.

As an alternative to the steps in this task, you can also use a pay service that does the tedious work of searching for hot items for you. One service is andale's What's Hot. To use andale's service, go to www.andale.com.

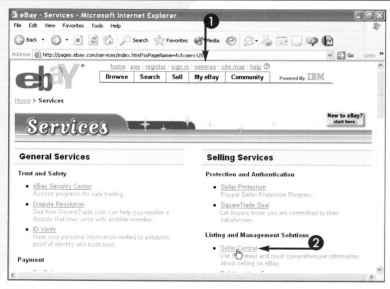

① In the eBay home page, click the services link.

The eBay Services page appears.

② Click the Seller Central link

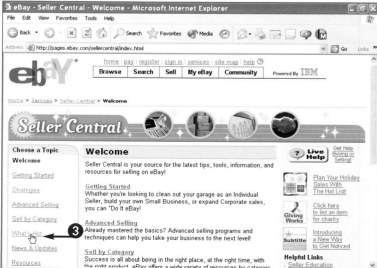

The Seller Central page appears.

③ Click the What's Hot link.

The What's Hot page appears.

④ Click the Hot Items by Category link.

● You may need to scroll down to access this link.

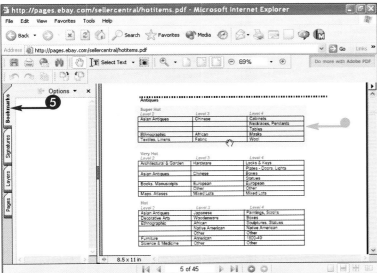

The Hot Categories Report, which is in Adobe Acrobat's pdf format, appears.

***Note:** If you do not already have the Adobe Acrobat Reader, eBay may prompt you to download it.*

⑤ Click the Bookmarks tab to view the report.

● You can see the Hot Products by category.

TIPS

Did You Know?

You can see previous lists of Hot Items on the Hot Items Folder in the eBay Community area. In any eBay page, click Community, and then click the Discussion Boards link. Next, click the Hot Items link. Click a specific category folder, and you can see the lists of Hot Items for that category.

The hot products in the Computers & Electronics category for the week of 09/25/03:

Desktop PCs
700MHz to 1GHz
400-650MHz
Gadgets & Other Electronics
Air Purifiers
Home Automation
Other Gadgets
Home Audio & Video
Wholesale Lots
Home Audio
Office Products
Calendars, Planners
Copiers & Supplies
Laminating Machines, Supplies
Presentation A/V
Portable Audio & Video
MP3 Players
Voice Recorders

Search
WHILE YOU SLEEP

You can use eBay's My Favorite Search feature to have the system regularly scan for a certain type of item. This is a convenient and timesaving way to locate a particular item without having to perform multiple manual searches. This technique is especially useful when you are not in a hurry, and can take your time to find an item over days, weeks, or even months.

You can give the search a name. For example, if your search is for a medium-sized, black cardigan, you can name the search black cardigan M. You can also

designate for how long you want eBay to e-mail you the daily results of the search — with options ranging from 7 days to 12 months.

You can opt whether eBay e-mails your search results using the E-mail me daily whenever there are new items option. You can also check the saved search anytime in the My Favorite Searches area located in My eBay's Favorites tab.

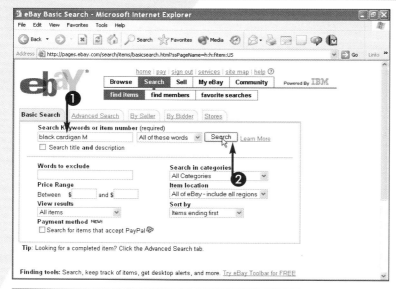

❶ In the Basic Search tab, type a search word or phrase.

❷ Click Search.

The search results appear.

❸ Click the Add to My Favorite Searches link.

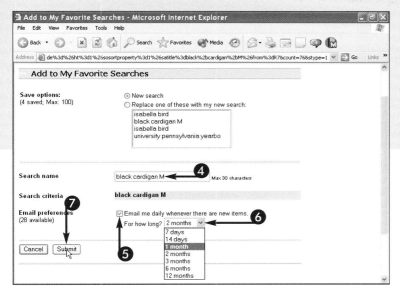

The Add to My Favorite Searches page appears.

④ Type a name for your search.

⑤ Click the Email me daily whenever there are new items option.

⑥ Click here and select a time frame for the search.

⑦ Click Submit.

eBay e-mails your Favorite Search results to you.

Note: *You must sign on to your e-mail service to check the Favorite Searches e-mail.*

TIPS

Did You Know?

When you find the item you want, you can delete its Favorite Search to make room for new searches. Click My eBay in the eBay home page, or any other eBay page, and then click the Favorites tab. Click the option next to the name of the search, and then click Delete. eBay lets you save up to 100 searches.

More Options!

If you especially like items from a specific seller or store, and you want to quickly and easily view new items, you can save them as favorites. In the My eBay page, click the Favorites tab, and then click My Favorite Sellers/Stores. Click Add new Seller/Store and type the seller's user ID or the store name. Then click Save Favorite.

Find eBay's
HIDDEN GEMS

You can find great items that other eBay users may miss by searching for alternate spellings and typo variations of words. Because many searchers overlook alternate spellings, fewer people view and bid on these listings, allowing you to find wonderful bargains.

For example, if you look for Lilly Pulitzer brand clothing, which tends to sell very well on eBay, you may want to search under the spelling Lily Pulitzer, as this is a common misspelling of the brand name.

Another common error sellers make is transposing two letters. You can almost always find items with this mistake. For example, try DNKY instead of DKNY, or Evlis instead of Elvis.

As an example, a recent search on DNKY brought up 24 listings, only three of which had bids. These listings without bids give you an opportunity to find bargains. Compare that to the correct spelling, DKNY, where, out of the first 50 items, 30 have bids.

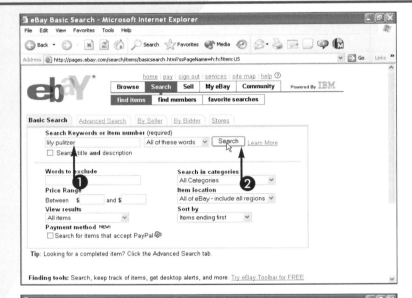

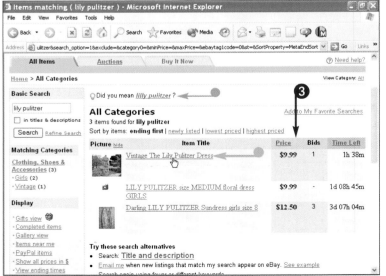

SEARCH FOR ITEMS WITH MISSPELLINGS

1 In the Basic Search tab, type a misspelled word or phrase.

2 Click Search.

Search results appear with misspelled listings.

● eBay prompts you for the correct spelling.

3 Search through the Price and Bids columns for auctions that still have low prices and bids.

● You can click these items to investigate further and to bid.

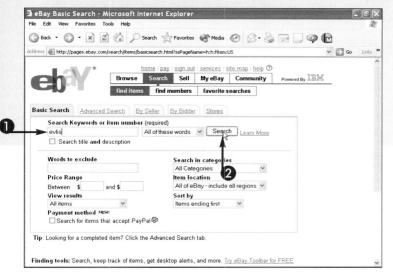

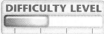
① In the Basic Search tab,
type a word or acronym
with transposed letters.

② Click Search.

The search results appear.

③ Search through the Price and Bids
columns for auctions that still have low
prices and bids.

● You can click these items to investigate
further and to bid.

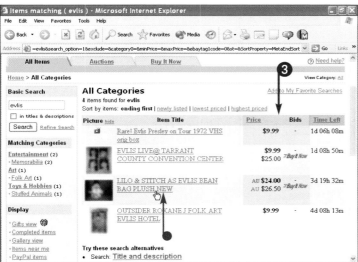

TIPS

eBay Savvy!

A misspelled item with a Buy It Now
option is great, because you can
buy it immediately at a low price
and prevent other typo-hunters from
finding it. For more information on
the Buy It Now option, see Tasks
#2, and #46.

eBay Savvy!

Try searching for both newly listed
and Buy It Now items to increase
your chances of finding a bargain,
because the good deals go quickly.
When you browse, look for the New
Today items.

Did You Know?

When you deliberately search for
items with incorrect spellings,
you can ignore the eBay search
engine's prompt near the top of
the page that suggests the correct
spelling.

Create photo albums of
SEARCH RESULTS

Have you ever scrolled through numerous eBay listings of similar items, clicking into each one to find the specific one that you want? You can reduce the time you spend finding items by using a tool called timeBLASTER, which was invented by an avid stamp collector who spent long hours on eBay. With timeBLASTER, you can reduce searches that take 20 hours a week to an hour a week. timeBLASTER is great for sellers, too. One sports trading card dealer uses a standing timeBLASTER search to monitor market prices.

timeBLASTER automatically searches eBay, downloads the item descriptions and photos, and creates photo albums of the results by neatly lining up rows of photos and item information. Instead of scrolling through many pages of listings and clicking each auction to see photos, you can view the search results in a compact, easy-to-view format. You can also easily bid on or watch an item directly from the Photo Album page.

Before you can use timeBLASTER, you must first download and install the timeBLASTER software from the Web site, www.timeblaster.com/tbeindex.shtml.

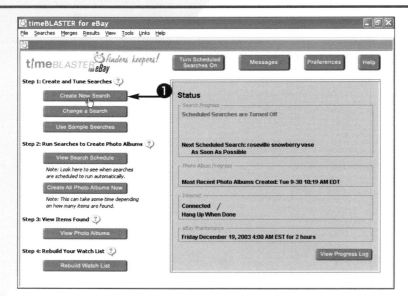

❶ In the timeBLASTER main page, click Create New Search.

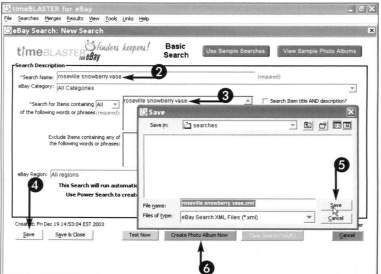

A Search Description window appears.

❷ Type a name for your search.

❸ Type the items for which you are searching.

❹ Click Save.

❺ In the Save dialog box that appears, click Save.

❻ Click Create Photo Album Now.

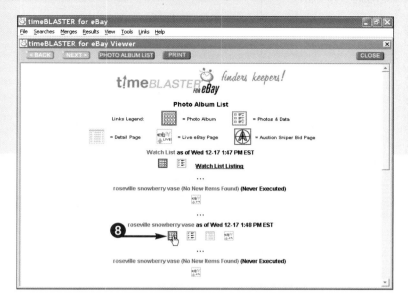

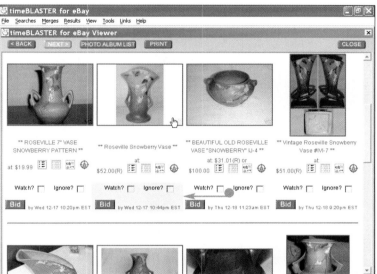

The timeBLASTER main page reappears, showing the status of the newly created search.

⑦ Click View Photo Albums.

The Photo Album List appears.

⑧ Click a photo album icon of an album you want to view.

The Photo Album appears, allowing you to view photos and titles of multiple items on one page.

● You can click the options to watch, bid on, or ignore an item.

TIPS

Did You Know?

The timeBLASTER software for eBay is only available for Windows PCs. You can view a free animated demonstration of how the software works on the timeBLASTER Web site. The example in the demonstration is of a search for Roseville vases, a popular collector's item. timeBLASTER offers a 30-day free trial. A one-year subscription to the service costs $39.95, and timeBLASTER pays you $4 for every friend you refer who buys a one-year subscription.

Did You Know?

You can run searches automatically by clicking Turn Scheduled Searches On from the main timeBLASTER page. Running a scheduled search allows you to do searches at night, or any time that is most convenient for you, so you can do other things while the search runs.

Find it fast with eBay's
SITE MAP

One of the easiest ways to find a particular section of the eBay site is to use the site map. Because eBay can be many layers deep in some areas, the site map acts as a valuable tool, displaying the broad array of features, services, and information available on the eBay site, and enabling you to navigate to a particular link. The site map can save you time and frustration in trying to find a specific part of eBay, because it compactly organizes all of the eBay links on one page.

You can access the eBay site map from any eBay page by using the link that appears at the top right of every page.

The site map is organized as a series of links under headings that describe every area on eBay, such as Browse, Sell, Search, Services, and Community. New features and areas are easy to find, because they are marked with a bright yellow NEW! icon.

① In the eBay home page, click the site map link.

The eBay site map page appears.

Links to all eBay areas appear in the lists on this page.

● Special items feature a don't miss! icon.

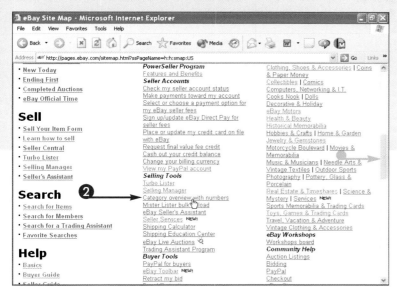

- You can scroll down to see the entire site map.

② Click the link that interests you.

This example uses the Category overview with numbers link.

DIFFICULTY LEVEL

The Category Overview with Category Numbers page appears, allowing you to find an eBay area that you may not otherwise notice.

- You can use the numbers in the Sell Your Item form to specify the category in which to list your item.

- You can click a main Category link to view the subcategories with numbers below it.

More Options!

If you cannot find what you need on eBay's site map, you can search eBay's Help section. Click the help link, located just to the right of the site map link on any eBay page. You search the help database by typing your search words in the box at the top of the help window, and then clicking Search Help. You can also browse a complete alphabetical list of help topics by clicking the A-Z index tab in the eBay Help Center window.

Did You Know?

If you still cannot find what you need using the site map or the eBay Help Center, you can use the Contact Us link, under eBay Help at the left of the Help Center search page.

Chapter 2

Using Smart Shopping on eBay

With all the competition for shopping on eBay, it helps to use some tricks to buy the items you want at the right time and for the right price.

You can use eBay's tools, such as the Watch an Item option, to mark an item you may not be sure you want to buy, but do not think you can find later in the sea of eBay items. You can also use tools like the eBay Toolbar Alert to set up an alarm on your computer so you know when your auctions are about to end.

To ensure you have all the important details you need about an item, you can use the Ask seller a question link.

Checking a seller's feedback rating is critical to your success as a buyer. You can save time finding negative or neutral feedback with tools like Gutcheck.

To find good deals, you can look for auctions that are about to end and have few to no bids, and you can use the Buy It Now feature when the price is right. You can also shop for items in other countries, for which you may have less competition.

Other things you can do to save money include buying items within your own geographical area, and buying several things from the same seller to save on shipping. Remembering hidden costs such as shipping, handling, and insurance helps you spend your money wisely.

Top 100

WATCH AN ITEM
you want to buy

You can track items that interest you by using the Watch this item feature. When you browse through many pages of listings, you may find it confusing to go back to an earlier page and find an item that interests you. The Watch this item feature makes it very easy to keep track of all the items you may want to buy, because you can mark an item on which you may want to bid, and then continue to browse for similar items before you decide to bid on one of them.

You can view a complete list of all the items you are watching in My eBay, under the Items I'm Watching heading. The list shows you the item numbers, titles, current prices, number of bids, time left in the auction, and the seller's user ID. You can even bid on the item directly from the Items I'm Watching list.

Once the auctions end for the items you are watching, you can delete them to make room for more items.

ADD AN ITEM TO YOUR WATCH LIST

① In a browsing or searching list, click a listing.

In this example, the item is a Tiffany-style lamp.

Note: For more on searching and browsing, see Chapter 1.

The details page appears for the listing.

● The photo and price of the item display.

● You may need to scroll down to view the description.

② Click the Watch this item link.

eBay tracks the item.

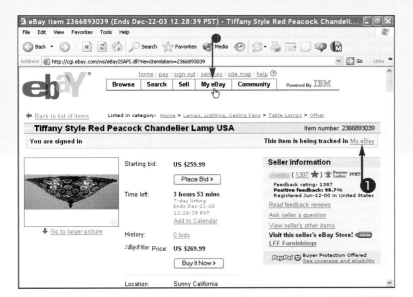

DIFFICULTY LEVEL

❶ Click the My eBay link.

● You can also access the My eBay page from any eBay page by clicking the My eBay link.

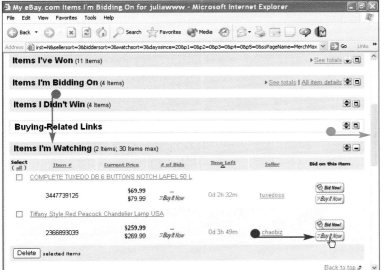

The My eBay page appears.

● You can view the item under the Items I'm Watching heading.

● You may need to scroll down the page.

● You can bid on the item directly by clicking the Buy It Now button (=Buy It Now).

TIPS

More Options!

For a quick, easy way to review items you want, you can use the My Recently Viewed Items or My Recent Searches features, which eBay displays at the bottom of search results and listings. Both features list the last 3 items you viewed or your last three searches.

Did You Know?

You can watch up to 30 items. As a reminder, eBay e-mails you a daily list of auctions that you are watching that end within 36 hours. If you do not want to receive this e-mail list, you can go to My eBay, click the Preferences tab, click Change my notification preferences, and then deselect the Item Watch Reminder option (☑ changes to ☐).

ASK A SELLER
a question

You can get more information about an item before you buy it using the Ask seller a question link. Because of privacy concerns, eBay does not publish a user's e-mail address, name, address, or phone number. Therefore, this link is the only way you can communicate directly with a seller, unless an auction is over and you win an item, at which point eBay sends your e-mail directly to the seller.

If the seller does not include key details in the auction's description, such as the measurements of an item of clothing, an item's age, or the shipping cost to your location, this option allows you to do further research. Getting detailed and complete information on an item helps you to avoid buying something you do not want.

eBay sends your question to the seller's e-mail address. The seller can then e-mail you back with the answers to your question. You can specify if you want to receive a blind carbon copy, or Bcc, of the e-mail for your records.

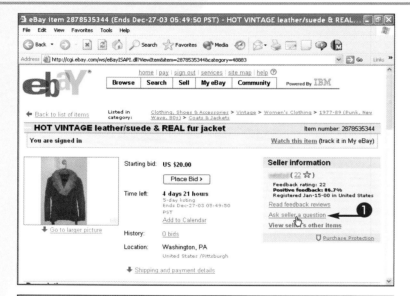

1 In an item listing, click the Ask seller a question link.

The Ask Seller a Question page appears.

● You can deselect this option if you do not want to receive a blind copy of the e-mail.

2 Type a question for the seller.

3 Click Send message.

- eBay confirms that your e-mail has been sent to the seller.

- If you selected the Bcc to myself option on the Ask Seller a Question screen, eBay tells you that you will receive it shortly.

DIFFICULTY LEVEL

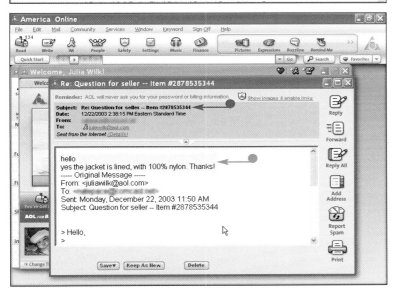

④ Launch your e-mail application and check your e-mail.

⑤ Open the e-mail from the seller.

- The item number appears in the subject.

- The seller's response helps you make a more informed decision about whether to purchase the item.

Did You Know?

You can request an eBay member's contact information during an active transaction. Also, in a successful closed transaction, winning bidders and sellers can request each other's contact information. To request contact information, click Search, and then click Find Members. Type the user ID of the member and the item number in the option boxes, and then click Submit. eBay tells you that it has processed your request, and e-mails you the contact information.

Caution!

It is against eBay's rules to ask a seller to sell you an item outside of the eBay system. Also, transactions outside the eBay Web site do not offer the same protections that eBay offers, such as buyer protection, dispute resolution, mediation, and feedback.

Save time with
FEEDBACK TOOLS

Before you bid on an item, it is critical to perform a thorough check of a seller's feedback rating to determine a seller's integrity. Located next to the seller's eBay ID, a seller's *feedback rating* tells you how many transactions a seller has completed, as well as what percentage of these transactions resulted in positive comments from buyers. eBay also allows you to read a seller's feedback comments.

To save time scrolling through hundreds of feedback comments, you can download the free Gutcheck tool at www.teamredline.com/gutcheck/fdefault.asp

and view just the negative and neutral comments together on one page. With Gutcheck, you can also easily see information about the auction that a comment references.

Preferably, the seller's percentage of positive feedback comments should be very high — 100 percent, or close to it. Keep in mind that even the best sellers have a few neutral or negative comments, especially if they complete numerous transactions. That is why it is important to read what those comments say.

① In an item listing, right-click the seller's feedback rating number or eBay ID.

② Click Get Gutcheck.

Note: The steps in this section assume that you have Gutcheck installed.

The Gutcheck software opens.

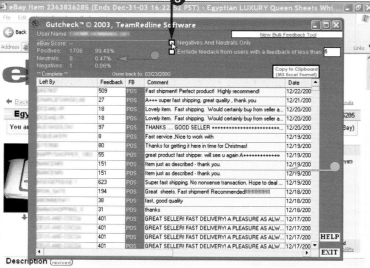

● You can see how many, and the percentage of, positive, negative, and neutral comments the seller has.

● A condensed list of the comments appears below the eBay score.

This example shows a seller with a good Positives feedback rating of greater than 99 percent.

③ Click the Negatives And Neutrals Only option.

The negative and neutral feedback ratings and comments appear, along with users' own feedback ratings.

④ Double-click the comment you want to view.

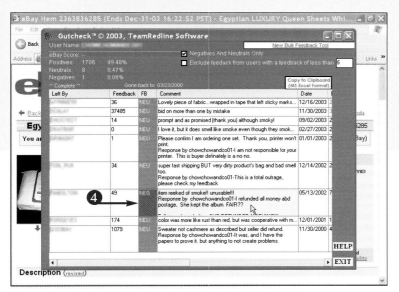

● The entire feedback comment from the buyer appears.

● The seller's follow-up comment also appears.

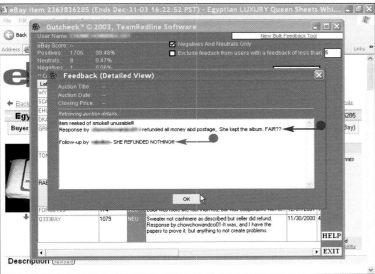

TIPS

More Options!

You can export your Gutcheck feedback data to other applications, such as Microsoft Excel. From the first Gutcheck feedback page, click the Copy to Clipboard option above the Date column. Gutcheck informs you that the data is copied to the clipboard. Open Excel and click Paste or press Ctrl-V.

More Options!

With Gutcheck's GiveSomeBack Bulk Feedback Tool, you can simultaneously leave multiple positive feedback comments for specific or all pending, transactions. You can also use a feedback comment from a stored list to avoid retyping commonly used feedback comments. You can download the Bulk Feedback Tool at www.teamredline.com/gsb. The Bulk Feedback Tool only works for positive feedback because most eBay buyers typically give negative feedback comments sparingly.

Buy regionally to
SAVE SHIPPING

You can save a lot of money on the shipping of heavy items if you find an item you want on eBay that is located near where you live. You can use eBay's Item location menu on the Basic Search tab to select the closest city to where you live and then perform a search. If you win the item, you can reduce the cost of shipping, or you can simply drive to the seller's location and pick up the item.

For example, if you want a bicycle and you live near the Washington, D.C., area, you can select that city in the Item location menu and perform a search. If

you can drive to other nearby locations to pick up an item, you can also perform additional searches for other cities near you.

You should check the item's description to find out if the seller permits you to pick it up in person. If this information is not in the description, you can use the Ask seller a question link. For more information on the Ask seller a question feature, see Task #13.

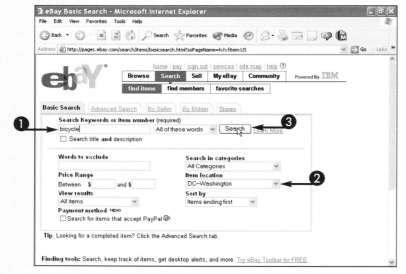

❶ From the eBay Basic Search page, type your search word or phrase.

❷ Click the Item location ▾ and then select a location.

❸ Click Search.

The search results appear, with a list of items located in the region you specified.

❹ Click the item you want to view.

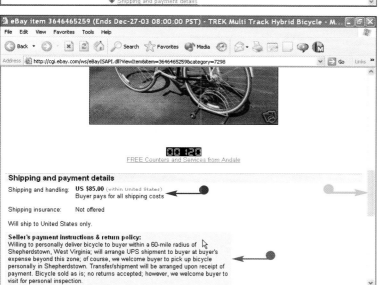

A description of the item appears, along with pictures of the item.

● The location of the item displays.

Note: *The item may actually be located in a town near the major center that you specified in your search.*

● You can scroll down to view more pictures of the item, if they are included.

● You can view the Shipping and handling cost.

● You can view any specified details about pickup and delivery.

Buyer Beware!

Although buying a heavy item regionally on eBay often makes sense, if an item is expensive or fragile and shipping is a fraction of its cost, sometimes you are better off searching the whole country or the world on eBay and paying for the shipping. You can use a special shipping service such as Craters and Freighters. For more information on shipping large, valuable, or fragile items, see Task #92.

More Options!

If you live near more than one city, you can perform more than one regional search in case the item you want is located in another city near you. For example, if you live in northern Virginia, you can search in Baltimore, Md., as well as in Washington, D.C.

Find unique items in
OTHER COUNTRIES

You can shop for items from around the world by using the Location/International options in the eBay Advanced Search page. This is a great way to find unique items that are hard to locate in your own country.

For example, you can search for authentic Celtic jewelry by using the Items located in option under Location/International heading to find items in Ireland.

If the seller does not state in the auction description that they ship to your country, you can use the Ask seller a question link to find out if they do. For more information on the Ask seller a question feature, see Task #13.

You can also use the Items available to option to search for items that sellers ship to your country, although this usually brings up a mixture of both local and international items.

Another way to find unique items is to select the Any country from the Items available to option. However, you may discover that sellers do not ship their items to your country, so you need to check the item description for shipping details.

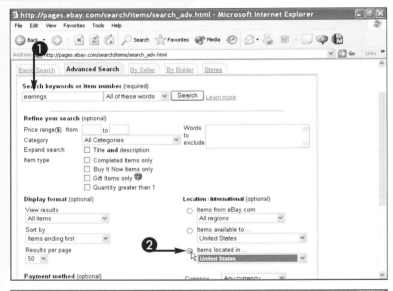

① In the eBay Advanced Search page, type your search word or phrase.

② Click the Items located in option.

③ Click here, and select a country.

④ Click Search.

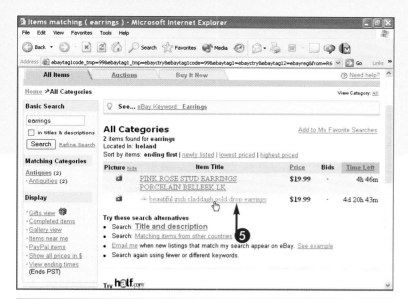

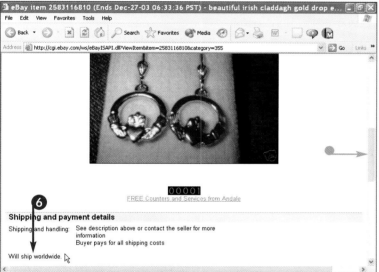

The search results appear for the list of items located in the country you specified.

⑤ Click the item you want to view.

The details page appears for the listing.

⑥ View the Shipping and payment details section to determine if the seller ships to your country.

● You may need to scroll down to see the Shipping and payment details.

More Options!

Another way to search for items in different countries is to go directly to the international eBay site of that country, using that country's domain name. For example, to look for items in Germany, you can go to www.ebay.de. For a list of eBay's worldwide sites, with links to each, scroll to the lower left of the eBay home page and look under Global Sites. However, remember that these sites appear in each respective country's native language.

Buyer Beware!

When you buy internationally on eBay, you must pay with whatever currency the seller specifies. You can view a currency converter at www.pages.ebay.com/services/buyandsell/currencyconverter.html. For more about international buying, go to www.pages.ebay.com/internationaltrading/findingitems.html.

GET BID ALERTS
with the eBay Toolbar

You can use the eBay Toolbar to receive a notice on your desktop, reminding you to bid on an auction on which you have already bid, and that is about to end. Called a *Bid Alert*, these notices are especially helpful when you bid on numerous items and want to expend less time keeping track of when their auctions end.

Although the eBay Toolbar is free, you must download the toolbar from www.pages.ebay.com/ebay_toolbar/ and install it before you can perform the steps in this task. Once installed, you can specify how many

minutes before the auction ends that you want to receive your Bid Alert.

You do not have to be online or have your browser window open to see the Bid Alert. The alert appears on your desktop and links you to the item's auction page on eBay.

eBay automatically removes ended auctions from your Bid List in the Bid Alert menu. However, if you win the auction, the item appears in the Items I've Won menu, which you access via the Items Won button.

SET BID ALERT PREFERENCES

① Click here, and then click eBay Toolbar Preferences.

The eBay Toolbar Preferences window appears.

② Click here, and select when you want eBay to send you a Bid Alert.

● You can click here and select an option to dismiss the notification.

● You can click here to receive Audio notification.

③ Scroll down and click Save Changes.

Your new eBay Toolbar settings take effect.

USING A BID ALERT

At the time you specified before the end of the auction, the Bid Alert appears on the lower-right corner of your desktop.

If you have the default Audio notification selected in your eBay Toolbar preferences, you hear a noise.

① Click the Bid Alert.

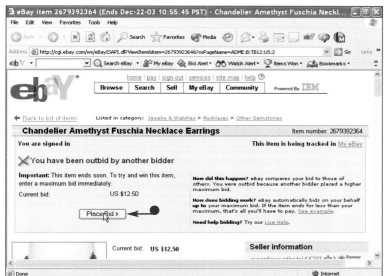

Your browser opens, and the item's auction page appears.

● eBay allows you to bid on the item before the auction ends.

More Options!

You can check the items on which you have bids at any time by using the Bid Alert menu. In the eBay Toolbar, click the Bid Alert icon (🔖). You can select an item from the menu to view the item's auction. eBay refreshes your Bid List when you bid on a new item. You refresh your bid list manually by clicking 🔖 and then clicking Refresh Bid List.

Did You Know?

You can receive watch alerts for your Watch List items. For information on how to watch an item, see Task #12. When an auction you are watching is about to end, eBay sends an audio notification, and an alert appears in the lower right corner of your desktop.

Shop for
LAST-MINUTE BARGAINS

You can take advantage of great deals by bidding on soon-to-end auctions with few or no bids. You can find a nice, low-price item that many eBay buyers overlook because of a poor title or misspelled name. For more on running a search for such items, see Task #9.

When you browse categories, you can sort the various auctions by their ending time to find appealing items with few or no bids. eBay displays auctions that close in the next five hours as going, going, gone. You can also sort listings by ending today, which shows you auctions with a closing date of today.

You can also apply these parameters with search results by simply checking the auctions that are ending first.

Although you can find some great bargains with the going, going, gone feature, items may have no bids for a good reason. For example, the item may have a flaw or be outdated. Always read the auction description carefully to make sure you do not bid on something you do not want.

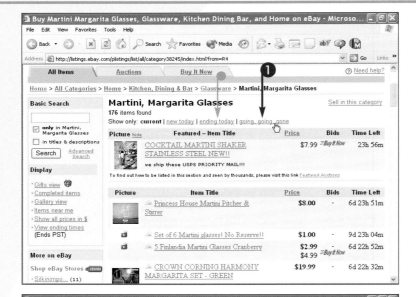

BROWSE FOR GOING, GOING, GOING ITEMS

1 In a browsing or searching list, click the going, going, gone link.

Note: For more on searching and browsing, see Chapter 1.

● You can click the ending today link for auctions that end today.

A list appears of auctions that end in the next five hours.

2 View the list of auctions for items you want to buy.

● The Price column enables you to quickly find items that have a low price.

● The Bids column allows you to see if any items have no bids or only a few bids.

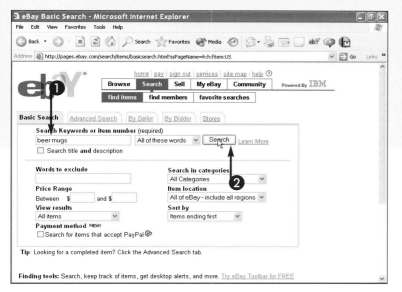

① In the eBay Basic Search tab, type your search word or phrase.

② Click Search.

DIFFICULTY LEVEL

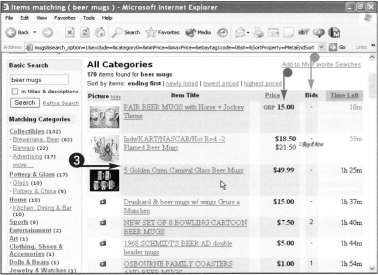

A list of auctions appears, sorted by the auctions ending first.

Note: This is the default sort setting for the search.

③ View the list of auctions for items you want to buy.

● The Price column enables you to quickly find items that have a low price.

● The Bids column allows you to see if any items have no bids or only a few bids.

More Options!

You can also sort items while browsing using the new today link, on the top of a browsing list, which shows listings that just started today. Sorting by new today is useful when you want to find good items that have just gone live, decreasing the possibility that other eBay buyers may view the same bargain.

eBay Savvy!

You can also check for items whose auctions are about to end and that have a Buy It Now icon (≡Buy It Now). When ≡Buy It Now appears next to an item that you want, you can buy it right away and not worry about losing the item to another bidder. For more information on using the Buy It Now feature, see Tasks #2, #9 and #46.

USING GALLERY VIEW
to quickly shop

Have you ever been in a situation where you need to find a gift quickly for that special someone? You can combine two options on eBay, the Gallery view and the Buy It Now features, to expedite your shopping.

The Gallery view option allows you to view the items in an eBay search or browse results list as neatly aligned rows of photos, and you can efficiently scan the pictures to see if there are any items you want.

When you combine the Gallery view option with the Buy It Now feature, you cannot only find what you want more quickly, but you can also purchase it right away.

To find Buy It Now items, you can use the Buy It Now option on the Advanced Search page, or the Buy It Now tab above a category name next to the All Items and Auctions tabs. The Buy It Now tab appears whether you are browsing or searching. For information about finding bargains with Buy It Now, see Tasks #2, #9 and #46.

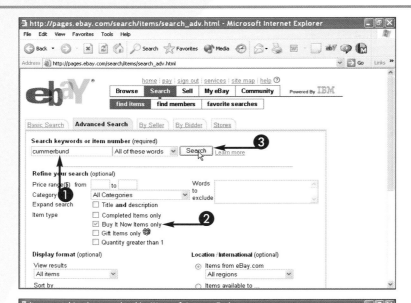

❶ In the eBay Advanced Search page, type your search word or phrase.

❷ Select the Buy It Now Items only option.

❸ Click Search.

The search results appear, with a list of Buy It Now items.

❹ Click the Gallery view link, located under the Display heading on the left side of the page.

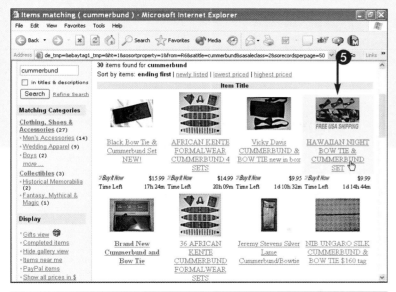

The items display in Gallery format, with the item photos horizontally aligned.

You can view the items more efficiently, expediting your shopping.

5 Click the item you want to view.

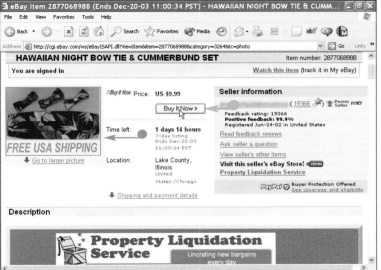

The details page appears for the listing.

● You can view a larger photo of the item.

● You can click Buy It Now and purchase the item right away.

TIPS

More Options!

Another way to quickly view photos of items is to use the timeBLASTER tool, which downloads photos of eBay items for offline viewing in a Photo Album format. For more information, see Task #10.

Did You Know?

Items can either have a Buy It Now price in addition to a starting bid price, or they can have only a Buy It Now price, with no option to bid — this is known as a *fixed-price listing*.

Did You Know?

The Buy It Now option disappears after a buyer places a bid, unless the auction has a reserve price, in which case the Buy It Now option remains until someone bids at or above the reserve price.

Buy multiple items to
SAVE ON SHIPPING

You can save money on shipping costs by buying several items from the same seller. It is usually cheaper to mail two items in one envelope or box than it is to ship two separately packaged items, so sellers usually offer to pass the savings to you.

Sellers try to get you to buy more from them by offering to combine shipping costs. If you need those other items anyway, it makes sense to buy them from the same seller and save money on postage.

For example, if you need both bubble wrap and padded mailers, and the seller offers both, it makes

sense to buy both at the same time and save money on shipping fees.

You can use the View seller's other items link under the Seller information heading to view the other items the seller offers.

You can also search using the words "combine shipping" with the titles and descriptions option selected, to find auctions where sellers offer savings on shipping.

For more information on using the title and description option, see Task #2.

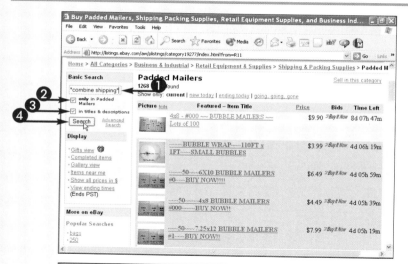

① After selecting an eBay category, type **"combine shipping"**.

② Click the only in *this category* option, where the category you selected replaces the words *this category*.

③ Click the in titles & descriptions option.

④ Click Search.

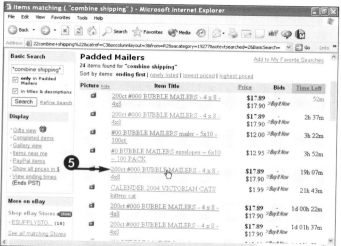

A list appears with items for which the sellers offer to combine shipping in their auction descriptions.

⑤ Click a listing.

A details page appears for the listing.

● Scroll down through the auction description to confirm that the seller will combine shipping.

● You can click the View seller's other items link under the Ask seller a question link to see if the seller offers other items you want to buy.

In this example, the seller allows you to buy multiple items to save money on shipping costs.

TIPS

eBay Savvy!

Look for opportunities to combine shipping even on items you do not buy regularly. Consider buying other, similar things you need from sellers you use regularly. If a seller does not specify whether they combine shipping, you can use the Ask seller a question link, covered in Task #13, to find out.

Did You Know?

When you buy multiple items regularly from a seller, you can add that seller as a Favorite Seller in your My eBay page to save on shipping. In the eBay home page, click My eBay, click the Favorites tab, and then click Add new seller/store. Type the seller's user ID in the appropriate box, and then click Save Favorite.

Factor in
HIDDEN COSTS

Although you can find many great deals on eBay, you should factor in hidden costs to determine if you really have a bargain. You can add up the less obvious fees associated with buying through an online auction, such as shipping, handling, and insurance.

On eBay, the buyer usually pays for the shipping costs. Some sellers also charge a handling fee, which is a value they place on their time to wrap, package, and send the item to you. Some sellers may offer insurance, although this is usually optional for buyers.

It is a good idea to read an item's description carefully to ensure that you understand all of the fees the seller charges. For example, if you win an auction for a pair of shoes for twelve dollars, shipping and handling fees may bring the total cost to acquire those shoes up to twenty dollars. If you can buy the same shoes at a store for eighteen dollars, you may be better off buying them at a store.

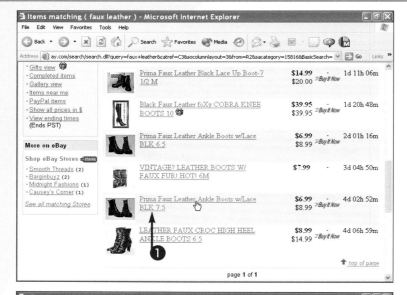

❶ In a browsing or searching list, click an item you want to buy.

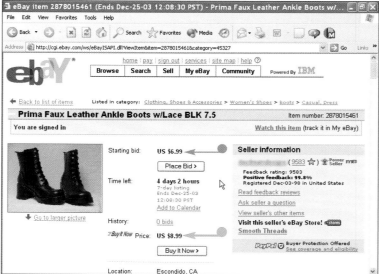

The details page appears for the listing.

● You can see the current bid price.

● You can also see the Buy It Now price, if applicable.

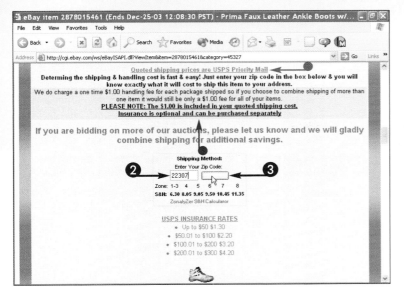

You can scroll down to view the shipping details.

- You can see if the seller charges a handling fee.

- You can see the seller's shipping method.

② Type your zip code in the option box of the shipping calculator.

Not all listings have a shipping calculator.

③ Click here.

- The shipping calculator displays your total shipping cost.

- If you want insurance, add that to the total cost of your purchase.

④ Add your bid price, the shipping costs, and handling and insurance, if applicable.

You can make an informed decision about the total cost of buying the item and having it shipped.

TIPS

eBay Savvy!

You can estimate shipping fees by using the United States Postal Service Web site, at www.usps.com, the Federal Express Web site at www.fedex.com; or the UPS Web site, at www.ups.com. To calculate these fees, you need your ZIP code and the seller's ZIP code, which is usually included in the end-of-auction e-mail. This is only an estimate, because sellers set the shipping fees, which they determine in different ways. For more information about shipping, see Chapter 9.

Buyer Beware!

Be sure to find out the shipping charges before you bid, as some sellers inflate their shipping charges. If the seller does not state the shipping charges in the listing, you can use the Ask seller a question feature, as discussed in Task #13.

Improve Your Bidding & Buying Strategies

Whether you intend to buy items at low cost through a Dutch Auction, or big-ticket items such as a house or car, the Advanced bidding strategies in this chapter show you how to soundly beat the competition.

Sniping techniques can mean the difference between winning and losing an auction. You can either snipe manually, or use a sniping service to snipe automatically. You can also take sniping to a new level by setting up bid groups that snipe similar types of items until you win. Another useful technique is to bid odd numbers to limit your chances of being outbid. You can also increase your chances of getting a low price by bidding on items in a Dutch Auction.

Not sure if a seller is offering you an item at a fair price? You have several options to research a particular item's price before bidding.

You can take advantage of the big-ticket items, such as cars and real estate, on eBay. eBay Motors offers an attractive alternative to the daunting negotiations that accompany buying a car at a dealership. You can use blue book pricing, to educate yourself about your car deal and to get a lower price. eBay Real Estate listings can help you find that dream home or timeshare vacation deal.

The eBay Giving Works charity section and the Live Auctions offer some of the most exciting auction items — including celebrity-signed merchandise and unique opportunities, such as a walk-on part on a television show — while allowing you to help a worthy cause.

Top 100

USING PROXY BIDDING
to your advantage

You can avoid paying too much for an item by simply taking advantage of the eBay default bidding system, known as proxy bidding.

With *proxy bidding*, you set a price that is the most you want to pay for an item. The eBay software places a bid that is only high enough to outbid the current bidder by the auction's bid increment, and no higher. If another bidder then outbids you, eBay places another bid that is only as high as it needs to be to outbid that bidder, given that your maximum

bid is high enough. eBay continues placing proxy bids until you are the high bidder or another bidder outbids your maximum bid.

eBay determines the bid increment by the current price of the auction. This means that you do not have to pay the most you may be willing to pay for an item, as long as another bidder does not bid as much as your maximum bid. For more information about advanced bidding strategies, see Tasks #23, #24, and #25.

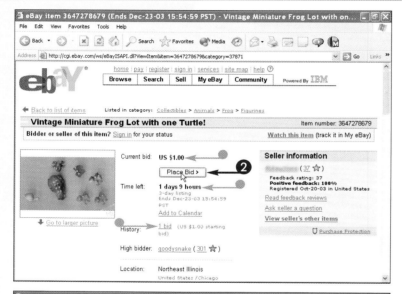

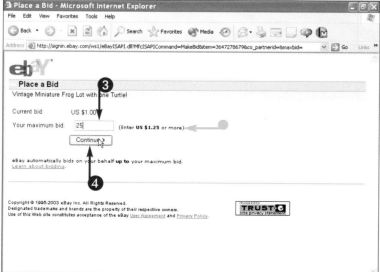

❶ Click on an item to view its details page.

Note: For more on accessing the details page for an item, see Tasks #1 and #2.

● You can view the Current bid price, the Time left in the auction, and the number of bids, if any.

❷ Click Place Bid.

The Place a Bid page appears.

eBay displays the Current bid.

● eBay displays the minimum amount you need to bid.

❸ Type the maximum amount you want to bid.

❹ Click Continue.

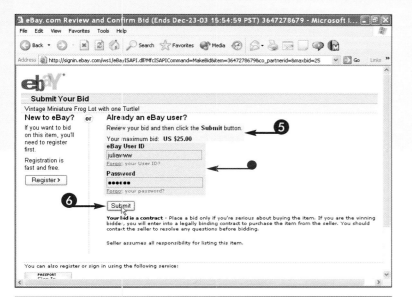

The Submit Your Bid page appears.

5 Review your bid to ensure that it is correct.

● If you are not signed in to eBay, eBay prompts you with a login.

6 Click Submit.

 # 22

DIFFICULTY LEVEL

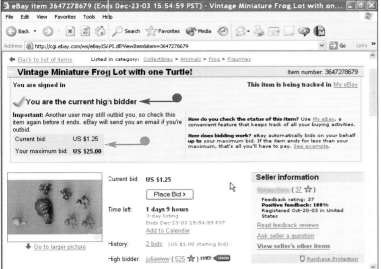

● eBay tells you if you are the current high bidder.

● eBay places a proxy bid that is just high enough to make you the high bidder.

TIPS

Did You Know?

eBay's bid increments vary, depending on the current price of an item. Here are the bid increments for various prices. If the winning bidder's maximum bid beats the second-highest maximum bid by an amount that is less than the full bid increment, you can be outbid by less than a full bid increment.

eBay Bid Increments	
Current Price	*Bid Increment*
$0.01 - $0.99	$0.05
$1.00 - $4.99	$0.25
$5.00 - $24.99	$0.50
$25.00 - $99.99	$1.00
$100.00 - $249.99	$2.50
$250.00 - $499.99	$5.00
$500.00 - $999.99	$10.00
$1,000.00 - $2,499.99	$25.00
$2,500.00 - $4,999.99	$50.00
$5,000.00 and up	$100.00

Snipe with
LAST-SECOND BIDDING

You can increase your chances of winning an item by bidding in the last seconds of the auction, a strategy known as sniping.

To snipe an item on eBay manually, you need to take note of the exact end time of the auction so that you can have your browser window open and ready to bid.

The speed of your Internet connection determines how many seconds before the end of an auction you need to place your bid in order to successfully snipe. Some bidders with fast connections wait until only

five seconds before the end of an auction to place a bid. Others prefer more time and may wait until 20 seconds or more remain.

One strategy, shown in this task, is to open two browser windows and place them side by side to keep track of the time. You need to refresh one of the windows regularly. Then with the other window, you can quickly place your bid.

You can also use sniping software to place a snipe automatically. For more information on sniping software, see Tasks #24 and #25.

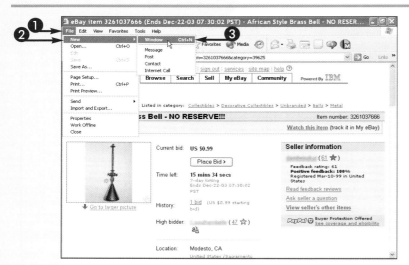

① In a details page that appears for the eBay listing that is about to end, click File.

② Click New.

③ Click Window.

You can also press Ctrl+N.

You may want to begin the sniping process at least a few minutes before the listing ends, to give yourself enough time to arrange the windows.

A second browser window appears.

④ Arrange the windows side by side by clicking and dragging the title bars, making sure you can see the Current bid, Time left, and the Place Bid button in each window.

● You can resize each window by dragging the bottom-right corner.

⑤ A minute or two before the auction ends, click Place Bid in one of the windows.

23

DIFFICULTY LEVEL

The Place a Bid page appears.

6 Type the maximum amount you want to bid.

7 Click Continue.

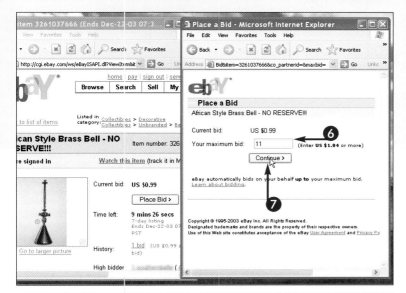

The Submit Your Bid page appears.

8 Click the Reload button to refresh the other browser window.

9 Repeat step **8** to continue refreshing the item details page so you can see how much time remains.

10 When you are ready to snipe, click Submit.

If your maximum bid is high enough, you win the auction.

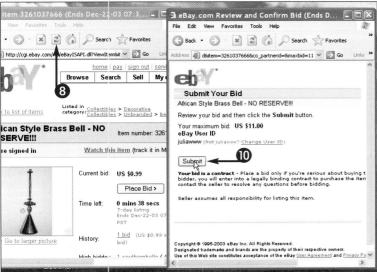

eBay Savvy!

To estimate the minimum time it takes your connection to snipe, refresh your browser and then note the Time left for the auction, which is in minutes and seconds. Refresh your browser again, and note the new Time left. The difference in seconds between the two numbers is the time it takes your connection to place a snipe.

Caution!

It is possible, although unlikely, that both you and another bidder may snipe the same auction. In that case, the winner is whoever places the highest maximum bid. It is also possible that the hidden maximum bid of an earlier bidder is higher than your maximum bid. If two snipers place the exact same bid, the winner is whoever places the bid first.

SNIPE
while you sleep

You can snipe an item automatically with sniping software, such as Auction Sniper, which does the waiting for you. This prevents human error and lets you do other things besides sitting by the computer.

To use Auction Sniper, you must first set up an account at www.auctionsniper.com/register.aspx. To place a snipe, all you need is the item number of the eBay auction you want to snipe, and the maximum you want to spend on that item. You can also enter a *lead time* — the amount of time before the auction

ends, in seconds, that you want AuctionSniper to place your bid.

One sniping strategy involves just placing a snipe with your sniping software, but not bidding on the item first; if you place a bid and then place a snipe, you just drive up the bid price by that much more.

Auction Sniper displays a message that you have won, and reflects this in the status. You can also receive an e-mail message informing you of your win, or see all your wins by clicking the Wins tab.

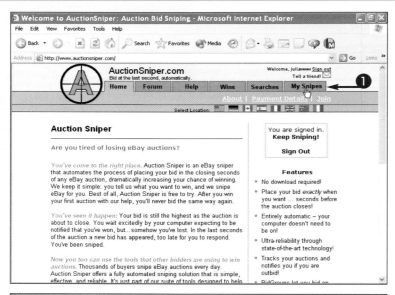

❶ In the Auction Sniper home page, click the My Snipes tab.

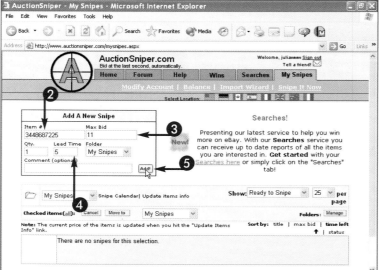

The My Snipes tab appears.

❷ Type the number of the eBay item you want to snipe.

❸ Type the maximum amount you want to bid.

❹ Type the lead time.

The default is 5 seconds.

❺ Click Add!

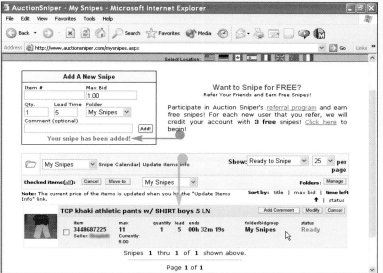

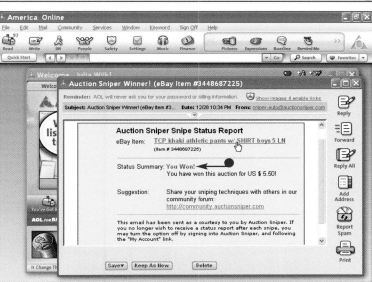

- Auction Sniper places your snipe and displays a message that confirms that your snipe has been added.

- Your snipe appears at the bottom of the page.

DIFFICULTY LEVEL

6 Launch your e-mail application and open the e-mail from Auction Sniper.

- Auction Sniper sends you an e-mail that tells you if you won the item.

Note: You may see a different screen, depending on your e-mail application.

To view your wins, you can also click the Wins tab, located at the Auction Sniper home page.

More Options!

You can use other sniping services, including Bidnapper, Bidsage, eSnipe, EZsniper, Hammersnipe, Justsnipe, Powersnipe, and Snipeville. For a comparison in table format of 11 different auction services, including their pricing, see Auctionsbytes at www.auctionbytes.com/cab/pages/sniping.

More Options!

You can keep track of your payments and feedback using the Auction Sniper Wins Tracker simply by signing in to Auction Sniper and clicking the Wins tab.

Did You Know?

Although Auction Sniper offers a free trial, once the trial is up, they do charge for this service. For more information on costs for the service, go to www.auctionsniper.com/payment.aspx. You pay only for auctions you win.

OUT-SNIPE SNIPERS
with advanced techniques

Rather than spend time sniping several auctions that you may lose, you can set up multiple bids at once. You can increase your odds of winning a certain type of item with Auction Sniper bid groups, which are specifically for several types of an item that is available simultaneously on eBay. This technique is not for a unique item. You use bid groups for items with a lot of competition, such as a popular laptop computer. Bid Groups are available as a feature from Auction Sniper's Web site at www.auctionsniper.com.

When numerous people bid on an item, they may try to snipe the item. Likewise, they may have a higher maximum bid set by eBay's proxy bidding system and unknown to you until the auction's end. For more on proxy bidding, see Task #22. For more on sniping techniques, see Tasks #23 and #24.

You can set up the software to bid until you win only one of that type of item, and then Auction Sniper cancels the other snipes so you do not buy items you do not want.

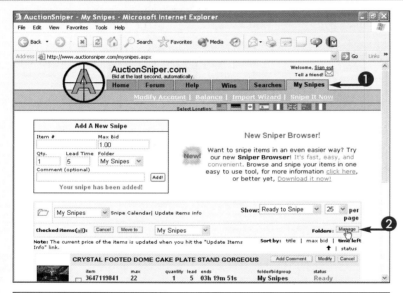

① In the Auction Sniper home page, click the My Snipes tab.

The My Snipes tab appears.

② Click Manage.

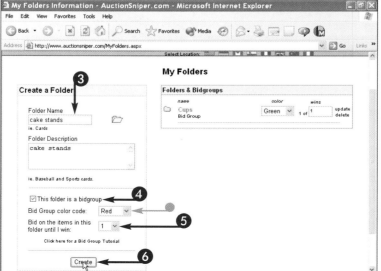

The My Folders page appears.

③ Type a folder name and description.

④ Click the This folder is a bidgroup option.

● To help distinguish your bid groups, you can color code them by clicking here and selecting a color.

⑤ Type the number of items you want to win in this bid group.

⑥ Click Create.

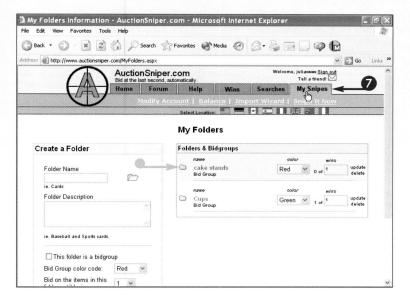

- Auction Sniper Bid Groups creates the folder.

7 Click the My Snipes tab.

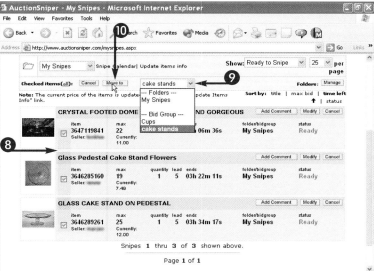

You can see the list of items you are sniping.

8 Select the items you want to move into the bid group folder.

9 Click here and select the bid group folder into which you want to move the items to snipe as a bid group.

10 Click Move to.

Auction Sniper moves your items into the bid group folder you specify and places snipes until you win an item.

TIPS

More Options!

You can toggle between the Auction Sniper and the eBay interface and easily place snipes with the click of a button by using Auction Sniper's browser. For more information see www.auctionsniper.com/sniperbrowser. aspx. Download the browser at www.auctionsniper.com/ download/AuctionSniper100.exe.

Did You Know?

Bid groups are also available via BidSlammer at www.bidslammer.com, and eSnipe, at www.esnipe.com. BidSlammer gives you three free snipes, after which you pay $0.25 for every item you win under $10.00, and 1 percent of the closing price for items over $10.00. eSnipe is free for 14 days, after which it costs $0.25 for items you won up to $24.99, 1 percent of the winning amount for items up to $1,000.00 — rounded down to the nearest penny — and a maximum of $10.00 thereafter. See www.bidslammer.com/help/?s=pricing for more information.

MAKE ODD NUMBERS
work for you

If you bid odd amounts, you can increase your chances of winning auctions. Many buyers bid in simple, round, whole-dollar amounts, without cents. Others try to outsmart the system by adding one penny to their bids. If you regularly bid odd numbers, such as $13.39 or $23.17, you increase your chances of outbidding others who bid amounts like $13.01 or $23.00.

Because other bidders' maximum bids are hidden until the auction closes, you must make educated guesses as to what they are bidding to try to outbid

them. For example, if the current bid of an item with one bid is $28.99, you may guess a bidder's obvious maximum bid, such as $30.00 or $30.01, and place a bid such as $31.05.

Of course, these strategies do not guarantee a win. If you prefer to keep your bid amount secret until the last few seconds of an auction, you can try sniping. For more information on sniping, see Tasks #23, #24, and #25.

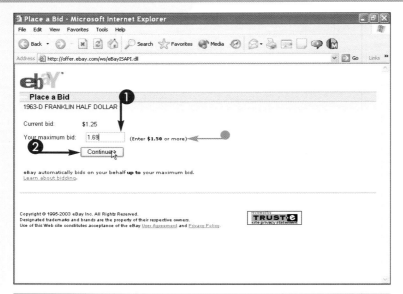

① In a Place a Bid screen for a listing, type an odd number of a maximum bid amount.

Note: See Task #4 to access this screen.

● eBay bases the minimum bid you must make on the current bid.

② Click Continue.

● eBay displays a message that you are the high bidder.

If no one outbids your odd number bid, you win the auction.

If you are outbid, you can place another odd number bid by following steps **1** and **2**.

CHECK PRICES
of common items

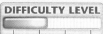

DIFFICULTY LEVEL

You can ensure you do not pay too much for an item on eBay by using a price comparison Web site such as Froogle.com. Froogle searches the Web to find products for sale online and presents you with the results in an easy-to-read format. You can go directly from Froogle's search results to a merchant's Web site to buy an item.

Froogle is owned by Internet search company Google, and uses Google's powerful search technology to find items from a wide range of online retailers.

You can find prices for items by browsing Froogle's search. You can also search within a certain category, or search the whole Froogle site.

When you check prices by combining both Froogle and eBay's Completed items options in the Advanced Search, you have a powerful tool for educating yourself about the best deals you can get for a given type of item.

For more information on using the Completed items option in eBay's Advanced Search, see Task #3.

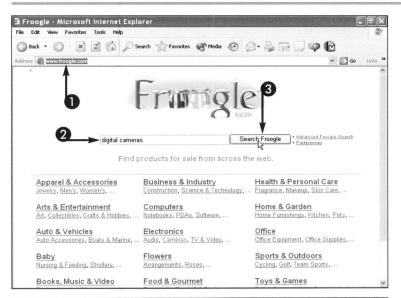

① Type **www.froogle.com** into the Address bar of your Web browser and press Enter.

The Froogle home page appears.

② Type your search phrase into the box.

③ Click Search Froogle.

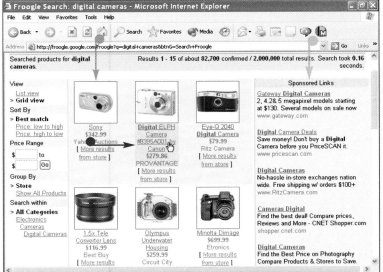

The search results appear.

● You can see photos and sale prices of items.

● The Sponsored Links on the right are ads.

● You can click an item link to go to the retailer's Web site and buy the item.

Get a low price with
DUTCH AUCTIONS

You can take advantage of the *Dutch Auction*, or *multiple item auction,* format to get a low price on an item because in a Dutch Auction, all winning bidders pay the same amount: the lowest successful bid. In a Dutch Auction, the seller offers multiple items that are identical. For example, if a seller has 100 party favors to sell, the seller may list a Dutch Auction of 10 lots of 10 party favors each. A Dutch Auction is a great way to buy things for which you need multiple quantities.

If you have more bids than available items in a Dutch Auction, bidders who offer the highest total bid price — which is the bid price times the number of items bid on — win the auction. Earlier successful bids beat later ones. However, you often find more available items than bids for a Dutch Auction, which means that all bidders pay the starting, and therefore the lower, price.

To identify a Dutch auction, you look for a number in the Quantity field in the item description that is 2 or greater.

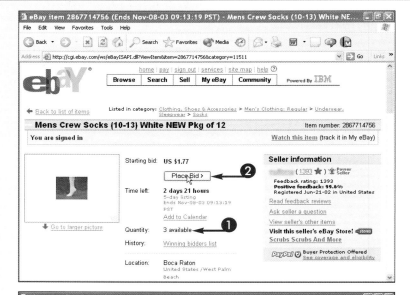

① In an eBay listing, look for a number of 2 or greater in the Quantity field, which indicates that this is a Dutch Auction.

You can use the Advanced Search tab's Quantity greater than 1 option to find Dutch Auction items.

Note: For more information about Advanced Search, see Task #2.

② Click Place Bid.

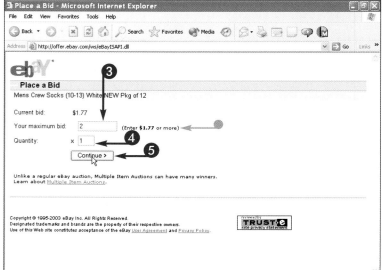

The Place a Bid page appears.

③ Type the maximum amount you want to bid.

• eBay displays the minimum bid you must make.

④ Type the quantity of items you want.

⑤ Click Continue.

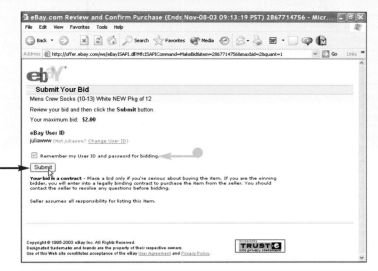

The Submit Your Bid page appears.

- You can click the Remember my User ID and password for bidding option if you intend to bid on other items before logging out of eBay.

6 Click Submit.

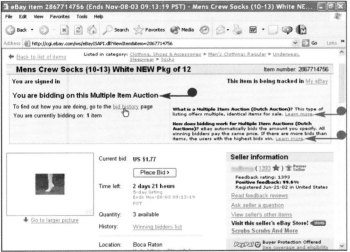

- eBay indicates that you are bidding on this Multiple Item Auction.

  In this example, you win the item for the minimum bid price as long as no more than two other bidders bid on this auction.

- You can click the Learn more links to find out more information about Dutch Auctions.

TIPS

Did You Know?

Besides Dutch Auctions, eBay offers other types of auction formats including regular auctions; reserve price auctions, where the seller designates a hidden minimum price; Buy It Now auctions; Ads, as in the Real Estate area; and Private Auctions, where bidders' user IDs do not display on the listing. For more on the various auction formats, go to pages.ebay.com/help/buy/formats-ov.html.

Did You Know?

If the seller offers you a partial quantity at the auction's end — or fewer items than the number on which you bid — you can refuse all of the items.

Did You Know?

You can see all the item's bids — including unsuccessful bids — at the end of the auction by clicking the Winning bidders list link in the item listing.

Buy a car with
EBAY MOTORS

You can get a great deal on a car and avoid the stressful negotiation process of traditional car dealerships by buying a car on eBay Motors.

You can buy a car either with the traditional auction format or the fixed-price Buy It Now format.

You should look carefully at the car's description, and assume the vehicle is being sold as is. Because of the higher dollar amount involved compared to most auctions, it is especially critical to check a seller's feedback. For more information on checking feedback, see Task #14.

You should consider using an escrow service, like the one at www.escrow.com, to protect yourself from fraud. But be aware there are fake escrow sites targeting online auto buyers.

If you bid on any automobiles over $15,000, you need to provide background and credit verification. This means you must have your credit card on file with eBay. eBay notifies you when you place a bid, so allow yourself extra time for credit verification if you bid near the end time of an auction.

❶ Type **www.ebaymotors.com** into the Address bar of your Web browser and press Enter.

The eBay Motors home page appears.

❷ Type the car you want, surrounding your entry with quotation marks.

❸ Click Search

● You can also browse the Categories.

The search results appear.

❹ Click a listing.

Note: For more on searching and accessing listings, see Task #1 and #2.

● In the listing of a vehicle you want, you can click the Read feedback reviews link to check the seller's reputation.

● eBay displays the Current bid, which is where your bidding must start.

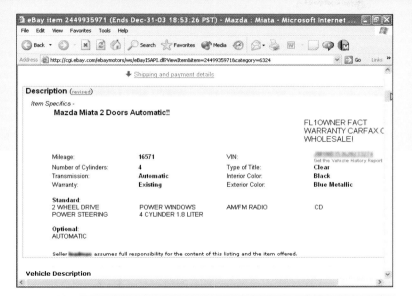

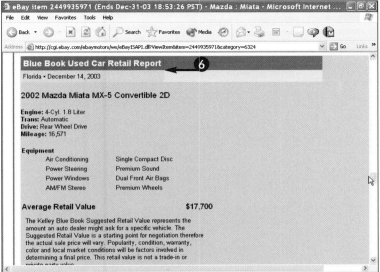

5 Scroll down to see a description of the vehicle.

The seller should include information such as the transmission type and mileage, as well as vehicle options.

Make sure you read the entire description to find out if the car has ever been in an accident or had body work done.

6 Scroll down to see if the seller included a report from the Kelley Blue Book.

You can go to www.kbb.com and verify the report yourself.

TIPS

eBay Savvy!

If you are unable to pick up the vehicle, you can use a delivery service, such as Dependable Auto Shippers, or DAS. DAS offers free shipping quotes at pages.ebay.com/ebaymotors/services/das-shipping.html.

eBay Savvy!

You can obtain a vehicle history report on any used car to find out information such as the accident history, or if the car has been in a flood. To obtain a report, click the VIN link on the vehicle description page. For eBay Motors users, a single Vehicle History Report costs $4.99, or you can receive ten reports for $9.99. You can view a sample vehicle history report at pages.ebay.com/ebaymotors/services/vehicle_history_report.html.

Find
REAL ESTATE BARGAINS

You can shop for a property anywhere in the world with eBay Real Estate. If you do your research and understand the listing details, you may find a good deal.

Different from the rest of the site, many eBay Real Estate listings are in an Ad format. With the Ad format, you provide your name, contact information, and any questions through the listing's Contact the Seller form to inform the seller of your interest.

In addition to residential homes, the other types of property for sale on eBay include land parcels and commercial real estate. You can also find timeshares and vacation rentals.

You can narrow your search by state or province, and by sale type, such as a foreclosed home or a new home. You can also select a number of bedrooms or bathrooms, and a price range.

Please note that eBay strongly recommends that you seek your attorney's advice before entering into any binding real estate transaction. For more information, see eBay's disclaimer page: pages.ebay.com/help/community/re_agreement.html.

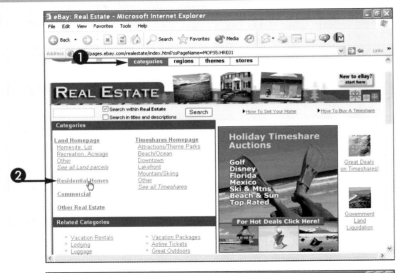

① Open the eBay Real Estate page by clicking the Real Estate link under Categories in the eBay home page.

② Click the Residential Homes subcategory link.

eBay also lists other types of real estate, including Timeshares, Land, and Commercial real estate.

The Residential Real Estate listings appear.

③ Click a listing that interests you.

This icon (▥) shows that this listing is an ad, not an auction.

● You can select a City, State, number of rooms, and Sale Type; type a price range and click Find to narrow your search.

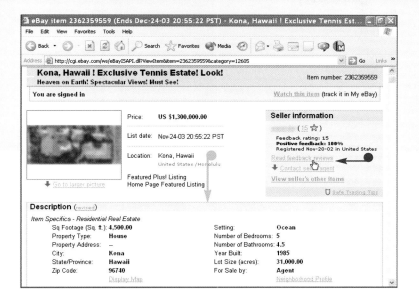

The details page appears for the listing.

● You can view the property description.

● You can click this link to read the seller's feedback reviews.

DIFFICULTY LEVEL

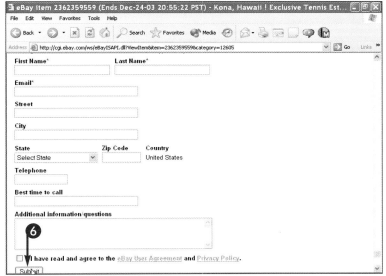

④ Scroll down to the Ready to contact seller/agent? section.

⑤ Type your personal information.

⑥ Click Submit.

eBay transmits your interest to the owner of the property.

Did You Know?

eBay also displays Real Estate listings in an Auction format, in which you click Place Bid to bid. A listing is in Auction format if it shows a number of bids in the Bids column — instead of the Ad icon — in the search or browse results list.

eBay Real Estate Auctions offer non-binding or binding bids. A note at the bottom of the listing tells you if the auction is binding or non-binding. With *non-binding auctions*, you can view properties in the familiar, auction-style format without committing to the seller to complete the transaction. *Binding auctions* are more likely to result in a sale, because the buyer is expected to complete the purchase in good faith.

Support a
GOOD CAUSE

You can buy items on eBay and support a charity of your choice at the same time by shopping at Giving Works, eBay's charity section. Giving Works offers many wonderful items, as well as services, and even some unique experiences, such as being *Redbook* magazine editor for a day, or attending *Entertainment Weekly's* Oscar Viewing Party.

You can also find many items signed by celebrities, such as a guitar signed by Nickelback and a signed CD from Clay Aiken.

You can search the eBay Giving Works section for items at www.pages.ebay.com/givingworks. You can also search for items benefiting a specific nonprofit organization by name, keyword, mission area, and geography, or browse the categories from that page.

You can bid on eBay Giving Works items the same way you bid on any other eBay items. Just find an item you like, sign in with your eBay account, and place a bid.

In the item description, you can see the percentage of the item's final price that the seller donates to the benefiting nonprofit organization.

① In the eBay home page, click the Charity link.

The eBay Giving Works page appears.

eBay displays a list of nonprofit organizations and charity auctions.

② Click the charity icon of your choice.

The charity listing page appears.

You can read the description of the charity and whom it helps.

You can read about the donated items.

DIFFICULTY LEVEL

③ Scroll down to see the actual item listings.

● You can click a listing that interests you and bid on it, thus donating money to the charity.

Item	Start	End	Price	Title	High Bidder/Status
3439206369	Nov-03-03	Nov-13-03 13:05:19	$600.00	The Ultimate Winter Tote by Hogan	☆
2962363381	Nov-03-03	Nov-13-03 13:10:22	$435.00	Allure Best of Beauty Basket	
2201160496	Nov-03-03	Nov-13-03 14:27:54	$192.50	Float Away Spa Package at the Away Spa & Gym	
2962380945	Nov-03-03	Nov-13-03 14:30:54	$75.00	Jean Paul Gaultier Luxury Basket	
2201166305	Nov-03-03	Nov-13-03 15:03:28	$510.00	Weekend at the Mayflower Inn, Washington, CT	
2962387161	Nov-03-03	Nov-13-03 15:04:05	$200.00	Rembrandt Teeth Whitening Session	
2201167309	Nov-03-03	Nov-13-03 15:08:07	$202.50	Gourmet Chocolate Tasting Party for 20	
2201167375	Nov-03-03	Nov-13-03 15:08:28	$355.00	A Night at The Peninsula Hotel in New York	
2962390233	Nov-03-03	Nov-13-03 15:19:15	$172.50	Bobbi Brown Cosmetics Basket	
2201169868	Nov-03-03	Nov-13-03 15:20:23	$250.00	Hair Makeover by Celebrity Stylist Ken Paves	☆

eBay Savvy!

As an eBay seller, you can donate your auction's proceeds to a designated charity. eBay works with MissionFish, a third-party nonprofit organization, to facilitate transactions between charities and sellers. To list an eBay Giving Works item, you must first register with MissionFish and list your items using the MissionFish Giving Assistant. After an auction ends, MissionFish forwards the funds to the designated nonprofit organization. To register with MissionFish, go to www.missionfish.org and click the Register to sell or Register to benefit link.

Did You Know?

If you pay over fair market value for an item from a nonprofit organization, the amount you overpaid may be tax-deductible. However, fair market value or below is not tax-deductible. Consult your accountant or tax advisor for specific advice.

Join the elite fray of
LIVE AUCTION BIDDING

You can bid in real-time auctions taking place in some of the world's most elite auction houses with eBay's Live Auctions.

In addition to offering exquisite and unique merchandise, Live Auction places you in contact with sellers who are highly reputable and experienced, so you can minimize your chances of having a bad transaction.

Before bidding in a live auction, you can prepare yourself by browsing live auctions either by the auction catalog or by categories. The catalog features all the lots available in a particular live auction.

You can search both live auction lots and categories at www.pages.liveauctions.ebay.com/search/items/search.html. Categories include Asian Arts, Books and Manuscripts, Furniture and Decorative Arts, Fine Arts, and Jewelry and Timepieces.

To participate in a live auction, you must first register, which you can do in the Browse tab at the top of any eBay Live Auctions page. Once you register, you can place absentee bids, or you can go to the live auction.

The Live Auction sellers each have their own terms and conditions of sale for each event, which usually include a satisfaction and authenticity guarantee.

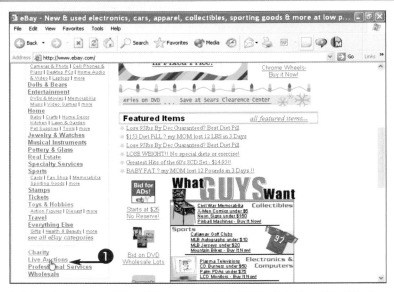

❶ In the eBay home page, click the Live Auctions link under Categories.

The Live Auctions page appears.

❷ Scroll down to the Special Events and Upcoming Auctions sections.

❸ Click View Live.

● You can also sign up for an upcoming auction by clicking Sign Up for this auction.

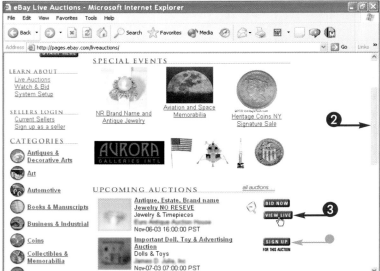

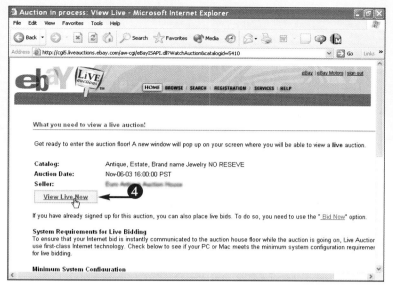

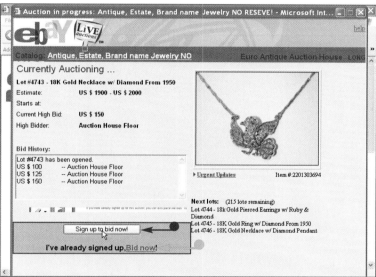

The What you need to view a live auction! page appears.

eBay displays the catalog and seller name.

④ Click the View Live Now link.

The Live Auction page appears with bids showing in real time.

● If you have signed up to bid, you can click the Bid now! link to place a bid.

● If you have not signed up to bid, you can click Sign up to bid now!.

Did You Know?

When you sign up to bid in a live auction, eBay displays the seller's terms and conditions of sale. For example, the buyer may need to contact the seller within a certain number of business days, or the seller may have a disclaimer about the auction items, such as that items are all sold as is. You must click the option (☐ changes to ☑) to indicate that you have read and accept the terms and conditions of sale. You can also check an option (☐ changes to ☑) to have eBay send you a reminder email about the auction. Click Continue. eBay then informs you that you have successfully signed up to participate in the upcoming live auction, and displays the catalog name, auction dates, and seller name.

Chapter 4

Paying For Items Painlessly

You can save time and please both buyers and sellers on eBay by using the right payment services. The tasks in this chapter show several available payment options and the advantages of each.

You should familiarize yourself with the wide range of payment options that you can use, from money orders to eBay's integrated payment service, PayPal. Many eBay buyers and sellers prefer PayPal for its ease of use and because it allows sellers to accept credit card payments, as well as transfer funds into and out of a designated bank account.

You can also earn discounts and even get eBay items for free by earning Anything Points, a promotional currency that works with eBay and PayPal.

In some cases you may need to use alternate payment services. For example, if a seller only accepts money orders, you can save time by ordering a money order online with the Auction Payments service. For items priced over $500, where you have a much higher risk, you can use an escrow service.

Although most transactions on eBay go smoothly, you need to know what to do when you encounter a problem. For example, you should follow the recommended procedures if you receive a misrepresented item. The SquareTrade service offers a valuable, impartial way to work out a positive solution to a variety of transaction problems when the recommended procedures fail.

You can build your own feedback rating so both sellers and buyers implicitly trust you.

Top 100

Find the right
PAYMENT OPTIONS

The payment options available for an item vary from seller to seller. You should know all these options so you can make a timely payment with as few problems as possible. Ideally, you should check the seller's payment instructions, which are usually in the Shipping and payment details section of the auction listing, before you place a bid. Consequently, if you win the item, you do not have to pay for the item with a payment method you do not prefer. To find what type of payments the seller accepts, you view the shipping and payment section of the auction listing, which you can access following the steps in Task #1.

Although sellers usually state their payment instructions in detail, if they do not, you can use the Ask seller a question link in the auction listing for more information. For more information about the Ask seller a question link, see Task #13.

Western Union Auction Payments

Some sellers may only accept money orders or cashier's checks, in which case you may want to consider the Western Union Auction Payments, an online money order service formerly BidPay at www.auctionpayments.com. The service starts at $1.95 for transactions up to $10.00 and under. For more information about Western Union Auction Payments, see Task #37.

Checkfree

An alternative to Paypal, Checkfree is located at checkfree.com, and is free to buyers, although the seller pays 1.85 percent plus $0.30 per transaction. Sellers may prefer Checkfree to PayPal because the fees are lower. The only drawback is that both buyers and sellers must have an account to use the service. To open an account, go to www.checkfree, and specify your financial institution. Select it by specifying a state in the appropriate option box.

Payingfast

You may want to use Payingfast to buy a money order for an item that cost $10 or less, because Payingfast's fee is lower than Western Union Auction Payments for such items. You find this service at payingfast.com. It starts at $1.75 for transactions up to $10.00. To use Payingfast, go to www.payingfast and follow the instructions.

Joseph McDonald
322 South St.
Berkley, IN 46576

313

Pay to the
Order of   eBay merchant $ 76.85

Seventy-six dollars and   85/100   Dollars

Small Town Bank
Small Town Bank of Ohio
Berkley, Ohio

For nehru jacket   Joseph McDonald

1080433367 833089361 8974

Paypal

Many sellers and buyers prefer PayPal, because it is integrated into the eBay Web site, and allows buyers to make payments quickly and easily. With PayPal, you can send cash to anyone who has an e-mail address. Buyers can pay by simply clicking on a PayPal link in the email they receive at an auction's end. Personal PayPal accounts are free, but Business and Premier accounts pay either a Standard rate of 2.9 percent of the transaction amount + $.30, or a Merchant rate of 2.2 percent of the transaction amount + $.30. For more information about PayPal, see Tasks #34 to #36.

Personal Check

You can pay with a personal check, but some sellers may require you to have a good feedback rating to do this. For more on feedback ratings, see Task #14. If you do pay with a personal check, remember that it may take longer to receive your item because it takes time for the check to arrive at the seller's by U.S. mail, and because sellers sometimes hold personal checks until they clear. Read the seller's payment instructions in the auction listing carefully to find out their policy on personal checks and to whom you should make the check out.

Other Payment Services

You can view a complete chart of the payment services, how they work, and their fees, on the AuctionBytes Web site at www.auctionbytes.com/cab/pages/payment.

Set up a
PAYPAL ACCOUNT

You can make it easier for yourself and your customers to pay for items on eBay by having a PayPal account. PayPal allows buyers to make online payments from their designated bank account or a credit card. PayPal is owned by eBay and is seamlessly integrated into the Web site as a payment option.

With a PayPal Premier or business account, you can accept credit card payments without paying the high overhead of a credit card merchant account. You can set up a PayPal account by going to their Web site at www.paypal.com and following the relatively simple steps to sign up for the account.

Once you have a PayPal account, you can pay for many auction items right away by simply using the Pay Now or PayPal link in the auction listing.

Not all sellers on eBay accept PayPal, so you may need to pay by personal check or money order. However, many sellers realize the value in accepting eBay buyers' favorite payment method. For more information on PayPal, see Tasks #35 and #36. For more on the various payment options, see Task #33.

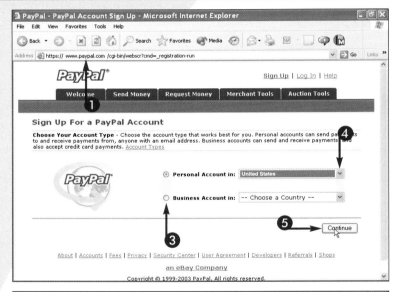

① Type **www.paypal.com** into your Web browser address bar, and press Enter.

② In the PayPal home pages, click the Sign Up link.

③ Click to select an account option.

④ Click here and select the country.

⑤ Click Continue.

The Account Sign Up page appears.

⑥ Type your name, address, and phone number.

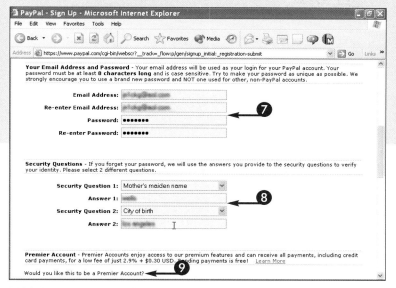

7 Type your e-mail address and password.

8 Select a security question and type an answer.

9 Select an account option.

10 Click Yes in the PayPal's User Agreement section.

Note: *You may need to scroll down to see this button.*

11 Click Sign Up at the bottom of the page.

A page appears, asking you to confirm your e-mail address.

12 To confirm your e-mail address now, follow the steps on the screen.

You can confirm your e-mail address at a later time, if you prefer.

13 Click Continue.

PayPal creates your account.

TIPS

Did You Know?

Personal accounts are free, but your buyers cannot pay with a credit card. However, personal accounts can use PayPal's Winning Buyer Notification feature, which automatically sends payment requests to your auction winner. PayPal business and Premier accounts accept credit card payments, but they cost 2.9 percent plus $0.30 per transaction to receive funds. If you qualify, you may receive a reduced Merchant Rate of 2.2 percent plus $0.30 per transaction.

eBay Savvy!

Premier PayPal accounts have access to PayPal's premium features, such as the ability to receive credit card payments. The cost is 2.9 percent plus $0.30. Sending payments is free. Sign in to PayPal and click the Profile tab on PayPal's main screen to upgrade from a Personal to a Premier account.

Add
PAYPAL FUNDS

You can transfer money to your PayPal account from your bank account. You can also accept payments from other PayPal users to your PayPal account. To transfer funds to your PayPal account, you must first add your account to PayPal and then verify your bank account. Electronically transferred funds become available in your PayPal account within three to four business days. PayPal sends you an e-mail confirming when you add funds to your account, as well as when eBay buyers pay you with PayPal for items they purchase from you.

If you receive an e-mail notification that a payment has been made to your PayPal account but the transaction does not appear on your History page, the sender may have typed an incorrect e-mail address. You should contact the sender and confirm that they have sent the payment to the correct address.

You should check your PayPal balance periodically to ensure that you have adequate funds to cover any eBay purchases. For more information on PayPal, see Tasks #34 and #36.

① Type **www.paypal.com** into your Web browser address bar, and then press Enter.

Note: You need to login to the PayPal site, if you have not already done so.

② In the main PayPal page, click the Add Funds tab.

The Add Funds tab appears.

③ Click the Transfer Funds from a Bank Account link.

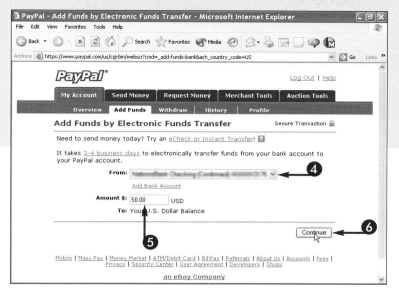

The Add Funds by Electronic Funds Transfer tab appears.

Note: *A form may appear to link your account to PayPal. Fill in the form and click Add Bank Account.*

# 35

DIFFICULTY LEVEL

④ Click here and select your bank account.

⑤ Type the amount you want to transfer.

⑥ Click Continue.

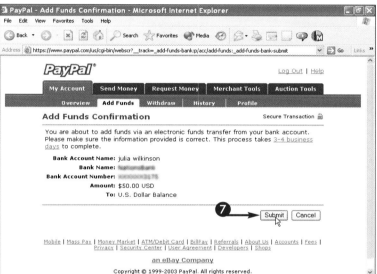

The Add Funds Confirmation tab appears.

Verify that the information is correct.

⑦ Click Submit.

PayPal adds funds to your account.

Did You Know?

After you sign up for PayPal you need to add and then confirm your bank account. You also need to confirm your e-mail address. To add your bank account, click the My Account tab and then click the Add Checking Account link. Fill out the Add Bank Account form and click Add Bank Account. PayPal e-mails you instructions on how to confirm your e-mail address and bank account. To confirm your e-mail address, simply launch your e-mail application, open PayPal's e-mail, and click the link. Type your PayPal password. To confirm your bank account, PayPal makes two small deposits into it and then asks you to confirm them by checking your bank balance after two to three days.

WITHDRAW FUNDS
from PayPal

You can use your PayPal funds in many different ways. For example, you can transfer the money you make from selling items on eBay into your bank account. PayPal does not charge for transferring funds into your bank account. You can also leave the funds in your PayPal account and use them to buy items on eBay.

Be aware that transfers from PayPal to your account are not instantaneous and that you may have a delay between the time you transfer funds and the time that they appear in your account. Although PayPal

shows the transaction as complete, your bank may not recognize the transfer, and as a result may not reflect the transfer. PayPal cannot verify when funds transfer to your bank account. If your transfer request has a problem, your bank may take up to one week to notify PayPal. PayPal e-mails you if they learn of any problems.

You cannot cancel a withdrawal from your PayPal account, so be very sure you want to withdraw the funds before doing so. For more information about PayPal, see Tasks #34 and #35.

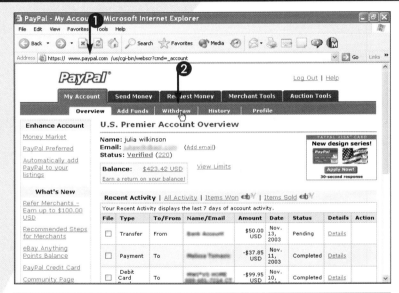

① Type **www.paypal.com** into your Web browser address bar, and then press Enter.

   Note: *You need to login to the PayPal site, if you have not already done so.*

② In the main PayPal page, click the Withdraw tab.

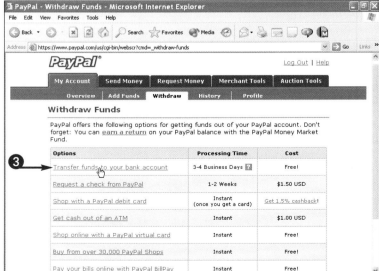

eBay displays your withdrawal options.

The processing time and cost appear for each option.

③ Click the Transfer funds to your bank account link.

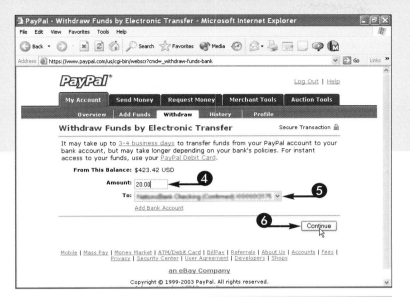

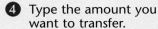

The Withdraw Funds by Electronic Transfer page appears and PayPal tells you it may take three to four business days to transfer funds.

④ Type the amount you want to transfer.

⑤ Click here and select the bank account you want to use.

⑥ Click Continue.

If you only have one bank account linked, your account name and number appears in the To: box.

Note: *If you have not yet linked your bank account to PayPal, you need to do so. See Task #35 for more information.*

The Withdraw Funds Confirmation page appears.

⑦ Verify that the information is correct.

⑧ Click Submit.

PayPal processes your transfer request.

More Options!
You can also request a check from PayPal, which takes one to two weeks and costs $1.50. Another option is to use a debit card, which allows you to receive 1.5 percent cash back on your purchases. To request the card, click the link on the bottom of any PayPal page.

eBay Savvy!
You can use your PayPal funds to purchase items from over 30,000 PayPal shops, through an online directory of businesses that accept PayPal. To access PayPal shops, click the Shops link on the lower right-hand corner of any PayPal page. You can also pay your bills online with PayPal BillPay. To use BillPay, click the BillPay link that appears on the bottom of any PayPal page once you log in.

Save time with
AUCTION PAYMENTS

You can avoid long, tedious waits at the bank or Post Office to purchase a money order by using Auction Payments, a Western Union service, to purchase them online with a credit, debit, or charge card. You can then purchase online auction items with the money orders. You access Auction Payments, which was formally BidPay, at www.auctionpayments.com. This service is especially useful if you win an auction for which the seller only accepts money orders instead of PayPal or personal checks. Auction Payments also allows both you and the seller to track the money order online.

You receive confirmations by e-mail when the money order ships. You also may receive your item more quickly when you use Auction Payments, because many sellers ship items as soon as they receive e-mail confirmation that Auction Payments has sent your money order.

Auction Payments bases the cost of the service on the amount of the money order, with fees starting at $1.95 for a money order of up to $10.00. Auction Payments limits money orders to $700 per item purchased.

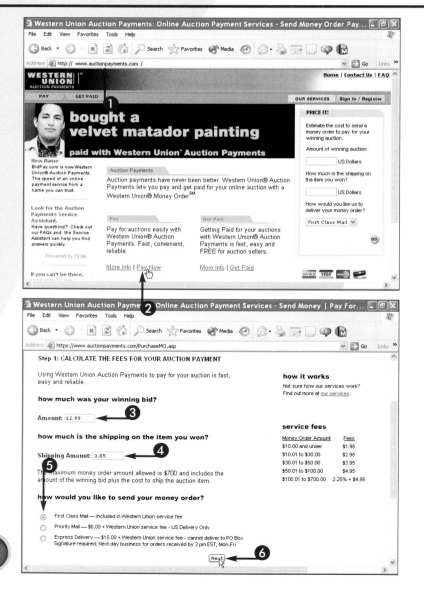

PAY FOR AN ITEM WITH BIDPAY

1 Type **www.auctionpayments. com** into your Web browser address bar, and then press Enter.

The Auction Payments home page appears.

2 Click the Pay Now link.

Auction Payments displays a page that calculates fees.

You may need to scroll down the page to complete the form.

3 Type the amount you bid.

4 Type the shipping for the item.

5 Click a shipping option for the money order.

6 Click Next.

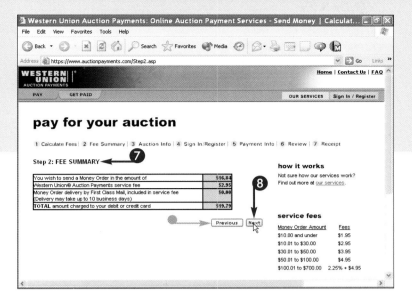

Auction Payments displays a summary of your fees.

⑦ Review the Fee Summary information for accuracy.

● You can click Previous and edit the amounts you have typed.

DIFFICULTY LEVEL

⑧ Click Next.

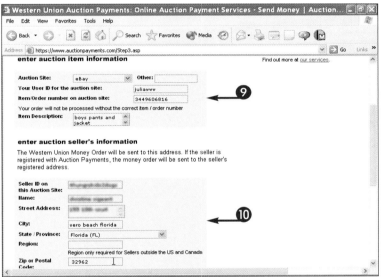

Scroll the page to enter auction item and seller information displays.

⑨ Type the Item information, including the auction site, your user ID, the item number, and item description.

⑩ Type the seller's information.

⑪ Click Next at the bottom of the page.

Auction Payments prompts you for your billing information and confirms your order.

TIPS

eBay Savvy!
You can check the status of your orders online. Click the Buyer Login link, and type your e-mail address and password. You can then modify your information, see the history and status of your orders, or place new orders.

Did You Know?
You need to include the seller's shipping fee and other fees in the principal amount of the money order. The principal is labeled Amount in US$ on the purchase money order form in the Pay for Your Auction page. Remember that the delivery charge on the form in the Pay for Your Auction page is for the shipment of the money order to the seller, and not for the shipment of the item you purchase from the seller.

Get discounts with
ANYTHING POINTS

You can pay for eBay items and seller fees with eBay Anything Points when you use PayPal. eBay Anything Points are promotional currency that you can earn from designated eBay partners, such as Hilton, Netflix, and *The New York Times*. You can also earn points with the eBay Anything Points credit card, which you can sign up for at anythingpoints.ebay.com. Also, sellers can offer Anything Points to buyers who use PayPal to purchase items from them.

One eBay Anything Point equals $0.01 toward the payment of an eBay item, providing the seller accepts PayPal as a payment method. Anything Points apply only to the final price of an eBay item, and not to shipping, sales tax, or insurance fees.

If you do not have enough Anything Points to purchase an item, you can spend the points you have, and pay the remaining portion using PayPal.

To use Anything Points, you need to first sign up for the program at anythingpoints.ebay.com. At this site, you can also view or spend your points, or get a complete list of the details for Anything Points.

EARN ANYTHING POINTS

① Type **anythingpoints.ebay.com/getpoints.html** into your Web browser address bar, and press Enter.

A list of eBay partners appears.

Note: *To earn Anything Points, you must first sign up for the program at anythingpoints.ebay.com.*

② Click the logo of the eBay partner whose points you want to earn.

The partner's Web page appears.

A list of products and services appears, along with details of the offer.

③ Click the ORDER NOW link to buy an item.

eBay guides you through the checkout process.

eBay awards you the designated number of Anything Points.

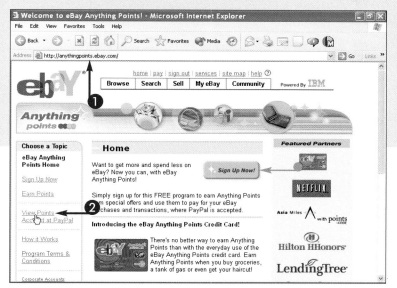

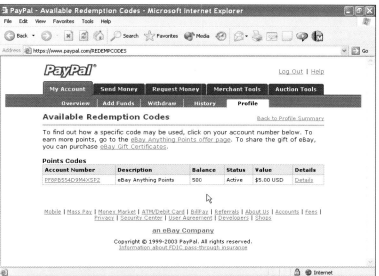

① Type **anythingpoints. ebay.com/getpoints. html** into your Web browser address bar, and then press Enter.

● You can sign up for Anything Points by clicking the Sign Up Now link or button.

② Click the View Points Account at PayPal link.

DIFFICULTY LEVEL

Note: If you have not already logged into PayPal, a prompt appears asking you to do so.

The PayPal Available Redemption Codes page appears.

PayPal displays your Anything Points balance.

TIPS

Apply it!

To pay for an eBay item using your Anything Points, click Pay Now on the eBay won item page, and then click the PayPal option. Click Continue, and follow the PayPal login process. On the Confirm Your Payment page, click Add/Select in the Redemption Code (Optional) section, which allows you to designate that the payment uses your Anything Points.

Did You Know?

To pay your eBay seller fees with Anything Points, click the My eBay tab, and then click Accounts. Type the amount in the PayPal payment text box and click Pay. Click the Redemption Code link, and your Anything Points balance appears. Select the option to use your Anything Points for the payment and click Continue.

USING ESCROW
to buy your item

You can protect yourself from seller fraud and ensure the quality of your purchase using an escrow service. An *escrow service* is a company that both buyer and seller trust to hold the buyer's payment until the buyer receives, inspects, and approves the item.

Both buyer and seller must agree to use escrow before the auction ends. You can check the seller's payment terms in the listing to see if they accept escrow. If you have any doubt, use the Ask seller a question link, discussed in Task #13, to ask if they accept escrow.

Although you can use escrow for any type of item once the seller agrees, you generally use escrow for items worth $500 or more because of the level of risk involved and because the escrow service generally charges you for using the service.

Make sure you research the escrow company you use. There have been cases of fraudulent Web sites made to look like real escrow services. eBay recommends that U.S. and Canadian users use escrow.com and recommends other escrow sites for users in other countries.

1 Click the services link at the top of any eBay page.

The eBay Services page appears.

2 Click the Escrow Services link under Payment.

The eBay Escrow Services page appears.

● You can click the Fees link to calculate your fees for using the service.

3 Click Start New Transaction.

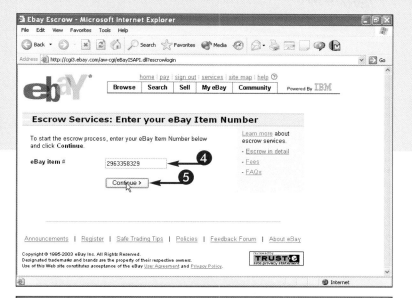

The Escrow Services: Enter your eBay Item Number page appears.

④ Type your eBay item number.

⑤ Click Continue.

 # 39

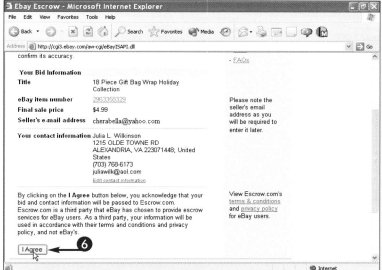

Your bid and contact information appear.

⑥ Click I Agree.

escrow.com initiates the escrow process.

TIPS

Apply It!

To calculate your escrow fee, go to pages.ebay.com/ help/community/escrow.html, and click the Fees link. In the Rates for eBay Customers page that appears, type the transaction value, indicate your method of payment, and then click Calculate Your Fee. Your escrow fee appears for this transaction. Fees for escrow vary, depending on the price of the item. For example, the escrow fee for a $500 item using a credit card is $37.

Did You Know?

Both seller and buyer must agree to the inspection period and the length of time the buyer has to examine the item, which can be from 1 to 30 days. If the buyer rejects the item, the seller has five days to examine the merchandise after the buyer returns it.

Troubleshoot
AFTER-SALE PROBLEMS

Although most transactions on eBay go smoothly, some unfortunately do have problems. To protect your important feedback rating, you need to handle problems carefully by following eBay's procedures.

Many sellers send a confirmation e-mail right away, including shipping fees, if necessary. If they do not, you can request the total amount using the Ask seller a question link in the item's listing page.

If the seller does not contact you within three days, as stipulated in eBay's Item Won e-mail, you can use eBay's Request a member's contact info form to get

the seller's phone number. For information about how to contact a seller, see Task #13.

If you get into a disagreement, you can try to resolve the problem with the SquareTrade service. For more information about SquareTrade, see Task #41.

If your attempts to resolve a problem do not work, you can file a fraud alert between 30 and 60 days after the auction ends. eBay then gives you instructions as to how file a protection claim, which you must file within 90 days after the auction ends.

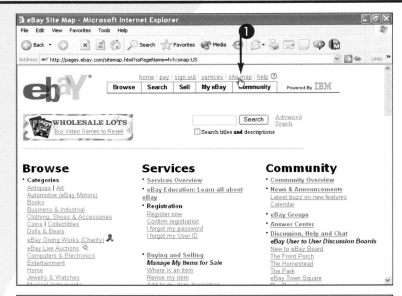

① In the eBay home page, click the site map link at the top of the page.

The site map page appears.

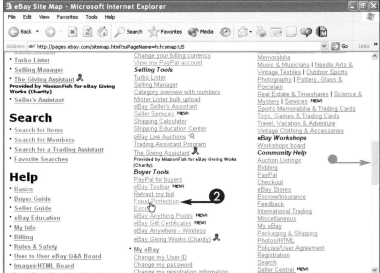

● You can scroll to the Buyer Tools section.

② Click the Fraud Protection link.

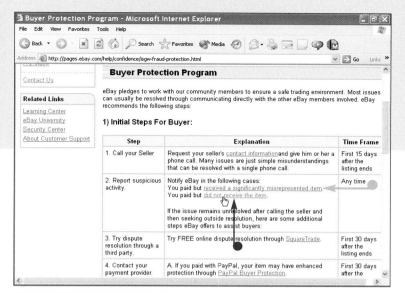

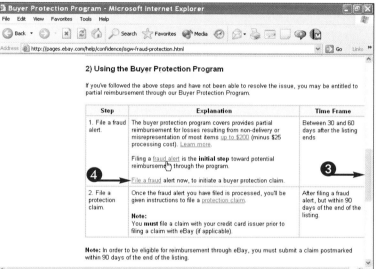

The Buyer Protection Program window appears.

● You can click the You paid but received a significantly misrepresented item link in the Report suspicious activity section.

● You can click the You paid but did not receive the item link in the Report suspicious activity section.

❸ Scroll down to the Using the Buyer Protection Program

❹ Click the Filing a fraud alert link to report non-delivery or misrepresentation of an item between 30 and 60 days after the auction ends.

eBay steps you through the complaint process.

Did You Know?

Most credit card companies offer 100 percent consumer protection for online fraud or misrepresentation. eBay also offers buyer protection on items up to $200, minus a $25 processing fee. If you pay with PayPal, you are eligible for up to $500 of coverage through PayPal's Buyer Protection program. To check if you are covered, look for the PayPal Buyer Protection icon in the Seller Information box on an eBay View Item page.

eBay Savvy!

Some eBay buyers complain that sellers give retaliatory negative feedback when they receive negative feedback. To protect your own feedback rating, leave negative or neutral feedback only as a last resort. For more information about the proper use of feedback, see Tasks #14 and #42.

Resolve payment disputes with
SQUARETRADE

You can have a trusted third party mediate a dispute between you and a seller or buyer when you use SquareTrade.

SquareTrade is an eBay-recommended service that provides mediation for auction transaction disputes. It allows both seller and buyer to voluntarily work toward a positive solution in a safe, neutral setting.

To start the process, you can file a case through the SquareTrade site for eBay users. SquareTrade then contacts the other party in your dispute and instructs you both how to proceed. All information and communication related to the case appear on a password-protected Case Page.

The next step is for both parties to try to work out a resolution by communicating with each other using SquareTrade's Direct Negotiation, a free, completely automated Web-based tool.

If you and the other party cannot resolve the dispute using Direct Negotiation, you can request a mediator's help. A *mediator* is a third party who helps both parties work through the issue and focus on a positive solution. If both parties agree, the mediator recommends a solution, and you can resolve the dispute.

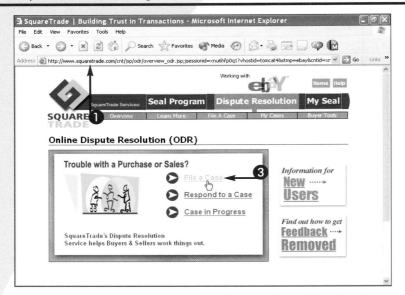

FILE A CASE

1 Type **www.squaretrade.com** here, and then press Enter.

The SquareTrade home page appears.

2 Click the eBay Buyers and Sellers involved in a dispute, Click here link.

The SquareTrade Online Dispute Resolution (ODR) page appears.

3 Click the File a Case link.

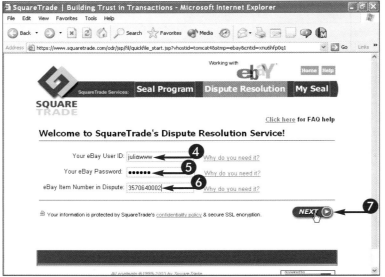

The Welcome page appears for SquareTrade's dispute resolution service.

4 Type your eBay user ID.

5 Type your eBay password.

6 Type the eBay item number in dispute.

7 Click Next.

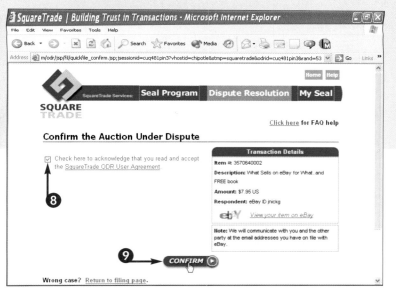

The Confirm the Auction Under Dispute page appears.

8 Click here to acknowledge that you read and accept the SquareTrade ODR User Agreement.

9 Click Confirm.

SquareTrade guides you through the mediation process.

DIFFICULTY LEVEL

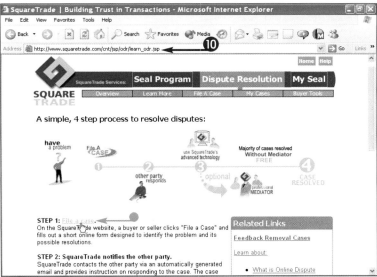

● The Type of problem page appears.

10 Click all of the options that apply to your situation.

SquareTrade guides you through the mediation process.

Did You Know?

SquareTrade allows you to suggest resolutions to your problem on its Step 3: Identify Potential Solutions page.

Did You Know?

You can get negative feedback removed or withdrawn. Select the option that you want feedback removed on SquareTrade's online form, and then explain the issues of your dispute in the Step 3: Identify Potential Solutions page. SquareTrade charges $20 for resolution services. For more information, click the SquareTrade link in the eBay site map, and then click Find out how to get Feedback Removed or Withdrawn button.

Using feedback to build
GOODWILL

Because buyers check feedback ratings before purchasing items, you can increase your desirability as a seller to eBay bidders by building a good feedback rating. You do this by giving positive feedback as often as possible to both your buyers and the sellers from whom you buy. As a seller, the more you give positive feedback to buyers, the more likely they return the favor. You can also request that your buyers leave feedback if they have not done so soon after purchasing an item.

In eBay's feedback forum, you can leave feedback concerning any transactions within the last 90 days.

You can also review and respond to feedback left about you. This lets you explain extenuating circumstances which may have led to a user leaving you negative feedback. You can also explain what you did to make up for it if applicable.

If you are new to eBay, one way to build your feedback quickly is to purchase many inexpensive items and be sure to leave positive feedback promptly.

For more information about feedback, see Tasks #14 and #42.

① In the My eBay home page, click the Feedback tab.

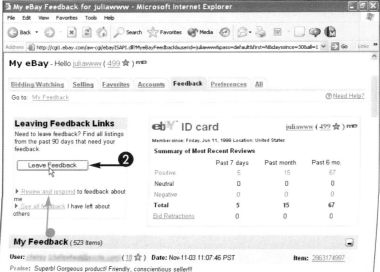

eBay displays your eBay ID card, with your positive, neutral, and negative ratings for the last 90 days.

② Click Leave Feedback.

● You can also respond to feedback by clicking the Review and respond link.

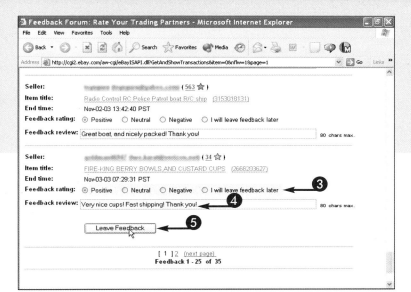

The Feedback Forum: Rate Your Trading Partners page appears.

③ Select an option for the Feedback rating.

④ Type your feedback comments.

⑤ Click Leave Feedback.

42

DIFFICULTY LEVEL

A new page appears, informing you that eBay has sent your feedback.

● The number of feedbacks you left appears here, along with eBay users for whom you have left them.

● If you want to leave additional feedback, you can click the Show all transactions link.

TIPS

eBay Savvy!

Be very careful about leaving negative and neutral feedback. eBay advises users to keep comments factual and to avoid personal comments. They also suggest that you try to resolve any disputes with your buyer or seller before leaving feedback. Some eBay users fear that if they are the first to leave feedback after a transaction, and it is negative, the buyer or seller may retaliate with negative feedback, whether it is justified or not. Therefore, they wait until the other party leaves feedback first.

Did You Know?

On the Feedback Forum, eBay tells you that once you leave it, you cannot edit or retract feedback. However, in some cases, you can get a piece of negative feedback removed with SquareTrade as explained in Task #41.

Chapter 4: Paying For Items Painlessly

Smart Selling on eBay

Selling items on eBay can be just as exciting as bidding on them because it brings a great deal of satisfaction — as well as extra cash. You can become a savvy seller by knowing what length to make your auction, the various listing options, and what to do when your highest bidder falls through. Adding pizzazz to your listing with a different design or color gives you an edge over the competition. Understanding listing fees and the pre-filled information feature saves you time and money.

Knowing how to list an item to match your situation is extremely important because listing formats determine how you conduct an auction. Regular auctions let buyers bid on an item until time runs out and the best bid wins. But if you want to set the prices of your item, you can use a Fixed Price auction. To allow bidding as well as the option of a set price, you can add a Buy It Now feature. If you have multiple identical items to sell, you can offer them in a single listing using a Dutch Auction.

To start your path as a smart seller, register on your My eBay page and become familiar with the eBay policies page, which lists legal standards you must follow. You can also ensure that eBay allows your item by checking it against the Prohibited and Restricted Items list. As the seller, you must follow the law, as well as eBay rules and guidelines. Failing to do so can lead to legal problems.

Top 100

Avoid problems with
TRADEMARK PROTECTION

When you sell items on eBay, you must consider trademark and copyright protection. eBay prohibits infringing materials, which can include copyrighted items such as written works, music, movies, television shows, software, games, artwork, and other images.

Intellectual property rights generally belong to the creator of the material. If you hold a copyright to materials being sold illegally on eBay, you can join the Verified Rights Owner, or VeRO, Program to help keep illegal copies of your work from circulating. Because eBay cannot verify if an item is auctioned illegally, the owners of such properties must be vigilant.

In 1997, eBay created the VeRO Program to enlist owners of intellectual property rights to help keep eBay safe from trademark and copyright violations. As a member of VeRO, you can report and request the removal of listings that infringe on your ownership rights.

As a seller, it is your responsibility to make sure that the item you auction does not infringe upon the rights of the owners. If you are unsure, you can check the VeRO Program participant's About Me pages.

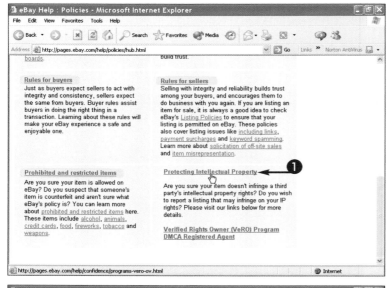

① In the eBay Policies page, scroll to the bottom of the page and click the Protecting Intellectual Property link.

Note: See Task #44 to learn how to view the eBay Policies page.

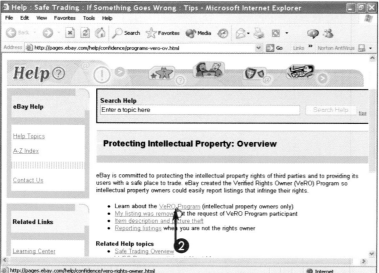

The Protecting Intellectual Property page appears.

② Click the VeRO Program link.

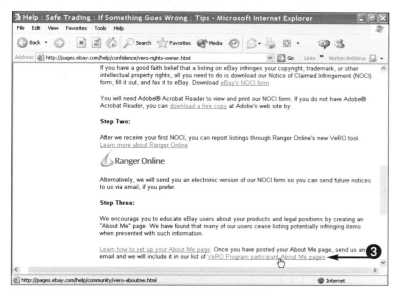

The eBay Verified Rights Owner (VeRO) Program page appears in a new browser window.

You can read more about the program.

③ Scroll down the page and click the VeRO Program participant About Me pages link.

43

DIFFICULTY LEVEL

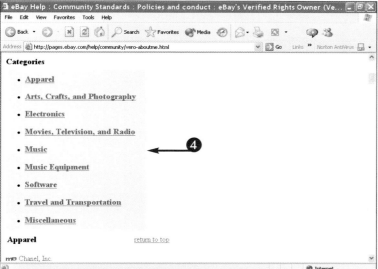

A list of categories appears.

④ Click a category.

eBay displays individual policies regarding copyrights and trademarks.

TIPS

eBay Savvy!

When you find it confusing to determine what constitutes illegal use, let common sense guide you. For example, if an eBay auction offers a DVD, and that movie is still in theaters, the DVD is clearly an illegal copy. Another example is a photograph, which is copyrighted, from a catalog being used to describe an item in a listing.

Caution!

If eBay removes your listing through VeRO, you receive an e-mail explaining why. To find out what you did wrong, consult the VeRO About Me pages. If you believe the rights owner is in error and the item was legal for trade, you can contact the owner directly and ask about the problem. The notification e-mail includes the rights owner's e-mail address.

EBAY ALLOWS YOUR ITEM

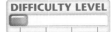

Before you start selling any items on eBay, you can check the policies list to make sure that eBay allows your items for auction. Some items, such as firearms, are absolutely prohibited. Other items may require some clarification before listing them on an auction. The eBay Web site features a variety of guidelines that you can consult regarding items you plan to sell.

Some of the eBay item restrictions are fairly obvious — you cannot sell hazardous materials, fireworks, or weapons and knives. Items such as autographed memorabilia require certificates of

authenticity. Because such items are easily forged, offering your buyers a certificate of authenticity can help reassure them that the item is legitimate.

DIFFICULTY LEVEL

If you end up selling an item that eBay does not allow, eBay or a user can report you for a listing violation. If you accumulate several violations, eBay can revoke your selling status.

If you have any doubts about whether or not the item that you want to sell is acceptable, consult the Prohibited and Restricted Items list.

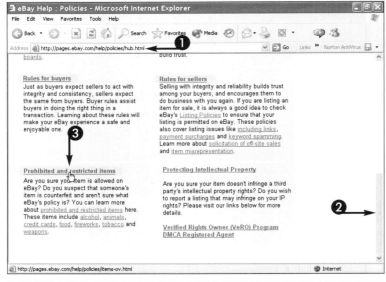

❶ Type **pages.ebay.com/help/ policies/hub.html** into your browser window and press Enter.

The eBay Policies page appears.

❷ Scroll to the bottom of the page.

❸ Click the Prohibited and restricted items link.

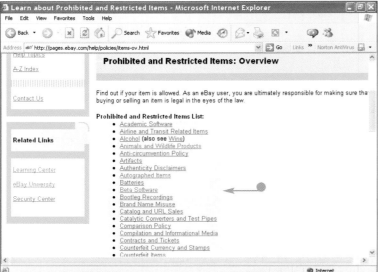

The Prohibited and Restricted Items list appears.

● You can click a link to learn more about eBay's policies regarding an item category.

Set an
AUCTION LENGTH

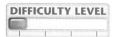

It takes practice and luck to determine proper auction length and timing. Depending on which length you choose — one, three, five, seven, or ten days — the auction ends at the exact time of the day in which the auction started.

For best results, enter an auction when the most potential bidders are online. Many experienced eBay users say that evenings and weekends are the best times to end an auction. If you plan to sell your items to eBay users overseas, you must compensate for the time zone changes when determining the auction start and end times.

You may also want to evaluate your own circumstances. For example, do you need to sell the item right away, or do you prefer to sell at a more leisurely pace? Some sellers believe that a ten-day auction attracts more potential buyers. Others say that a shorter auction appeals to impatient buyers, those unwilling to wait ten days to buy an item. Many buyers also look for shorter auctions around major gift-buying holidays. In general, the more popular an item is, the shorter the auction.

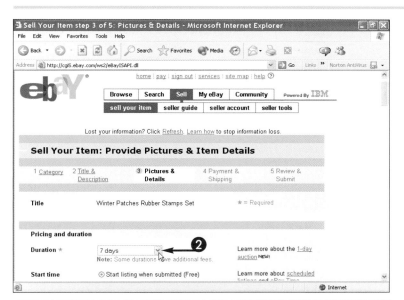

① Begin filling out the eBay seller's form to create an auction listing.

Note: If you are new to selling, go to the eBay help pages to learn how to become a registered seller and set up an auction.

② On the Sell Your Item: Provide Pictures & Item Details page, click here.

By default, eBay assigns a seven-day auction unless you specify otherwise.

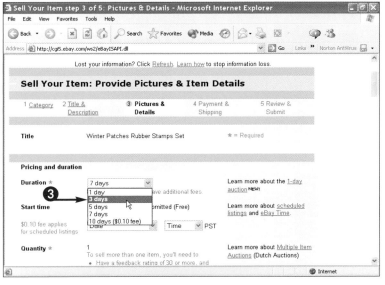

③ Click an auction length.

Note: A ten-day auction incurs an additional fee.

eBay assigns the length to your auction.

④ Finish filling out the seller form and post your item.

Note: For more information about listing items, see Tasks #68, #76, and #77.

Determine when to use
BUY IT NOW

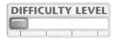

DIFFICULTY LEVEL

The Buy It Now option allows buyers to purchase an item without going through the actual bidding process, allowing your bidder to end an auction early by paying the listed prices. Essentially, your item becomes a real time-saver for impatient buyers, but still displays as a regular auction item.

When you add the Buy It Now option, a special button appears on the auction page. The option is only available until someone makes a bid on the item, at which time the button disappears.

When determining a reasonable price for your Buy It Now auction, you need to do some research. Setting the price too high drives off potential bidders who find that the price exceeds what they want to bid. If you set the price too low, you risk selling the item for less than it is worth. For more information about researching prices for your items, see Task #3.

eBay charges 5 cents for using Buy It Now for auction listings, but not for Buy It Now Fixed-Price listings. For more on Fixed-Price listings, see Task #47.

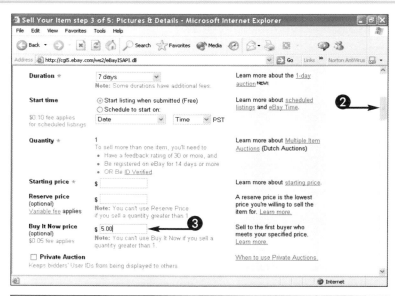

① Fill out the eBay sellers form to create an auction listing.

② In the Sell Your Item: Pictures & Item Details page, scroll down to the Buy It Now price box.

③ Type the amount for which you are willing to sell the item.

Note: You cannot use this option if the quantity of the item you are selling is more than one.

④ Finish filling out the seller form and post your item.

● When you post your auction, the Buy It Now button appears along with the Buy It Now price.

Note: The Buy It Now button disappears if someone places a bid on the item.

Create a
FIXED-PRICE LISTING

#47

DIFFICULTY LEVEL

You can use the new eBay Fixed-Price listing option to bypass all the bidding and offer a set price to anyone who looks at the item listing. Fixed-Price listings allow for an immediate transaction for both the buyer and seller without waiting for an auction to end. You use this listing to ensure that your item does not sell for less than its value, or to sell multiple items at the same price.

When you use the Fixed-Price listing, eBay lists the item with the Buy It Now feature, a button that appears on the item description page that lets buyers

purchase the item with a single click. To use the new Fixed-Price listing option, you must be an established eBay seller, with a feedback rating of 30 or more.

Although both Fixed-Price listings and Buy It Now auctions show the Buy It Now button, a Fixed-Price listing shows only the Buy It Now button, whereas a Buy It Now listing offers both a Place Bid and a Buy It Now option. For more information about the Buy It Now feature, see Tasks #19 and #46.

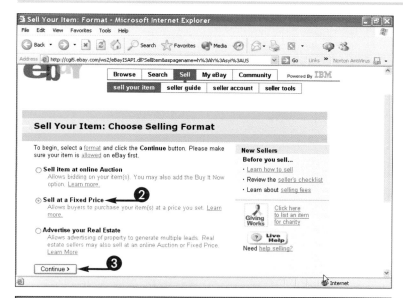

① Fill out the eBay Sell Your Item form to create an auction listing.

② In the Sell Your Item: Choose Selling Format page, click the Sell at a Fixed Price option.

③ Click Continue and resume setting up your item listing.

④ In the Sell Your Item: Provide Pictures & Item Details page, scroll down to the Buy It Now price box.

⑤ Type the amount for which you are willing to sell the item.

eBay assigns the fixed price to your auction.

⑥ Finish filling out the seller form and post your item.

SELL IN BULK
with Dutch Auctions

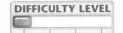

To sell a quantity of the same item quickly, consider offering a Dutch Auction — also called *multiple item auctions* — a format that allows multiple bidders to bid on a set quantity of identical items. For example, to sell ten tape measures without the Dutch Auction feature, you must sell them as a lot using a regular auction and hope for a good price, or set up ten different auctions for each item. However, if you offer the ten tape measures in a Dutch Auction with a minimum price, you leverage your selling potential and only have to set up one auction listing.

What makes Dutch Auctions unique is the winning bid price — all winning bidders pay the lowest successful bid. If you have more buyers than goods, the earliest successful bidders win the auction.

DIFFICULTY LEVEL

eBay does not allow a seller to list more than ten identical items as regular auctions, so in the example, you must use a Dutch Auction format. You can also use a Fixed-Price format or sell through your eBay Store, if you have one.

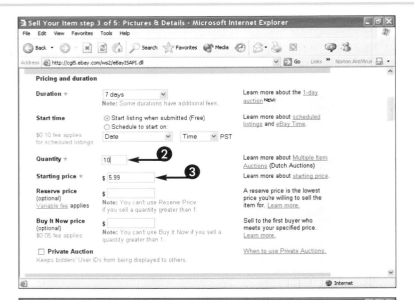

❶ Fill out the eBay Sell Your Item form to create an auction listing.

❷ When you get to the Quantity box in the Sell Your Item: Provide Pictures & Item Details page, type an amount.

❸ Type a starting price.

eBay assigns Dutch Auction status.

❹ Finish filling out the seller form and post your Dutch Auction.

Note: In order to sell items in a Dutch Auction, you must have a feedback rating of 30 or more or be ID-Verified. See Task #14 for more on feedback.

● The auction listing displays the quantity available.

The quantity being more than one item identifies this listing as a Dutch Auction.

Protect your item with a
RESERVE

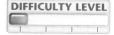

If you do not want to sell your auction item below a particular price, you can assign a reserve price to the item. A *reserve price* is the lowest price for which you are willing to sell the item and is hidden from the bidder in the auction listing. You must make this price higher than the minimum bid price. Keep in mind that setting the reserve price too high may discourage buyers from continuing to bid for the item.

When you assign a reserve, eBay displays the phrase "Reserve Not Met" on the auction page. When the bidding reaches the reserve price, the phrase disappears. If none of the bidders meet the reserve price by the end of the auction, you reserve the right not to sell the item below the reserve price.

Be warned, however, that adding a reserve price to an auction incurs an additional listing fee. If your item sells above the reserve price, eBay refunds the fee. If the item fails to sell, eBay does not refund the fee.

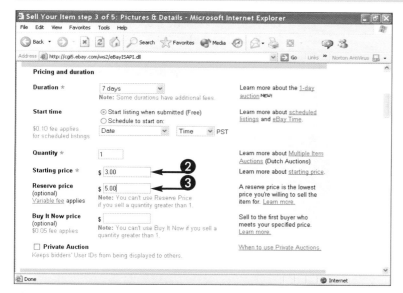

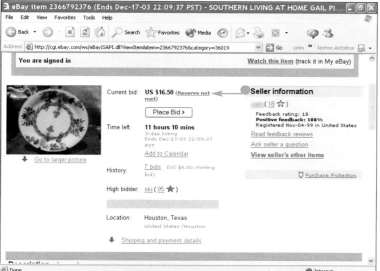

① Begin filling out the eBay Sell Your Item form to create an auction listing.

② When you get to the Starting price box, type a minimum price.

③ In the Reserve price box, type the minimum amount you will accept as a final sale price.

eBay assigns the reserve status to your listing.

④ Finish filling out the seller form and post your reserve price Auction.

● The reserve phrase displays in your auction listing until the reserve price is met.

Save money on
LISTING FEES

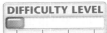

If you incur extra fees by adding too many extra features to your auctions, you may reduce your profits by spending more than you intended. To help you limit your costs, evaluate the effectiveness of a feature before adding it to your listing.

You can save some money on your eBay listing fees by thinking creatively. For example, if you decide you really must add a starting price or reserve price to an item, first check out the insertion fees chart on eBay to see a breakdown of fee prices. If you planned to

sell the item in the $10 price range, you may save money if you pay attention to how eBay defines its insertion fee brackets. Items priced from $1 to $9.99 cost $0.35 to list. Items priced from $10 to $24.99 cost $0.60 to list. As a result, by listing your item at $9.99 instead of $10, you save $0.25.

DIFFICULTY LEVEL

It is a good idea to regularly check the Fees Overview page on eBay to keep up with any fee changes.

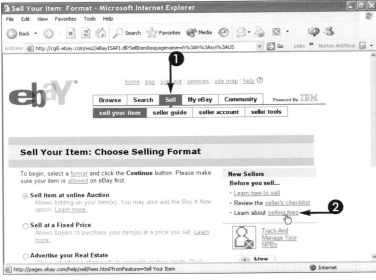

① From the eBay home page click Sell.

The Sell Your Item page opens.

② Click the Learn about selling fees link.

Note: You can also access the page by typing selling fees in the Help pages search box.

The eBay Fees Overview page appears.

● You can scroll through the page to view current fee tables, such as the Insertion Fees table.

● Alternatively, you can click a link at the top of the overview page.

BACKGROUND COLOR

DIFFICULTY LEVEL

By default, eBay auction pages use a white background. With some HTML and JavaScript coding, you can add extra interest to your auction by assigning a unique color background to your page. Anything you can do to make your auction seem more distinct can draw a buyer's attention. Color backgrounds can also display your personal style.

To designate a background color, you can enter HTML coding into the auction description text box when you fill out the seller's form. Valid HTML colors

include teal, blue, aqua, fuchsia, green, lime, maroon, red, purple, yellow, olive, and silver. Type any of these color names in your HTML code to specify the corresponding background color. If you are familiar with hexadecimal numbers, you can also use six-digit color codes that mix varying amounts of red, green, and blue.

When adding a background color, be careful that the color does not interfere with the buyer's ability to read your item description and instructions.

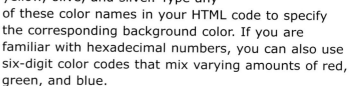

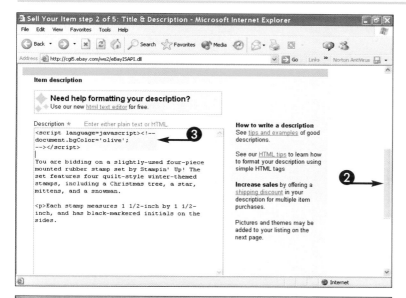

① Begin filling out the eBay seller's form to create an auction listing.

② Scroll down the Sell Your Item: Title & Description page to the description text box.

③ Type **<script language= javascript><!— document. bgColor='X';— ></script>**, where *X* is the color you want to use.

This example uses olive.

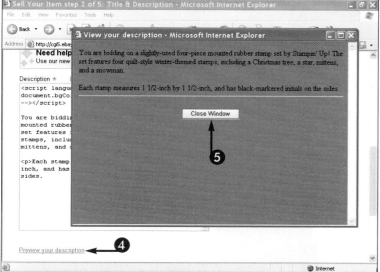

④ Scroll down the page to click the Preview your description link.

A separate browser window appears, displaying your description with the background color.

⑤ Click Close Window.

The browser window disappears.

⑥ Continue filling out the information for your auction.

Jazz up your listing with
LISTING DESIGNER GRAPHICS

You can add interest to your auction listing by using graphics with the eBay Listing Designer feature. For an extra fee, you can add a graphical theme to make your listing more attractive to potential buyers. A Listing Designer theme sets a default font and background color for your listing that controls the appearance of the description area.

eBay's Listing Designer themes include holiday themes, themes related to collectible items — such as clothing — and generic graphical themes that add color and liveliness to your description area. The Listing Designer also lets you choose from a variety of layouts to customize the appearance of any photos that you display in the auction. For example, you can select a layout that displays your item photo prominently in the description area.

As with all features that enhance your listing, remember to consider if the price of your item justifies the fee for a design.

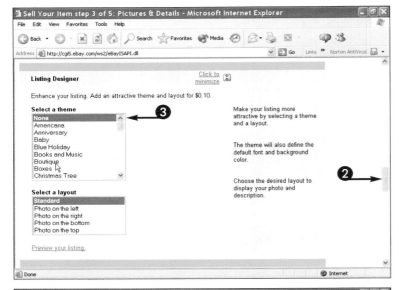

❶ Begin filling out the eBay seller's form to create an auction listing.

❷ In the Sell Your Item: Provide Pictures & Item Details page, scroll to the bottom of the page to view the Listing Designer options.

❸ Click the theme you want to apply.

● A preview appears for the theme design.

❹ Click a layout.

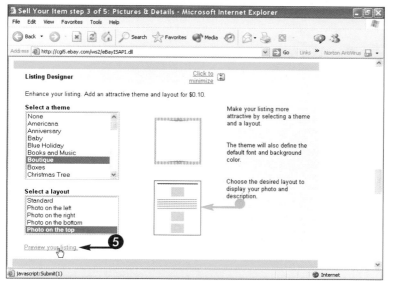

- A preview appears for the layout design.

⑤ To preview how your description looks with the theme and layout, click the Preview your listing link.

DIFFICULTY LEVEL

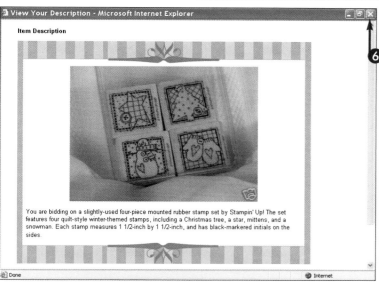

A preview window appears and displays your listing text and photos.

⑥ Click the Close button.

The preview window closes.

⑦ Continue filling out the information for your auction.

TIPS

Did You Know?

If you include HTML tags and JavaScript in your auction listing description, you can still use the Listing Designer themes and layouts. Keep in mind, however, that if you set font color tags, you should make sure that the colors do not conflict with the theme colors. For more on using HTML tags with your listing, see Task #68.

Did You Know?

You can also add your own graphics to an auction description. Graphic elements should never replace a photo of an item, but if you do not mind paying the extra fees to list them, you can add graphic files just like you can add photo files.

Save time with
PRE-FILLED INFORMATION

You can make the process of listing your item much shorter by using eBay's Pre-filled Item Information feature. The feature is free, and it allows you to quickly and automatically place specific information in your auction's listing. The feature sometimes even provides a photograph for use in your listing, as in a book cover, which can save you from the especially time-consuming task of creating and editing your own picture.

The Pre-filled Item Information screen appears in the listing process after you select a category and subcategory for your item and is only available for certain types of items, such as books or movies.

Examples of the type of details the Pre-filled item Information feature can add include a book's cover photograph, author, ISBN, and publisher. A third party provides the pre-filled information to eBay, so eBay recommends that you confirm the accuracy of the information before including it in your listing.

Note that you still need to add your own personal description to your auction listing to elaborate on your own item's specific features or flaws.

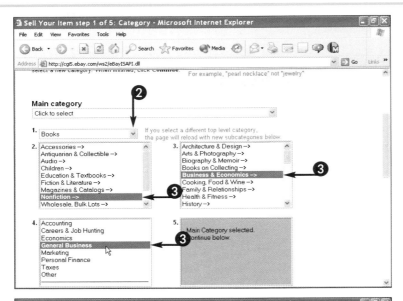

① Begin filling out the eBay seller's form to create an auction listing.

② At the Sell Your Item: Select Subcategory screen, click here and select a category for your item.

③ Click the various subcategories that best describe your item.

④ At the bottom of the pages, click Continue.

The Sell Your Item: Choose a Listing Option page appears.

eBay presents you with a List with Pre-filled information option.

⑤ Click here and select the Title, Author, or ISBN option.

⑥ Click Continue.

● You can also opt to list the standard way by clicking this Continue.

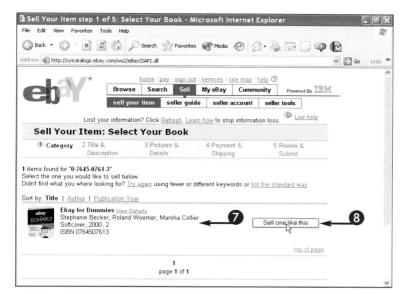

The Sell Your Item: Select Your Book page appears.

Note: *Although this example uses a book, you can use this feature for DVDs and CDs, but the options may list differently.*

⑦ Check that the listed information matches your item.

Some items have multiple versions or dates.

⑧ Click Sell one like this.

The Sell Your Item: Describe Your Item page automatically lists all important information about your item.

⑨ Click the Subject menus and select appropriate options.

⑩ Complete the remaining listing process.

eBay lists your book with the pre-filled information.

Did You Know?

eBay offers another time-saving listing feature called Item Specifics in some categories, which are available as options for your selection in the Sell Your Item: Describe Your Item form. For example, in the Women's Pants subcategory, eBay provides options for Style, such as Khakis.

Did You Know?

amazon.com also allows you to use pre-filled information to sell certain types of items. First, create a seller account. In an amazon.com item page, click Sell yours here. Select a condition, such as Used: Acceptable. Type a description in the comments box, and click Continue. In the Enter the price for your item page, type a price, and your ZIP code, then select a shipping method. Confirm the details and click List item for sale.

Make a
SECOND-CHANCE OFFER

If your winning bidder fails to complete a sale, you can make a second-chance offer to the next-highest bidder, if you have one. You can also offer the item to any underbidder if you have duplicate items available. This allows you to sell more than one item for one listing fee. A second-chance offer allows you to leverage the bidders in an auction and sell an item without having to relist the item, or pay additional listing fees. You pay only a Final Value Fee if the bidder accepts the offer.

You can create a second-chance offer immediately after a listing ends, and for up to 60 days afterward.

However, bidders can opt not to receive the offer. For this reason, you should first attempt to complete the sale with the original winning bidder before making a second-chance offer.

You can create a Second-Chance offer from your closed listing's page. A Second Chance Offer link is only available for closed items with at least one underbidder.

Second-Chance offers are not available for Multiple Item Auctions, also known as Dutch Auctions.

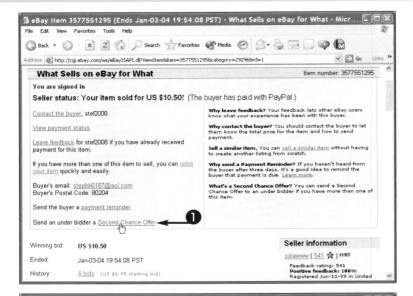

① From your item's closed listing page, click the Second Chance Offer link.

This link only appears for closed listings that had at least one underbidder.

The Second Chance Offer page appears.

● You can read the rules for using a Second Chance Offer.

② Type the Item number.

③ Click Continue.

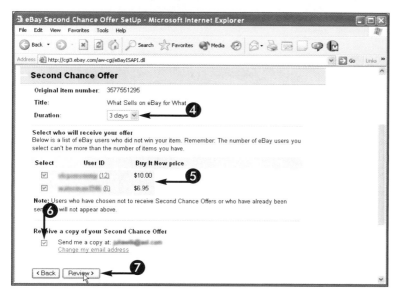

The Second Chance Offer setup page appears.

④ Click here and select how long you want the offer to last.

⑤ Click to select the bidders to whom you want to make the offer.

⑥ You can click this option to receive an e-mail copy of your offer.

⑦ Click Review.

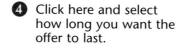

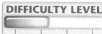
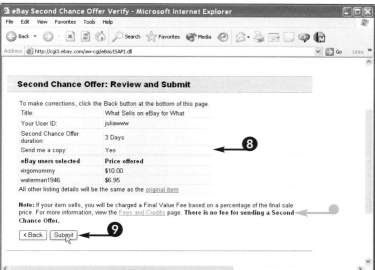

The Second Chance Offer: Review and Submit screen appears.

⑧ Review your offer details for accuracy.

● eBay charges a Final Value Fee if your item sells.

⑨ Click Submit.

eBay sends a Second Chance Offer to the designated underbidders.

TIPS

Did You Know?

You can make a Second Chance Offer to underbidders in a reserve price auction that ends without the reserve price being met. In addition, eBay refunds the reserve fee to you if the bidder accepts your Second Chance Offer. For more information about eBay's Second Chance Offer, go to pages.ebay.com/help/sell/second_chance_offer.html.

Did You Know?

You can leave feedback for your original winning bidder as well as for the buyer or buyers in your Second Chance Offer sale. Your buyers can also leave feedback for you. eBay protection services covers Second Chance Offer sales. For more on eBay's fraud protection and related programs, see Task #40. For more on giving and receiving feedback, see Tasks #14 and #42.

Chapter 6

Using Effective Seller Tools

When you use the eBay marketplace as a seller, you gain access to a whole new world of eBay areas and expertise. To help you gain more experience, this chapter shows you some practical ways to sell more efficiently online.

Savvy eBay sellers know that it pays to invest in a quality image-editing program. Whether you take a snapshot of your item with a digital camera and download it to your computer, or scan a picture, you should edit the picture in an image-editing program to make your item look its best. Most image-editing programs offer features to cover up imperfections in a photo's quality, to improve tone and contrast, and to crop out parts of the picture that detract from the subject.

Another way to optimize your selling potential is to take advantage of eBay's tools, such as the auction scheduler, and the free counters that track how many people visit your listing page. These tools are available on the seller's form when you create a new auction listing.

eBay also offers several additional tools that you can download, such as the popular Turbo Lister, which enables you to prepare listings offline.

Another way to sell more efficiently is to take advantage of the many third-party auction tools available on the Web, such as DeepAnalysis and andale. These tools help you examine eBay data, for example, to find hot items, and marketing values for various items.

Top 100

Using Photoshop Elements to
EDIT A PICTURE

Because photos show the buyer exactly on what they are bidding, a good photograph of your item is your most powerful selling tool on eBay. To show an accurate representation of your item, take clear and well-lit color photographs. You can then use a photo-editing program to improve your photo's quality before posting it in your auction listing. To avoid after-sale problems, the photo should clearly show any flaws in the item.

Photoshop Elements 2.0 is one of the best photo-editing programs on the market today.

Retailing for less than $90, the program can handle all of your photo-editing needs for eBay auctions. For example, you can use Elements to edit picture size, and improve focus, brightness, and contrast. You can also use the Auto Levels feature to quickly adjust tone and contrast. Finally, you can crop your image to eliminate extra background, and to minimize the file size, making the photo faster to load in your auction.

When you finish editing the picture, you must then save it as a GIF, JPEG, or PNG file to upload to the eBay Web site.

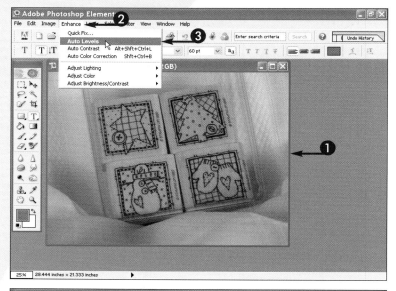

ADJUST TONE AND CONTRAST

① Launch Photoshop Elements, and open the image file that you want to edit.

② Click Enhance.

③ Click Auto Levels.

Note: You can use similar commands in other image-editing programs.

Elements corrects the shadows, midtones, and highlights of the image.

55

① Open the image file that you want to edit in Elements.

② Click the Crop tool.

③ Click and drag a cropping boundary around the area you want to crop.

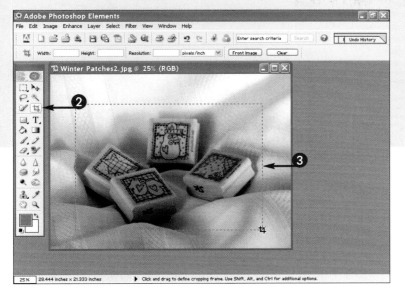

● You can drag the side and corner handles to adjust the size of the cropping boundary.

④ Click the Checkmark icon.

Elements crops the image, deleting the pixels outside of the cropping boundary.

TIPS

eBay Savvy!

You should use a neutral background when taking a picture of an eBay auction item. A busy background, such as a pattern, distracts the viewer's focus from the item. It is also a good practice to shoot an item from a flattering angle instead of straight-on, so the viewer can see more than one side of the item. If you are selling a collection of items, include at least one photo of all the items together. Be sure to take several snapshots so you can choose from among the best for posting in the auction listing.

More Options!

Some other popular image-editing programs include IrfanView, free at www.irfanview.com; Jasc Paint Shop Pro, $79.00 at www.jasc.com; and Ulead PhotoImpact, $89.95 at www.ulead.com/pi.

COPYRIGHT
your auction photographs

If you take a good photograph of your auction item, other eBay users may use your photograph in their own auctions. Although eBay disapproves of this behavior, which infringes on copyright laws, it is not uncommon to see photographs used in other sellers' auctions. To prevent this, you can place a text line discreetly in the image.

Most photo-editing programs, including Photoshop Elements, offer a text-editing feature that you can use to add your user ID number and a superimposed copyright symbol to the photo. If someone co-opts

your image for use on their site, bidders can clearly see that the image does not belong to the seller.

If someone does use your image without your permission, you can contact eBay and report the infringement, including the auction item number as well as your original auction item number. However, you must enroll in eBay's VeRO program for eBay to take action on your behalf. For more information about VeRO, see Task #44. eBay may take a few days to investigate, at which point they may remove the auction and notify the seller of the offense.

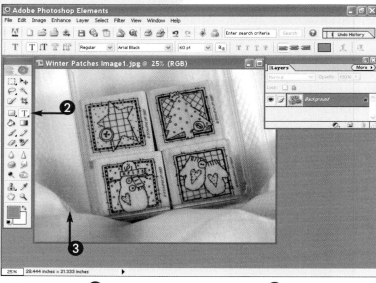

① Open the image file to which you want to add a copyright symbol in Photoshop Elements.

② Click the Type tool.

③ Click where you want the line of text to appear.

Elements creates a new layer for the text.

④ Click here to select a font, style, and size for your text.

⑤ Click the Color box.

The Color Picker dialog box appears.

⑥ Click a color range, and then click a color for the text.

⑦ Click OK.

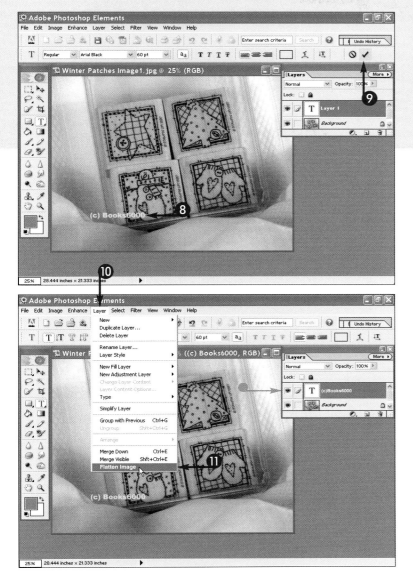

8 Type your copyright text.

To create a copyright symbol, type **(c)**.

9 Click the Checkmark icon or press Enter.

The text layer displays the text you have typed.

10 Click Layer.

11 Click Flatten Image.

● Elements merges the text layer with the image layer.

TIPS

Caution!

When selecting a color for text, be sure to make it a color that does not conflict with the image or distract the buyer from viewing from the item.

Did You Know?

You can change the opacity level of a text layer in Photoshop Elements to create a more transparent copyright line of text in your photo. Click the text layer in the Layer palette, click the Opacity slider at the top of the palette, and then drag to a new opacity setting; a setting of 50 percent makes the text half as opaque as the 100 percent setting. This lower opacity setting allows the photo layer beneath the text layer to show through, yet still displays legible text over the image.

Track listing visits with a
FREE COUNTER

You can use a counter on your auction listing page to keep track of how many people view your listing. Counting the number of visits can help you determine the marketability of your item, as well as how popular or unpopular your item is with other eBay bidders. You can use counters from third-party sources, or you can use a free counter from andale.

andale counters count every visit to your item listing, even if a person looks at your item more than once. The andale counter has two different designs from

which you can choose. You can also keep the counter hidden from the bidders' view. Counters appear as graphics at the bottom of your auction listing page.

If you want to hide your counter, visitors see only a Thanks for Looking graphic instead of the usual counter graphic. With a hidden counter, only you, the seller, can see how many people visit your listing.

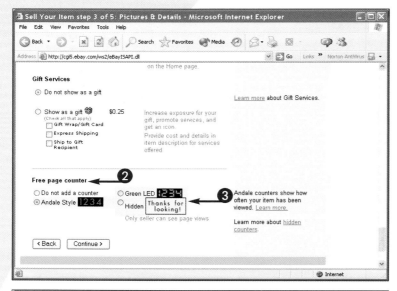

① Begin filling out the eBay seller's form to create an auction listing.

② In the Sell Your Item: Pictures & Details page, scroll to the bottom of the page to locate the Free page counter section.

③ Click a counter style.

④ Finish filling out the seller form and post your item.

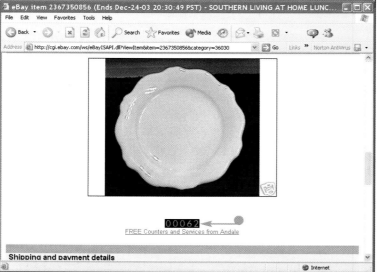

⑤ View your finished listing page in a Web browser.

● The auction listing displays the counter.

Start an auction with the
SCHEDULER

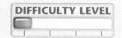

You can use eBay's built-in scheduling feature to help you schedule auctions for the best times, even when you are not around to post your listings. For a small fee, the eBay scheduler allows you to pick a day and time to start the auction. You can use the scheduler to schedule up to 3,000 auction listings, up to three weeks in advance.

For example, if you know you are going to be out of town when you want to begin a seven-day auction, you can use the scheduler to designate the date and time for you. You may find that your item sells best when you start an auction on a particular day of the week, or that your item gets more bids when an auction closes at the end of the day rather than earlier. The scheduler allows you to select the date and time that works best for your particular item.

In addition to the eBay scheduler, you can also find third-party schedulers that you can use to list your items.

DIFFICULTY LEVEL

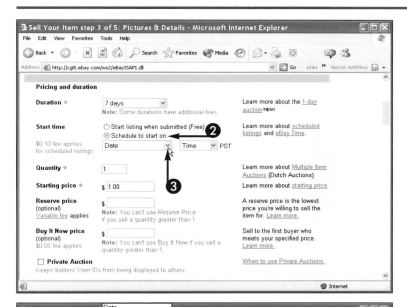

❶ Begin typing information in the eBay seller's form to create an auction listing.

❷ In the Sell Your Item: Pictures & Details page, click the Schedule to start on option.

❸ Click here.

❹ Click a start date.

❺ Click here and select a start time.

Finish typing in your information into the seller's form and post your item.

eBay posts your auction at the designated date and time.

Create auction listings with
TURBO LISTER

You can use the eBay Turbo Lister program to give your eBay auction listings a more uniform and professional appearance. You can download Turbo Lister for free from eBay, and build your auction listings offline. When you are ready to post the auctions on eBay, Turbo Lister posts the listings for you.

Turbo Lister offers you a choice of several themes. You can also select from several layouts for photo placement in your listing. You can add your description text and format it just as you would

format text with a word-processing program. You can also view your listing in HTML format and add HTML tags to your text.

One of the most attractive features in Turbo Lister is the ability to duplicate listings for similar items without having to retype your information. For example, after you design and type a listing for a collectible item, you can duplicate that same listing for a second, similar item and then make small changes to describe the second item.

1 Double-click the Turbo Lister shortcut icon.

Note: A Turbo Lister shortcut icon appears on the Windows XP desktop after you install the free Turbo Lister program, which you can download from eBay.

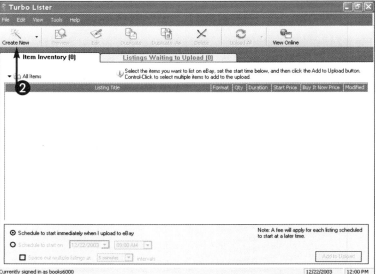

The Turbo Lister program window appears.

Note: At first use, you must set up your eBay account to work with Turbo Lister by following the onscreen prompts.

2 Click the Create New button.

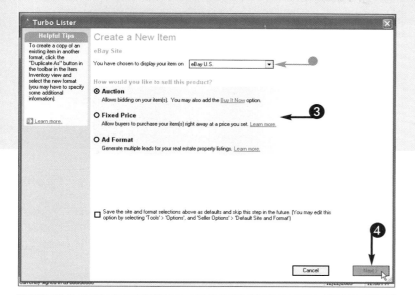

The Create a New Item page appears.

③ Click the type of auction you want to create.

● To post your auction on another eBay site, you can click here and select the location.

④ Click Next.

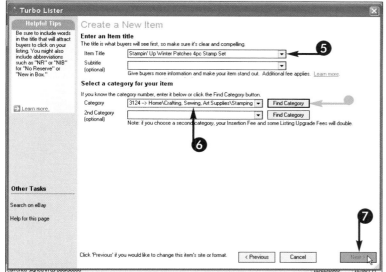

The next Create a New Item page appears.

⑤ Type a title that describes your item.

⑥ Type a category number.

● You can also click Find Category and select your category.

⑦ Click Next.

The Design Your Listing page appears

Did You Know?

You can download a copy of Turbo Lister for free from eBay. Click the Community tab on any eBay page, and then click the eBay Downloads link at the bottom of the eBay Community page. Click the eBay Turbo Lister link and follow the prompts for downloading the software onto your computer. After installing the software, a shortcut icon for Turbo Lister appears on the Windows desktop — Turbo Lister does not currently support the Macintosh platform. You can double-click the icon to open the program.

eBay Savvy

Turbo Lister can also import delimited data files, which means that you can use database core programs, such as inventory-management programs or order-accounting programs, with Turbo Lister.

Create auction listings with
TURBO LISTER

If you plan to sell items frequently on eBay, you can definitely benefit from downloading Turbo Lister. Turbo Lister helps you sell your items more efficiently, and you always have a list of your auctions ready to view or edit.

Turbo Lister presents a sellers' form similar to the one on the eBay site; however, creating your listing with Turbo Lister is much faster than creating an online eBay listing. You can relax and check your work for errors without the pressure to complete

your listing online. You can also save your work and edit it later before posting the auction on eBay.

Turbo Lister's themes and photo layouts are the same as those available with the Listing Designer feature on eBay's online sellers' form. You are charged a small fee per auction for using Listing Designer with Turbo Lister. Other items that you apply in Turbo Lister still incur a fee on eBay, such as adding a second category, adding a Bid Now option, or including more than one photo with the listing.

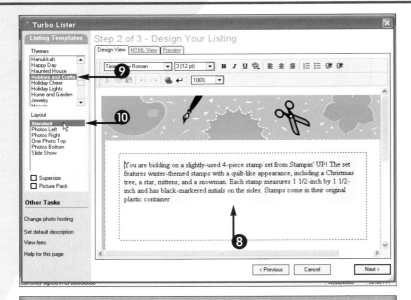

⑧ Type your auction listing text.

⑨ Click a theme.

⑩ Click a photo layout.

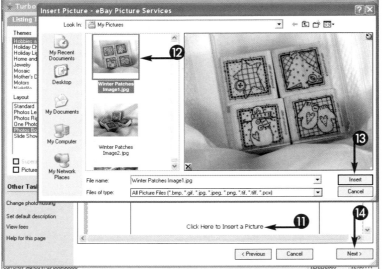

⑪ Click Click Here to Insert a Picture.

The Insert Picture dialog box appears.

⑫ Click the picture that you want to add to your auction listing.

⑬ Click Insert.

The Insert Picture dialog box closes.

⑭ Click Next.

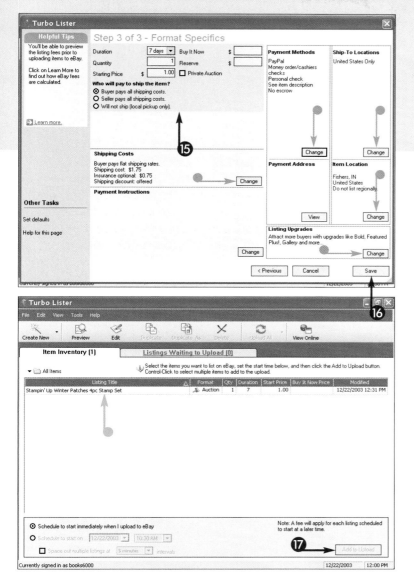

The Format Specifics page appears.

⑮ Type information in the form just as you would the eBay sellers' form, specifying auction duration, price, and payment methods.

● You can click Change to edit information.

⑯ Click Save.

● Turbo Lister saves the listing to your Item Inventory list.

You can continue adding more auction listings to your inventory.

⑰ When you are ready to post the listings, select the listings and click Add to Upload, log onto the Internet, and upload your auction to eBay.

eBay Savvy!

When you upload your auction listings from Turbo Lister to eBay, eBay schedules the auction to start at the time you upload. If you prefer to start an auction at a later time, you must use the scheduler, which incurs a listing fee. For that reason, you may prefer to log into your Internet connection and upload the listings at the most convenient time for your auctions. Remember that the start time on eBay's listing form is in PST — Pacific Standard Time.

Did You Know?

Every time you upload listings to eBay from Turbo Lister, the program also checks for system updates. Any updates display in an update status message.

Research auctions with DEEPANALYSIS

You can use a variety of third-party auction tools to research the eBay marketplace. For example, a search for the keywords "auction tools" using a Web search engine such as google.com displays a variety of shareware and freeware tools that you can download and use, including the popular DeepAnalysis program from HammerTap.

DeepAnalysis is an eBay market research program that you can use to analyze and extract auction sales information and eBay statistics. You can download a trial version of the program. Once you install the program, you can specify what sort of auction data you want to research. DeepAnalysis helps you to log into eBay and extract the data. DeepAnalysis then displays the data by seller and item.

The program also features a Statistics tab for viewing eBay statistics about the item that you are researching; however, this feature is only available to registered users of the program.

You can use the full version of DeepAnalysis to view sell-through rates, see the average sale price per item, view average bids per item, and create reports about the data you analyze.

① Double-click the DeepAnalysis shortcut icon.

Note: A DeepAnalysis shortcut icon appears on your desktop after you download and install the trial version of the program from www.hammertap.com.

The DeepAnalysis program window appears.

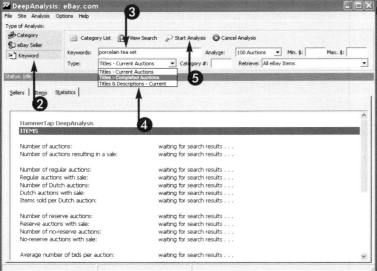

Note: If a prompt appears asking you to register the trial version before proceeding, click Evaluate to continue.

② Click the type of analysis you want to perform.

③ Type the keywords.

④ Click here and select an auction type.

⑤ Click Start Analysis.

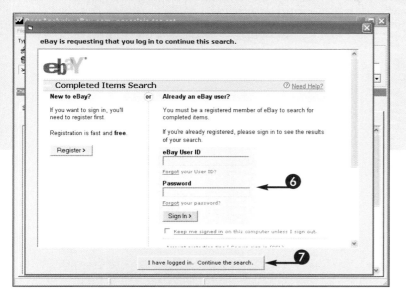

DeepAnalysis displays a window with the eBay login.

6 Type your user ID and password.

7 Click I have logged in. Continue the search.

#60

DIFFICULTY LEVEL

DeepAnalysis analyzes the site.

This process may take a few minutes.

● The results appear in the Items and Sellers tabs.

● After viewing the results of the analysis, you can click the Close button to exit DeepAnalysis.

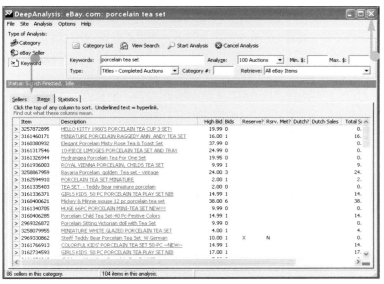

eBay Savvy!

With a tool like DeepAnalysis, you can quickly see which eBay sellers are doing well in the marketplace and examine their techniques and product lines. You can also use the data you research to find out which categories work best for your own items and find out which items receive the most bids.

Did You Know?

Growing along with eBay are numerous eBay industries, people, and companies dedicated to improving and developing products that help eBay users. Auction management software, also a growing industry, helps users to track inventory, maintain customer communication, and simplify transaction checkout. Online auction management service providers are also growing in popularity, and allow sellers to manage their auctions from a Web site rather than their own computers.

Determine the
BEST AUCTION DAYS

Although there is no magic formula for determining what times and days are the best for online auctions, some users argue that certain days are better than others. For example, the AuctionBytes Web site offers a useful calendar that you can reference when determining which days are best to start your auctions, with weather-related icons that identify good days and bad days.

The AuctionBytes calendar lists optimum days to end auctions, based on the number of days you set for your auction listing. For example, starting a three-day auction on a Monday is good because Thursday is considered a good day to end your auction.

However, be aware that anomalies exist with any eBay formula; no one can predict with any certainty when a bidder may bid on an item. Trial and error is best gauged from your own experiences when selling items online. You may find that the market for your item contradicts popular eBay listing theories completely.

DIFFICULTY LEVEL

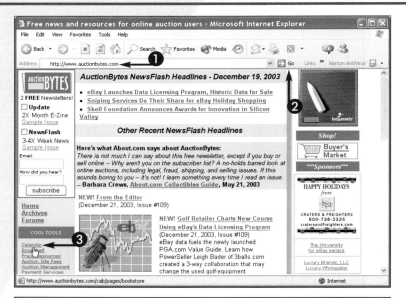

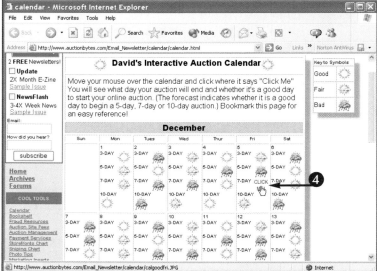

❶ In the Address bar of your Web browser, type **www.auctionbytes.com**.

❷ Click Go or press Enter.

The AuctionBytes Web page appears.

❸ Click the Calendar link.

The auction calendar page appears.

❹ Move the mouse pointer over an auction listing icon and click when the icon changes to text Click Me.

A Web page displays information about that particular type of listing and auction length.

View eBay
SELLER NEWSLETTERS

A great way to stay current with the latest news about any particular eBay auction category is to view the online category newsletter. Called *newsflashes*, the electronic newsletters offer information about upcoming events, seller tips, and special offers.

Published monthly, eBay newsletters are made for a variety of unique categories. For example, the Antiques Seller Newsflash is specific to online antique sellers, while the Entertainment Seller Newsflash is specific to entertainment products. Each newsflash lists the hottest-selling items for that particular category, as well as links to useful eBay tools and

information. Be sure to look at the newsflash each month to find out the latest news about your category of interest.

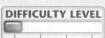
DIFFICULTY LEVEL

You can sign up to have the newsletter delivered to your e-mail address. You can also subscribe to more than one newsletter. If you are new to selling items on eBay, start by subscribing to just one or two newsletters until you are ready to explore other categories. For information various industry newsletters, see Task #100.

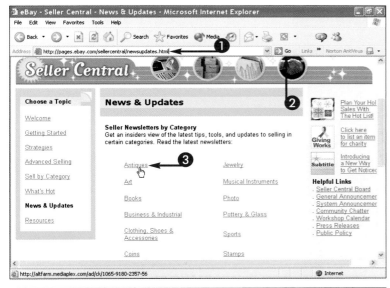

① In the Address bar of your Web browser, type **http://pages.ebay.com/sellercentral/newsupdates.html**.

② Click Go or press Enter.

The News & Updates page appears.

③ Click a category that interests you.

eBay displays the online newsletter page for that category.

● You can click this link to sign up to have the newsletter sent to your e-mail address.

Chapter 7

Boost Your Sales with Advanced Selling Techniques

Once you master the basics of selling on eBay, you can learn new skills to manage and increase your sales.

If you consistently sell enough items on eBay, you can earn the prestigious title of PowerSeller, which brings many benefits, such as icons that you can use in your auctions, a dedicated message board, and a health care program.

As you sell more items, your image fees may add up, especially if you list multiple images of each item. You can save money by using third-party image-hosting companies, such as inkFrog.com. You may also want to display multiple images of your items in a slideshow format.

eBay's tools, such as Selling Manager, can help you keep track of sales, archive sales records, and download statistics into a format that you can read with accounting applications, such as Microsoft Excel. Selling Manager also enables you to expedite the many chores associated with eBay sales, such as contacting buyers, managing payments, and tracking shipments.

You can improve the appearance of your auctions by using basic HTML tags to make your auction look much more professional.

You can create an even more professional image by opening your own eBay Store, which enables you to use listing management tools and many cross-promotion features.

Another option you have is to create a Store using Vendio's tools, which allows you to sell items on eBay as well as other online marketplaces.

Top 100

Benefit from
POWERSELLERS

You can benefit from PowerSellers as both a buyer and a seller. As a buyer, when you bid on a PowerSeller's listing, you know you can trust the experienced PowerSeller to handle the transaction professionally. You find PowerSeller listings by adding the word "powerseller" to your other search words. See Chapter 1 for more on performing searches. As a seller, if you earn the PowerSeller title, you can enjoy benefits such as a health care program, enhanced customer service, and an exclusive discussion board.

eBay grants the title of *PowerSeller* to users who sell at least $1,000 worth of merchandise, with a minimum of four average total listings, for three consecutive months. A PowerSeller's feedback rating is at least 100, of which 98 percent is positive. eBay designates a PowerSeller with a special icon next to the user's ID, in the user's item listings, and on the user's About Me page.

You can read about how others became PowerSellers, and find out their success secrets, in eBay's PowerSeller of the Month story, located in eBay's Community Discussion Board areas.

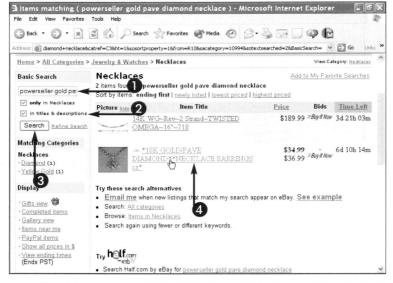

VIEW A POWERSELLER LISTING

① Type your search words and the word **PowerSeller** into eBay's search engine.

Note: For more on searching and browsing, see Chapter 1.

② Click the in titles & descriptions option.

③ Click Search.

The search results appear for items sold by PowerSellers.

④ Click an item.

The details page appears for the item.

● The PowerSeller's feedback rating and percentage of positive feedback appear here.

The PowerSeller icon appears here.

● You can click the PowerSeller icon to go to the PowerSeller area at pages.ebay.com/services/buyandsell/welcome.html.

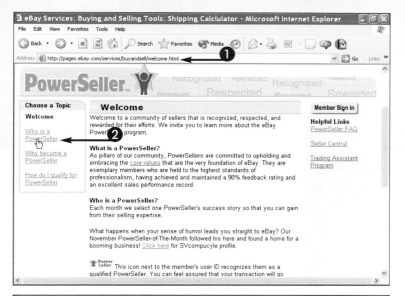

① Type **pages.ebay.com/ services/buyandsell/ welcome.html** into the address bar of your Web browser and press Enter.

The PowerSeller page appears.

② Click the Who is a PowerSeller link.

DIFFICULTY LEVEL

The PowerSeller of the Month page appears.

The page displays the PowerSeller of the Month success story.

Did You Know?

eBay has five different types, or tiers, of PowerSellers, based on gross monthly sales. eBay notifies eligible members each month by e-mail.

PowerSeller Tiers	
Tier Name	*Qualifying Gross Monthly Sales*
Bronze	$1,000
Silver	$3,000
Gold	$10,000
Platinum	$25,000
Titanium	$150,000

Did You Know?

If you no longer meet the criteria to keep your PowerSeller status, eBay alerts you via e-mail. You have 30 days to get your account back to the PowerSeller level, after which eBay disqualifies your account from the program. However, you can still attain PowerSeller status in the future.

Save money with
IMAGE-HOSTING

Because eBay charges for each picture you upload to host auction images, you can save money on eBay's image-hosting fees by using a third-party image-hosting service. The first image on eBay's image-hosting service is free, but each subsequent image costs $0.15. Thus, your picture fees can add up to a significant amount of money. For example, if you upload four images for each auction, and you list ten auctions each week, your image-hosting fees on eBay is $4.50 each week, or about $18 every month.

With the same number of images, you can have a service, such as inkFrog.com, host your images for one flat rate of $4.95 each month — a savings of $13 each month, or more, depending on how many auctions you list. inkFrog also offers other pricing plans.

Remember not to make your photo files too large — ideally under 50 kilobytes — or they load slowly on eBay. See Task #55 to crop your image.

Before you can perform the steps in this task, you must first register for at inkfrog.com. For more on slideshows, see Task #65.

① Log in to the inkfrog.com Web site.

The inkFrog picture & auction management page appears.

② Click the Upload Images link.

The Images Section appears.

③ Type the filename and pathname of the image you want to upload.

● You can also click Browse and then select the image from the appropriate folder in your hard drive.

Note: *To make sure that your image is eBay-ready, see Task #55.*

④ Click Upload Images.

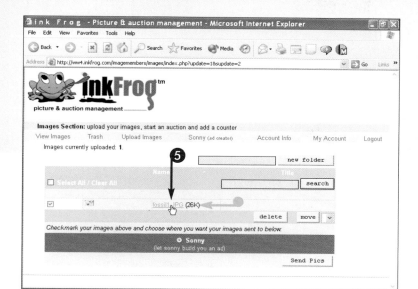

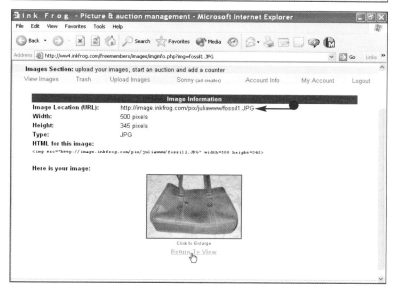

inkFrog tells you that your image is uploaded.

● The file size appears here.

Remember that if your file size is larger than 50KB, the image loads slowly on eBay.

❺ Click the filename link.

● inkFrog displays the image location, or URL.

inkFrog hosts your picture.

You can type the URL into the Picture URL box on eBay's listing page to add the picture to your eBay auction.

More Options!

You can use other third-party image-hosting services, such as SpareDollar, Vendio, or andale. SpareDollar offers 50MB of image storage space that holds approximately 1,000 images, for $4.95 a month. andale offers a $3 monthly plan for up to 50 images. You can read about their pricing plans at www.sparedollar.com/corp/pricing.asp., www.vendio.com/pricing.html, and www.andale.com/corp/pricing_corp.jsp. Shop around and decide which is best for you. Consider the volume and size of images you host each week or month.

More Options!

inkFrog offers a premium plan at $7.95 each month, which includes 400 images and auction listing tools, such as professional-looking templates. It also offers a pro plan at $12.95 each month, which includes 1,000 images, thumbnails, cropping, and bulk-listing tools.

Add multiple images in
SLIDESHOW FORMAT

Using eBay's image-listing options, you can increase your sales by showing your prospective buyers different angles of an item using multiple images in a slideshow format. eBay buyers are savvy, and like to know exactly what they are getting. For example, they bid more confidently if they can view both sides of a garment instead of only the front view.

You can upload up to a total of six images with eBay's image-hosting service. The first image for an auction is free. Each additional image is $0.15.

Rotating the images in slideshow format costs an additional $0.75.

Because costs for images and a slideshow add up, you should make sure that the estimated final price of the auction item justifies adding them. For example, you may decide that it makes sense to post multiple images and a slideshow for an item worth $50, but not for an item worth only $10.

For more information about image hosting, see Task #64.

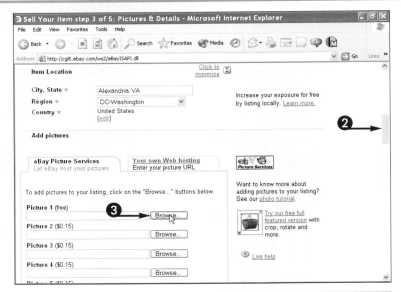

① In the eBay home page, click the Sell tab.

eBay guides you through the Sell Your Item process.

② In the Sell Your Item: Pictures & Item Details page, scroll to the eBay Picture Services tab.

③ Click Browse.

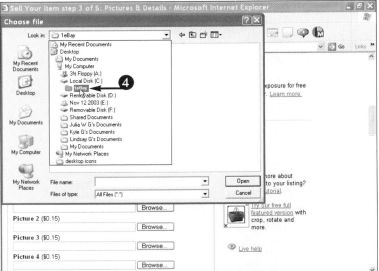

Note: If this is the first time you use eBay Picture Services, a pop-up box appears, prompting you to download software

The Choose file window appears.

④ Double-click the folder that contains your photo file.

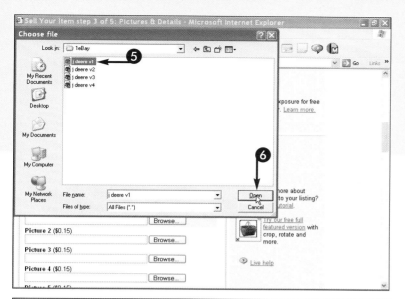

The folder displays the files.

5 Click the file you want to upload.

6 Click Open.

#65

DIFFICULTY LEVEL

● The photo appears in the Picture 1 box.

7 Repeat steps **4** and **5** for each additional photo you want to add.

8 Select the Slide Show option.

9 Continue the listing process by completing the Sell Your Item form.

eBay adds a slideshow of the selected images to your listing.

TIPS

Did You Know?

You can use between two and six images to create an animated effect with a slideshow. Keep in mind that you cannot have still pictures and a slideshow in the same listing with eBay's picture services. You can also increase the size of your pictures — or *super size* them — up to 880 pixels wide by 600 pixels high, for $0.75. Images must be at least 440 pixels wide by 330 pixels high to qualify for the Supersize Picture option.

More Options!

You can create slideshows with third-party image-hosting companies, such as WebShots at auctions.webshots.com. WebShots offers a range of plans, from $9.99 a year for 20 photos to $249.99 a year for 1,000 photos. For more information about third-party image hosting, see Task #64.

Using statistics to
MEASURE SALES

If you sell items regularly on eBay, you may find keeping track of all your sales records for business and tax purposes time-consuming and difficult. The Selling Manager tool makes this tedious chore a lot easier.

You can download your sales records with eBay's Selling Manager tool in a comma-delimited file format, so that you can read them in a software application, such as Microsoft Excel. You can also retrieve an immediate estimate of your total active and past sales with Selling Manager's Quick Stats, which measures weekly or monthly profits, as well as tax records.

You can download sales records for periods ranging from yesterday to the last 90 days, or select a specific date. Because eBay only retains sales records for four months, you should download them at least that often to ensure that you have all the information you need for the entire tax year.

Selling Manager costs $4.99/month. For more information about Selling Manager, see Task #67. For a tour of Selling Manager, go to Selling Manager Tour at pages.ebay.com/selling_manager/tour.html.

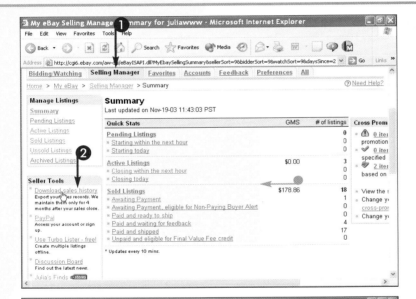

① In the My eBay page, click the Selling Manager link.

The My eBay Selling Manager Summary page appears.

The Quick Stats listings display here.

● You can view how many pending, active, and sold listings you have and total sales for each.

② Click the Download sales history link.

The My eBay Download Sales History page appears.

③ Click the date range option to define the data you want to download.

● You can click this option and select a date range.

In this example, the date range is From the Last 90 Days.

④ Click Download.

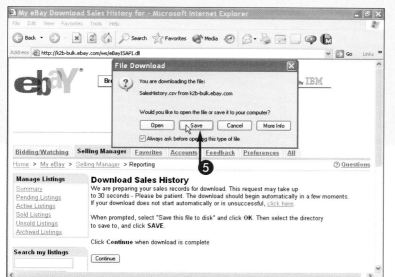

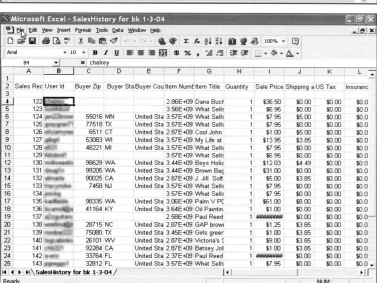

The File Download dialog box appears.

⑤ Click Save.

eBay walks you through the process of saving your data.

⑥ Open your spreadsheet application and open the file containing your data.

You can view your sales statistics with an application.

More Options!

Sales Manager can help you keep track of when you ship items and when buyers pay for them. You can mark sold items Paid, Shipped, or Paid & Shipped. From the Selling Manager tab, click the Sold Listings link. Click the option next to an item (☐ changes to ☑), and select an option, such as Mark Paid & Shipped. Click Confirm Status. Sales Manager tells you your sales record status is updated successfully.

Did You Know?

Some third-party tools, such as Vendio at www.vendio.com and andale at www.andale.com, also allow you to organize statistics. andale's Sales Manager tool shows you what percentage of your sales is successful, and your top five most successful products by average selling.

Get organized with
SELLING MANAGER

You can save time on many administrative tasks and be more efficient and organized with eBay's Selling Manager, an online tool that enables you to track and manage sales. With Selling Manager, you can easily keep track of items that have sold, been paid for, and shipped; relist items in bulk; archive auction records; and print invoices and shipping labels directly from your sales records. You can also export your sales records to files on your computer, which is useful for keeping your tax records.

Selling Manager is most useful for sellers with medium- to high-volume sales. If you have low-volume sales, then you may not need Selling Manager. You get the most out of Selling Manager if you use it in tandem with eBay's free Turbo Lister tool.

To sign up for Sales Manager, go to pages.ebay.com/selling_manager/products.html.

You can try Selling Manager for free for 30 days. After the free trial, Selling Manager costs $4.99 each month. For more information about Selling Manager, see Task #66.

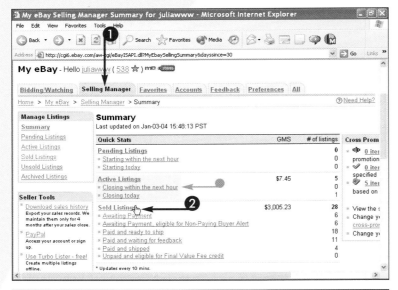

❶ From the My eBay page, click the Selling Manager tab.

Note: This tab appears only after you subscribe to Selling Manager.

The Selling Manager Summary page appears, with a summary of your stats.

● You can click here to view your Archived Listings.

❷ Click the Sold Listings link.

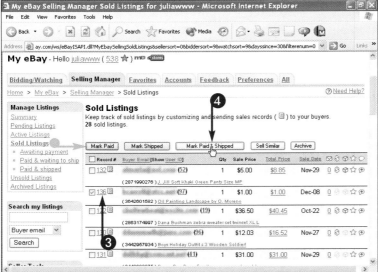

❸ Select an item or items.

❹ Click Mark Paid & Shipped.

● You can also click just Mark Paid, or Mark Shipped.

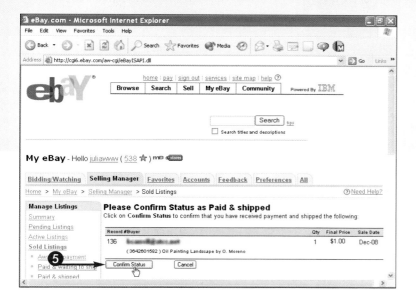

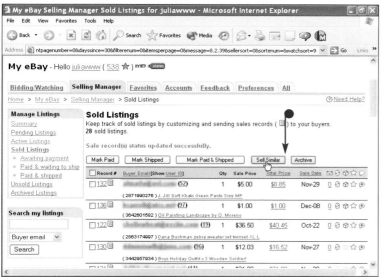

The Please Confirm Status as Paid & shipped screen appears.

⑤ Click Confirm Status.

Sales Manager tells you your sales record status is successfully updated.

Sales Manager updates the numbers on the Summary page, next to Paid and shipped.

● You can click Sell Similar or Archive.

Sales Manager helps you keep track of your payments and shipments.

TIPS

More Options!

If you are a high-volume eBay seller and list hundreds of items a month, you can use eBay's Selling Manager Pro, which offers all the features of the regular Selling Manager tool, as well as inventory management. These tools can help you to: determine your products' success ratio and average selling price; send and track feedback and invoices; use customizable seller e-mail templates; and bulk e-mail to buyers. For a complete list of Selling Manager Pro features, go to pages.ebay.com/selling_manager_pro/faq.html. Selling Manager Pro is free for 30 days and then costs $15.99 monthly.

Did You Know?

If you use Seller's Assistant Basic, you can upgrade to Selling Manager for free. Get more information about how to upgrade at pages.ebay.com/selling_manager/upgrade-info.html.

Improve your listings with eBay's
HTML EDITOR

You can format your listings so they are clear, well organized, and have a nice appearance, using basic HTML attributes. Your prospective bidders take you more seriously when your listings look professional, and this can lead to more sales.

eBay makes it very easy to use HTML, because it provides a small HTML text editor within the auction-listing page.

To use the embedded HTML editor, you simply select from a menu of buttons that represent different HTML attributes, and highlight the text to indicate to which words you want to apply those attributes.

The HTML editor allows you to do things like place your text in bold and italics; select a font, size, and color for your text; center or right- or left-justify it; or create bulleted or numbered lists.

Even if you do not use a lot of HTML tags in your listings, using even a few basic tags can make the difference between one long, monotonous piece of text, and a series of neatly separated and defined paragraphs.

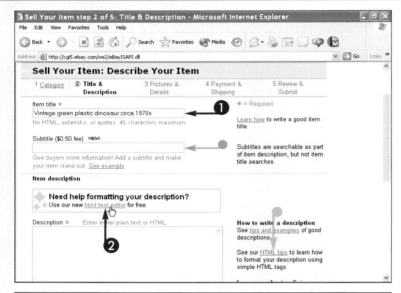

❶ In the Sell Your Item: Describe Your Item page, type your item's title.

● If you want to add a subtitle, type it here.

❷ Click the html text editor link under the Item description heading.

● You can click here for HTML tips.

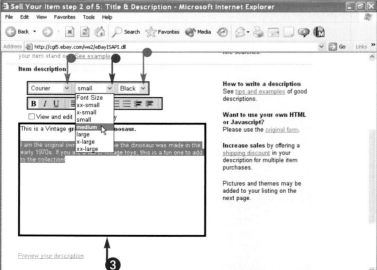

The HTML text editor appears.

❸ Type your text into the text box, selecting what you want to change.

❹ Click a formatting option.

● You can click here and select a font size.

● You can also click options to change text font and color.

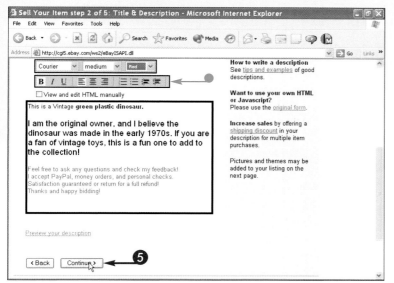

- You can click these options to change the format of your text.

B	bold
I	italic
U	underline
≣	bulleted list
≣	numbered list
≣	center
≣	right-justify
≣	left-justify

5 Click Continue.

Your item description appears with the designated HTML attributes when eBay users view it.

This example shows where text has been changed to bold, medium font, and red color to emphasize different parts of the listing.

More Options!

In the Sell Your Item: Describe Your Item page, you can click the HTML tips link under the Item description heading to learn how to add a `<p>` tag to separate your paragraphs, a `<br>` tag to start a new line without skipping a space, and the `<hr>` tag to add a horizontal rule with your text above and below it. You can also create different-size headings with the `<h1></h1>` through `<h6></h6>` tags.

Did You Know?

The Web offers a number of free HTML tutorials. For example, www.pagetutor.com, www.htmlgoodies.com, or Dave's HTML guide at www.davesite.com/webstation/html. You can also do a search for HTML tutorials in your favorite search engine.

Market your goods with
AN EBAY STORE

When you open an eBay Store, you can create your own unique presence on eBay, and instill greater confidence in your customers that you are a reputable seller. An eBay Store is an area within eBay that a seller can customize with graphics and their own designated categories. You can also use the eBay Store listing-management tools to receive monthly reports on your sales performance.

eBay Stores give you the following advantages: your own directory page and search engine; a chance to feature the store on the main Stores page;

promotion on every one of your item listings and on the related Stores area within eBay's search results pages; and a general eBay Stores link in the eBay home page.

To qualify for opening an eBay Store, you must have a minimum feedback rating of 20, or be ID-verified. A basic eBay Store costs $9.95 each month.

Even if you have an eBay Store, you may also want to list items within the non-store part of eBay. This is because eBay Store items do not currently appear in the eBay main search engine.

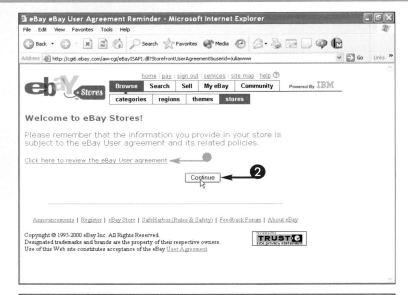

❶ In the eBay site map link at the top of the page, click the Open an eBay Store link under eBay Stores under Services.

Note: *To access the site map, see Task #11.*

The Welcome to eBay Stores! page appears.

● You can click this link to read the eBay User agreement.

❷ Click Continue.

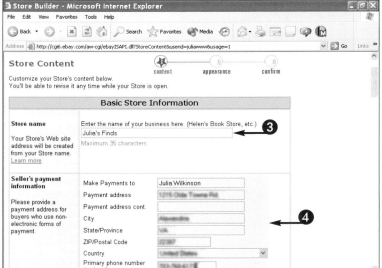

The Store Content: page appears.

❸ Type your Store name.

❹ Type your name and address.

eBay guides you through the Store-building process.

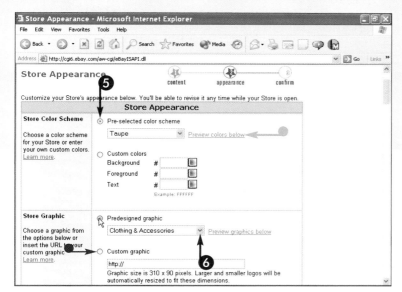

At the Store Appearance page, you can select the store's design.

5 Click a pre-selected color scheme.

● You can click this link to preview the colors

6 Click here and select a predesigned graphic.

● You can click this option to upload a custom graphic, if you have one.

DIFFICULTY LEVEL

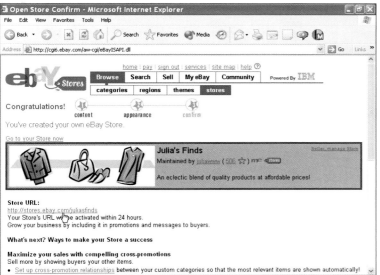

eBay continues to step you through the rest of the listing process.

eBay displays your Store URL and tells you it will be activated within 24 hours.

More Options!

In addition to the Basic Store, eBay offers Featured Stores for $49.95 a month, and Anchor Stores for $499.95 a month. Featured stores get priority placement in the eBay Stores home page, the Shop eBay Stores section that appears on eBay's search results pages, and the eBay Stores Directory for the appropriate categories. With an Anchor Store, eBay gives your Store 1 million page visitors monthly, and priority placement in the Shop eBay Stores section and the eBay Stores Directory pages.

Did You Know?

You can make changes to your Store after you create it by using the Store Builder tool. To make changes, go to your Store's home page, click the Seller, manage store link, and then select the Edit your store option.

Create your own store with
VENDIO

You can sell directly to your customers from a customized Store that works with many automated selling features by using Vendio, a third-party auction service provider. Vendio's interface allows you to sell items directly from a Web site, as well as through eBay or other online selling sites, such as Amazon and Yahoo, or any combination thereof. Vendio Store also sends daily information about all of the available Store items to Froogle.com, Google's shopping engine.

Vendio Store prices start with the Bronze Plan at $4.95 each month plus 1% of the items' final values.

However, the maximum final value fee you pay for each item sold is $4.95. For example, if you sell an item for $1,000, you pay a fee of $4.95, rather than $10, which is 1 percent of $1,000.

The Vendio Store Gold Plan costs $14.95 each month plus $0.10 for each sold item. For each pricing plan, you can list an unlimited number of items.

To perform this task, you need to first register for a Vendio store from the site at www.vendio.com. For more information about Stores, see Tasks #69 and #71.

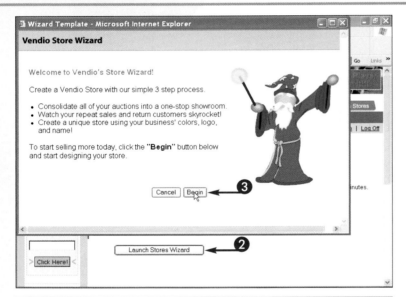

① Register for Vendio at www.vendio.com.

When registration completes, the Welcome to Vendio Stores! page appears.

② Click Launch Stores Wizard.

The Vendio Store Wizard page appears.

③ Click Begin.

④ When Vendio prompts you for your name, address, and e-mail, click Next.

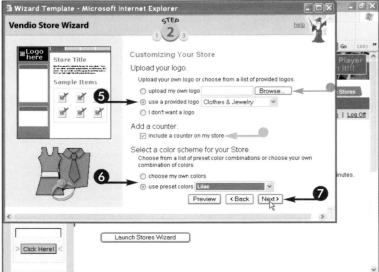

The Customizing Your Store page appears.

⑤ Click an Upload your logo option.

● You can upload your own logo by clicking Browse.

● You can select the counter option.

⑥ Click a color scheme.

⑦ Click Next.

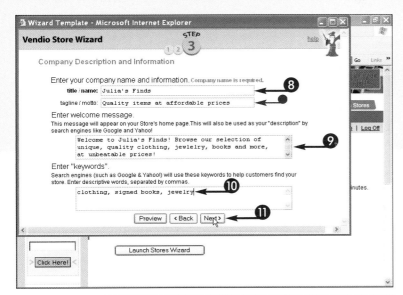

The Company Description and Information screen appears.

8 Type a store name.

● You can type a store tagline.

9 Type a store welcome message.

10 Type your store's keywords.

11 Click Next.

The Vendio Store Wizard guides you through the rest of the signup process.

Vendio creates your Store.

More Options!

To list items on eBay from your Vendio Store, you must sign up for Vendio's Sales Manager. Sales Manager speeds up your listing process by saving your shipping, payment, and marketplace preferences, allowing your buyers to calculate their shipping fees, and managing the many post-sale tasks. To sign up, go to www.vendio.com/tours/sm/index.html, and click FREE TRIAL. The cost ranges from $12.95 each month plus a $0.05 listing fee and 1-percent final value fee, to $39.95 each month plus a $0.10 listing fee. Vendio also offers a pay-as-you-go plan for $.10 per listing plus 1 percent final value fee, and free images.

More Options!

Vendio also offers a tool called Customer Manager that helps you manage customer e-mails. For more information, see www.vendio.com/my/cm/promo_cm.html.

Cross-promote your
EBAY STORE ITEMS

One of the great features of an eBay Store is that shoppers can see thumbnail images at the bottom of a Store listing of items that you designate. They can then go directly to one of those items if they are interested in it and bid on it, which can lead to more sales for you. You can designate what types of items you cross-promote using the Manage your Store area.

You have several options for cross-promoting. You can cross-promote items by Selling format, such as Buy It Now items only or Store inventory items only.

You can promote items with Gallery images first, or only items with Gallery images. You can also select items by when they end, such as those ending soonest or ending last. Or, you can have eBay show your highest-priced items first.

For information on cross promoting by Store category, see Task #72. For more on eBay Stores, see Task #69. You can also attract eBay buyers to your auctions using Keywords by eBay and your About Me page as illustrated in Tasks #73 and #75.

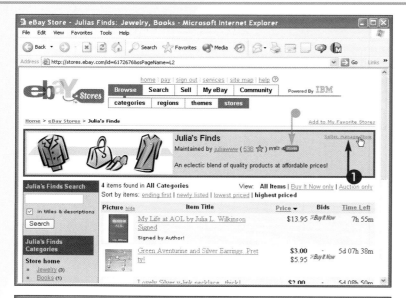

① From your eBay Store main page, click the Seller, manage Store link.

● You can click the Stores icon near the top of the My eBay page to get to your store, or just click the stores icon from any of your eBay listings.

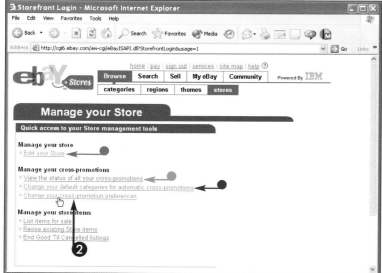

The Manage Your Store page appears.

② Click the Change your cross-promotion preferences link.

● You can click here to view the status of all your cross promotions.

● You can click here to change your default categories for automatic cross-promotions.

● You can click here to edit your store items.

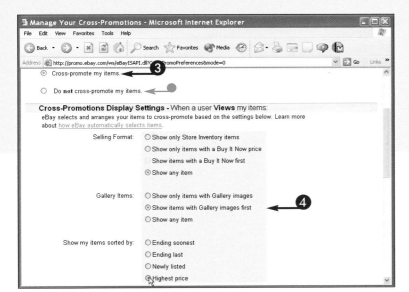

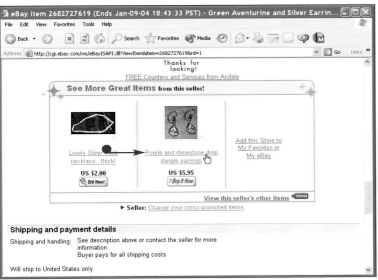

DIFFICULTY LEVEL

③ Click the Cross-promote my items option.

● You can also choose Do **not** cross-promote my items.

④ Click your cross-promotions settings when a user views your items.

⑤ Click Save My Changes at the bottom of the page.

eBay saves your cross-promotion settings.

● eBay users see your designated cross-promoted items in your listings, and can click on an item's link to bid on it.

More Options!

To quickly cross-promote your eBay Store, include item descriptions that encourage users to view your other Store items. Prospective bidders can click the eBay Stores icon to access your Store. To make this technique effective, list auctions as well as fixed-price Store listings, because fixed-price Store listings do not appear in eBay's regular search, but Store items in regular auction format do.

More Options!

You can select options for When a user Bids on or Wins your items, in addition to the options for when a user Views your items. From the Cross-promote my items link, scroll down past When a User Views my items. You can select to cross-promote your items by Selling format, by Gallery images, or by ending times.

Manage
CROSS-PROMOTED ITEM CATEGORIES

Using eBay's Store Merchandising Manager, you can boost your Store sales by designating which types of items your eBay Store cross-promotes to eBay users.

eBay shoppers can see thumbnail images at the bottom of a Store listing of items in the same category, or of items in the category that you designate. eBay automatically cross-promotes items that are in the same Store category, but Merchandising Manager lets you change which categories of items you want users to see when they view and bid on your items.

In most cases, you may want to promote items in the same category. For example, from a listing in a Books category, you may want to promote other items in the Books category. But in some cases you may want to promote an item that complements a particular item, but is in a different category. For example, you may want to promote a book light in a book listing.

For more information about cross-promoting your eBay Store items, see Task #71.

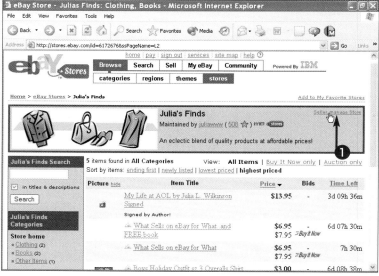

❶ In your Store page, click the Seller, manage Store link.

The Manage your Store page appears.

❷ Click the Change your default categories for automatic cross-promotions link.

● You can also click links to view the status of all your cross-promotions and to change your cross-promotion preferences.

The Default Categories for Automatic Cross-Promotions page appears.

③ Click the change default categories link under the category you want.

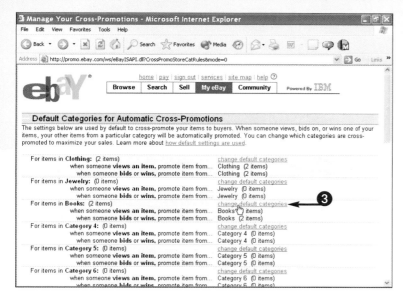

The Change Default Categories for Automatic Cross-Promotions page appears.

④ Click here and select a category that users see when they view an item.

● You can specify to promote an item when someone bids on, or wins an item.

⑤ Click Save My Changes.

eBay promotes items from the category you designate for items in that category.

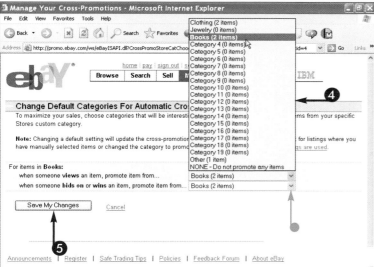

TIPS

More Options!

You can see which of your Store items have manual and which have automatic cross-promotions, and which ended items have had their cross-promotions replaced. To do this, in the Manage your Store page, click the View the status of all your cross-promotions links.

Did You Know?

You can turn cross-promotion of your items on or off, and specify different cross-promotion display settings. From the Manage your Store page, click the link. You can select various display options, such as Show only items with a Buy It Now price, or Show any item. You can also select how you want to cross-promote Gallery items and how to sort cross-promoted items; for example, by Ending soonest or Highest priced.

Maximize Your Item's Exposure

eBay and some third-party developers offer many ways to attract attention to your items to increase your sales. One way to promote both your auctions and your business is to set up an About Me page. The About Me page is the only place on eBay where you may post links to your Web site, or other Web sites.

You can also use eBay's Gallery feature, which offers a good value at only $0.25. With Gallery, eBay users can preview a photo of your item when searching and browsing, and therefore are more likely to view the auction.

You can buy your way to a better placement within eBay's many pages, using a Featured Plus! Listing for an extra $19.95. You can also time your auctions more strategically using the eBay Merchandising Calendar, and create your own banner ad using Keywords on eBay.

Other tactics, while not as high profile, can also be effective, such as using the bold listing option, and mentioning your other auctions within your auction text.

Sophisticated techniques, such as andale's Gallery tool, showcase thumbnails of your other auctions in your listings. You can also list a strategic item to attract attention to all your auctions and gain buyers' confidence with a SquareTrade Seal of Approval.

Experiment to see which techniques work best for you, and watch your sales increase.

Top 100

Emphasize listings with your
ABOUT ME PAGE

You can attract viewers to your auctions and post links to outside-eBay resources by using your About Me page. Although eBay does not allow members to post links to their own Web sites in auction listings, it does allow the posting of such links on members' About Me pages.

eBay users can access your About Me page by clicking the blue-and-red me icon next to your eBay user ID. You can place text in your auction listings that directs people to your About Me page.

Some eBay sellers use the About Me page to post helpful information and resources about their field of

expertise. For example, several purse experts use the About Me pages to showcase information about how to tell authentic brand bags from fake bags. You can do the same thing with your About Me page, giving eBay buyers a reason to come to your page, and therefore getting more eBay buyers to follow links to your auctions.

This task assumes you already have an About Me page. For more information about the About Me page, see pages.ebay.com/help/feedback/about_me.html.

① From the services link at the top of the eBay home page, click the About Me page link.

The About Me: Create Your Own eBay Personal Page section appears.

② Click Create and edit your page.

If not already created, eBay guides you through the process of creating an About Me Page.

③ In the Edit Your About Me page, type text about yourself and your business.

● You can type links to your Web site in the box using HTML.

Note: For more information about using HTML, see Task #68.

④ Click Preview your page.

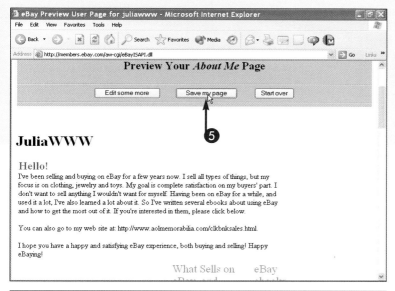

You can see how your new About Me page appears.

⑤ Click Save my page.

eBay saves your About Me page.

eBay tells you Your About Me page is ready for sharing.

● You can click this URL to view your About Me page.

eBay buyers can view the information about your business and click the link to get to your Web site.

More Options!

You can select various layouts for your About Me page. These include two column, three column, and centered — where the text extends across the page instead of in columns. Once you select a layout, you can type your information, and then you can preview and save your page. To start creating your page, click the services link at the top of any eBay page, and then click the About Me page link.

eBay Savvy!

eBay offers special HTML tags, available at pages.ebay. com/help/account/html-tags.html, that can enhance your About Me page. For example, you can use the `<eBayUserID>` tag to enhance the appearance of your eBay user ID. For more information about using HTML, see Task #68.

Give shoppers a preview with
GALLERY

When you use the Gallery feature, you can show eBay shoppers a miniature image, or thumbnail, of your auction item when they browse or search in your lists of items. According to some reports, you can get from 25 percent to 200 percent more bids by using the Gallery feature. At a cost of only $0.25, the Gallery feature may be your best investment in your auction beyond the basic listing fees.

Because your items are competing against so many other items on eBay, anything that you do to help them stand out increases the chances that people will bid on them. Some shoppers browse through so many pages of listings so quickly that they may not even take the time to view your item if you do not use the Gallery feature.

You can choose the Gallery feature on the Sell Your Item: Pictures and Details page during the eBay listing process. After you submit your listing, eBay may take a few minutes to recognize your item in its search engine.

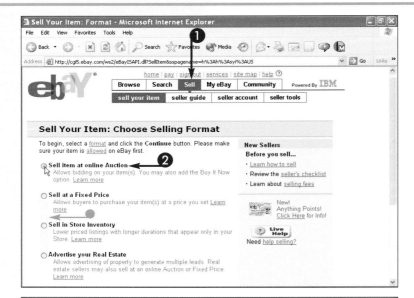

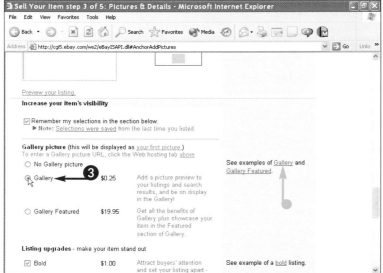

LIST YOUR AUCTION

① In the eBay home page, click Sell.

The Sell Your Item page appears.

② Click the Sell item at online Auction option.

● You can also select the Sell at a Fixed Price, the Sell in Store Inventory, or the Advertise your Real Estate options.

eBay guides you through the listing process.

③ In the Sell Your Item: Pictures and Details page, select the Gallery option.

The Gallery option costs $0.25.

● You can click this link to view an example of a Gallery listing.

eBay continues to guide you through the listing process.

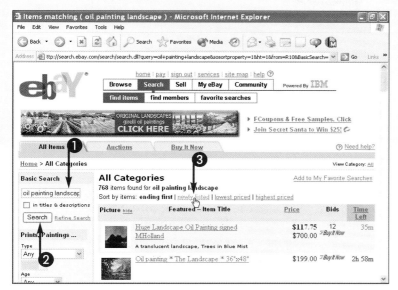

VIEW YOUR AUCTION

1 In the eBay category where you list your item, or eBay's main Search page, type keywords from your item's title in the Search box.

2 Click Search.

eBay lists items similar to your items.

3 Click the newly listed link.

The most recently listed auctions appear.

You can view your item with a Gallery preview.

eBay shoppers see this photo preview when they browse or search.

 **More Options!**

You can use the Gallery feature when you shop on eBay. Try browsing with the Gallery view feature, instead of viewing the search results in the default view. To do this, click the Gallery view link on the left side of an eBay search or browse results page under the Display heading. eBay displays auctions on the page in horizontal rows of gallery images, allowing you to view many photos of items on one page. For more information about the Gallery View feature, see Task #19.

eBay Savvy!

Although the Gallery feature is relatively inexpensive, if your profit margins are slim, the Gallery option may not be worthwhile for you.

Place your item on eBay's
HOME PAGE

Every day, eBay features specific categories and subcategories on its home page, the first page people see when they navigate to www.ebay.com on the Web. You can take advantage of the top-level exposure those categories receive, and therefore get more exposure for your own items, by using eBay's Merchandising Calendar. The eBay Merchandising Calendar is a schedule of which categories eBay plans to feature on its home page in the upcoming weeks. You can plan to list items that match those items

during that time. You can find this calendar in the Seller Central section of eBay, located under What's Hot in Seller Services and on the eBay site map.

Because the schedule is subject to change without notice, you may want to check the calendar shortly before you plan to list the items for which you want front-page category exposure. eBay says they make every effort to update the calendar as soon as any changes occur.

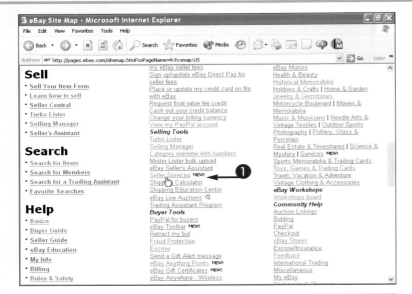

1 In the eBay site map, click the Seller Services link.

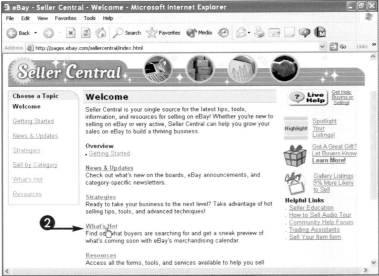

The Seller Central page appears.

The News & Updates link and other resource links appear.

2 Click the What's Hot link.

The What's Hot page appears.

A link appears to Hot Items by Category.

③ Click the Merchandising Calendar link.

The Merchandising Calendar page appears.

eBay lists which categories it will feature in upcoming weeks.

By listing the types of items specified during the weeks listed, you ensure that your items' categories receive maximum exposure on the eBay home page.

Note: *For more information about emphasizing a listing, see Tasks #73 and #76.*

TIPS

eBay Savvy!

To immediately receive front-page exposure for auctions, make a note of which categories eBay promotes on a given day and quickly list any inventory you have that fits into those categories. For example, if the home page promotes Fisher Price toys, you can quickly list one you have to sell and benefit from eBay's top-level category exposure.

eBay Savvy!

You can time your auctions to maximize their effectiveness by using the David's Interactive Auction Calendar at www.auctionbytes.com/ Email_Newsletter/calendar/calendar. html.

More Options!

For $39.95, you can receive a link to your item directly on the eBay home page with the Home Page Featured listing option. For more information about the Home Page Featured listing option, see Task #77.

Using bold and highlighting to
EMPHASIZE AUCTIONS

You can make your item stand out in the sea of auction items on eBay by using the Bold or Highlight Listing upgrade. These options are especially helpful when eBay has many items similar to yours, and you do not want your item getting lost in the sea of competition. By some estimates, placing the title of your auction in bold text, or in highlighted format, increases your chances of receiving more bids by as much as 25 percent to 35 percent.

The bold listing option costs $1.00, which is a good deal when you sell an item that is of a high-enough estimated final sale value to justify the cost of the feature. The highlight listing option is more expensive at $5, which you can only justify for more-expensive items.

You may not want to use bold or highlighted text for every listing. For low-priced items or rare items without much competition, the added fees for emphasized text may not be worth it. You can experiment with your auctions to see where these options are most effective.

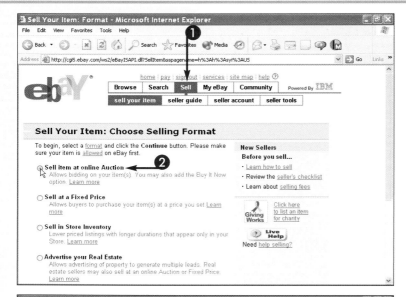

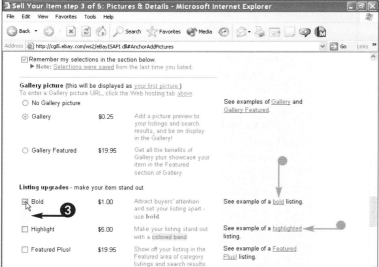

SELECT THE BOLD OR HIGHLIGHT OPTION

1 In the eBay home page, click Sell.

The Sell Your Item page appears.

2 Click the Sell item at online Auction option.

eBay guides you through the listing process.

3 In the Sell Your Item: Pictures and Details page, select either the Bold or the Highlight option.

The Bold listing option costs $1, and the Highlight option costs $5.

Note: *For more on the Featured Plus! option, see Task #77*

● You can click these links to see an example of the emphasized listing.

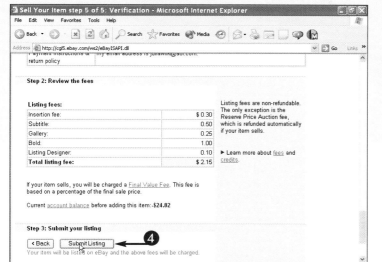

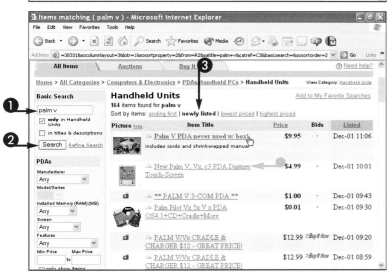

eBay continues to guide you through the listing process.

④ At the end of the listing pages, click Submit Listing.

eBay tells you that you have successfully listed your item.

VIEW FORMATTING

① In the eBay category where you listed your item, type search words that describe your item.

② Click Search.

③ Click the newly listed link.

● The search results appear with your item listing in emphasized text.

More Options!

You can also use HTML to apply bold formatting to parts of your item description text to make it stand out. For more information about using HTML in auction listings, see Task #68.

Did You Know?

eBay sometimes changes fees for additional features, such as bold and featured listings, so check the eBay Announcements section at www2.ebay.com/aw/marketing.shtml periodically, or pay close attention to the prices on the Sell Your Item form. eBay reduced the fee for bold listings in regular U.S. auctions from $2 to $1 in March 2003. eBay also reduced the fees for bold text in eBay Stores, depending on the duration of the eBay Store listing. For more information, see pages.ebay.com/community/news/changes.html.

Maximize visibility with
FEATURED AUCTIONS

You can use the Featured Auction listing option to increase the visibility of your auctions. When you apply the Featured Auction option to your listings, they appear above the other auctions in their category.

eBay currently offers two kinds of Featured listings. The first kind, Featured Plus!, costs $19.95. Featured Plus! auctions appear at the top of the listings page for that category. eBay also randomly selects Featured Plus! auctions for display in the Featured Items section of related category pages.

The other type of Featured listing is the Home Page Featured Auction listing, which costs $39.95, or $79.95 for multiple-quantity listings. When you select the option, your item appears at the top of eBay's all featured items page. Several lucky auctions randomly appear on the eBay home page in the Featured display section, and in the Featured Items section of related category home pages.

For other ways to emphasize your listings using formatting, see Tasks #68 and #76.

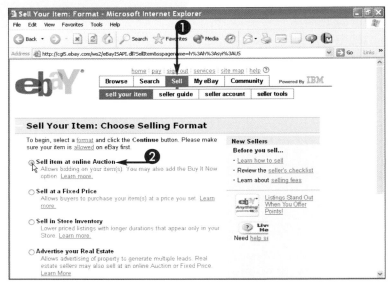

1 In the eBay home page, click Sell.

The Sell Your Item page appears.

2 Click the Sell item at online Auction option

eBay guides you through the listing process.

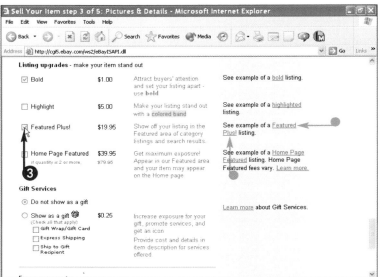

3 In the Sell Your Item: Pictures and Details page, click the Featured Plus! option.

eBay tells you that the Featured Plus! option costs $19.95.

● You can click this link to see an example of a Featured Plus! listing.

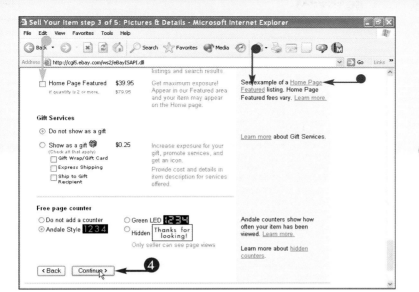

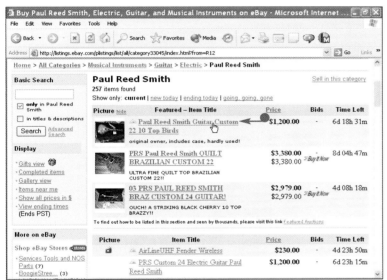

- Alternatively, you can click the Home Page Featured option for $39.95.

- You can click here to see an example of a Home Page Featured listing.

④ Click Continue.

eBay guides you through the rest of the listing process.

To view your Featured listing, navigate to the category in which your item is listed.

In this example, the category is Paul Reed Smith Electric Guitars.

- Your item appears in the Featured Auctions section above the non-featured items.

TIPS

Did You Know?

You need to scroll to the bottom of the eBay home page to see the Home Page Featured Items. Conditions for using the Featured Items options include that the auction item cannot be of an adult nature or in poor taste. For a complete list of prohibited items, see cgi3.ebay.com/aw-cgi/eBayISAPI.dll?Featured, or click Feature my item on the eBay site map, located under Buying and Selling. For more on what items eBay allows, see Task #44.

Call attention to your
OTHER AUCTIONS

One of the easiest ways to notify eBay shoppers about all your other auctions is to write a sentence or two in your auction descriptions that invite people to view your other auctions. Calling attention to other auctions is especially effective when you list a popular or otherwise attention-getting item, and when your other auctions are for related items.

You can use bold, italics, or other HTML tags to highlight the sentence that describes your other auctions. eBay shoppers can then go to your other auctions using the View seller's other items link,

located in the blue Seller information box. eBay buyers can also access your eBay Store, if you have one, through its link, which appears beneath the View seller's other items link. For more on using HTML tags, see Task #68.

To perform this task, you should know how to create a basic eBay listing. This task builds on this knowledge by showing you how you can use text to point bidders to your other auctions.

For more information about attracting eBay buyers to related auctions, see Task #79.

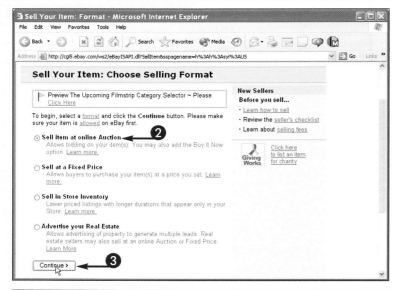

REFERENCE YOUR OTHER AUCTIONS AS A SELLER

1 In eBay's home page, click Sell.

   Note: To access this screen, see Task #77.

2 In the Sell Your Item: Choose Selling Format screen, click the Sell item at online Auction option.

3 Click Continue.

   eBay prompts you to select a category and steps you through the auction listing process.

4 In the Sell Your Item: Describe Your Item form, type text that invites buyers to other auctions.

   Note: To create auction descriptions, see Task #68.

5 Click Continue.

   eBay steps you through the listing process and lists your item.

#78

DIFFICULTY LEVEL

① In your item's listing page, look for text referring to the seller's other auctions.

② Scroll up the page to see view the Seller Information section.

③ Click the View seller's other items link.

If the seller has an eBay Store, the link appears here.

TIPS

eBay Savvy!

You can create a direct link to your other auctions in your item's listing page. Go to any of your auctions and click the View seller's other items link. Copy the URL that appears in your browser address window and paste it into your new auction's description. Add the `<a href=` tag in front of the `http` tag, the `>` tag after the `50`, and the `</a>` tag at the end. For example, where xxxx is your seller ID, type the following:

```
<a href=http://cgi6.ebay.com/ws/eBayISAPI.
dll?ViewSellersOtherItems&userid=xxxx&
include=0&since=-1&sort=3&rows=50>Click
HERE to see my other auctions!</a>
```

More Options!

Although you cannot post links to your Web site in your auctions, you can post them in your About Me page, which is discussed in Task #73.

Showcase thumbnails of
RELATED AUCTION ITEMS

You can use andale's Gallery tool to show eBay shoppers thumbnail images of your related auction items. This enables eBay users to view small images of your other auction items from your auction descriptions. When eBay shoppers can easily view and access your other auctions, it means increased sales for you.

andale, at www.andale.com, is a third-party auction management service with products that enable you to list and research your auctions, and analyze your sales. You can purchase Gallery as a separate service from andale, or combine it with some of andale's other tools.

andale provides graphics templates so you can customize the look of your Gallery. You can also select whether to have your thumbnail images available from a button in your listing, or directly embedded into your listing.

andale Gallery costs $5.95 a month for up to 200 listings, and an extra $5.95 for each additional set of 200 listings. andale provides their counter service free of charge when you sign up for the Gallery feature.

To perform this task, you must first sign up for the andale Gallery service at www.andale.com.

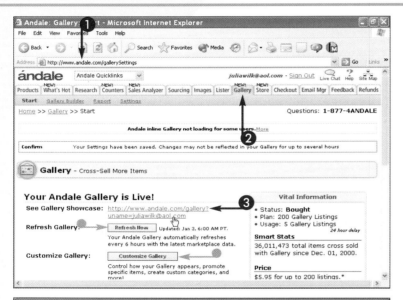

1 Type **www.andale.com** into your Web browser address bar, and press Enter.

2 Click the Gallery tab.

● You can click these options to reload your gallery at any time or to set your gallery's design.

3 Click the See Gallery Showcase link.

Your Gallery Showcase appears.

● You can click this menu and select a category option.

4 Click an auction link to view one of your eBay auctions.

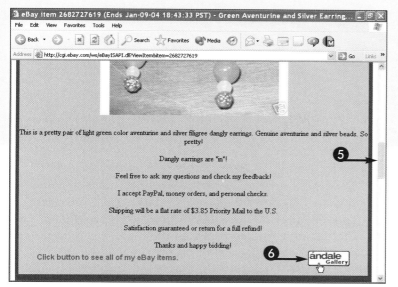

Your eBay auction opens in a new window.

5 Scroll down to the Description section.

6 Click andale Gallery.

andale displays thumbnail images of your other auction items.

● Buyers can see your other auctions and click a link to bid on one.

TIPS

More Options!

You can customize your Gallery so your thumbnail images show directly beneath your item's photo in an auction page, and set other display options. From the andale Gallery page, click Customize Gallery, and then select the Gallery in listing option, which displays up to fifty items in your listing. Click Continue. You can select an option from a menu of design themes, color themes, and fonts. You can also select an option to place the Gallery in the bottom or the top of the listing. You can type a business name and promotion text. Click Continue. You can select an option to feature up to eight items, and select custom categories to display in your Gallery. Click Done to save your settings.

Appeal to buyers with SquareTrade's
SEAL OF APPROVAL

You can attract more buyers to your auctions and inspire more confidence in your bidders with a SquareTrade Seal of Approval. SquareTrade Seal benefits include automatic insertion of the seal into your eBay listings, notification when you receive negative feedback, and up to $750 in buyer protection. You also receive activity reports that show you when buyers view your auctions the most as well as buyer alert e-mails that tell bidders you are a SquareTrade Seal Member who cares about giving them a positive buying experience.

To sign up for a SquareTrade Seal of Approval, go to the SquareTrade home page at www.squaretrade.com. The SquareTrade Seal costs $7.50 each month after your 30-day free trial. You can also prepay $67.50 for a year, saving 25 percent off the monthly fees, and get the premium features, which include sales reports, discounts off mediation services, and increased buyer protection.

For more information about using SquareTrade, including mediating a dispute, see Task #41.

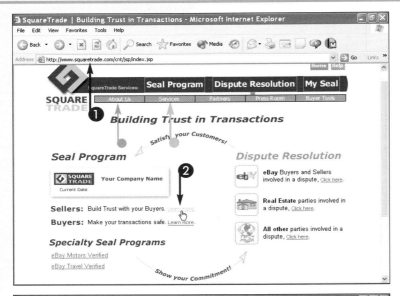

① Type **www.squaretrade.com** in the Address bar of your Web browser, and press Enter.

● You can click here to read about the SquareTrade company.

● You can click here to read about SquareTrade's services.

② Click the Learn more link.

The SquareTrade Seal Overview page appears.

● You can scroll down to read about the Seal Program's benefits.

③ Click Apply Now.

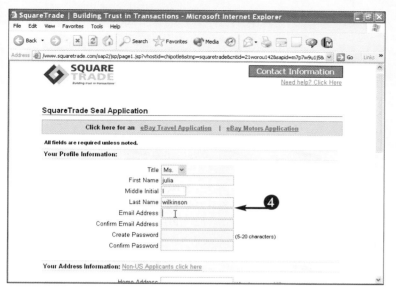

The SquareTrade Seal application page appears.

④ Type your profile information into the form text boxes.

SquareTrade guides you through the application process.

SquareTrade thanks you for applying and informs you that it will send you an e-mail to confirm your identity.

When SquareTrade confirms your identity and activates your account, you receive the SquareTrade Seal of Approval, and eBay inserts the SquareTrade logo into your auction listings.

TIPS

More Options!

You can get a customized SquareTrade Seal to use in your auctions. SquareTrade personalizes the Seal with your eBay user ID and that day's date on your eBay listings. That way, buyers know that the Seal is really yours. The personalization protects you from unauthorized use of your Seal.

More Options!

A Business Reporting Center is coming soon to SquareTrade. It features over 20 reports in chart format to help you analyze your sales. The reports help you to keep track of how your business performance changes from month to month, and how your auctions compare to those of other sellers in the same categories. The reports are updated daily, and you can export the data to Microsoft Excel or other spreadsheet programs.

ATTRACT TRAFFIC
to your auction

You can attract bidders who search for auctions using related words by running ads with Keywords on eBay. eBay shoppers use the search box millions of times each day, so Keywords on eBay ads can significantly boost your auctions' visibility. Your banner ad runs on the search results page that eBay members see when they perform searches using the same keywords or phrases that you specify.

You can link your ad to an auction, to multiple auctions, or to your eBay store. The Keywords on eBay site guides you through the creation of your ad banner. If you prefer, you can upload a banner of your own.

You can designate your budget for the ad campaign, and your bid for the ad's cost per click. You only pay when someone clicks on your ad. eBay automatically pauses your campaign when the auction to which the campaign is linked ends. Be careful not to spend more than you can afford, especially with your first campaign.

To perform this task, you must first go to the Keywords on eBay Web site at ebay.admarketplace. net, and register for the service.

① Type **ebay.admarketplace.net**, in the Address bar of your Web browser, and press Enter.

The eBay Keywords home page appears.

② Log into the site.

Your Campaign Summary appears, with information about any current or previous campaigns.

③ Click the Create New Campaign tab.

The Create New Campaign page appears.

④ Type a Campaign Name in the text box.

⑤ Type an amount for your campaign budget.

The minimum budget is $20

⑥ Click Proceed to Keyword Group.

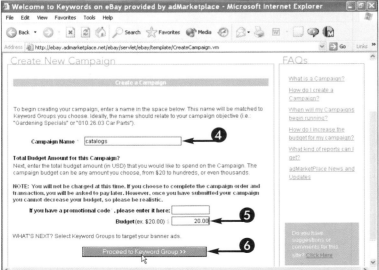

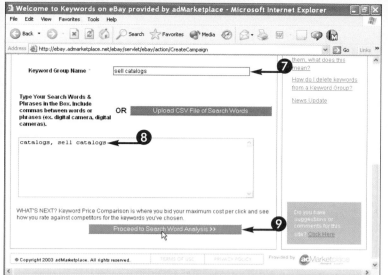

The Keyword Group page opens.

⑦ Type a Keyword Group Name in the text box.

⑧ Type your keywords or phrases in the text box.

⑨ Click Proceed to Search Word Analysis.

DIFFICULTY LEVEL

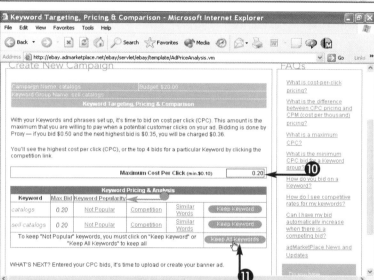

⑩ In the Keyword Pricing and Analysis section, type a maximum cost per click amount.

● You can click here to review the popularity of your keywords.

⑪ Click Keep All Keywords.

eBay guides you through the rest of the ad creation process.

When a buyer types one of your keywords in an eBay search, they see your banner ad.

Boost all auctions with a
STRATEGIC ITEM

You can attract more bidders to all your auctions by listing just one special item that attracts a lot of attention. Even if your other items are not as unique or expensive as your strategic item, more bidders are likely to view these auctions. Many eBay sellers agree that this strategy works very well for getting bids for their other items.

If you have a limited inventory of big-ticket items, you can spread out your strategic auctions over time. In this way, your other auctions benefit from being listed with the attention-drawing items for the longest period of time.

You can use various methods to attract bidders to your other auctions: bidders can simply click the View seller's other items link; you can reference the other auctions in your strategic auction description; or you can use the andale Gallery tool to showcase thumbnail photos of your other items. For more on cross-promoting your auctions, see Tasks #71 and #72.

This task assumes you know how to list an item. For more information on listing an item, see Task #68 and Chapter 5.

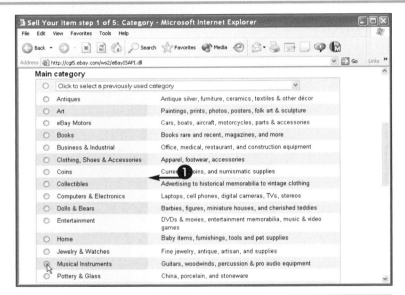

LIST A STRATEGIC ITEM AS A SELLER

① In the Sell Your Item: Select Category page, select the main category option for your strategic item.

Make the strategic item expensive or attention-getting, similar to a store window display item.

eBay steps you through selecting a subcategory.

② In the Sell Your Item: Describe Your Item form, type words in your auction description that describe your strategic item.

You can mention any special details, including the item's retail value.

Note: For more on attractive auction descriptions, see Task #68.

③ Click Continue.

eBay steps you through the listing process and lists your item.

DIFFICULTY LEVEL

① In the item listing page for a strategic item, you can scroll down to the counter stats, which show the number of visits your auction has received.

In this example, over 500 people viewed this item, which is a high number of people.

② Scroll up to the Seller Information section.

③ Click the View seller's other items link to check the seller's other auctions.

Buyers who are attracted by your strategic item may bid on a seller's other items.

TIPS

eBay Savvy!

To learn the techniques of successful sellers, consider viewing their auctions for up to the past two weeks. You can do so by clicking the Search tab, clicking the By Seller tab, and then typing the seller's eBay user ID in the text box. Select the All option next to Include completed items, and then click Search. You can also learn by participating in the eBay Community Forums. For more information about eBay's Discussion Boards, see Tasks #93 to #96.

eBay Savvy!

To improve the click-through rates in your auctions, you can add text to the title and description that reference an item's brand, age, or retail value. You can also use eBay abbreviations to conserve space in an auction title.

Smart Shipping for Sellers

Packaging and shipping items are among the least favorite tasks that eBay sellers must perform. However, with the tools described in this chapter, you can lighten your workload considerably in this area of your business.

For example, you can easily look up shipping rates online, or use flat rates, thus eliminating the need to estimate shipping rates altogether.

You can empower your customers to find out their own shipping information by placing a shipping calculator in your auction listing. eBay customers also appreciate clearly written shipping and packaging terms. You can keep your costs down by using services like U-PIC's discount shipping insurance, ordering low-cost supplies, and even getting free packing

supplies. You can pass these savings on to your customers and give yourself an edge over other sellers.

Shipping entails risk for both buyers and sellers. As a seller, you can protect yourself against loss by ordering delivery confirmation, insurance, or both. Of all the shipping-related tasks, the least enjoyable for most eBay users is waiting in line at the post office. You can eliminate this task by buying and printing your own stamps. You can then either drop off your packages at given locations or have your mail carrier pick them up. Special shippers such as Craters and Freighters, can handle the shipping of large or awkward items. Once you are familiar with the various shipping services and methods that are available, you can decide what works best for you.

Top 100

Create good
TERMS OF SALE

You can attract more bidders to your auctions if you clearly state your packaging, shipping, and return policy in your auctions. You can also save time answering e-mails from prospective bidders if you place as much detail in your auctions about your terms of sale as possible. Although eBay prompts you for terms of sale details in the Sell Your Item pages, consider repeating them in the item description area.

Be sure to state what types of payment you accept, how you charge for shipping, and your return policy. Many sellers charge separately for handling or

packaging, so it is a good idea to be clear about those details. You risk getting negative feedback if you surprise buyers with added costs on top of what they pay for shipping. To determine shipping costs, see Task #84. To include a shipping calculator in your listing, see Task #85.

One successful eBay seller suggests phrasing your sale terms positively — "I accept PayPal and money orders" — rather than negatively — "NO personal checks!" — because negative wording may scare off bidders.

❶ In the eBay home page, click Sell.

The Sell Your Item: Choose Selling Format page appears.

❷ Click the Sell item at online Auction option.

eBay prompts you to select a category in the next screen.

❸ Click Continue.

The Sell Your Item: Describe Your Item page appears.

❹ Type a title for your item.

● You can type an optional item subtitle.

❺ Click ☑ and select the specific options that describe your item.

172

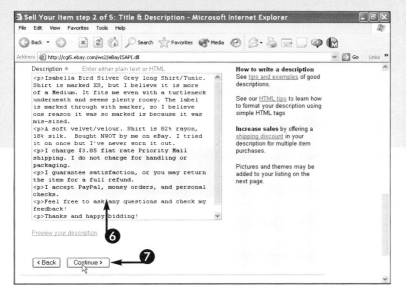

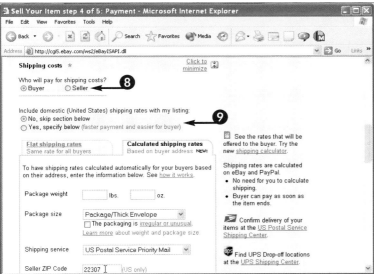

DIFFICULTY LEVEL

6 Type your shipping, return, and payment policy in the item description text box.

Note: For more on adding HTML tags to make your text more interesting, see Task #68.

7 Click Continue.

In the Provide Pictures and Item Details page, eBay guides you through setting an auction duration, starting price, and picture details.

The Enter Payment & Shipping page guides you through selecting the payment methods you want to accept.

8 Click to specify who pays for shipping.

9 Click whether to include shipping rates.

For more on shipping rates, see Task #84.

TIPS

eBay Savvy!

Because buyers may be very sensitive to how much you charge for shipping, consider charge an exact amount — which involves weighing the item and looking up the shipping cost to the destination ZIP code. Exact amounts help you avoid negative feedback from buyers who think you overcharge for shipping. If you charge for handling or packaging costs, clearly state so in the auction description. For more information about calculating shipping costs, see Tasks #84, #86, and #92.

eBay Savvy!

When you buy on eBay if you do not see the shipping cost specified, you can use the Ask seller a question link on the item's listing page. For more information about the Ask seller a question feature, see Task #13.

Retrieve
SHIPPING INFORMATION

You can easily determine the shipping for an item by using the United States Postal Service, or USPS, Web site, which has a shipping calculator for both domestic and international items. Once you know the correct postage, you can place it on your packages and eliminate waiting in line at the post office by either handing the package to your mail carrier or placing it directly in a mailbox or other postal pickup location. You need to know your package's weight and destination ZIP code. You can calculate postage for a postcard, letter, envelope, or package.

The USPS Web site asks you to specify the size of the package. If the length of the longest side of the package plus the distance around its thickest part equals 84 inches or less, the USPS considers the package a regular size. If it is more than 84 inches but less than or equal to 108 inches, the USPS considers it a large package.

You can indicate any special characteristics your package has, and choose from different types of mail services, such as Express, Priority, or Parcel Post.

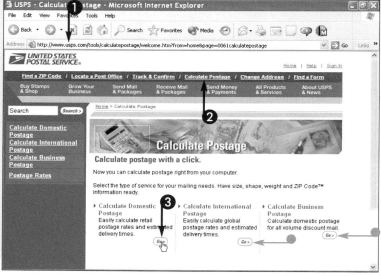

① Type **usps.com** into the Address bar of your Web browser and press Enter.

The USPS home page appears.

② Click the Calculate Postage link.

The Calculate Postage page appears.

③ Click Go under Calculate Domestic Postage.

● You can also click Go for international or business postage.

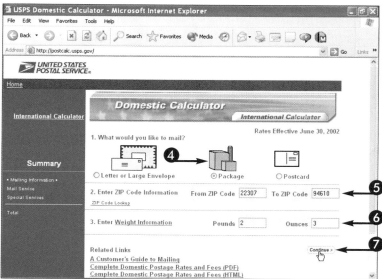

The Domestic Calculator page appears.

④ Click to select an item to mail.

⑤ Type your ZIP code and the destination ZIP code.

⑥ Type the weight of your item.

⑦ Click Continue.

174

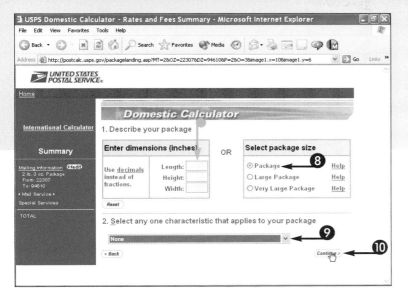

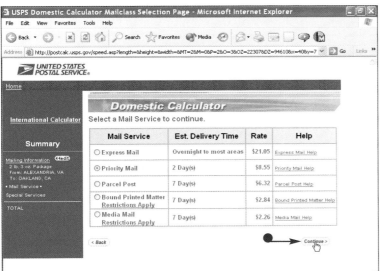

8 Click a package size option.

● You can also type the dimensions of your package.

9 Click the package characteristic arrow ☑ and select an option, if applicable.

Package characteristics range from less than 6 inches long to a film case over 5 pounds or with strap-type closures.

DIFFICULTY LEVEL

10 Click Continue.

A table appears with shipping rates for most types of mail service, and estimated delivery times.

● You can click Continue to add special services to your package.

Note: For more on the services that USPS has to offer, see Task #88.

TIPS

More Options!

You can also use the United Parcel Service, or UPS. You can obtain shipping and tracking information at their Web site, www.ups.com. To find shipping rates, go to www.ups.com/content/us/en/shipping/index.html and click the Estimate Cost link.

eBay Savvy!

You can find assembled links about shipping methods and costs on the AuctionBytes Web site at www.auctionbytes.com/Yellow_Pages/Postman/postman.html.

More Options!

You can add special services to your package on the USPS site, such as certified mail, insurance, registered mail, collect on delivery — or COD — and return receipt for merchandise. To select a special service, click Continue on the Mail Service page that contains shipping rates. The Special Services page appears. You can also select None of These options.

Place a
SHIPPING CALCULATOR
in your listing

You can save time and money and increase your customers' satisfaction by placing a shipping calculator in your auctions. This allows customers to determine their own shipping costs, and prevents e-mails from buyers about shipping fees. The calculator can also save you from making errors in estimating shipping on your own.

eBay offers a shipping calculator option in its Sell Your Item forms. eBay's shipping calculator determines United States Postal Service and United Parcel Service shipping charges based on the buyer's ZIP code

within the United States. Buyers can then see the shipping calculator in your listing in the Shipping & payment details section, under the item description.

Although eBay's shipping calculator supports most eBay auctions, it does not calculate shipping for outside of the United States or for shipping services that are not shown within the calculator, such as UPS Next Day Air. eBay's shipping calculator also does not calculate the shipping costs of multiple items purchased from one seller. For information about calculating your shipping costs using the USPS Web site, see Task #84.

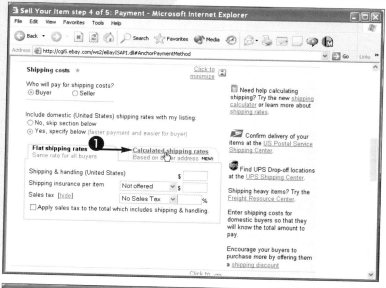

① In the Sell Your Item: Enter Payment and Shipping page, click the Calculated shipping rates link.

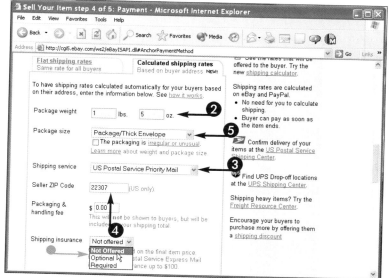

The Calculated shipping rates tab appears.

② Type the weight of the package.

③ Click the Package size and Shipping service ☑, and select the options you want.

④ Type the seller's ZIP code.

● You can click here and select an insurance option.

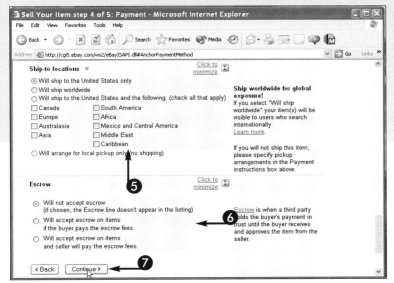

⑤ Scroll down and select a ship-to location option.

⑥ Click an escrow option.

The default setting is Will not accept escrow.

Note: *For more information about escrow, see Task #39.*

⑦ Click Continue and fill out the remainder of the Sell Your Item form.

eBay lists your item.

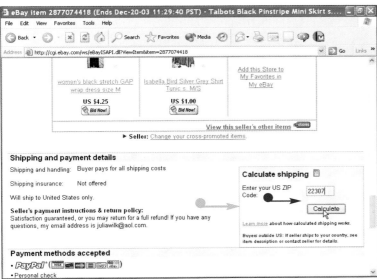

● When bidders view your listing, a Calculate shipping section appears.

● Bidders can type their ZIP code and click the Calculate button to compute their shipping costs.

TIPS

More Options!

You can choose from several third-party shipping calculators. AuctionInc's aiShip calculates both UPS and USPS rates, and works with all listing tools. To find out more, go to www.auctioninc.com and click Learn More! under aiShip Shipping Calculator. aiShip costs $0.10 for each auction sale, with a maximum charge of $9.50 each month. aiShip does not charge for unsold auctions or for calculator hits.

You can also use the free shipping calculator at www.beesonware.com/shippingcalculator.

Did You Know?

eBay's shipping calculator also computes insurance and taxes. Because the item's final price determines the rate, the calculator only shows the shipping insurance rate when the auction ends. For more information about eBay's shipping calculator, go to pages.ebay.com/help/buy/ship-calc-buyer-overview.html.

Save time and money with
FLAT RATES

You can spare yourself the trouble of looking up each item's shipping information by using flat shipping rates in your auctions. A *flat rate* is a consistent rate that is meant to be close to an item's actual shipping cost.

Although some eBay shoppers may expect exact shipping rates, many understand that flat rates can save sellers time and money — savings that a seller can pass on to buyers. If you inform prospective bidders by placing a clear notation in your auction description that you charge a flat shipping rate, buyers can decide if they want to bid on your auction

if they find the shipping amount acceptable. One eBay seller has used flat rates in over 750 auctions, with no buyer complaints.

Flat-rate shipping is especially useful for sellers who list similar types of items that tend to have the same shipping cost.

However, you may not want to use flat-rate shipping for large, heavy items where a margin of error in shipping can add up to a significant amount of money. For more on large, valuable and fragile items, see Task #92.

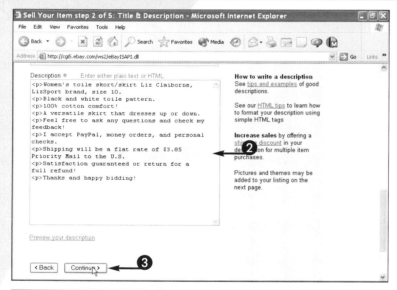

❶ In the eBay home page, click Sell.

The Sell Your Item: Choose Selling Format page appears.

Note: *For more information about creating a listing see Task #68.*

❷ Scroll down the Sell Your Item: Describe Your Item page, and type information about your flat rates in the item description text box.

❸ Click Continue.

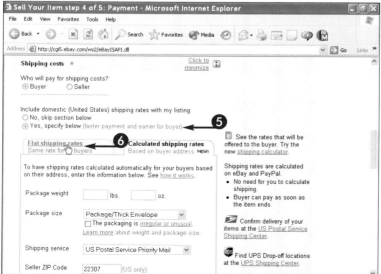

❹ Fill out the Sell Your Item: Provide Pictures & Item Details page, and click Continue.

Note: *For more information about this page, see Tasks #65 and #68.*

The Enter Payment & Shipping page appears.

❺ Scroll down and at the Include domestic shipping rates with my listing section, click the Yes, specify below option.

❻ Click the Flat shipping rates tab.

178

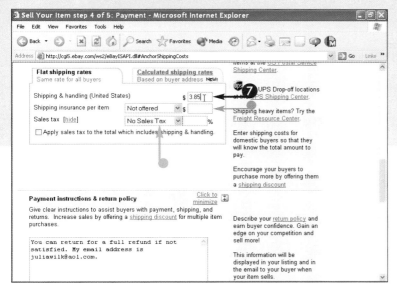

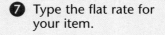
The Flat shipping rates tab appears.

7 Type the flat rate for your item.

● You can type a rate for shipping insurance.

● You can type a rate for sales tax.

DIFFICULTY LEVEL

8 Click Continue.

eBay guides you through the remainder of the listing process.

● When a buyer views your listing, your flat shipping rates appear.

---

eBay Savvy!

There are different ways to determine flat rates. One seller uses the average cost of shipping the same product to three parts of the country, and then adds $1. This seller sells items with similar weights.

Another seller bases the cost of shipping on the Zone 8 ZIP codes shipping rate, and recovers postage, but not packaging, costs for buyers in Zone 8. If a buyer is in Zones 5 to 7, the seller recovers packaging but not handling costs. If the buyer lives in Zones 1 to 4, the seller recovers postage, all packaging materials and a small labor charge. To help in calculating flat rates, you can get a postal zone chart at postcalc.usps.gov/Zonecharts.

Print your
OWN STAMPS

You can print stamps and mailing labels from your own printer, thus eliminating long waits at the post office. You can also get free delivery confirmation with Stamps.com.

To use Stamps.com, you must first sign up for the service and download the free software from the Stamps.com Web site. Stamps.com then appears as an icon on your desktop.

Stamps.com offers two different pricing plans: The Simple Plan, which costs 10 percent of your printed postage, with a minimum of $4.49 of purchases each month; or the Power Plan, which costs $15.99 each

month, in addition to your actual costs for postage. If you buy over $150 worth of postage a month, consider using the Power Plan.

With either plan, you receive a 29-day free trial, with $10 or $20 in free postage during the trial. You also receive a free postal supplies kit, which includes a Getting Started Guide, a sheet of NetStamps labels, a sheet of Internet postage labels, and a sheet of adhesive shipping labels. If you do not cancel this service, Stamps.com charges you on day 30 for using the service.

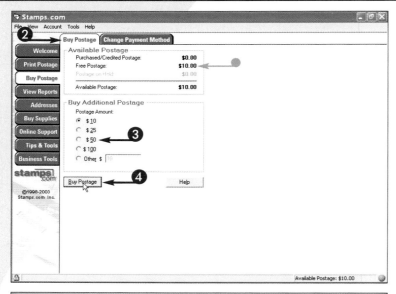

BUY POSTAGE

❶ On your desktop, double-click the Stamps.com icon and log in.

❷ In the Stamps.com home page, click Buy Postage.

● The Buy Postage page appears, showing your free postage credit.

❸ Click a Postage Amount option.

❹ Click Buy Postage.

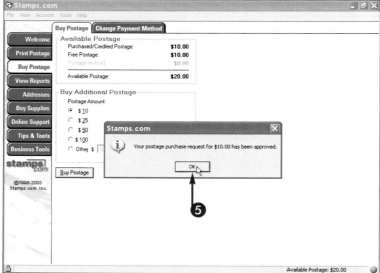

A dialog box appears, telling you that your postage purchase request has been approved.

❺ Click OK.

⑥ Click the Print Postage tab.

A Postage Printing Options dialog box appears.

Stamps.com explains your different postage printing options.

⑦ Click OK.

⑧ Click a tab for the type of postage that you want.

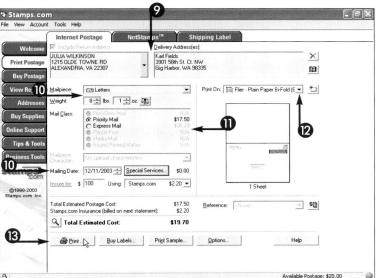

⑨ Type the return and delivery addresses.

⑩ Click here and select a mailpiece, weight, and mailing date.

⑪ Click a Mail Class option.

⑫ Click here and select the paper for printing.

Your total estimated cost appears.

⑬ Click Print.

Your postage prints.

TIPS

Did You Know?

Stamps.com offers several pickup and drop-off options. If it is not too large, you can give the package to your local mail carrier, or drop packages into any street mailbox. If you need to add Registered Mail or USPS insurance, you can take the package to your local post office. For an additional $12.50, you can schedule a pickup for an unlimited number of packages; this option is only available for Priority Mail, Express Mail, and Parcel Post. You can schedule a pickup online, or call 800-222-1811.

eBay Savvy!

Stamps.com offers a Hidden Postage feature for Power Plan customers, which allows sellers to print shipping labels without the actual postage value on the label. Sellers find they get fewer complaints about shipping charges with this feature.

PROTECT YOURSELF
with delivery confirmation and insurance

You can ensure that your packages arrive safely, and help protect yourself from dishonest bidders, by purchasing delivery confirmation and insurance. You can also request a return receipt so that the shipping service contacts you when the package arrives.

You can get delivery confirmation at a local post office for between $0.45 for Priority Mail and $0.55 for First-Class and Parcel Post.

The Postal Service does not charge additional fees for online delivery confirmation because the United States Postal Service receives an electronic record of your transaction. However, the online delivery

confirmation service is only available to those who use online shipping labels, which are available at http://sss-web.usps.com/ds/jsps/index.jsp.

The insurance fees for merchandise are $1.30 for between $0.01 and $50 worth of merchandise; and they range from $2.20 for from $50.01 to $100 worth of merchandise, to $11.20 for $1,000 worth. The USPS charges $11.20 plus $1 for each $100 over $1,000 for between $1,000 and $5,000 worth of merchandise.

This task assumes that you have already performed the steps to retrieve the shipping information for your package per the steps in Task #84.

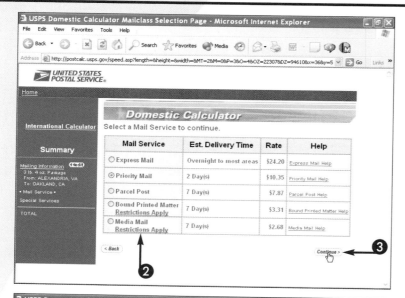

① Using the Calculate Postage link in **usps.com** determine your package's shipping information.

Note: To determine your shipping information using USPS's Domestic shipping calculator see Task #85.

② In the Domestic Calculator page, click the option you want.

③ Click Continue.

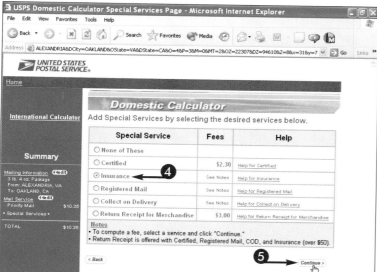

The Special Services page appears.

④ Click the Insurance option.

You can also select one of the other Special service options.

⑤ Click Continue.

182

#88

DIFFICULTY LEVEL

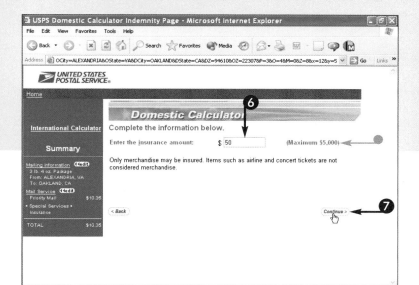

The insurance amount page appears.

6 Type the amount for which you want to insure the item.

● The maximum insurance amount is $5,000.

7 Click Continue.

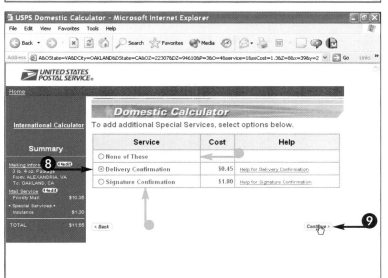

An additional Special Services page appears.

8 Click the Delivery Confirmation option.

● You can also select None of These or Signature Confirmation.

9 Click Continue.

USPS displays your total cost, including the cost for delivery confirmation and insurance.

Did You Know?

You can use the Delivery Confirmation option with: first-class packages that weigh 13 ounces or less; Priority Mail packages; Parcel Post; media mail — or book rate; bound, printed matter; or library mail. For more information, go to www.usps.com/send/waystosendmail/extraservices/deliveryconfirmationservice.htm.

Did You Know?

You can also use Delivery Confirmation with extra services, such as: Return Receipt for Merchandise; Insured Mail; Registered Mail; Collect on Delivery — or C.O.D.; Special Handling; Merchandise Return Service — where you pay the postage for items sent back to you; Return Receipt; or Restricted Delivery — where only a specified person can receive the piece of mail. For more information, go to www.usps.com/send/waystosendmail/extraservices/deliveryconfirmationservice.htm.

Using U-PIC to
INSURE PACKAGES

You can save 60 percent to 80 percent on insuring packages by using Universal Parcel Insurance Coverage, or U-PIC. Depending on how many packages you send, you can save hundreds, or even thousands, of dollars each year on your insurance costs.

U-PIC is a discounted insurance service for packages that you ship with major carriers, such as the United Parcel Service, the U.S. Postal Service, and Federal Express. Although the carrier ships the package, it is insured by U-PIC. U-PIC has no minimum requirements, and offers different programs for different types of shippers.

To use U-PIC, you must first fill out the Request to Provide Coverage form on the U-PIC Web site. U-PIC reviews your form and contacts you to determine what U-PIC program best suits your needs. After U-PIC approves you for coverage, they send you a policy and a supply of claim forms. Then, instead of declaring value with your carrier, you do so with U-PIC.

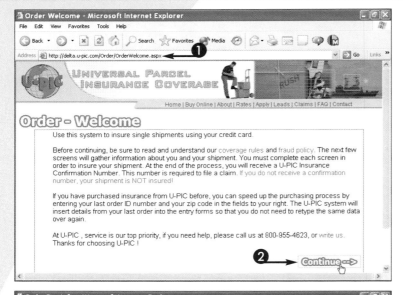

① Type **delta.u-pic.com/Order/OrderWelcome.aspx** into the Address bar of your Web browser, and press Enter.

The U-PIC Order Welcome page appears.

② Click the Continue link.

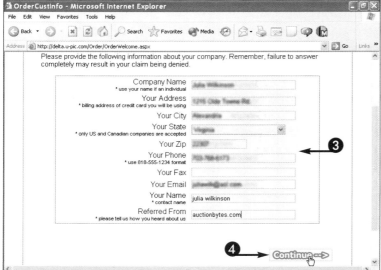

The Customer Information section appears.

③ Type your name, address, phone number, e-mail address, and other requested information.

④ Click Continue.

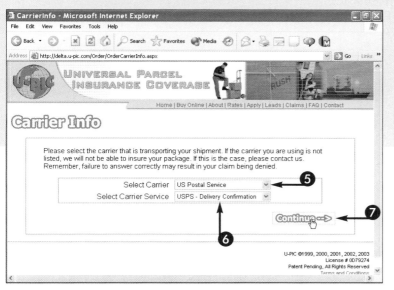

The Carrier Information page appears.

#89

⑤ Click here and select a carrier option.

⑥ Click here and select a carrier service.

⑦ Click Continue.

U-PIC gives you the price to insure your package and guides you through the rest of the order process.

When you are finished, an Insurance Confirmation page appears, with the details of your order.

⑧ Click Continue.

U-PIC finalizes your order.

More Options!

After submitting your personal information with U-PIC in the first order, you do not need to retype this information for future orders. When you type a previous order ID, along with your ZIP code for security, U-PIC automatically fills in the appropriate fields for you.

Did You Know?

At any time during the U-PIC order process, you can click Stop, I'd like to quit link. U-PIC does not process your order until it has your billing information. Until you receive an order ID and confirmation, your package is not yet insured.

Did You Know?

On the Carrier Service Page, make sure that you select which type of carrier service you want, as the services have different levels of risk, and therefore different costs.

Using eBay to purchase
PACKING SUPPLIES

Almost every type of packing supply that you need is available on eBay, and you can save a lot of time by purchasing them online. Because many sellers offer good deals, you can also save money. eBay sellers offer everything from bubble wrap and tissue paper to Tyvek mailers and packing boxes.

Because eBay is a ready-made market for shipping supplies, you can get good deals from eBay vendors who sell in bulk. You can also buy multiple packing items from the same seller in order to save money on shipping fees. Several eBay Stores also

specialize in packaging supplies, and you can use the link to a seller's eBay store, if applicable, to search for more items from a seller. Although you do have to pay shipping fees for packing supplies that you buy on eBay, the dollar value in terms of time saved makes it worthwhile to buy the supplies online.

For more information about obtaining good deals on shipping supplies, see Task #91. For more information about buying multiple items from the same seller to save on shipping costs, see Task #20.

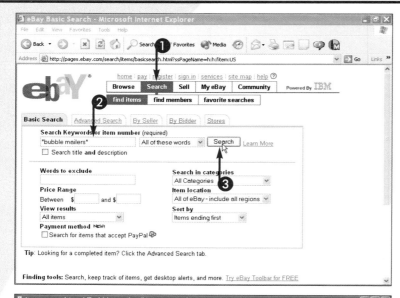

① In the eBay home page, click Search.

The Search page appears.

② Type the search word or words that describe the shipping supplies that you want.

③ Click Search.

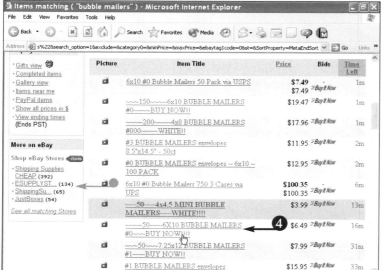

eBay lists the search results.

● You can click here to view the eBay Stores that offer related items.

④ Click an item listing.

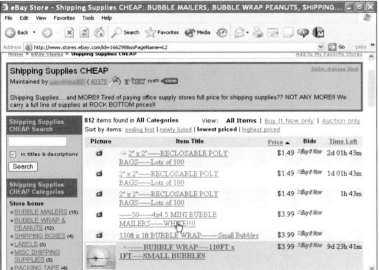

The details page appears for the listing.

A picture of the item appears along with its description.

⑤ Click the seller's eBay Store link to search for related shipping supplies.

The seller's eBay Store page appears.

You can buy more shipping supplies and ask the seller to combine shipping costs, thus saving you money.

More Options!

Other places to find good deals on shipping supplies include www.papermart.com, www.packagingprice.com, www.uline.com, and www.vikingop.com. You can also check your local dollar store for attractive and inexpensive boxes. Some retail establishments, such as grocery stores, offer boxes, which they no longer need, for free. Check with the store management about their policy on free boxes.

More Options!

For more information about packing and shipping supplies, and recommendations about good eBay shipping supply sellers, go to the eBay Community Discussion Board on Packaging & Shipping. From the eBay home page, click the Community button, then click Discussion Boards, and then click the Packaging & Shipping link under Community Help Boards. For more on Community Help Boards, see Chapter 10.

Order
FREE SUPPLIES

You can get free packing and shipping supplies from the United States Postal Service when you order Priority Mail or more-expensive services, such as Express Mail. You can order them online, and USPS delivers them to you for free.

The USPS.com Web site offers many types of supplies, including cardboard boxes of various sizes, Tyvek mailers, postal tape, mail stickers, and labels. Some of the supplies are for special-sized items, such as long tubes that are ideal for mailing posters and some works of art.

You can also get supplies for different types of mail, such as Priority Mail, Express Mail, and Global Express Mail.

If you use Parcel Post shipping, you cannot receive free USPS supplies, and you still need to buy postage for your packages.

You must only use the free USPS supplies for the type of mail service for which they are intended. Before you check out your free supplies, you must agree that the packaging is solely for sending the type of mail on the supply label, as misuse is a violation of federal law.

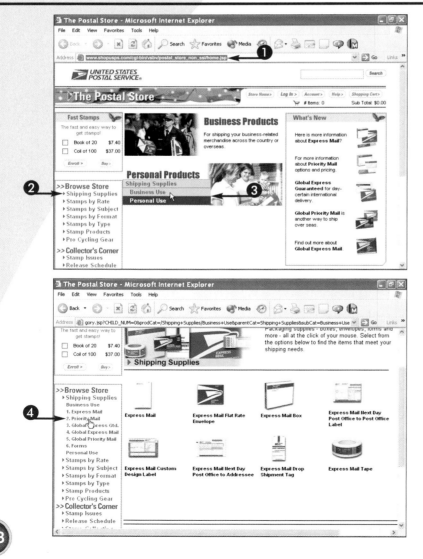

① Type **shop.usps.com/cgi-bin/ vsbv/postal_store_non_ssl/ home.jsp** into the Address bar of your Web browser, and press Enter.

The Postal Store page appears.

② Click Shipping Supplies.

③ Click the option that applies to you.

You can select either the Business Use or the Personal Use option.

The Shipping Supplies page appears.

④ Click the link to a supply type that you want.

This example selects Priority Mail.

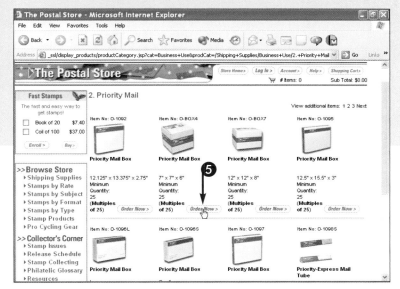

The Priority Mail page appears.

⑤ Click Order Now for the item you want.

The Shopping Cart page appears.

You can review or change the item quantity.

The USPS does not charge for these supplies.

⑥ Click Checkout.

USPS.com guides you through the rest of the checkout process, and delivers free shipping supplies to you.

TIPS

More Options!

You can also get free supplies from the United Parcel Service, or UPS, Web site. Type **www.ups.com** into your Web browser Address bar, select the option for your country, and then click the arrow icon. Click the Order Supplies link. You can view the available supplies, and click the Get Now link to order them.

Did You Know?

The USPS ships supplies through Priority Mail, and may take three to five business days for delivery to domestic addresses, and three weeks to arrive to foreign addresses.

eBay Savvy!

For another free source of packing supplies, use the plastic bags from your grocery store. They are ideal, lightweight packing materials, and using them saves you from having to throw them away.

Send
LARGE, VALUABLE, OR FRAGILE ITEMS

In some cases, you may need to ship large, valuable, or fragile items. The packaging and shipping company Craters and Freighters specializes in these items, and offers free pickup at your location, as well as free insurance. You can get an online shipping quote from Craters and Freighters at www.craters andfreighters.com.

To get a quote for packaging and transporting the item to anywhere in the 48 contiguous states, you need to know the item's destination address, weight and dimensions, value, and when you want the item to arrive. You can also receive a quote for just the transportation or the packaging.

Although Craters and Freighters can be more expensive than other shipping services, in some cases they offer advantages, such as in-home pickup, and experience in dealing with very large and valuable items. Their rates are best on items that are too big for UPS to ship.

You must register for the Craters and Freighters service before you can receive an e-quote or use their service.

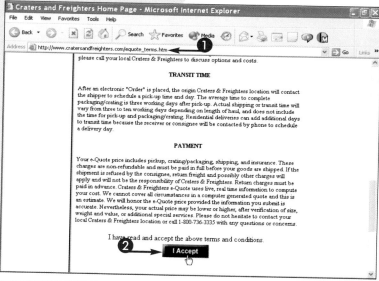

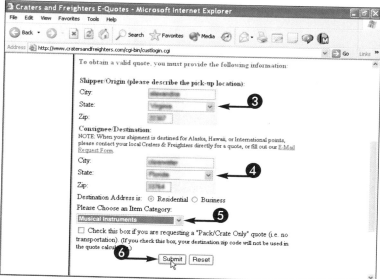

① Type **www.cratersand freighters.com/equote_terms. htm** into the Address bar of your Web browser, and press Enter.

A page of quote terms appears.

② Read the terms and click I Accept.

③ Type the city, state, and ZIP code of the shipment origin and destination.

④ Click an option for the destination address type.

⑤ Click here and select a category for the item.

⑥ Click Submit.

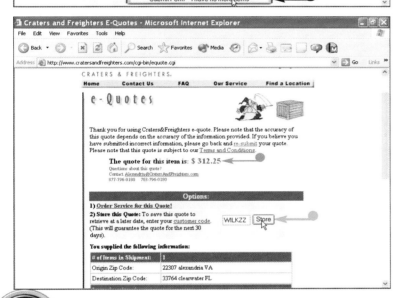

The Description section appears.

92

7 Type the dimensions and a declared value for your item.

8 Click a shipping option.

9 Type a description of the item.

10 Click here and select a subcategory.

11 Click Submit Form — I have no more items.

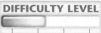

DIFFICULTY LEVEL

● A shipping quote appears.

● You can click Store to save this quote.

TIPS

More Options!

You can also send large and heavy items through other shipping services. With UPS, you can send packages that are up to 150 lbs, which measure up to 130 inches in combined length and girth. Oversize and very heavy packages may require special pricing. For more information, go to www.ups.com/content/us/en/resources/prepare/guidelines/index.htm.

Other shipping options include Federal Express at www.fedex.com/us and the United States Postal Service at www.usps.com. You can get rates by going to and clicking the rates button. For more information on calculating USPS rates, see Tasks #84 and #85.

More Options!

If you register your auction on the Craters and Freighters Web site, then Craters and Freighters lets your bidders determine their packaging and shipping costs directly from your auction listing. Go to www.cratersandfreighters.com/equote_auction_main.htm for more information.

Chapter 10

Tap into the eBay Community Gold Mine

You can find a wealth of information and resources in the eBay community. Other auction users are not only a valuable source of information, but also of friendship and support. The eBay Discussion Boards cover a wide range of topics, so you can easily find one or more boards that interest you.

For a smaller, more-specialized community, you can join an eBay Group and share items like photos and polls with fellow group members.

You can read discussions in the boards, as well as start new topics. You can navigate the boards in several ways, such as from the oldest or the most recent post. The Boards Search tool is an excellent way to uncover information that may otherwise be difficult to find.

If you need help immediately, you can use eBay's Live Chat Boards, which show the responses of other eBay users right away. You can also explore the topics in eBay's Help boards. eBay community members are extremely helpful, and some member experts even compile comprehensive resources and links in their About Me pages.

You can learn new skills with eBay University's online or offline classes. You can also explore the many resources for online auction users on the Web outside of eBay. Some of these sites offer helpful, free newsletters.

You can easily navigate all of the Community boards as well as the entire eBay site using the eBay site map.

Top 100

Find a Home
IN THE DISCUSSION BOARDS

You can learn more about the types of items you like to buy and sell as well as meet friends who share your interests by becoming a part of eBay's Discussion Boards community. The boards are full of knowledgeable eBay users from various fields of interest, ready help new members.

The eBay Category-Specific Discussion Boards contain every type of item you may want to sell or buy, and range from animals to vintage clothing. You can scan the list of categories and decide which interests you the most.

Before you post to a Discussion Board for the first time, read the eBay Board Usage Policies, available in each board's Welcome message. You may also want to *lurk* — read posts for a while without posting — to get accustomed to the topics that the board users discuss. For example, for some questions, the board's regular users may already have a long list of answers, or FAQs. If you are courteous, message board users should receive you warmly.

For more information about the eBay Discussion Boards, see Tasks #94 and #96.

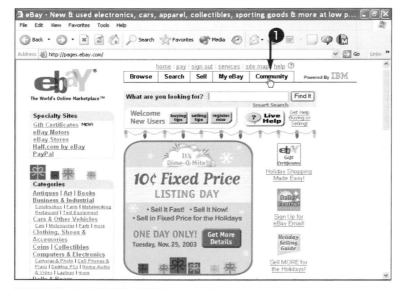

1 In the main eBay home page, click Community.

The eBay Community page appears.

● You can click this link to go to the Chat area.

● You can click this link to go to the Answer Center.

2 Click the Discussion Boards link.

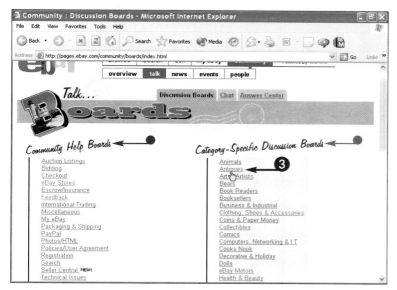

The Discussion Boards page appears.

- A list of links to Community Help Boards displays here.

- A list of links to Category-Specific Discussion Boards displays here.

3 Click the link of a Category that interests you.

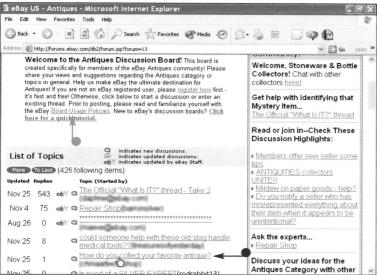

The Discussion Board page for that category appears with a Welcome message.

- You can click this link to read the Board Usage Policies.

- You can click a topic to read it, and join the Category's community by reading and posting messages.

TIPS

More Options!

To post a message on a Discussion Board, click Login at the bottom of the Board. A new screen appears, and eBay prompts you to log in. Once you log in, an Add Discussion link appears at the bottom of the board. Click the link to make a new post. You can also reply to an existing message by clicking the link to the message to which you want to reply, clicking Post Message, typing your reply in the Your Reply box, and then clicking Post Message.

Did You Know?

eBay staff highlight discussions that are particularly helpful or fun. You can find links to these discussions on the right side of the Discussion Board screen, under the category's Community heading.

Browse the
DISCUSSION BOARDS

To find the useful information you need on the eBay message boards — such as tips on where to find inventory, and sales techniques from fellow sellers — you must know how to navigate the boards. You can then move easily through discussions to read the posts and get the information you want.

When you click a Discussion Board topic, the first message that appears is the one that started that topic. After that, the messages are numbered sequentially in the order eBay users post them.

You can scroll through the messages using the More button at the bottom of a page of posts. In some cases, you can also scroll forward by a given number of posts using a button with that number on it. For example, if the button has a 25 on it, it scrolls you forward 25 posts. If there are many posts in a given topic, you can use the Recent button to go to the most recently posted messages. This helps you to avoid having to read messages that are weeks or months old.

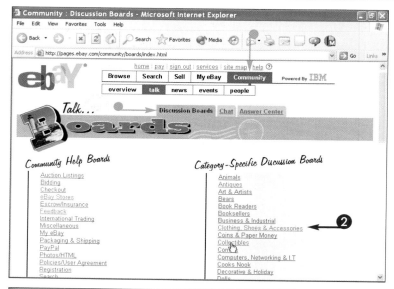

❶ Type **pages.ebay.com/ community/boards/index. html** into the Address bar of your Web browser, and then press Enter.

● You can also click Community in eBay's home page, and then click the Discussion Boards tab.

❷ Click the Discussion Board that interests you.

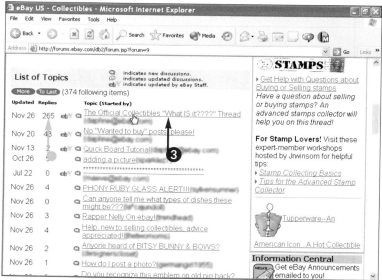

The Discussion Board page appears for the category that you selected.

A list of topics appears.

❸ Click the topic that interests you.

● The number of posts in to the topic appears here.

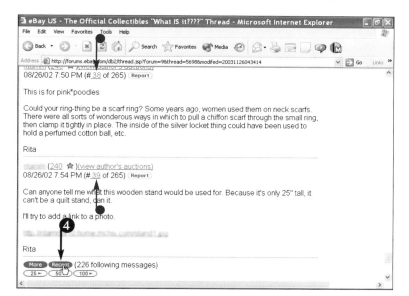

- The page appears for the topic you select with the first messages at the top of the page, in order from original message to most recent.

  You can scroll down to the bottom of the page to use the navigation buttons to quickly read the posts.

④ Click Recent.

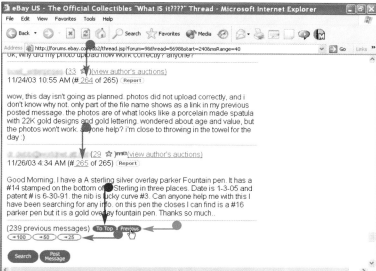

- The most recent messages appear.
- You can click Previous to see the page of messages before this page.
- You can click To Top to go back to the first messages in the topic.
- You can click a numbered button to scroll back by that number of posts.

 TIPS

More Options!

You can also search the Discussion Boards for keywords. To do so, click a Discussion Board link, and then click Search at the bottom of the topic page. In the search form that appears, type the word or words you want to find. Click Search, and eBay displays links to all the topics that match your keywords.

eBay Savvy!

Some Category Discussion groups have games and contests, informally run by other board users, designed to attract users to their auctions. You can read the boards regularly to find out when the contests are run.

You can receive more information about using the Discussion Boards by accessing the eBay Board help tutorial at http://forums.ebay.com/db1/thread.jsp? forum=120&thread=65945.

Get answers with
LIVE CHAT

If you have an urgent question, such as about an auction that is about to end, you can receive immediate help using the Chat Boards. Chat Boards allow you to view timely advice from eBay members as soon as you type a question.

Unlike Internet chat rooms, eBay's Chat Boards do not automatically refresh your screen: You must manually do this with the Reload button. Once you refresh, you see the most-recent messages, ranging from the last 5 minutes to the last 24 hours. The

most recent chat room messages display on the top of the page, and the chat threads disappear two weeks after the last post. You must be signed in to eBay to make a chat room post.

Once you sign in on eBay, you can choose from several chat rooms, including the original chat room, The eBay Café; The AOL Café, for AOL users; Discuss eBay's Newest Features; and an Images/HTML Board for help with photos and images in your auctions. The eBay Q&A Board is great for general questions.

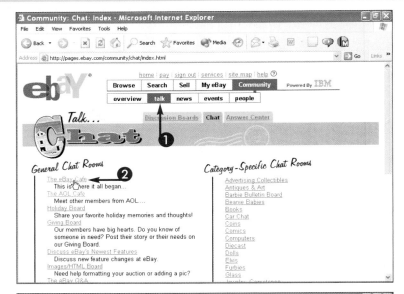

① In the eBay Community page, click the talk tab.

The eBay Chat page appears with a General Chat Rooms and a Category-Specific Chat Rooms list.

② Click a chat room link.

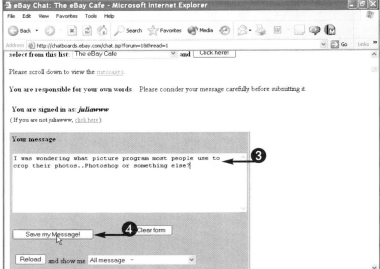

The selected chat room appears.

③ Type a message in the text box.

④ Click Save my Message!.

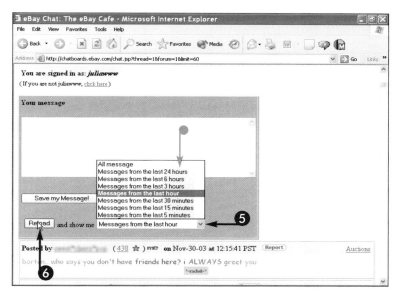

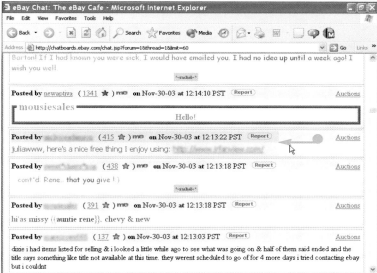

The page refreshes, and eBay sends your message to the chat room.

5 Click here and select a viewing option.

● The options range from the last 5 minutes to the last 24 hours.

6 Click Reload.

eBay refreshes the chat room page.

The most recent chat messages appear on the top of the page, which is the opposite of the default order for eBay's Discussion Boards.

● You can see if anyone has replied to your chat room posting.

TIPS

Did You Know?

The time-date stamp next to a member's eBay ID at the top of their post shows when they posted their chat message. The time is in Pacific Standard Time, or PST. You can also click the Auctions link to the far right of the time-date stamp to display that member's eBay auctions.

More Options!

eBay has many category-specific chat rooms about everything from advertising collectibles to trading cards. Category-specific chat rooms are often close communities that offer help and resources to members. For example, in the eBay Advertising Collectibles Chat Room, members post a Welcome Message with this link to helpful collectibles resources: www.signtech-rta.com/acboardlinks2. htm. This link includes links to sites about collectible Absolut Vodka ads, a Pepsi Cola Collectors Club, and a Cereal Box Archive.

Get answers with
MESSAGE BOARDS

You can receive answers to your eBay questions using the Community Help Boards, located in the main Boards page, to the left of the Category-Specific Discussion Boards. These message boards are a great place to post questions about any subject, from eBay auction listings to shipping, because so many helpful members reply to these boards regularly.

You can also scan these boards to see if similar questions to yours have already been asked and answered. In fact, you may want to first search a specific message board for the word or words about

which you have a question, because someone has probably already asked it and the answer is on the board. For information on how to search the boards, see Task #94.

The eBay Community Help Boards are in alphabetical order, starting with Auction Listings and ending with Trust & Safety (SafeHarbor).

If you are a beginner, or have a basic question, you may want to post your question on the New to eBay board, located under General Discussion Boards, beneath the Community Help Boards.

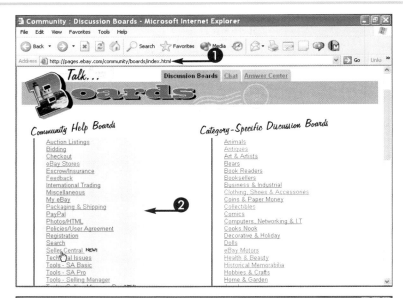

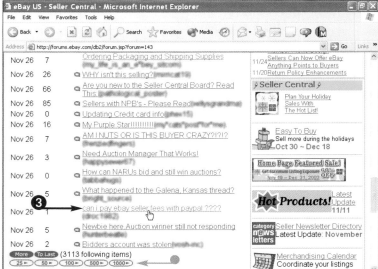

① Type **pages.ebay.com/ community/boards/index. html** into the Address bar of your Web browser, and then press Enter.

You can also click Community in the eBay home page, and then click the Discussion Boards link.

② Click a Community Help Board appropriate to your question.

This example uses the Seller Central Board link.

The Community Help Board page appears, with a list of topics.

③ Click an appropriate topic for your question.

● You can use the navigation tools to move through the board.

Note: *If an appropriate topic does not exist, you can create a one following the steps in Task #93. For more on navigating the boards, see Task #94.*

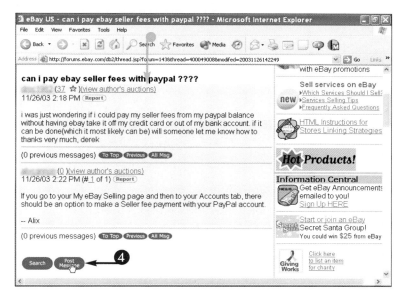

The topic appears.

- You can read the question and any answers that users have posted.

④ Click Post Message.

A page appears where you can reply to the message.

⑤ Type your question or reply in the Your Reply text box.

⑥ Click Post Message.

eBay posts your message to the list of existing messages.

TIPS

eBay Savvy!

Because eBay changes its features and policies regularly, it is crucial for both sellers and buyers to keep up-to-date on these changes. You can find valuable information about changes to eBay features and policies in the eBay Community area at eBay's General Announcements Board, located at www2.ebay.com/aw/marketing.shtml. You can find updates about any technical problems that the eBay site may experience, as well as system maintenance and downtimes, at the System Announcements Board, located at http://www2.ebay.com/aw/announce.shtml.

Did You Know?

Several newsletters and Web sites outside of eBay report on the fast-paced auction industry and offer free information that keeps you informed about the constantly changing eBay environment. For more about outside auction communities and newsletters, see Tasks #99 and #100.

Using eBay University to
TAKE CLASSES

You can improve your eBay skills by taking a class at eBay University. eBay University offers both offline classes, which you attend in person, and online classes, which you can access from your home computer. The main eBay University page is located at pages.ebay.com/university/.

Online eBay University classes address topics ranging from Getting Started — the basics of bidding and buying — to Enhanced Listings and Completing the Sale. Online Classes cost $19.95, and you can register for them online at ebayu.vitalstream.com/c1/registration1.html.

You can sign up for offline classes at pages.ebay.com/university/classes.html. In the eBay University Attend Classes page, you can select from a list of cities and dates where the classes are available.

Currently, eBay offers two different offline courses: Selling Basics, which includes opening a seller and PayPal account, creating listings, and setting prices; and Beyond the Basics, which covers more advanced topics, such as starting and marketing an eBay business, using listing tools, and packing and shipping your inventory.

REGISTER FOR OFFLINE CLASSES

① Type **pages.ebay.com/university/** into the Address bar of your Web browser, and then press Enter.

The eBay University page appears and displays the different courses it has to offer.

② Click the Learn More link for class that interests you.

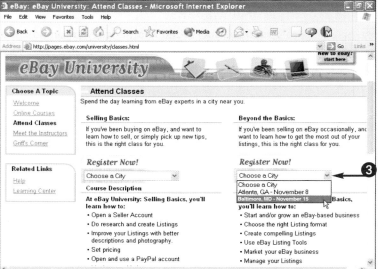

The Attend Classes page appears, displaying a description of the course that you selected.

③ Click here and select a city and date for class registration.

eBay guides you through the registration process.

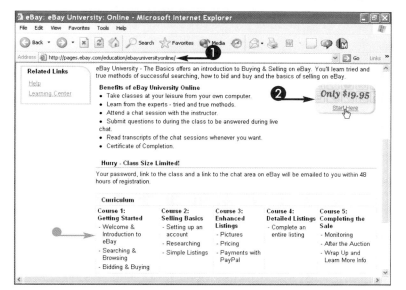

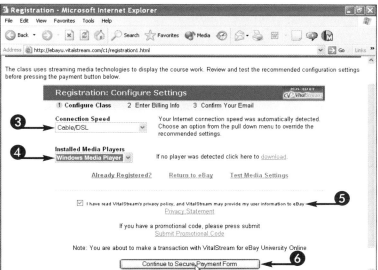

1 Type **pages.ebay. com/education/ebay universityonline/** into the Address bar of your Web browser, and then press Enter.

The Introducing eBay University Online! page appears.

● You can scroll through the Course descriptions.

2 Click the Start Here link.

The eBay University Registration page appears.

3 Click here and select a connection speed.

4 Click here and select an installed media player.

5 After reading the Privacy Statement, click this option.

6 Click Continue to Secure Payment Form.

eBay guides you through the registration process.

More Options!

You can take online classes about a wide range of eBay-related topics with eBay Workshops. eBay posts the archives of previous workshops on eBay at members. ebay.com/aboutme/workshopevents. Recent workshop topics include Collectibles, PayPal, Holiday Selling, and Seller's Assistant Pro Post-Sales Basics.

Did You Know?

If you have specialized knowledge, you can host your own eBay Workshop. For example, a vintage clothing merchant hosted a workshop and shared his tips for success. Tips included very specific and anecdotal examples, such as that certain plastic aprons from the 1950s sell for over $100, and that 1950s Christian Dior for Holt Renfrew dresses can sell for as much as $300 today on eBay. For more information about eBay Workshop, e-mail workshopevents@ebay.com or go to http://members.ebay.com/aboutme/workshopevents.

Network with
EBAY GROUPS

You can connect with other eBay users who share your interests or geographical location by joining an eBay Group. eBay Groups offer an excellent way to learn more about your field of interest and to get to know your fellow eBay users in a more personal community than that offered by a typical eBay Discussion Board.

People in the same eBay Group can develop their own community by using tools such as polls, photo albums, and calendars.

The eBay Groups home page allows you to view the different categories of groups that are available.

Groups are sorted into categories, such as: Collectors Clubs, for those who share a particular collecting or selling passion — for example, for Coins, Pottery/Porcelain, or Stamps; Seller Groups, for different types of sellers, such as PowerSellers and Store Owners; and Regional Groups, with different groups listed by state.

You can browse the list of eBay Groups in the eBay Groups home page, located at groups.ebay.com. You can also search the Groups by keyword or ZIP code to find the type of group you want to join.

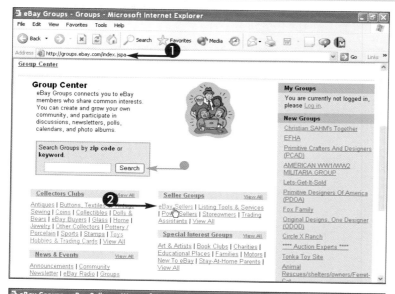

① Type **groups.ebay.com/** into The Address bar of your Web browser, and then press Enter.

The eBay Group Center page appears.

● You can search the Groups by typing a ZIP code or keyword and clicking Search.

② Click a subcategory link for a Group that interests you.

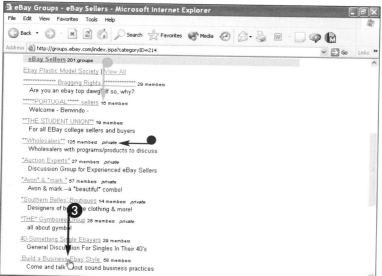

The eBay Group list appears for the category you select.

● eBay displays the number of members each group has.

● eBay displays whether each group is private or public.

③ Click the link for a group that interests you.

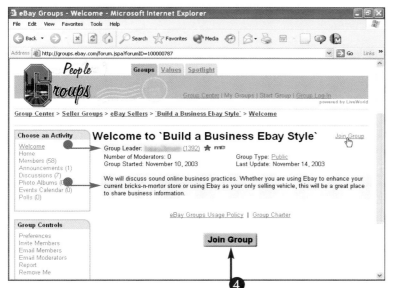

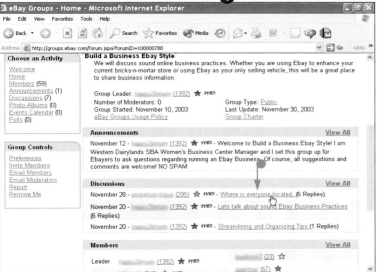

The eBay Groups page appears for the group you select.

- eBay displays the Group Leader's ID and a description for the group.

④ Click Join Group.

If you have not yet logged in, then eBay prompts you to do so.

The eBay Group Discussions list appears.

- You can click a discussion link to read the discussion or to post a message.

 TIPS

More Options!

eBay Groups can be either public or private, and are marked accordingly in the list of Groups. If you want to join a private Group, the Group Leader can invite you to join, or you can request to join by clicking the Join Group link in that Group's page. In the screen provide, type the reason you want to join and click Send Request. eBay tells you that your request has been sent, and the Group Leader contacts you if the Group grants you membership.

More Options!

For more information on participating or moderating an eBay Group, go to the eBay Groups Information Center at groups.ebay.com/forum.jspa?forumID=1254 and join the group. There you can find Group Controls, such as Preferences, Invite Members, and Remove Me.

Find outside
AUCTION COMMUNITIES

You can find valuable resource information about the sometimes-confusing array of auction tools — such as photo-hosting and listing-software services — and other auction-related topics at online communities such as AuctionBytes and the Online Traders Web Alliance, or OTWA. You can receive information from these sites that you may not find on eBay because they discuss third-party developers as well as alternative auction sites to eBay, such as Amazon, ePier, and Yahoo.

For example, the AuctionBytes site provides a message board community, where you can network and share information with other auction users, as well as several resource tables that present information clearly. You can view the Auction Management Services at a Glance chart, which shows the major auction management companies, such as andale and Auctionworks; the auction sites they support; and their prices. You can also view a chart that compares online storefront vendors, and a table that compares the various auction-site seller fees, from Amazon and eBay to Yahoo.

For more information about message boards and networking with other users, see Tasks #96 and #98.

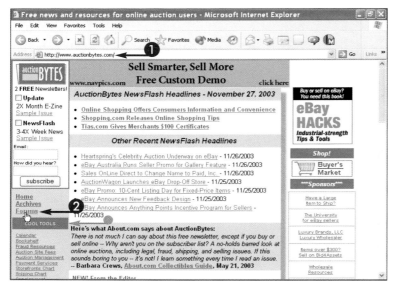

USING AUCTIONBYTES

① Type **www.auctionbytes.com** into the Address bar of your Web browser, and then press Enter.

The AuctionBytes Web site appears.

● You click here to access resources, including recommended books, fraud resources, and a chart of fees and services.

② Click the Forums link.

The AuctionBytes Forum Index page appears, with a list of forums.

③ Click link of a forum that interests you.

The Forum page appears, allowing you to read and post messages.

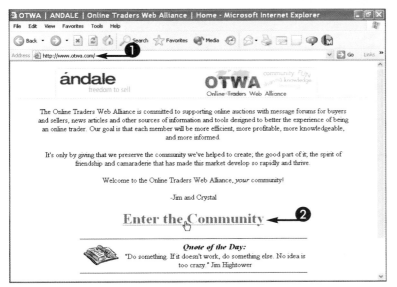

99

1 Type **www.otwa.com** in the Address bar of your Web browser, and then press Enter.

The OTWA page appears.

2 Click the Enter the Community link.

DIFFICULTY LEVEL

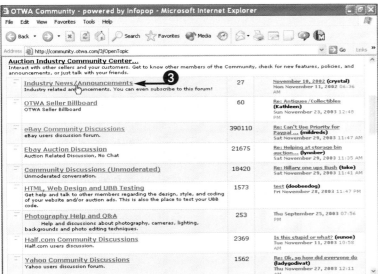

The OTWA Forums page appears.

A list of Forums displays, including the andale Community Center, Auction Industry Community Center, and the Antiques, and Collectibles Arena.

3 Click a Forum link.

The Forum page opens, allowing you to read and post messages, and participate in the OTWA Community.

TIPS

More Options!

To post a message on the AuctionBytes boards, in the AuctionBytes home page — located at www.auctionbytes. com — click the Forums link. Select a Forum and click the link. Select a topic from the list and click the topic link to open it and read the messages. Click post reply to respond to a message, or click the new topic button to start a new discussion.

Success Story!

AuctionBytes has specialty collectors' forums where people share successes and tips. In one topic about collectible postcards, a user tells about selling postcards of roadside attractions from the 1950s to early 1960s for $20 to $50 each.

Stay informed with
INDUSTRY NEWSLETTERS

To keep up with the constantly changing world of online auctions, you can subscribe to some of the auction newsletters.

You can subscribe to monthly, weekly, or daily newsletters, depending on the frequency that suits you. Examples of what you can learn from auction newsletters include advice from collectibles experts, packing and shipping tips, and new features on eBay and other auction sites. Many of the newsletters focus on maximizing your profits and selling tips. One recent newsletter featured articles about selling event tickets on eBay, and writing compelling auction copy.

Monthly newsletters include: The Auction Seller's Resource, at www.auction-sellers-resource.com;

Auction Gold, at www.auctionknowhow.com/AG; Cool eBay Tools at www.coolebaytools.com; and Creative eBay Selling, at www.silentsalesmachine.com.

Weekly newsletters include AuctionBytes, at www.auctionbytes.com and The Auction Guild's TAGnotes, at www.auctionguild.com.

AuctionBytes provides a daily newsletter, AuctionBytes NewsFlash, which you can subscribe to at www.auctionbytes.com.

You can also search newsletter back issues on some sites, such as AuctionBytes. For more information about online auction communities, see Task #99.

Although this example uses AuctionBytes, you can use the steps in this task for other newletters.

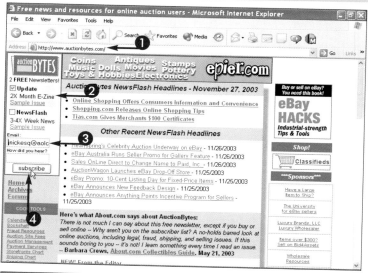

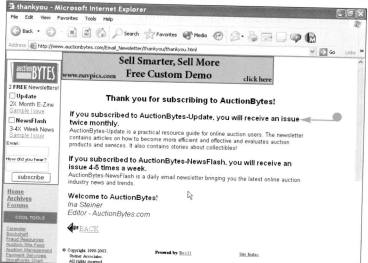

SUBSCRIBE TO A NEWSLETTER

❶ Type the newsletter URL into the Address bar of your Web browser, and then press Enter.

❷ In the newletter Web site, select the options for the newsletter you want.

❸ Type your e-mail address.

❹ Click subscribe.

● The Web site informs you that your subscription is active for the newsletter that you selected.

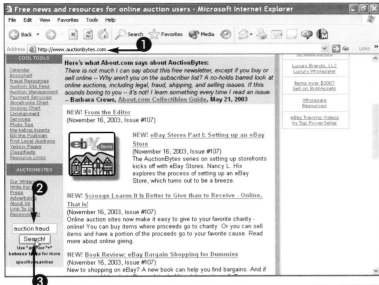

In this example,
the newsletter is
AuctionBytes.

1 Type **www.auction
bytes.com** into the
Address bar of your
Web browser, and
then press Enter.

The AuctionBytes Web site
appears.

2 Type your word or words
into the Search text box.

3 Click Search!.

The search results list appears.

● You can click an article link to read
more about the topic.

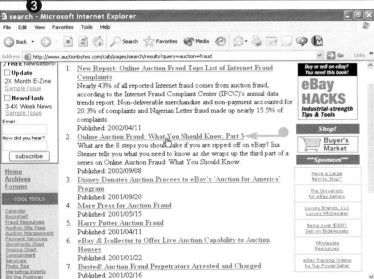

More Options!

You can search the Internet for more auction-related
newsletters. Try conducting a search using the Google
search engine, at www.google.com, or the Yahoo directory,
at dir.yahoo.com/Business_and_Economy/Shopping_and_
Services/Auctions/Industry_Information.

Did You Know?

eBay also has its own monthly general community
newsletter, The Chatter, available at pages.ebay.com/
community/chatter. The Chatter includes hints, articles
about eBay members of note, and profiles of eBay staff.
The newsletter also offers interviews with representatives
of popular collectible manufacturers, such as Precious
Moments figurines and Fenton Art Glass. You can read
past issues of The Chatter by clicking the Chatter Archive
link, available at the lower left side of the main Chatter
page. For information about eBay's Category-Specific
newsletters, available for some eBay categories, see
Task #62.

INDEX

Symbols

" (quotation marks) characters, Basic Search keywords, 4–5

A

About Me page
- seller's personal information, 150–151
- seller's Web site links, 161

accounts
- PayPal money transfers, 76–79
- PayPal setup, 74–75

acronyms, misspelled item bargains, 20–21
ad banners, Keywords on eBay, 166–167
Ad format
- bid process, 61
- real estate auctions, 64–65

Add to My Favorite Searches, add/delete items, 18–19
Adobe Acrobat, Hot Categories Report, 17
Advanced Search
- access methods, 6
- Buy It Now Items only, 6–7, 42–43
- Completed Items only, 7, 8–9
- Gallery View, 153
- Gift Items only, 6–7
- Location/International list, 36–37
- Quantity greater than 1, 60–61
- Sort by list, 7
- Sort by menu, 8
- Words to exclude, 6–7

after-sale problems, 86–87
aiShip Shipping Calculator, 177
alerts
- Bid Alert, 38–39
- watch alerts, 39

Anchor Stores, market service, 141
andale
- Gallery, related auction item thumbnails, 162–163
- hit counters, 116
- image-hosting service, 131
- statistics capability, 135

Any country, international search, 36–37
Anything Points, PayPal, 82–83
Asian Arts, Live Auctions category, 68
Ask seller a question link, 30–31
Auction format, real estate bid process, 65
Auction Payments (Western Union), payment service, 73, 80–81
Auction Sniper
- bid groups, 56–57
- browser interface, 57
- snipe service, 54–55

AuctionBytes
- auction communities resource, 206–207
- calendars, 124
- NewsFlash newsletter, 208
- weekly newsletters, 208

AuctionInc's aiShip calculator, 177
auctions
- hit counters, 116
- length issues, 97
- links between, 160–161

- related item thumbnails, 162–163
- schedulers, 117
- strategic item, 168–169

Audio notification, Bid Alert, 38–39
automobiles
- eBay Motors, 62–63
- vehicle history reports, 63

B

background colors, 103
backgrounds, image guidelines, 113
bank accounts, PayPal money transfers, 76–79
banner ads, Keywords on eBay, 166–167
bargains
- hidden cost considerations, 46–47
- last-minute auctions, 40–41

Basic Search
- end first items, 41
- Gallery View, 153
- Item location link, 34
- Matching Categories list, 14–15
- misspelled items, 20–21
- My Favorite Searches, 18–19
- Only in this category, 15
- Search title and description, 4–5
- Sort by list, 7
- titles-only limitations, 4–5
- transpositions, 20–21
- versus Browse, 2, 12–13

Bcc (blind carbon copy), seller questions, 30–31
Bid Alert, eBay Toolbar element, 38–39
bid groups, snipe method, 56–57
bidders, By Bidder market research, 10–11
Bidnapper, snipe service, 55
BidPay. *See* Western Union Auction Payments, payment service
bids
- Auction Sniper, 54–53
- automobile purchases, 62–63
- Bid Alert, 38–39
- bid groups, 56–57
- charity auctions, 66–67
- Dutch Auctions, 60–61
- increments, 51
- last-minute auction bargains, 40–41
- last-second, 52–53
- non-binding, 65
- odd amount advantages, 58
- price comparisons of common items, 59
- proxy, 50–51
- real estate, 64–65
- real-time auctions, 68–69
- reserve price, 101
- snipe methods, 52–57

Bids column, item interest information display, 9
Bidsage, snipe service, 55
BidSlammer, bid groups, 57
binding bids, real estate auction, 65
blind carbon copy (Bcc), seller questions, 30–31
boldface text, item emphasis method, 156–157
Books and Manuscripts, Live Auctions category, 68

INDEX

INDEX

INDEX

There's a Visual™ book for every learning level . . .

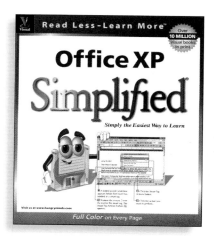

. . . all designed for visual learners—just like you!

Top 100 Simplified® Tips & Tricks

Tips and techniques to take your skills beyond the basics. Full color.

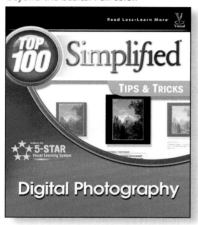

Visual Blueprint™

Where to go for professional level programming instruction. Two-color.

 Read Less—Learn More®

Visual

For a complete listing of Visual books, go to wiley.com/go/visualtech

Also available:

- Windows XP: Top 100 Simplified Tips & Tricks, 2nd Edition
- Photoshop Elements 3: Top 100 Simplified Tips & Tricks
- Mac OS X v.10.3 Panther: Top 100 Simplified Tips & Tricks
- eBay: Top 100 Simplified Tips & Tricks
- HTML: Top 100 Simplified Tips & Tricks
- Office 2003: Top 100 Simplified Tips & Tricks
- Excel 2003: Top 100 Simplified Tips & Tricks
- Photoshop CS: Top 100 Simplified Tips & Tricks
- Internet: Top 100 Simplified Tips & Tricks

Also available:

- HTML: Your visual blueprint for designing effective Web pages
- Excel Programming: Your visual blueprint for creating interactive spreadsheets
- Unix for Mac: Your visual blueprint to maximizing the foundation of Mac OS X
- MySQL: Your visual blueprint for creating open-source databases
- Active Server Pages 3.0: Your visual blueprint for developing interactive Web sites

- Visual Basic .NET: Your visual blueprint for building versatile programs on the .NET Framework
- Adobe Scripting: Your visual blueprint for scripting in Photoshop and Illustrator
- JavaServer Pages: Your visual blueprint for designing dynamic content with JSP
- Access 2003: Your visual blueprint for creating and maintaining real-world databases

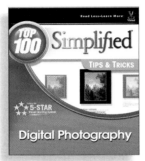
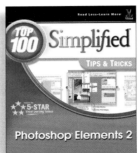
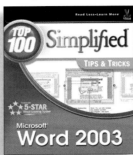

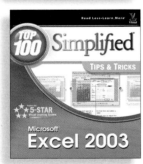

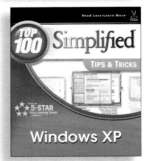
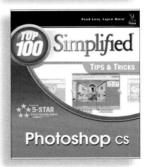
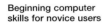

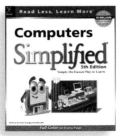

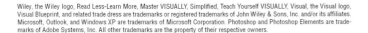